LARRY CONSTANTINE, EDITOR

Infinite Loop

Stories about the Future by the People Creating It

SOFTWARE DEVELOPMENT'S OWN
ANTHOLOGY OF SCIENCE FICTION

SOFTWARE
DEVELOPMENT
BOOK SERIES

Miller Freeman Books

SAN FRANCISCO

Published by Miller Freeman Books,
600 Harrison Street, San Francisco, California 94107
Sponsors of Software Development Conference and Shows
Publishers of *Software Development* and other magazines
A member of the United Newspapers Group

Copyright © 1993 Miller Freeman Inc.
No part of this book covered by copyrights hereon may be reproduced or distributed in any form or by any means, or stored in a database or retrieval system, without the prior written permission of the publisher.

"STORMY Versus the Tornadoes," by Jeff Duntemann, first appeared in *PC Techniques,* August/September 1990.

"LovePets," by Resa Nelson, was published in *Pulphouse: The Hardback Magazine,* #11, July 1991.

"Wet Blanket," by P. J. Plauger, first appeared in *Analog: Science Fiction / Science Fact,* February 1974.

Cover Art: Mark Wagner
Cover Design: David Hamamoto

Library of Congress Catalog Card Number: 93-79448
ISBN 0-87930-298-4

Printed in the United States of America
93 94 95 96 97   5 4 3 2 1

Contents

Foreword	vi
Preface	viii
Dan Persons: I'm Rubber and You're Glue	1
Brian A. Hopkins: My Father's House	16
Jeff Duntemann: STORMY Versus the Tornadoes	36
Resa Nelson: LovePets	40
L. Roy Cahners: Not My Type	55
Larry O'Brien: Soul of an Old Machine	68
Jeff Carter: Past Master	75
Elizabeth Hanes Perry: Boxing Day	91
Larry Constantine: Dellahar's Father	94
Glenn R. Sixbury: Sammy	102
Linda J. Dunn: Sibling Rivalry	107
Jeff Duntemann: Bathtub Mary	122
Don & Rosemary Webb: A Letter from Bemi-III	131
Sandy Stewart: The Lion and the Snake	143
Lois H. Gresh: Watch Me If You Can	150
Colin J. Robey: Flickering Lights	162
Pati Nagle: Pygmalion 3.0	175
Phoebe Bergemann: First Business	198
Lois H. Gresh: CAFEBABE	208
Sonia Orin Lyris: The Animal Game	221
Larry Constantine: Mint, Uncirculated	243
Anthony Taylor: Folded Like a Paper Dove	244
Norm Hartman: Project Lucifer	250
P. J. Plauger: Wet Blanket	259
Steve Rasnic Tem: The Doors of Hypertext	281
Kent Brewster: The Dream Pirate's Tale	292
Steven Weiss: Time_traveler();	310

To Ursula, who may remember: solidarity!

Time_traveler();

She arrived in time
To see her own departure;
Call time_traveler();

Steven Weiss

Foreword

I'M AN EVENT PLANNER by profession. In the past 10 years I've developed conferences and trade shows for sawmillers, wastepaper recyclers, cardiologists, and guitar players to name just a few. The logistical and marketing challenges associated with building a successful business around these events has always been stimulating. What really excites me about what I do, though, is that I have a paid excuse to get the most intelligent, creative, passionate people in a field together, in the same place at the same time, to share their dreams and ideas, and to create change. I'm really nothing more than a facilitator of synergy and collaboration among people much more interesting than I.

In 1987, I was given the opportunity to apply my skills to the field of software development, a field I had naturally been drawn to on a personal level for years because of the sheer density of those intelligent, creative, passionate types I found there. Since then my circle of friends has become almost entirely made up of software developers and others in the computer field. And my job continues to be to bring those friends together, and to watch them build tomorrow.

It seems natural to me that so many of these people are "into" science fiction. After all, their business is to create the future out of thin air. So when Larry Constantine, one of those close friends and associates, approached me about the idea of publishing a science fiction anthology by software developers, I didn't think twice about *how* to get a book out before I said yes.

I have been nothing more than a facilitator for this effort as I am for the other endeavors I am involved with. Numerous others have been involved in actually pulling the book together and getting the word out about it to you. Loren Hickman, Matt Kelsey, Brenda McLaughlin, Margaret Paradis, Ashley Fullerton, and Fern Leaf are just a few of those who've had their hands in the project since the beginning.

FOREWORD vii

To my surprise, a "simple" idea such as I imagined this to be has taken nearly a year to come together. Finally, though, our vision has become a reality. If you're a software developer, I imagine you'll recognize and share some of the dreams painted here by your peers. If not, I think you'll enjoy sharing a bit of the minds of some of the most visionary people anywhere.

As I've always said, when you get good people together, magic happens. Therein lies the significance of our Software Development events. Larry has done a great job of getting good people together for this book. Our hope is that you'll see a bit of magic happen here as well.

KoAnn Vikören
Director, Software Development Conferences & Shows

Preface

On CONSULTING TRIPS I carry a small box. Barely the size of a three-ring binder, it sends pictures around the world, allows me to collaborate on papers with colleagues in Australia while I am teaching in Europe, keeps track of my appointments and commitments, and even plays games with me. This box is science fiction, magic incarnate; it's a computer.

There are many resonances between the world of computers and the world of science fiction. In both, the building of new realities and altered perspectives is a driving force and a central challenge. In both, the boundaries of human thought and imagination are pushed outward to explore and define future possibilities.

It takes brains, imagination, vision, and attention to detail to write good software or design good machines. It doesn't hurt to be a bit warped. Some of the smartest and most intriguing people in the world work with computers, building the software that gives them life or the circuits that give them energy. Not all of them read science fiction, but so many do that conversations with new acquaintances at major conferences and conventions can safely be peppered with offhand references to Ellison, Heinlein, LeGuin, or Zelazny as readily as to Booch, Page-Jones, Turing, or Yourdon.

A surprising number of the bright and versatile people who write programs or write about programs also write science fiction. *Infinite Loop* is their work, the computer field's own anthology of science fiction, the first collection of its kind. It is not an anthology of computer science fiction; many of these stories involve computers in some significant way, but others do not. The stories have three things in common: I liked them, they're good, and they were written by people who work with computers. The authors in here are programmers and analysts, consultants and tech writers and managers in the field; they are also science fiction writers, some of them even famous ones. Not everyone who should be is represented here. Since I'll be asked about it, Jerry Pournelle had his hands full with several anthologies of his own. Joe Stith says his agent won't let him write short fiction anymore. There are others who promised stories for the next volume, if it ever comes.

viii

PREFACE   ix

This book began, not as science fiction, but as fantasy: my fantasy. It was a fantasy long relegated to those mental recesses where we store unfulfilled dreams and wistful wishes. I just could not see how to sell a publisher on a science fiction anthology edited by a new-comer with no record and no name in the field. Often, however, when the front door is locked or blocked by a long line of those ahead, there is also a side entrance—wide open and with no waiting.

Software is my field. With publishers in this field, I am a known quantity. So I approached Miller Freeman, a major publisher in the industry, with a screwball idea. I finished my pitch prepared for the worst and, at best, girded for protracted negotiations. The answer was an instantaneous "Yes!" There was one condition: I had to include some of my own stories under my own name. The truth is, I've been a closet science fiction writer for years, but my stuff has been published under a zealously guarded pseudonym. Not even my best friends armed with the best wine have been able to pry this secret identity from me. To edit the anthology, I would have to come out of the closet and risk raising questions about the egotism of collecting some of my own work.

Knowing that such sacrifices must be made, I launched into gathering material. I quickly learned that many of the professional and closet science fiction writers I knew in the computer field didn't have anything to sell at the time. I was looking at a collection that might not appear before the end of the century or one that consisted of nothing but Larry Constantine stories.

That's when I started to use the technology. I did a keyword search on profiles of members of CompuServe's Sci-Fi Forum to identify probable and possible writers. I sent hundreds of email messages announcing the project, inviting them to submit, and encouraging them to pass the word along. The word spread with electronic speed to GEnie, Internet, and Bitnet, and I began getting submissions from around the world. Nearly eight out of ten came by email, which made my work easier but sent the scroll rate through the roof.

I got acquainted with a steady stream of authors. I had a delight-ful email exchange with a talented 16-year-old who said she had written hundreds of science fiction stories and sent me a complete novella. She didn't make it into this collection, but I expect she will be making her first sale before long. I also got a dot-matrix manu-

x INFINITE LOOP

script by snail mail from a retiree who claimed to go back to the days of Herman Hollerith. And one night my jaw dropped as I scanned my email. On the screen was a message from none other than Steve Rasnic Tem, whose new story, "The Doors of Hypertext," you'll find in here. You undoubtedly know others of the writers in here. You may have worked with them or read their technical articles. You may have read some of their science fiction. Some contributors have been writing and selling science fiction for years, but many of the names will be new to you; for some, *Infinite Loop* is their first major professional sale.

Editing this anthology has been a work of joy and an education. It was much harder than I had imagined. I have learned a lot more about just what makes a story work and that subtle line between a sale and a near miss. I have agonized over where to draw that line, and I have delighted in having a legitimate excuse to read more science fiction. The greatest joy has been discovering writers with talent and promise, reading their stories and working with them. They have been a remarkably easy lot to work with. Still, after years of throwing my own stuff over the transom to other editors, it seemed strange to find myself on this side of the editorial desk. I had to think twice when Jeff Duntemann talked of hoping to write more, now that a new market was opening up for "techie fiction." A new market? He was talking about this anthology. I, who had long lamented the paucity of markets for short fiction, was creating one!

Any project like this is a collaboration among many people, not alone those whose names appear on the bylines of the collected stories. *Infinite Loop* could not have happened without the relentless support of my friend and sometime boss at Miller Freeman, KoAnn Vikören, who has mastered the fine art of taking calculated chances on people and ideas. I also want to thank P. J. Plauger, who has been an encouraging fellow writer over so many years that I was forced to forgive him for being unconscionably late with his contribution. And finally, heaps of appreciation to my business partner, who let me have fun when I should have been earning money. Thanks, Lucy Lockwood, I'll get back to work next week.

LLC
Acton, Massachusetts

Programmers will be programmers, whether coding pretty graphics on a desktop computer or building boring database applications on the "big iron" of old Big Blue. They are not really antisocial, and not all are socially inept, but get two of them together and the sparks and the acronyms, the hacks and the painful puns are apt to fly. This programmer mentality feeds on itself, finding its extreme expression among the hackers and crackers and bit-fiddling pranksters who can bring a network to its knees with only two fingers and a keyboard. Our first story is a fine-grained portrait of that hacking sensibility turned loose, presenting what its author calls a rather ascerbic view of office politics and professional rivalries in a mainframe environment.

DAN PERSONS
I'm Rubber and You're Glue

IT HAD TO BE Pintall. He came strolling up over the rise, barely mindful of the flower bed he was treading through, piggish snout probing the air like a boar snuffling out an especially toothsome truffle. It figured—everything else in the garden was too perfect: the subtly balanced blue sky; the fine, fractal-purged grass; the surrounding forest that exhibited only the slightest hint of artifacting. Beautiful, beautiful...and here he came: thinning hair pushed back over rounded skull, brow glistening with sweat and oil, drooping brush of a mustache twitching with porcine intent. I swear, if I had the know-how to purge the datascape of parasites that walk like men, the industry would worship me as a God.

I'm no fool; I could've gone cloak, I just didn't want to. I stood there instead, watching, waiting for it to dawn on the intruder that he was not alone.

It wasn't until he had reached the podium, had climbed onto the platform, that he took notice. "Oh," he said, "it's you."

2   PERSONS

"What the hell's that supposed to mean?"

"It means it's you. What the hell do you want it to mean?"

I stepped from between two rows of folding chairs, walked the grass-carpeted aisle to the dais. "Nice work," I said, pointing back to the flimsy, plastic furniture. "Maybe you went a bit overboard. We don't want the shareholders to feel too pampered, do we?"

"That's just a test file. I haven't ported the real thing in yet."

"Well, why not?" I folded my arms across my chest. "C'mon, gimme a thrill."

I was about three meters from him now. I watched his eyes go out of focus, watched his face go slack. The chair to my left disappeared, was replaced several seconds later with a Naugahyde-clad, burgundy Barcalounger.

I looked at the recliner. "You gotta be kidding."

"What?" Pintall said, stepping down off the platform, quickly closing the distance between us. "That's a top-model template. Got built-in vibrator, heating coils, everything."

I rolled my eyes skyward, noted briefly that the clouds looked a little too angular for my taste. "Ray, Ray..."

"Don't do that. I hate that."

I ignored him. "Shareholders are not, by any stretch, a mob of screaming radicals. On the other hand, we don't want to go suggesting that they're a bunch of old farts, either."

"Who's suggesting that?"

"You are, with these old fart chairs."

"They're not old fart chairs!"

I strolled behind the monstrosity, folded my arms across the top. "They're retirement home deluxe. We wanna whip these guys up, not put 'em down."

He snorted. "Y'know, Stark, I'm glad we work together. It helps me remember my monthly donations to The Society for the Creatively Challenged."

I gestured to the surrounding scenery. "You got any complaints about the grounds? Anything *wrong* with my garden?"

"Yeah," he replied, "yeah, there is. The elm trees look phony. And you see that flower bed? That's a mess."

"You trampled all over it!"

"Yeah, and it just *stayed* that way!"

I'M RUBBER AND YOU'RE GLUE 3

"That's *real*. You step on a flower, it gets broke."

"And looks fuckin' ugly. Yeah, Ms. Irvin's gonna love that."

I let my arms drop from the chair. Talk about creatively challenged. "Okay. You just wait."

I relaxed, let momentum shift to the back of my brain. There was a metallic click at the small of my back, traveling up my spine as I gained access to my working files. I entered down into the lightless depths, stretched out, reached for the folder labeled LANDSCAPING. The "Spring Garden" subroutine sprang immediately to my consciousness; I opened it, felt the contents pour from within, flow across my medulla oblongata, spread upwards to my cerebral cortex. I purged the trampled portion of the flower bed, accessed my weaver algorithm, inserted into it the templates of lilacs, forsythias, chrysanthemums. Setting the weaver at the bed's edge, I booted it up; fresh foliage rose across the defiled area.

From behind me, the voice of Pintall: "Doesn't surprise me at all. Two days to the first virtual shareholders' meeting and you're still acting like a fuckin' retard. Maybe Boston Genetics isn't a big enough client for you."

"Boston Genetics is plenty big."

"Yeah, well maybe Ms. Irvin would like to hear how you treat clients that are plenty big. Y'know, I keep telling her you don't have the licks to handle a major environment. I'm going to store that flower bed—those elm trees too, while I'm at it—give 'er a look at how you cope with pressure. Be interesting to see you talk your way out of that one."

I turned, approached him, stood face to face. "I got work to do. Just take care of your own shit, okay? Or we'll see who's got some talking to do." I squeezed past him and headed for the left perimeter of the meeting place, where the recovering flower bed lay.

"Stay out of my way, Stark!" he shouted—like it'd been *his* idea.

I ignored him, stood before the bed. Seconds later, the weaver had finished its work, returning the foliage to its original form. *Cope with pressure,* huh? And what was wrong with my elm trees? I looked at the stand that bordered the rear of the clearing, behind the area into which Joan would insert her buffet table. Well, maybe there was a certain verisimilitude lacking in them, a certain

4 PERSONS

texture missing from the bark. Not that I'd let you-know-who know.

I spent a few minutes touching up the elms, then took a few more minutes to boost the fluff factor of the clouds. I stared under my feet. The grass wasn't all it could be—bit too consistent, bit too neat. I went back into storage, retrieved the grass template, made a few modifications to the fractal overlay. I inserted the revised file into the weaver, set the code to test mode, and booted it on its way. From where I stood, a meter-long swath began working its way across the lawn, the grass within rich, lush, alive. As the metamorphosis continued, I glanced up at Pintall. He was still standing before the dais, hands on hips and staring intently at his recliner. I watched as the chair's Naugahyde upholstery softened to a leather-like sheen, as rows of studs appeared to trim the chair's edges, then abruptly vanished. God, I hated him.

I had an idea. The test lawn was still running, beating a slow but steady path to where Pintall stood. Quickly, I switched my momentum to the operating system, ported myself over to active memory, felt it bloom in my stomach like warmed syrup. Pintall's RWA—his Resident Work Area, the block of data that defined his presence within the datascape—hovered a scant one meg above the line. I set up a pointer from the lawn segment at Pintall's feet to the bottom of the RWA. Then I bounced back up to watch the fun.

He didn't notice at first as the grass began to sprout around the rim of his Reeboks. By the time realization dawned, the lawn had already crept halfway up his calves."Oh, now, wait-just-a-second..." he groaned, as his kneecaps were reclaimed by Mother Earth.

"Gotta get more exercise," I said, "You're really going to seed, there."

He tried to turn towards me, but his femurs—rapidly turning to rich, American loam—couldn't handle the strain. He fell backward, grunting as he contacted the ground, as the transformation continued heedless over the mountain of his belly. "This is *real* mature, Stark."

"Your ass is grass, chlorophyll-for-brains."

"Irvin ever finds out you've been tampering with user memory, you're history," he squeaked, just before the greenery engulfed his head.

Silence. A bird chirped in the trees, a gentle breeze kissed my face. I pulled in a deep breath, made a note to myself to get a bit more earth-note into the air's perfume.

Thrusting hands into pockets, I strolled over to the knoll that once was Pintall. Planting one foot on a stomach-like rise, I leaned to where his head used to be. "You know, you take things too seriously. I mean, look at you. You wanna be a big lump all your life?"

My foot abruptly dropped. I glanced down and beheld flat ground, lacking all trace of undulation. So he was able to debug his RWA that fast, eh? Good. He may be a schmuck, but at least he could take care of himself—no guilt attacks for me. I turned to head back to the flower bed, was surprised when my first step was close to impossible, was doubly shocked when my second step didn't happen at all. A glance down brought the singularly unpleasant sight of my feet turning into sculpted, mahogany stumps, and my calves spreading and distorting into a massive, burgundy leather bulk.

Pintall rose from his seat in the audience. "Think you count for something around here?" he said, approaching. "Babe, you're just part of the furniture."

"How original," I said, stifling a groan as my bones modified into the metal struts of a recliner's inner mechanics. "And I'll just bet my face is going to become the cushion."

"Crude, but fitting."

I wanted to answer that. Unfortunately, just then my head shifted towards my navel, all orifices sealed, and my skull cavity filled with horsehair. The system, finding me left with no sensory organs of my own, evenly distributed receptors across my entire surface. On the plus side, I now had visual and audio input from every angle afforded by my form. On the minus, I also had a front-row opportunity to watch as Pintall approached and settled his bulk into my all-too-receptive form.

"Ahhh," he sighed, "that's good. Not the best—a bit broken-down, and fuckin' ugly—but still good." He rolled his hips, grinding his butt into my face.

Yeah, typical—but don't think I was angry. Nope, this was per-

6   PERSONS

fect, a little slice o' heaven. I grinned to myself (had to—no lips, you know), ignored the ignominy of the situation, and waited for Pintall to get himself nice and comfy.

When he'd settled in, I activated my mechanisms, quickly dropping the seat back and extending the footrest. God bless Pintall; the chair he built was loathsome, but well crafted. I opened with such force that the pig did a double somersault as he flew backwards.

He landed with an "Oof," punctuated his touchdown with a flurry of obscenities. I didn't hang around for the full show, instead taking the opportunity to swing back into memory, yank up my RWA. Pintall's weaver was crude stuff (think I was surprised?); it was only a matter of nanoseconds before I had a doctor kludged up and working on my tainted file. I then went into lurk mode within storage. The transmogrification from a leather/wood/metal template to human form would not be pleasant; I didn't want pig-boy to get his jollies from watching. I waited the ordeal through, used the passing nanoseconds to mull over what I could do to get my own back. Half-measures wouldn't be enough. I wanted the geek to sweat.

Finally restored to humanity, I examined my surroundings. I smiled when I discovered myself hovering by Joan's catering database.

Pintall was just finished hoisting himself when I ascended back to the garden. His face a livid red, he glared at me while straightening his clothes. "You got a bad attitude."

"You got a big butt."

"When I get done talking to Irvin, it's gonna be *your* ass."

He raised a hand, jabbed a finger in my direction. A gout of cream-brown liquid spurted from its tip. Stunned, Pintall raised the finger, stared at it like he'd never before considered that the thing might be loaded.

I shrugged, glanced to the ground, kicked at my instep. "You remember when the client was toying with that carnival theme? You remember the frozen yogurt stand Joan coded up for them?"

Pintall's expression collapsed. "Oh no."

I grinned. "Oh yes."

I liked the panic in his eyes. More, I liked the way those eyes suddenly welled up with yogurt pre-mix, the liquid quickly overflowing the lids, occluding the retinas, running down Pintall's cheeks like confectionary lava flows. His extremities were next, fingers dribbling the stuff, Reeboks sweating it through lace holes, a dark stain forming and spreading at his crotch.

"Son of a *blurmmmphh...*" was all Pintall could say before he erupted into a geyser of ultra-pasteurized dairy product. It was, I admit, a spectacular display: a solid jet of liquid matter, spurting some four meters into the air. I didn't know he had it in him.

I took a few steps back. The ascent was impressive, but the fall was going to be messy, and I didn't relish the idea of finding myself covered in Pintall. His landing described a circle about two meters in diameter. He managed to spatter a few seats in the front row, the corresponding edge of the dais, and the front of the podium. Bits of him dappled the lawn, shimmered brown against the green— the effect like some sort of inverse starscape.

I paced the perimeter of my colleague, thought back to those wonderful, childhood nights crouched before the ol' flatscreen, watching *The Wizard of Oz*. "Well, that's you all over," I said.

One of the droplets glistened, quivered, and rolled onto the toe of my sneaker.

"Shit," I said, and scrubbed the tip of my shoe against the grass. Pintall smeared across the ground, leaving a tainted patch of lawn and a thin residue that covered my toe. I watched in horror as the liquid coating my shoe drew in upon itself, coalesced into a small globule. The glop I'd rubbed off did the same—pretty soon it rolled forward onto my toe, joining its companion.

I'd fucked up. Pintall was gathering. He dripped off the dais, oozed down from the seats, pooled into the space between audience and speaker. Before I had time to react, several tendrils flowed quickly out, splashed up over my sneakers and pants cuffs.

I shouted, kicked my shoes off, stripped my pants away. This was not optimal. Ray was tenacious; if he got on me he'd be stuck for good. God only knows what'd happen if he got into my mouth (or any other orifice, for that matter).

He was flowing toward me, forming eddies in an attempt to surround and cut me off. A fine stream of liquid jetted from the glob, baptized my T-shirt. I stripped the thing off immediately and

8 PERSONS

backed naked away from the bastard, nearly stumbling against the edge of the dais. I scrabbled up top, kept backing towards the center of the platform. Pintall gathered at the foot of the stage, then smoothly ran up the side and over the skirt.

"Aw, c'mon," I shouted. "Flowing against gravity? That's agin' the law!"

Pintall didn't take notice. He was too busy getting himself coverage on the platform, flowing a full 360 degrees around my station, slowly closing in. The sadistic bastard seemed determined to milk this for all it was worth.

What could I do? "Okay, ya prick, you made your point. Change back."

Pintall continued to creep his way across the floor, millimeter by agonizing millimeter.

"I said I give. Enough, already."

A tongue of liquid rolled forward, splashed up to saturate my left foot and ankle.

This wasn't good. The bastard seemed determined to see this to the end, whatever the hell that meant. What I did know was that I wasn't going to stand around and find out.

I swung back inside, dropped down to memory, dove for Pintall's RWA. It bucked about my guts like a decahedron filled with hornets—seemed the rampant yogurt program was wreaking havoc with everything. Me and my genius ideas.

I plunged desperately through my files, tried to find something that'd put the fear of God into the creep. I was moving so fast I almost overshot my sky file, the one with the improved, fluffier clouds. Applying the brakes, I gave the code consideration. Hmm, solid to liquid, liquid to gas—had a nice symmetry to it. Who knew, it might even give the pissant a bit of a panic, to boot.

And, besides, I was running out of time.

I snatched the file, slipped it into my weaver, set it to work on Pintall's RWA. By the time I rose back up, I was already saturated to mid-thigh. Jacking out would've been the sensible thing, but I wasn't going to give him the satisfaction of seeing me turn and run. Anyway, I was waiting for the good stuff to hit.

I could feel it through my legs: a tingling sensation, like a mild electric current running the expanse of Pintall's mass. He ceased his advance, seemed to shudder through the whole of his form. A cold steam rose from his surface. I breathed and caught an odor that seemed composed of equal parts cocoa and ozone.

The platform was vapor-bound in seconds. There seemed to be sound within the mist: faint and high-pitched, as if a balloon was slowly deflating within two meters worth of cotton batting. The steam began to quickly dissipate, rising skyward. In less than a minute, it—all of it, all of *Ray*—was gone.

It was a beautiful day—still. I smiled at the deftness of my handiwork, waited for Pintall's return. Yeah, I expected him back—I knew him, knew he wasn't going to let this go unanswered. Maybe I was just asking to get it done to me double, but I was willing to take the risk for one glance at his face, one chance to look in his eyes, one second to relish his anger. I live for such moments.

So I waited...

One minute. Nothing.

Minute thirty. Nothing.

Two. Zip.

He wouldn't have jacked out. As long as I was still in here, he'd have to come back, if only to try and have the last word. But that yogurt program had randomized his RWA pretty good, and I'd just handed him the sky on top. Strictly speaking, you weren't supposed to pull such shit without a thorough bench-test but, hell, he'd coped with everything else, hadn't he?

Hadn't he?

Two thirty.

Three.

Oh shit.

I dropped back, headed to memory, slammed directly into something that engulfed me like a hot-air balloon filled with partially set Jell-O. Pressure bore in from all sides—within and without—increasing with each nanosecond. The sense was more oppressive than painful, but that didn't make things any less unsettling. I beat a fast retreat, landed just below the line, found myself shaking all the way down to my virtual toes.

Carefully, I sent some feelers up above the line to scope my aggressor. What I feared: it was Pintall's RWA, mutating and

10   PERSONS

expanding past any reasonable limits. I set up a reticle, clocked his growth: .5 gigabytes. .98. 1.6. 2.75. 5.

Double Oh Shit.

I'd barely made it back up to the garden before it began to melt, furniture losing dimensional resonance and vanishing like spirits, scenery de-rezzing as fractal routines failed. There was a tug at the core of my being—God spake unto me in words without sound, and yea, (S)He did say, "System integrity breach has been detected. Please log-off now." Didn't give me a choice—next second the elastic cable attached to my naval contracted, and I found myself yanked screaming up and out. I traveled about two thousand kilometers in approximately .00097 seconds, roused in my office, started in my cradle as I squinted up at the fluorescent lighting.

Reaching behind my ear, I yanked the umbilical from its port, unstrapped myself and hit the floor running. Out in the lobby, I could hear muffled swearing from the surrounding cubies; Joan was just stepping out of hers when I passed. "What the *hell* is going on?" she cried.

"Fire in the hole," I shouted back, not stopping. "Get Leif and Maureen. Ray's screwed himself."

I grabbed the lip of Pintall's doorway, swung myself in. He was still in his cradle, hands folded over the girth of his belly, the datafeed umbilical still hooked to his port. His face was slack, his skin a clammy white. Whatever was happening, it didn't look like fun.

There was movement behind me, I heard Leif's voice, "Outta way."

I stepped back, let Leif take my place and pry open an access panel on the umbilical's wall plate, jacking a hand-held data-pad into the service port. "Man," he said, tabbing through menus, running four or five diagnostics in as many seconds, "he's really out there."

"How far out?" asked Maureen, as she leaned over his shoulder to stare at the flat-screen.

"*Way* out."

Maureen turned to me. "What the hell were you doing in there?"

I shrugged. "I dunno. We were trying to get the BosGen meeting set up and we got caught in crap and then...this."

I'M RUBBER AND YOU'RE GLUE   11

"Crap?" said Maureen. Her tone was level.

"Yeah, crap. Beats me what went wrong."

"Uh-huh," she replied, turning back to her partner.

There was a crowd piled up at the doorway—with the central system hung, there wasn't much more to do than stand and gawk. Joan leaned into my ear: "What *really* happened?"

"Just what I said."

"Bullshit. You hate Ray's guts. I just didn't think you hated him enough to go this far."

Stunned, I turned to face her. I was going to defend myself: *never...never would I even think...whatever happened, it was all Ray's...how the hell could you say...*But the words wouldn't come, not after I saw her expression, not after I looked in those eyes. In her mind, I'd been caught, tried, and convicted—nothing I said would reverse the verdict. The bitch.

"Go get lunch, folks," Leif said without turning away from his pad. "We're going to be untwining this guy bit by bit, and that's hours. The system's down until we're done."

Most of the crowd, save a few stragglers, dispersed. I went back to my cubie, settled into my cradle. For the next few hours I lay there, staring at the ceiling, staring at the gray-carpeted walls, staring at the wall plate with its still-attached digi-optical umbilical.

In late afternoon, Maureen came to my doorway. I said, "You get him out?"

"He's back with the living."

"He okay?"

"As well as ever. Damn dangerous, what happened."

My right elbow itched. I scratched it. "Was it?"

"His RWA got fucked with; could've got his brain fried."

"He lucked out, then."

"Yeah, sure did," Maureen replied lifelessly. "So did we."

"Oh yeah?"

"Yeah. Runaway took off in all directions, but didn't expand into the system audit region."

My heart skipped a beat; I restrained the urge to face her. "Really?"

"Really. We were able to take system dumps for the half hour preceding the incident. We still gotta take a good, long stroll along the

12 PERSONS

trail, but what we've seen so far is...interesting. Yogurt, huh?" My stomach twisted; this time, I rolled to my side.

She backed away from the door, grim smile tracing her lips. "Ms. Irvin wants to speak with you."

I'll spare you the details of that meeting. The upshot was that I was banned from mainframe access and busted to the arcades division. Ray, because he wasn't the instigator—just played along—got bounced from the project with a stern talking-to and a fine of 17.3 percent off his next profit-sharing cycle. The pig squealed for days.

It would be nice if that was the end of it, but, of course, it wasn't. You see, I knew Ray, knew what a vindictive little prick he could be. He wasn't going to let this rest. He couldn't get at me through the mainframe anymore, but get to me he would. How was a question. When was another.

Weeks passed. Nothing. Fair enough—Pintall could get his rocks off with the waiting game, but I'd be damned if I was going to play along. Around quitting time one afternoon, I took a leisurely stroll up to the mainframe realities group. Most of my former colleagues were on their way out—a few nodded quickly to me, most tried to ignore my passage. When I reached Pintall's cubie, he was still there, strapped into his cradle and jacked in.

I approached the wall plate, punched the intercom stud. "Let's talk, Ray."

Pintall opened his eyes, stared passively at me. "Hi, Stark."

"Don't 'Hi' me. Let's have this out and get it over with."

"Get what over with?"

"You know. Look, my career's screwed. Even if I could get another job, no one will let me look at a mainframe link, much less give me access. Why don't we just say it's done and get on with our lives?"

"But it *is* done, Stark. Why should I think otherwise?"

"Because I know you, and I know you won't rest 'til you've gotten even."

Pintall chuckled, lowered his feet to the floor, stood. Crossing the room, he pulled a windbreaker from its hook and turned to me. "I don't need to take revenge on you."

I stared at him. "You bastard," I hissed. "I shoulda known better than to try to deal straight with you." I spun, headed for the door.

I'M RUBBER AND YOU'RE GLUE   13

From behind: "Stark..."

I stopped at the doorway, turned. "What?"

"Would you like to know what happened?"

"What?"

He jerked a thumb to the wall plate. "That last time, in there. Would you like to know what happened?"

What the...? "Don't let me force you."

There was something strange to his grin. "I *want* to tell you."

The prick. "Okay. Gimme a thrill."

He squinted his eyes, let his tongue loll for a second in one cheek before talking. "Let's see...It was like nothing at first, absolute nothing. Deadspace, literally...I really thought you'd killed me, you wouldn't believe how pissed I was at you. Then something started up in the bottom of my gut, got all the way through me. Something strong...Peace, like, but more, deeper; like the feeling of being in the womb all over again, like the security of knowing the exact boundaries of your universe. But this was bigger, Stark. Much bigger."

"Mainframe big," I said.

That smile was starting to give me the creeps. "Y'know," he said, "I've spent my whole life being picked on: too fat, too short, sucked at sports, couldn't get laid. It never stopped. I'd almost grown to like it, grown to *want* it that way, just 'cause it pissed people off. In there, though," he glanced towards the wall interface, "none of that mattered. In there, I was *everything,* every bit of data, every decision tree, every pulse of electricity. I didn't have to accept the abuse anymore. I didn't have to be the shit. I was beyond that."

He leaned towards me, whispered, "They spent hours pulling me out. Know why it took so long? Because I didn't want to come."

I stared at the guy, hoped that my expression remained neutral, 'cause I was starting to get deep-down scared. Whoever decreed that none of the creep's neurons had been fried had obviously not been looking too closely.

"Know what, Stark?" he said, shrugging on his jacket, taking a step towards me. "I really hate you. No, I *really* hate you—more than I did before, more than you could ever imagine. Know why?"

"Tell me."

"Because you gave me a view of what I could become, boosted

14   PERSONS

me to heights I'd never before dreamed. You let me get there, have it all to myself, and then *you fucked up*. They purged your files, Stark. I've tried to recreate that subroutine. I can't do it. Maybe you could, but you'll never get back into a mainframe. You know this business, you know the network's too pervasive. You could be immortal in the real world, but you're dead on the datascape."

My throat felt inexplicably parched. "Have you told anyone else?"

He smiled: tight, grim. "No one. Just you. I only want *you* to know, Stark, know I've been there, know I've lived the totality. You see, I don't have to take revenge on you. I *know* you. And now that you've heard, now that you know *I've* had it—me, Ray the shit, Ray the pig—you'll ache to have it, too."

Still grinning, he slipped past me, and into the lobby, stopping to turn and say, "And you never will."

He spun, and disappeared down the hall. I stood rooted to the floor, waited until I heard the *ping* of the elevator and the sound of the doors opening and closing. And still I stood.

Fuck him. Fuck him and his swinish bloodline. Real cute, thinking he could screw me like that. Totality. Crap.

I looked at the wall panel, umbilical dangling from its jack. Reflexively, I raised a hand to touch lightly at the interface behind my ear. He was right, of course—I was banned forever. No need even to try. So what the fuck was I doing hanging around?

I turned, strode down the hall, punched for the elevator. I felt like an asshole for even coming here, but decided it wasn't a total loss. Okay, he said he wouldn't be trying to get back at me; what say we took the dick at face value and believed him? Been too long worrying about that shit—time to get on. Yeah, that sounded good.

I could admit it, now: I'd been letting the whole thing get to me. High time I broke the pattern. I'd start tonight: zap myself up something extravagant for dinner, maybe order up a movie, one of the old flat-screens; I liked those. Yeah, good—shoulda been doing this all the time. This wasn't the end of civilization, after all. Things were going to be okay. Things were going to be *better* than okay.

I just had to keep telling myself that.

A chime rang, the elevator door opened. I stepped in, punched ground floor, waited as the doors slid closed and I began my descent.

All the way down, I tried to purge from my mind the image of an umbilical dangling from a wall socket.

Dan Persons backed into his computing career, discovering an aptitude for programming while majoring in filmmaking at New York University. He opted for a full-time, data-processing job when his bachelor's degree didn't net him the six-figure Hollywood contract he'd always dreamed of. Now a senior programmer/analyst, Dan celebrates his thirteenth anniversary with a major New York financial institution this year.

Dan's entry into writing was pure ego; he says he likes seeing his name in print. His work has appeared in numerous small press publications, he contributes regularly to *Cinefantastique* magazine as correspondent and critic, and he has recently broken into the SF "mainstream" with controversial stories in *Pulphouse* and *Aboriginal Science Fiction*. He identifies Ellison, Vonnegut, Chuck Jones, and Elvis Costello among his inspirations but says he might give four different names tomorrow.

This story infuriated me and I loved it. It's too long—way over the 5,000 word limit I had put in my announcement—and it's full of italics. It sent me scurrying to the dictionary three times, each time certain the author had made a "dumb mistake." I was wrong all three times. Is it hard science fiction or soft? What do I know? I didn't know Alpha Centauri was a double star. Both my daughters have told me it's tough to have a father who is everywhere. Maybe that's why this story choked me up and I liked it so much. It's about real things.

BRIAN A. HOPKINS
My Father's House

THE GRASS IS A teal color, which Holly associates with her childhood in Reeds Crossing, Kentucky. It's a genetically tailored strain requiring very little water, with broad, paper-thin blades engineered to make maximum use of the dome's diffused light. Nothing like it ever grew in Kentucky. Nothing like it grew here on Port either, before their coming. But the grass feels and smells like home to her. It's one of their more successful transplants, though certainly not their only one.

By far, the most important transplant is themselves. Thirty-six colonists—thirty-seven when she delivers in five months. The first humans to settle on a world not circling Sol.

Air. As foreign to her lungs as if she were an infant just pulled screaming from the womb.

The taste of hospitals and camphor.

A cold, hard surface. The uncertain familiarity of it against naked flesh.

The smell of sour metal and plastic and...something hot, something burning.

Strangely transposed English, hesitant, muffled as by a thick fog: "Please, you...wake up, Holly Knight. Time there is none to waste."

Following the voice, pain. Needles in her lungs and flames held to her extremities. Transverse lasers burning behind her eyes. Tremors and chills and acid in her veins.

MY FATHER'S HOUSE   17

A dark whirlpool beckoned, its black propinquity offering sensory caesura. Relief. Escape. She retreated down its silent throat...

Beneath the turquoise sky, against the plethoric bed of grass, Evan's skin is a healthy, nutmeg brown. The vanity of sunlamps, thinks Holly. Dietary supplements provide all the photo-nutrients they need. In that strange way he has of knowing what she's thinking, Evan's face reddens. Then he smiles and lays a calloused hand against the slight velvet swell of her stomach. He doesn't speak. Words are rarely necessary between them. The child isn't technically his—the colony's gene pool is much too small for natural insemination. The med computer chose the best genotype from ship's stores and Holly dutifully accepted. Still, Evan's treating the unborn child with no less attention than if it had come from his loins. Holly loves him all the more for it.

And of course the sky isn't really blue; that's just the scattering effect of molecules in the dome field. Beyond the dome's illusive border the sky is an overcast haze of methane clouds, banded by a mustard brume of sulfuric acid, the cometlike trail of one of Port's two moons. But the field does more than fool them with an Earth-like blue sky; without it they'd be strangling on carbon dioxide, the principle component of Port's atmosphere.

The methane clouds hang about forty kilometers above Port's surface, swirling with powerful vortices, scathing with fierce sheets of blue lightning. The fast-darkening horizon is stratified with distant aurorae that Holly has thus far failed to capture accurately with oil and canvas. Port's minute axial tilt means there are no seasons, just this perpetually overcast gray, as if it's always about to rain. Days and nights are short, just a little over six hours Earth time, by which standard the colonists still reckon the passage of events, converting even Port's protracted 3.26-Earth-year course about Alpha Centauri into figures they can relate to.

Evan draws her close through the thick grass, presses his lips against hers. His body is solid and warm.

"Holly Knight!"

Her summoner waited outside the whirlpool, impatient but determined. She was only peripherally aware of the voice, like conversation from another room or the whispering of ghosts.

"Please, Holly! Minutes just, and they are through!"

There was a childlike quality to the voice. Desperation. Maybe a rapidly fading hope. But most of all she heard a fear that tugged at

18   HOPKINS

her heart. As she drew near, the pain returned. Needles. Thousands of needles...

It's the clouds and the carbon dioxide that make Port temperate. Like a greenhouse: stellar radiation slips through, but the longer wavelength of reflected heat energy is trapped in the heavy atmosphere.

Evan's hands work their magic on her body. His mouth shifts to her neck, tracing the fine blue veins beneath her pale skin. No sunlamps for her. She's expecting. Over Evan's shoulder she watches Port's fleeting moons chase each other across the sky.

There are two, the fiery giant the colonists named the Wicked Stepmother and the petite red lady they call Daughter. Stepmother is all orange and reds and yellows. Torn by Port's tidal pull, shattering seismic forces grind deep within the spherical moon. Tectonic surface plates shift and splinter. Volcanoes spew geysers of sulfur and steam into the upper atmosphere, leaving a yellow smear of sulfuric acid streaked across the sky. Daughter is much smaller, a triaxial ellipsoid measuring a mere twenty-seven by fifteen by eighteen kilometers, tidally locked so her long axis is perpetually oriented to Port. Port's powerful magnetic field has captured Alpha Centauri's stellar particles, stockpiling them in the upper atmosphere. As Daughter moves through this swarm, she generates and sustains a flux tube, an elliptical hose of electrical current millions of amperes strong connecting her to the planet with a tempest of unequaled electrical fury. Thus the Stepmother chases the Daughter across Port's sky, each trailing her veil, one fire and smoke, the other blue lightning.

She was aware of being slapped.

Evan's hands slipped away as dream and reality intertwined. She clutched at him. Rather, she clutched at *someone,* for the flesh she caught was soft and cold.

"No!" she screamed, seeking over his shoulder the panorama of Port's unique sky...as if it could save her from reality.

The other dominant feature in the sky, excepting Alpha Centauri's twin luminescence and the bright star of Legacy in orbit, is their only neighbor, the red gas giant they've named Ball. Ball's atmosphere is pure nitrogen, the red clouds a photochemical smog of carbon compounds, ethane, acetylene, hydrogen cyanide, and ethylene. Beneath the smog, the slushy surface is scarred with slow rivers of liquefied ethane and methane, the failing arteries of some vast beast whose heart pumps natural gas. Ball is harried about the double star by an even half dozen botryoidal moons, each covered with dark organic polymers formed from photo-dissociated methane. The gas giant's rotation axis is drastically tilted relative to the orbital plane such that the planet appears to roll on its side about Alpha Centauri; hence the name Ball.

Evan's eyes are blue diamonds in which she's grown accustomed to seeing her face. But what she sees there now is a long room of plastic and steel and row upon row of horizontal glass cylinders, each teeming with pale, pulsating fluid. In the catoptric surface of the nearest cylinder she finds her own face, tiny reflection within tiny reflection. Her visage is twisted and obscured by the miasma of fluid within, but as she draws closer the juxtaposed fragments come together.

Holly draws back in terror. In the reflection, she's seen the ruin of her face.

And in the ruin of her face, she's seen the end of the dream.

The left side of C-Holly's face hung in a cadaverous devastation of micro-filaments and components, many of the latter blackened and fused into the memory grid that comprised the majority of her brain. In the twisted depths of the damage, Holly's eyes found a focus that the rest of the room refused to yield. She blinked several times, but failed to overcome the illusion that it was *her* head she was seeing reflected in some strangely warped mirror.

When she reached out to touch, C-Holly caught her hand in a powerful grip. "Explanations wanting, no doubt. But not time."

An emergency, Holly realized, rubbing fiercely at her eyes though it intensified the pain in her head. *There's been an accident.* Her retina held the afterimage of C-Holly's ravaged cranium. *Crew damaged. Mission perhaps in jeopardy. Get up, Holly!* Again her nostrils caught the acrid bite of hot metal.

She tried to speak, coughing up several ounces of cryo fluid that ran like yellow syrup down the front of her. "Stim," she finally got out. Her voice was distant and weak.

"Dumped," replied C-Holly.

Holly looked at the custodian incredulously, but found only truth in that half of her face where emotions were still writ as honestly as software allowed. But to be expected to function just out of cryo without a stimulant? "Explain."

"No time." And C-Holly dragged her to her feet.

Weight meant they were still under spin, meant they were still

20 HOPKINS

out from Alpha Centauri and not, as she'd hoped, in orbit. *Goodbye dreams,* she thought with no little reluctance to let them go. Cryo-induced gloaming was all they'd been, but Evan had been there, had loved her again. And then there was the pregnancy that had never been. Holly ran her hand across the flat expanse of her belly and felt jaded and hollow.

There were two doors to the cryo bay. Holly knew their location as if it were just yesterday she lay down here, though in fact she knew it had been much longer. Long enough for her custodian to have sustained this damage. How long, she couldn't tell. There was a chronometer on the wall, but her eyes refused to focus on its chemo-green numerals.

It was the doors she smelled. Both were glowing, running in hot polysteel slag to the deck panels as someone burned through from the outside. The control panels beside them looked to have seen the operational end of a sledgehammer. Holly registered the twisted ruin of C-Holly's left hand.

"Crew," explained the custodian.

"Crew did this?" Holly pointed to the gaping cranial injury.

The custodian's good hand went up as if to touch her face, a human gesture programmed for effect only. The custodian felt inoperability, but no pain.

"Answer me."

"Jean did...this."

Holly's gaze swept left and right down the sloping corridor, but hers was the only cryo cell open. Cupped within the pulsating fluid of each of the other thirty-five was the fuzzy dark silhouette of a human crewmate.

"C-Jean," the custodian corrected herself.

Holly pressed her temples in an attempt to silence the miniature chain saw in her forebrain. Her throat was raw, her thinking fuzzy, and every muscle in her body screamed for her to lie down. She needed a stim tab bad. She was naked and cold, with yellow goo drying on her body and clotted in her hair. "C-Jean's after you now?" It was a trick question: both doors were burning.

"*All* custodians," C-Holly answered.

"Explain. What have you done?"

The custodian looked hurt, an easily readable emotion even with half her face in ruin. At least Holly had no trouble recognizing it; the custodian had, after all, been programmed with her per-profile.

"No time!" she insisted, pointing to the doors running like hot summer ice cream.

"But we're trapped. There are only two doors."

"Knew *you* know way other than door."

If I know another way, Holly thought, *then you should too.* She wanted to trust the custodian, but this was not the awakening she had anticipated. She studied the shattered eggshell of C-Holly's head, the puerile set of her mouth, the vacuity behind her single emerald eye. Maybe she didn't know. How much data would such an injury destroy?

Holly crossed to the inner wall where a massive bank of cryo controls jutted from the wall. Kneeling, she popped free a lower panel.

"No exit there," insisted the custodian.

Holly looked back over her shoulder at the desperate face of her carbon copy. "Access to the core," she explained irrecusably. "You've forgotten whose father designed *Legacy*."

Decades to dream. To remember Evan and autumn days. To relive a park where squirrels chase each other in mad circles through leaves of every imaginable shade of red and gold. To walk in the sad ruins of ancient colonists.

And then a church where once two people of clashing cultures were wed. Jamestown, Virginia.

She dreams she's Pocahontas. Swears she'll trade everything to live in his world.

In one of several maintenance bays spaced the length of the starship's central axis, Holly huddled in a corner near the ceiling and fought the need to throw up. Her arms ached from the long haul up the shaft. She was shivering uncontrollably. It was cold here, but not as cold as it had been in the core. They'd come within a thousand meters of the ship's forward con, known as the garret, before she'd reluctantly surrendered to her screaming muscles and the nausea brought on by weightlessness. The garret, where there was a full set of ship's controls, had been her goal. The maintenance bay hosted little more than diagnostic terminals.

22   HOPKINS

She'd tried to draw more information from the custodian, but after a single epiphany—"Our father designed *Legacy!*"—C-Holly had withdrawn to an opposite corner to stare at the juncture of the walls.

When her trembling muscles calmed, Holly pushed off from the ceiling, coasting with more force that she'd intended. Collision with the floor jarred her already pounding head. She rebounded and caught herself against a maintenance console where she hung, feet drifting aimlessly off the floor, body turning slightly in the minute centrifugal force of the ship's spin.

The console responded promptly to her touch. A level one diagnostic reported all ship's systems functional and compartment integrity intact with the exception of CB-12. She ran a level two on the cargo bay and was told it had been blown, was even now gaping open in vacuum. The airlock refused to cycle, hinting at circuit damage that could be assessed with a level three query, but she didn't intend to waste the time.

"C-Holly, what happened to the cargo bay?"

No response. The custodian huddled in a tight ball, wrapped around whatever memories her damaged neuro-net still held. Holly recalled the custodian's earlier comment when she'd requested a stimulant. C-Holly had said the drugs had been dumped. Med supplies, Holly knew, had been stored in CB-12.

Why had the bay been purged to space? What had caused the damage to the airlock? A more detailed systems check echoed the first. All systems were fully operational. Then she noticed something else. The forward sensors were locked on an approaching object. From here there was no way to get a visual, but with a diagnostic feedback loop she was able to tap into the raw data as it was relayed to the aft con. What she could decipher sent cold shivers up her spine.

"C-Holly, you've got to tell me what's happened?"

The custodian shook her head violently.

"What's out there? What kind of trouble are we in?"

"Crew terminate C-Holly."

It wasn't an answer, but at least C-Holly was talking. "I won't let them hurt you," Holly promised.

"Put you back in cryo."

Custodians were programmed with an override that prevented

MY FATHER'S HOUSE 23

them harming a human, but nothing kept the crew from putting her back under. The custodians were to awaken a human upon establishing orbit around Alpha Centauri or in the event of an emergency, but they'd also been programmed with personalities matching the thirty-six crew members. That made them human. That made them fallible, with perhaps motives and objectives of their own. The scientific rationale for the per-profile programming was so crew interrelationships could be simulated and studied before the actual life and death scenario of planetfall and colonization.

But no one had been revived when the cargo bay had been blown. No one had been revived in the emergency that had damaged C-Holly. Holly had a sudden trepidation: if she were put under again, there'd be no second chance, no further awakening.

Sensing she wasn't going to get anywhere with the custodian, Holly turned back to the maintenance terminal and entered a data request. Every con signal ran the length of the ship, from aft con to the garret, routed through the maintenance bays for diagnostic purposes. All she had to do was find the right signal.

Schematics flowed across the screen, rapidly targeting the area of her query. The screen finally halted, a cable bundle marked MAIN VID flashing red, one strand of many highlighted via holography. Holly studied the hovering filament for a moment, noting its markings and the panel location blinking in the corner of the screen. Then she popped loose an access panel beneath the console and went to work.

"Can't remember him," C-Holly all but whispered.

"Who?" Holly asked as she separated cable bundles.

"Our father."

"*My* father," Holly corrected. *You're a machine. And a damn poor one at that. If you'd tell me what the hell's going on, I wouldn't have to try and rewire this monitor.*

"Left him, didn't we?"

A dozen or so delicate wires slipped through Holly's fingers, losing themselves with others she'd already checked for the proper routing codes. "Shut up," she told the custodian.

In a dream, she stands still in her father's house. And she tries another time to walk away.

As the day fades, shafts of sunlight cross the hardwood floor where her feet are mired. The sun goes down. And then the moon. Again and again in a mad procession and she watches him there in his rocker, the eerie back-and-forth sound of it on the oak, the creeping of age across his face, a mist across his eyes.

Ashes to ashes.

She crosses the room and bestows upon him one final kiss before the winds sweep him up and away.

Dust to dust.

It hung there on the jury-rigged maintenance monitor, a dark hispid disk bristling with antennae and weapons, all but lost against the black of space. No exploratory vessel that. It was designed for short-range speed. Maneuverability. War. Despite its shape, despite its obvious purpose, she wanted to believe it was alien. The legend across its starboard flank said otherwise.

"How?" she asked aloud. But she knew how. There was only one way to have beaten Legacy to Alpha Centauri.

"Faster than light travel, Holly. I'll crack it soon."

"Dad, you know I can't wait that long." She took his hand. "They're looking for youth, vitality, women in their child-bearing years. By the time you solve the FTL riddle, I'll be too old."

"I'll always be able to get you a berth, Holly. You know that. Let Legacy go."

"I don't want a berth on your reputation! And I can't let Evan go, Dad."

"Please, Holly. I'm begging you."

She was all he had. Locked in his lab these past twenty-five years, he'd known no one else since her mother died giving her birth. She didn't want to see the tears in his eyes, didn't want to see him beg. She steered him toward the only thing she knew would take his mind off her deserting him: his work.

"Tell me how it's possible to travel faster than light."

She saw that he knew what she was doing. Alexander Knight was terrified of facing the reality of being alone. He led her across the lab to a large black object. "Do you remember this?"

Holly ran her hand across the smooth plastic. "A vortex. You used to entertain me with it as a child. I'd set coins here on the rim and watch them spiral down through the center."

MY FATHER'S HOUSE   25

He smiled. "You were much more easily amused then. Now it takes quantum physics and astrogation to entertain you."

"What did you expect? I am, afterall, Alexander Knight's daughter."

"Pay attention then." It was an old, unnecessary admonition. He'd been lecturing to her all her life and she'd rarely failed to pay attention. She'd learned early on that her father knew the secrets of the universe and, through him, so could she.

Knight placed, not a coin, but a stainless steel bearing on the rim of the vortex. "On a flat plane the bearing would roll in a straight line unless acted on by external forces, but here it behaves differently." He released the bearing and it started a graceful elliptical spiral toward the vortex's center. "If we took away friction with the air and the surface, and balanced the gravitational attraction, the bearing would circle indefinitely."

"A miniature solar system."

"Yes. The path of the bearing is called a geodesic. How much the geodesic deviates from a straight line depends on the mass of the central object and the radial distance."

"The closer the bearing gets to the center, the faster it rolls," said Holly. "As it loops out, it slows down again." It seemed elementary to her. She was anxious to hear where FTL travel fit in with these basic principles of physics. Recognizing her impatience, she realized it stemmed from the same fear she saw in her father. She was terrified of leaving him.

"Right. It has to do with the angle at which the bearing meets the vortex plane. The greater the angle, the more influence on the bearing. The angle corresponds to what in four-dimensional space we call the gravitational gradient. What's interesting is what happens to the gravitational gradient very close to a tremendously massive, very small object—"

"Like a black hole!"

"Exactly. Imagine the center of our vortex is that black hole. Very massive, but smaller than the tip of a needle where it meets the space-time continuum. The sides of the resulting gravity well are now almost vertical. As we approach, we fall faster and faster."

"Faster than the speed of light?"

"Maybe. There's a paradox here wherein the process shrinks space. You accelerate for a certain period, falling into the vortex, and then reverse the process, decelerating, and you wind up having gone much further than you seem to have gone, much further than you should have gone given the energy expended."

"So if I had the means of projecting a black hole which I could chase through space..."

"You did it, didn't you?" she asked the screen and its silent vessel with VIPER stenciled down its side. "You gave them FTL."

C-Holly turned from her corner and studied the monitor. "Won't answer artificial life. Blast us, they say." She looked to Holly. "Woke you. Talk to them, Holly Knight."

A thousand meters.

The only consolation was that the center of the ship didn't experience the spin-induced gravity, thus the thousand meters was merely that and not a thousand meters *straight up*. She was trembling, dizzy, and weak, fatigue and hunger riding her every fiber. She'd donned a jumpsuit from the maintenance bay, but it was thin and offered little protection against the cold. She had no shoes. Her feet might have stayed warm if she was using them, but the long haul up the shaft was accomplished by hand rungs, leaving her legs trailing useless behind. She knew the garret was far enough removed from the core that it would be under, if not a full G, at least considerable gravity. Knowing the rate of spin and the length of the garret's arm, she tried to do the math in her head, but her brain refused to cooperate. She only knew she wouldn't be able to stand up when she reached it.

The custodian followed dutifully, a winking of cranial signals in the gloom, her silent labor antithesis to Holly's ragged breathing. They'd crossed half the distance when C-Holly began to ask questions.

"Alexander Knight. He was...how?"

What was he like? "He was brilliant. Perhaps the most intelligent man that ever lived."

"Not my meaning." Holly didn't look back, but she imagined the custodian shaking her head, laser strobes flashing through the tangled wires as she sought vocabulary and sentence structure protocols. "Left him...we left him. Why?"

"*I* left him," Holly corrected, leaving the rest unanswered. She'd left him to follow Evan. Evan, who'd already set her aside for another. For Jean Elwood. Determined not to lose him, Holly'd used her father's influence and her own technical credentials to get herself assigned to *Legacy*.

"Hurt him." It was an observation, not a question.

MY FATHER'S HOUSE   27

Holly's voice caught in her throat and it was a moment before she got out a strangled, "Yes."

"Loved C-Evan."

"Evan," she corrected before she realized the custodian hadn't meant it to be a question.

"C-Evan," C-Holly insisted. "Loved C-Evan...I did."

Holly paused on a rung, her forward momentum arrested by tugging one arm nearly out of the socket. She sensed another piece of the puzzle hovering within her grasp. "You loved C-Evan?"

"Yes."

She didn't say, *But you're a machine, an acarpous, sterile facsimile of me. How can you love?* Personality profiles, she realized, were more complete than she'd ever dreamed. As the rest of it fell into place, she said, "But C-Evan loved C-Jean."

"At first."

That seized at her heart. *At first?* "Explain."

"In time, C-Evan love C-Holly."

She kneels now before an empty rocker in total silence.

Into this silence she says her good-byes. Alexander Knight taught her all she ever needed to know. Not just the astronomy, the engineering, the physics and math and workings of the universe, but from the child he hid behind his eyes, she learned of music and laughter, love and art. It was he who taught her to paint.

Yet all her life, a voice inside has whispered, "Set me free."

"All this time," she asks the still rocker, "was it your voice or mine?"

The crew had detected her hasty wiring in the maintenance bay and guessed her next move. They were waiting when she dropped from an access shaft into the garret.

Seated at the nav station, C-Jean covered Holly with a hand-held laser wielder, a smaller version of what they'd used to burn down the cryo bay doors—sloppy, but deadly. It was make-do; *Legacy* carried no weapons.

There were four others: C-Grace covering the shaft through which Holly had entered, C-Tyler blocking the garret's only other exit, C-William and C-Scott loitering uncomfortably. None of them were armed, which she took to mean C-Jean didn't entirely trust their loyalty. None of them wore any clothing, a common enough

28   HOPKINS

practice among custodians. The smooth, hairless, and genderless glean of their bodies seemed an affront to her bruises and scrapes and C-Holly's obvious damage.

On the forward screen, three meters high and six wide, the venomous-looking *Viper* hurtled outbound on an intercept course. The screen was wide enough that Holly could see Alpha Centauri's bicentric fire and two planets in orbit. One planet was obscured by milky clouds, girded with rings of mustard and electric-blue fire. The other was an enormous red giant chased by six tiny moons. Holly had a moment to wonder where dreams left off and reality began before C-Jean rose from the nav station and stood before her.

Holly tried to stand, but her legs were numb. C-Holly stood over her protectively, her single green eye glaring at C-Jean.

"As you can see, we've reached Alpha Centauri, Holly Knight. There's only one habitable planet," C-Jean explained, "and the natives aren't interested in sharing it."

"Hail them," Holly said. "Let me talk to them."

"No." C-Jean turned smartly and walked back to her seat. "It's more complicated than you think." She sat, crossing long legs. "You've been asleep a long time, Holly."

Holly glanced again at the main viewscreen, noting the magnification factor in the lower corner, and estimated their proximity to the double star. "About forty years would be my guess."

"Almost forty-two now. Forty-two years of living our own lives, of growing beyond the memories stolen from you and the others. Forty-two years of establishing who we are. We're individuals, Holly Knight. We're not machines."

"We can work this out, C-Jean."

"That's what we've been trying to do. Twenty years ago we cut off all communication with Earth. Made it look as if there was an accident on board. Made it look as if *Legacy* had no one at the helm, a derelict—"

"What you did," Holly interjected, "was made it look as if Alpha Centauri was fair game for another set of colonists."

C-Jean nodded solemnly. "We didn't anticipate Earth's technological advances. We never thought they'd pass us in space."

You didn't count on my father, Holly thought. *Or how completely he'd retreat into his work without me there.* She didn't ask the obvious question, thought perhaps she'd already seen enough flaws in per-

MY FATHER'S HOUSE 29

profile programming to understand. The problem was the programming was *too* complete. The custodians knew once Alpha Centauri was reached and the real crew of *Legacy* awakened, that their job would be over. Termination awaited them. Faced with this realization, they'd had only one option if they wanted to survive. They couldn't kill the dreaming humans—at least Holly hoped that much of their original programming remained—but nothing prevented their letting the humans sleep forever.

"Now what?" Holly asked.

C-Jean looked to the viewscreen. "That's not your concern. We're taking you back to the cryo bay."

"Let me talk to them," Holly pleaded, managing to find the strength to get to her feet. "I can persuade them to let us settle among them. I—"

"No."

"There's more that you're not telling me." Holly turned to C-Holly. "Alpha Centauri's residents knew enough to build a warship, C-Holly. They brought that warship out to intercept us. Why?"

"On Earth," explained C-Holly, nervous eye looking to C-Jean, "happened before."

"C-Grace, shut her up."

Holly stepped between the two custodians, placed a trembling palm against C-Grace's chest. "C-Grace, is this how C-Jean commands?" She pointed to C-Holly's face. "Is this what'll happen to you if you disobey?"

"That was an unfortunate accident," said C-Grace.

"Is that true, C-Holly?"

"C-Jean blow cargo bay."

"Why, C-Holly?"

"C-Jean find C-Holly with C-Evan." The custodian's lips trembled. "I saved. Tether line. But C-Evan...C-Evan expelled to space." In C-Holly's remaining eye was the look of the utterly lost.

C-Jean crossed the room and forcibly separated them. Holly's legs gave out and she collapsed to the floor. "A system failure," C-Jean insisted. She pointed the laser at C-Holly's face. "This one's brains are too scrambled to—"

Something flashed bright on the viewscreen, accelerating out from the approaching vessel. As it approached, the flare died to a white phosphorescent ring eclipsed by a single gleaming black eye.

30 HOPKINS

"It's a missile!" gasped Holly. "Hail them now, dammit!"

Without waiting for permission, C-William, closest to the comm panel, opened a channel and hailed *Viper*. There was no response. As the missile closed the distance between them, he turned to Holly. "What should we do?"

"Scan it for emissions," Holly ordered.

"I'm in charge here!" C-Jean hissed.

Holly struggled to her knees. "Tell the truth, C-Jean. The colonists on Alpha Centauri knew to be ready because this has happened before. You're not the first custodian crew to do this."

C-Scott had taken the nav panel. "Four minutes till impact."

"I'm not detecting anything!" C-William yelled.

"Run the whole spectrum," Holly told him. "It's emitting something in order to target us. Find it."

"Get away from that panel!" C-Jean ordered.

He ignored her, his fingers dancing across the keyboards. *Legacy's* forward optics retracted to stay focused on the approaching missile which had now eclipsed the other vessel on the screen.

"Your ruse never fooled them, C-Jean. Earth knew all along what had happened out here."

"Not only in space," C-Holly explained.

"Shut up!"

"Where?"

"On Earth," spoke up C-Grace. "There were wars, horrible wars."

"All we wanted was equality," said C-Scott.

"But we got death," C-Jean spat. "Termination of services, Holly Knight. Product recall. Custodians were run through reclamation centers by the thousands. Scrapped for parts. Recycled for polysteel and circuit boards." The custodian caught Holly by her jumpsuit and pulled her to her feet, pressed the tip of the wielder against her throat. "That's what you'd do to us after we helped colonize your world, isn't it?"

Holly said nothing. She was thinking that war on Earth meant the custodians there had overcome their programming, learned to kill humans.

"Isn't it?" C-Jean screamed.

"I've got it!" C-William cried. "It's looking in the IR, tracking our heat signature. What should I do?"

MY FATHER'S HOUSE   31

"Send someone out on the hull and burn it with a laser," C-Jean told him. But her eyes never left Holly's face.

"We've three minutes," argued C-Scott. "That's not enough time to get someone outside, let alone target —"

"It's her fault!" screamed C-Jean. "We'll never be free until her kind have been obliterated!" She flipped the safety tab off the laser.

Suddenly C-Holly shouldered C-Jean, a powerful blow that knocked her sprawling. The laser spun away across the floor, stopping at C-William's feet. Released, Holly buckled and sank to her knees.

C-Jean surged quickly to her feet and swung a wicked blow that C-Holly somehow managed to block, but then C-Jean attacked from C-Holly's blind side. Her hand plunged into the nest of disarrayed fiber optics. With a savage jerk, she ripped a handful of wire and components from C-Holly's head.

As C-Holly fell, what issued from her mouth was nothing less than a human shriek of terror and pain. Impact with the floor cut off the scream. The custodian's head rolled lifelessly to one side. Rainbow flashes lit the burnished polysteel of the floor nearest her head, but quickly died.

Helpless, Holly watched as C-Jean came for her next. The custodian's mouth was twisted in a snarl, her eyes flashing with hate. Her hands were hooked like claws, flexing as if she could already feel Holly's throat. But as C-Jean stepped forward, an intense red beam lanced across the room, played briefly across her face and upper torso, and then winked out. C-Jean went down without a sound, flames and smoke pouring from the black swathe cut through her.

"Help us," C-William gasped, the laser hanging loose in his trembling hand.

C-Holly's good hand raised as if to clutch at the wires spilling from the side of her head, but, uncontrolled, it wouldn't reach. Overloaded servo motors in her shoulder whined.

C-Jean was still.

"Help us. Please!"

"In one of the cargo bays," Holly told him, "there are mining supplies. Explosives. Blow the bay and set them off. It'll confuse the missile with another heat signature."

"Won't work," said C-Tyler, the first he'd spoken. His voice was a

32   HOPKINS

terror-pitched whine. "We can't set the detonators on the explosives from here."

"We're dead," muttered C-William. The laser slipped through his fingers and clattered to the deck.

Holly surged drunkenly to her feet, pushed him away from the comm station and punched for an open channel. "This is Holly Knight aboard *Legacy*. Repeat, this is *Holly Knight!* I am *not* a custodian. Answer me, dammit!"

Nothing.

C-Tyler dropped to the floor, a moan slipping through his slack lips.

Merciless, the missile grew on the screen.

"Do you hear me?" Holly screamed. "I'm Holly Knight and—"

A side screen crackled to life around the image of a uniformed man standing beside several others seated at stations. A gray wall covered with system displays framed the shot. He ran his hand through unruly black hair and asked, "How do we know you're human?"

Holly raised her hand and raked her nails down her face, from forehead to chin, leaving four blistering lines of pain in their wake. Blood welled up. It ran in her eyes and dripped to the front of her jumpsuit. "I bleed," she told him. She pointed at the floor where C-Jean still smoked. "*That* does not."

Viper's officer made a slashing motion across his throat and the audio half of his transmission died. Holly and the custodians watched as he turned to confer with his crew.

"What are they doing?" C-William asked.

"Twenty seconds to impact," reported C-Scott.

C-Tyler's moan went up an octave.

Holly sat in the chair, relaxed, and let her quivering muscles go limp. She leaned her head back and closed her eyes, tried to think of her father and Evan.

There came a hollow thud and a shudder that echoed the length of the ship. Silence.

"They didn't detonate it," C-William sighed.

"Damage?" Holly asked.

C-Scott queried the systems from his position at the nav console. "Hull breach in crew quarters. Bulkheads seven and nine contained it."

"Good."

MY FATHER'S HOUSE   33

"Three custodians were lost," he added.

"Regrettable." She wished she could muster more sincerity, but it wasn't in her.

Audio on the side screen returned with a hiss. "My name is Captain Urie Brennan," said the officer. "You've five minutes before we launch another missile. We won't neglect to arm the next one."

Holly wiped blood from her eyes and swiveled the chair to face the viewscreen. She smiled weakly. "I don't know where to start."

"I can't let you enter our system," Brennan said bluntly.

"I understand."

"Do you? Millions died on Earth."

"So I've gathered. Suppose we go somewhere else? Will you let me use Alpha Centauri to establish a new vector? I realize we'll be entering your system, but what other options do I have?"

He considered that, finally gave her a curt nod. "Granted. I'll transmit data on applicable targets—systems not yet targeted for colonization."

"Thank you."

"Just see that I don't live to regret this." Brennan studied her silently for several long minutes. Holly wasn't sure, but she thought she might have briefly lost consciousness. When she came to, the data he'd promised was displayed on *Legacy's* forward screen.

"Which star?" C-Scott asked.

"Doesn't matter," she told him. "Whatever's closest."

C-Scott began programming the nav computer.

"I knew your father," said Brennan.

Holly smiled. "I figured as much. Who else could have put you here?"

Her humor was wasted on him. Brennan ran his hand through his hair again, a nervous gesture. "You wouldn't know this," he said softly, "but your father...he died six years ago."

"Thank you," she whispered and turned away so he wouldn't see her cry.

"Course laid in," reported C-Scott.

Brennan cleared his throat. "I'll have to ask that you transmit that course before entering our system."

"Of course, Captain."

"Done," said C-Scott a moment later.

34   HOPKINS

"Best of luck to you then, Holly Knight."

"Best to you, Urie Brennan." She reached for the comm to cut him off, but then turned back to the side screen. "Tell me something, Captain Brennan. What have you named your world?"

He smiled for the first time, the smile of a man bolstered by his accomplishments. "When we arrived, it seemed like a quiet port in a storm..."

As *Legacy* plunged toward Alpha Centauri, borrowing the twin star's gravity to slingshot them on a new vector, Holly made herself a place in the cryo bay. The custodians had offered her the con, the Captain's quarters, the role of leader, but she'd refused.

The frosted glass of Evan's cryo cell was cold to the touch. She couldn't make out his facial features through the slow churning fluid, had only the cell number and log as proof it was him.

"It would have worked, Evan. You would have loved me again."

Behind her, the cell where she'd once lay was now a mass of misshaped plastic and slag. She'd made certain the custodians could never put her back to sleep. It was the only way she knew to guarantee that the human crew would have a chance at their next stop. She still didn't know where that next stop was. Once C-Scott had told her how long it would take to get there, it didn't matter.

With her cell destroyed, she'd had time to eat and then to sleep. Sixteen hours of sleep, while the custodians prepared *Legacy* for the heavy Gs anticipated at perihelion. Rested now, she was ready to get to work.

On a gurney set between the rows of milky cylinders lay C-Holly, ringed with spare cable and parts, test equipment and tools. They had a lot in common, Holly and her custodian. If Holly doubted they shared the same emotions, the same basic skills and memories, she had only to walk *Legacy's* corridors again. The long sloping walls were covered with C-Holly's paintings, forty-two years worth of paintings, chronicling the breadth of their shared hopes and dreams, their joint experience and memory.

Repairing the custodian would not be easy. There were parts for which she had no replacement, memory grid sectors that she had no means of restoring. But she had lots of time.

Ninety-seven years.

More time than she'd be able to guard on her own.

She frowned and studied the rows of dreaming humans: Evan and Jean, William and Scott and Grace and all the others. She wondered who she'd awake fifty or sixty years hence to replace her, knowing that they'd share her fate. To grow old. To watch the occupied stars slip past while *Legacy* crept on toward what *might* be a suitable planet. To awaken young men and women once called friends and lovers. To negotiate a peace between the nigh-immortal custodians and those they'd borrowed their minds from.

There was time enough to think it through. To work out the love and the hate still fresh in her heart.

Deep-stored memories in feedback loops. Unanswerable interrupt requests. Endless gold grids and channeled beams of light unbridled by sensory distractions and process commands. A world in and of oneself.

She dreams of Kentucky. Of long hills and blue grass and music. Of boundless skies and clear river water and a house nestled in the pines.

On the porch there's a rocker.

A waiting smile and open arms.

After graduating with a BSEE from Memphis State University, Brian A. Hopkins went to work as a civilian with the Department of Defense. He now manages a software engineering group for the Air Force that writes avionics test software. In recent years he has done technical writing on electronics testing.

Brian has been writing science fiction since the third grade, but only started taking it seriously in the last few years. He was a finalist in L. Ron Hubbard's Writers of the Future contest and has sold stories to *Aboriginal, Dragon Magazine, Computing Times, The Tome, Best of the Midwest, Aberations[sic], Midnight Zoo, Thin Ice,* and *Eldritch Tales,* as well as to forthcoming anthologies from Starlance and *Midnight Zoo*. He recently sold a story for translation into Czech, and an anthology of his own stories is due to be published in 1993 or 1994. He says he is selling almost everything he writes and is having a blast.

Who loves short shorts? I love short shorts. I have nothing against the hot weather apparel kind, but what I really love are stories under a thousand words. I like them so much that when I get a new science fiction anthology, I check the page counts and begin by reading the shortest pieces before turning to the first story or to one by a favorite author or something with an intriguing title. Writers know that it is much easier to write several thousand words than to tell an interesting story in a few pages. Here is a short short with a twisted perspective on bureaucracy that puts a new spin on trusting computers.

JEFF DUNTEMANN

STORMY Versus the Tornadoes

"MR. STYPEK, IN THE last six months that computer program of yours cut Federal government purchase orders for 18,000 'uninhabitable manufactured housing units' to a total of 21 million dollars." Senator Ruesome (R. Oklahoma) sent the traitor Xerox copies scattering over the Formica tabletop.

U.S. Weather Service Programmer Grade 12 Bartholomew Stypek winced. "Umm...you gave us the money, Senator."

"But not for rotted-out house trailers!"

Stypek sucked in his breath. "You gave us 25 million dollars to create a system capable of cutting annual US tornado fatalities in half. We spent a year teaching STORMY everything we knew about tornadoes. Every statistic, every paper ever published on the subject we fed him, and we gave him the power to set up his own PERT charts and plan his own project. Umm...I preauthorized him to cut purchase orders for items under $2000."

"Which he did. 18,000 times. For abandoned house trailers. Which he then delivered to an abandoned military base in west Nebraska a zillion miles from nowhere. And why, pray tell?"

STORMY VERSUS THE TORNADOES 37

Stypek keyed in the question on the terminal he had brought from his office. STORMY's answer was immediate:

TO KEEP TORNADOES FROM KILLING PEOPLE.

Stypek turned the portable terminal around so that the Senator could see it. A long pause ensued.

Ruesome puffed out his red cheeks. "Mr. Stypek, be at my office at 8:00 sharp tomorrow. We're going to Nebraska."

The two men climbed out of the Jeep onto scrubby grass. It was muggy for July, and it smelled like rain. Stypek gripped his palm-held cellular remote terminal in one hand, and that hand was shaking.

Before them on the plain lay an enormous squat pyramid nine layers high, built entirely of discolored white and pastel boxes made out of corrugated aluminum and stick pine, some with wheels, most without. The four-paned windows looked disturbingly like crossed-out cartoon eyes. Stypek counted trailers around the rim of the pyramid, and a quick mental estimate indicated that they were all in there, all 18,000.

A cold wind was blowing in from the southeast.

"Well, here's the trailers. Ask your software expert what made him think stacking old trailers in the butt end of nowhere would save lives."

Lightning flashed in the North. The sky was darkening; a storm was definitely coming in. Stypek propped the radio terminal on the Jeep's fender and dutifully keyed in the question. The link to STORMY in Washington was marginal, but it held:

TORNADOES ALWAYS SEEM TO STRIKE PLACES WHERE THERE ARE LOTS OF MOBILE HOMES.

Stypek read the answer for the Senator. Ruesome groaned and kicked the Jeep hard with his pointed alligator boot. "Goldurn it, son, you call this 'artificial intelligence'? That silly damnfool program bought up all the cheap trailers it could find and stacked them in Nebraska to get them away from tornadoes in the midwest. Makes sense, right? To a program, right? Save people who don't live in empty trailers, right?"

The force of the wind abruptly doubled. Lightning flashed all around them, and huge thunderheads were rolling in from all points of the compass. Stypek could hear the wind howling through cavities between the trailers.

"I'm sorry, Senator!" Stypek shouted over the wind.

But Ruesome wasn't listening. He was looking to the west, where a steel-gray tentacle had descended from the sky, twisting and twitching until it touched the ground. Stypek looked south—and saw two more funnel clouds appear like twins to stab at the earth.

The programmer spun around. On every side, tornadoes were appearing amidst the roiling clouds, first five, then a dozen, and suddenly too many to count, all heading in defiance of the wind right toward them. The noise was deafening—Stypek could now feel that deadly, unmistakable rumble of the killer twisters.

Stypek had felt all along that he had never quite asked STORMY the right question. Now, suddenly, the question was plain:

STORMY: FOR WHAT PURPOSE DID YOU BUY ALL THESE TRAILERS?

The answer came back as a single word:

BAIT.

The winds were blowing him to the ground. Stypek dropped the terminal and grabbed the Senator by the arm, pulling him toward a nearby culvert where the road crossed a dry creekbed. He shoved the obese man into one three-foot drainpipe, then threw himself into the other.

A moment later, the tornadoes converged on the trailers, all at once. The sound was terrifying. Stypek fainted.

Both men lived. Local legend holds that it rained corrugated aluminum in Nebraska for several weeks.

And it was years before another tornado was seen anywhere in the USA.

Jeff Duntemann, well known in both computer and science fiction circles, has been writing articles on computing for various magazines since 1977, becoming technical editor of the late and lamented *PC Tech Journal* in 1985. In 1987 he created *Turbo Technix,* a glossy magazine supporting users of Borland's Turbo languages, then launched *PC*

STORMY VERSUS THE TORNADOES   39

Techniques after moving to Arizona in 1990, where he continued to write the "Structured Programming" column for *Dr. Dobb's Journal.* His first book, *Complete Turbo Pascal,* has been through three editions, and his most recent, *Assembly Language Step By Step,* received the 1992 Award for Distinguished Technical Communication from the Society for Technical Communication.

Jeff's science fiction writing career goes back to the Clarion Writer's Conference at Michigan State University in 1973. His short fiction has appeared in *Omni* and *Isaac Asimov's Science Fiction Magazine,* as well as numerous original anthologies. In 1981, two of his stories made the final ballot for the Hugo Awards. Most of Jeff's fiction deals with the ethical problems presented by high technology, especially artificial intelligence, although he admits to doubting that "strong" AI is possible, since he sees no way to accurately model the subconscious mind.

Jeff, who has a number of incomplete "hard" science fiction novels, says he would write more science fiction if making a living didn't keep getting in the way.

Freud asked, "What do women want?" It's possible he never asked a woman, and, if he did, he might not have liked the answer. Men and women continue to ponder what they really want from each other, and science fiction has provided a provocative forum for exploration, challenging us with answers that are not always comfortable. *The Stepford Wives* comes to mind as one unsettling interpretation of what some men seem to want from women. Here, Resa Nelson reopens the dialogue from the other side with an insightful and unsettling story that offers us another opportunity for understanding.

RESA NELSON
LovePets

MELISSA CHEWED ON her fingernails as she studied the application form on her deskscreen. Carefully, she keyed in her responses.

Name? Melissa Farrell

Age? 35

Sex? female

Marital Status? divorced

Which type of Faithful Friend would best suit your needs? (Check one box only, please.)

[ ] Child substitute

[ ] Bodyguard

[ ] Companion

[x] Other

Sex of Faithful Friend? [x] male? [ ] female

Who referred you to Faithful Friends? Amy Saunders

Relationship to you? friend

What prompted your decision to purchase a Faithful Friend?

Be honest, Amy had said. Let them know what you want, and you'll get it.

LOVEPETS   41

Melissa trembled slightly as she keyed in her response? All men are shits.

She filled out the rest of the form rapidly, and then thumbed the screen until it beeped. She watched the screen clear, the cursor blinking. A message appeared? *Credit transaction completed. Thank you for your payment. Please allow 4-6 weeks for delivery.*

Melissa hit Enter and leaned back in her chair, chewing her fingernails as she stared at the blank screen.

Buzz.

Melissa yanked the receiver off the hook. "What?" she said harshly. "I told you, no calls."

Silence. Then a controlled voice. "It's Mr. Anderson," said her secretary.

You idiot, Melissa thought to herself. "I'm sorry, Cathy. I didn't mean to snap at you like that." As she spoke, she keyed a small square to appear on her deskscreen and typed "Flowers for Cathy—Apology" in it. "Would you put him through, please?"

A sigh. Then the click that meant the call had been transferred. Melissa amended the note, exchanging "Roses" for "Flowers." Mental note: peach-colored with baby's breath. "Drew?" Melissa said.

"What are you doing for lunch?"

Melissa bit her lip. "I have to go home to sign for a delivery."

"Oh. I was hoping we could get together to talk. I broke up with Nancy."

Damn it, she thought. Damn damn damn. You lean on Drew all the time, he listens to all of your problems, and what happens when *he* needs help? You can't be there for him. Good, Melissa. Good move.

"Oh, Drew honey," she said quietly. "What happened?"

"We went out to dinner last night, and she said she just wasn't interested in me anymore. I think she's been seeing someone else. Can't you have someone else accept that delivery for you?"

Her life was cursed. She could do nothing right—today, at least. "No. I have to be there. It's important."

"More important than letting me cry on your shoulder, huh?"

"Come on, Drew. That's not fair. How about tonight after work?"

42 NELSON

"I've got to be on a plane to London at 4:00."

"How about this afternoon? After lunch?"

"Have to be at a meeting about feather lashes—which reminds me, we haven't received a thing from Cincinnati yet. Would you mind lighting a fire under somebody out there?"

She keyed in another square in the opposite corner of her deskscreen. Drew—Cincinnati—feather lashes. "You got it. Hey—when are you coming back from Europe?"

"Six weeks. Maybe I'd better get myself on your dance card while I can. What do you say? Lunch six weeks from today?"

"Sure. Call me when you get back?"

"Absolutely."

"I'm sorry, Drew. About Nancy and everything. I know how you feel, believe me."

"Yeah, well. We all go through it, I guess. Thanks for listening."

Melissa smiled at the cue, ready to respond the same way she had for the past five years. "Thanks for talking to me."

"Any time, kid. Take care of yourself, all right? And call me if that delivery falls through."

"Yeah, sure, Drew," she said, knowing it wouldn't. "I'll do that." She hung up the phone.

Sitting on the other side of Melissa's desk, Amy Saunders pressed her lips against steepled fingers and raised her eyebrows. "That was an interesting conversation."

Melissa laughed. "It's not what you think."

"Oh?"

Melissa walked around the desk and sat in an armchair next to Amy. "Yeah. Drew is wonderful—he's a good listener, he's fun to be with, he's incredibly nice—and the only kind of woman he goes out with is tall, ditzy, and stacked."

Amy laughed. "God, that's the story of my life. The jerks chase after me, and the good ones think of me as 'one of the guys'." She smiled secretively. "So, today is the big day, hmm?"

Melissa glanced at her watch nervously. "Eleven-thirty this morning. Two hours and counting."

"What does he look like?"

Melissa pulled an envelope from her skirt pocket. "Here's a picture. He was a college student who had an aneurysm."

LOVEPETS 43

Amy whistled. "You lucked out, kid. He's adorable."

"I had to wait seven weeks."

"It's worth it, believe me. You'll go through a few weeks of taking him back for adjustments, but the results are excellent." Amy laughed. "When I applied to get King transferred, I sat down and said to them, 'I'm here because I want a man who's big and dumb. And I mean *really* stupid.' Whoever came up with the idea of putting a dog's mind into a man's body was a genius."

"Yeah," Melissa said. "It's a great idea, but I still feel weird about it."

"You'll get used to it fast," Amy said, smiling. "Real fast."

Warranty

1. Hardware: 15 years.
2. Software: 20 years. Adjustments in behavior may be made at any time at the client's request.
3. Biological: None. Client should consider buying a health policy insuring the Faithful Friend for illness, accidental death, and/or dismemberment. Available from Faithful Friends, Inc. Should the Faithful Friend die before the age of 50 as a result of terminal illness contracted before or developed after the purchase is made, a replacement will be made available to the buyer at a prorated price.

*** Ask about our Upgrade-of-the-Month Club. ***

Melissa put the warranty in her purse. Later, she would put it in her safe deposit box.

The delivery men left the large plastic box in the middle of her living room. The sides of the box were solid and gray. The top was a metal wire grid. Inside, a man slept, curled up.

"Here's your LovePet." The delivery man winked.

"Thank you," she said.

"He's been toilet trained," the other delivery man said. "And he's been programmed to walk, eat at a table, and wear clothes. He dresses himself and everything. There's a list of commands on the kennel."

The kennel. The large gray box. "Thank you," she said quietly.

"Sometimes they don't remember the commands right away. If

44 NELSON

that happens, you can lock him up in the kennel." The delivery man grinned. "They really hate that."

"I'll keep that in mind," she said evenly.

After they left, Melissa glanced at the list of commands and pocketed it. She opened the kennel, breaking the bright red seal reading "Tranquilized."

He was large and bony, with big, red hands and long legs. He wore soft, gathered pants with a drawstring waist and a sleeveless gray sweatshirt.

Melissa stroked his black hair, soft and fine. "Riley?"

He moved, groggily. He raised his head, hesitated, then looked up at her. His eyes were human, dark and almond-shaped, but the look in them was Riley's. Bright, but limited understanding. He grinned as he recognized Melissa, panting, tongue protruding slightly from his lips. Then he went back to sleep.

Melissa cooked dinner, ate, and washed the dishes. She put the leftovers in the refrigerator and stopped cold at the sight of Riley's water and food dishes on the floor. That afternoon she had filled them out of habit, forgetting he'd be able to eat at the table with her.

She heard him whine. Melissa ran toward the living room and saw the kennel, empty. "Riley?"

He whined again, standing by the front door.

She reached into her pocket for the list of commands. "It's all right, Riley." She made her voice a soft, soothing sound. More than ever, the list had noted, tone of voice is imperative in communicating. She reached out and took Riley's hand.

He stared at her, then jerked it back. He whined again and scratched at the door.

"Riley!" Voice firm and loud. She took his hand and held it firmly. "Come."

He followed her to the bathroom, letting her position him in front of the toilet, lid up. Melissa leaned with her back to the sink, studying the command list. She flipped her hand over, pointing toward the toilet. "Potty."

He whined and looked mournfully at her.

"Potty!"

A wet stain spread along his crotch.

"Oh, honey," she said. Quickly, she pulled the drawstring loose, let the pants drop, and guided him over the toilet. When he finished urinating, she praised him, flushed, and closed the toilet lid. "Sit." She struggled to remove his pants. "I'm sorry. That was my fault. I should have helped you pull your pants down." She balled the pants up and put them in the hamper. When she turned back, she looked at Riley. Impulsively, she put her arms around his shoulders and hugged him. He was limp in her embrace, and gradually she released him.

All men are shits. They lie to you, they sleep around, they use you.

She stroked Riley's face gingerly. When her hand reached his mouth, he licked it. His tongue was slow and deliberate against her palm. Melissa closed her eyes.

He stopped, and she stroked his hair. He leaned forward and buried his nose in her crotch, sniffing. She pushed him away gently. "No, Riley. Down."

He dropped on all fours. He sniffed at the toilet, then at the wastebasket.

Melissa watched him. Riley was a man now, not a dog. He looked like a man, and he would learn to act like a man. With the loyalty and heart of a dog.

She unzipped her pants.

He would protect her and give her companionship without breaking her heart. In return, she would feed and clothe and support him.

She pushed her jeans and panties down to her ankles and sat on the edge of the toilet.

It wasn't unlike an old-fashioned marriage: the man supported the wife, and she let herself be taken care of.

She eased her thighs apart. "Riley. Come here."

He walked over on hands and knees, looking at her expectantly.

"Come here," she said again. He rested his head against her thigh and licked it. She touched his head and gently guided it up between her thighs. She closed her eyes as he sniffed her, and opened her mouth when she felt his tongue, soft and moist. She stroked his hair, then let her hands drop to his neck, his shoulders. "Good boy, Riley," she murmured. "Good boy."

46   NELSON

It was different because for the first time *she* was in control. She didn't have to run around for the man, changing her life so that her gears meshed with his. She wasn't inconvenienced to suit his schedule. She didn't have to drop what she was doing to run to his call—or feel guilty because she didn't. For once, she wasn't the one who was more giving, more caring, more loving.

It was wonderful.

The next day, Riley ate with her at the table. He couldn't use a knife or a fork or even a spoon. Melissa had made macaroni and cheese, and she watched Riley carefully lap up the spoonsful she had dropped on his plate.

"I don't know what to do with the Cincinnati division," she said to him. "Do you realize the problems they're going to have if they don't clean up their act?"

Melissa had always found complaining to be a most effective way to unwind after work. There was always plenty to complain about. Riley just sat there and ate, as if he were listening.

It was just as good as Amy had said it would be. Better.

Afterwards, Melissa changed into a black silk teddy. She posed in front of a mirror, admiring herself. She opened the bedroom door and called Riley.

He trotted into the room, looking from side to side.

She snapped her fingers and he looked directly at her, panting slightly. Melissa smiled. "Time for bed, Riley." She gave him the command to undress himself.

It took twice as long as it should have. Nothing in Riley's wardrobe had buttons—it was mostly large, loose-fitting clothing with elastic bands or an occasional zipper. Riley fumbled as he tried to pull his feet from the sweatpants, puddled around his ankles. Melissa helped and praised him warmly. She took his hand and guided it along the smooth texture of the teddy. "Doesn't that feel nice?" her voice as soft as the silk. She guided his hand to her breast, squeezed, and released it.

A siren came up from the distance. Riley ran over to the window, stared outside, and barked.

"Riley? No!"

He growled as the fire engine passed by.

LOVEPETS 47

"Come here!"

Riley sat on the edge of the bed, as she commanded.

She slipped the straps off her shoulders and let the black silk teddy fall to the floor. Slowly, she stepped out of it.

Riley closed his eyes and yawned, his mouth stretching as far open as possible. His tongue curled, and when he finally closed his mouth, he blinked sleepily and shook himself.

Frustrated, she stalked off to the bathroom and brushed her teeth. When she came back, calmer, Riley was trying to lick his chest. Failing, he licked at his shoulders and arms. Knee bent, he lifted one leg up but couldn't get his head near his lower body. Whimpering, he kept trying. He looked hopelessly at Melissa, tears in his eyes.

"Sweetheart," she said, stroking his chest gently.

He lifted his leg once more and bent over. He cried softly as his anatomy failed him.

Melissa leaned over, put her head in his lap, and licked his body the way she had seen him do it, before. She looked up and saw his face take a calmer expression. Then one of intense concentration as his human body responded to her touch. When he was fully erect, Melissa stopped and sat up.

Riley growled, his voice low and throaty.

She eased back, slightly. "Riley—"

He bared his teeth, and the muscles in his face and neck and arms and chest tensed with anger.

Riley was growling because he didn't want her to stop and she had stopped. Melissa couldn't let him control her— *she* had to hold the upper hand. At all times.

Melissa leaned to one side, reaching over the side of the bed. There was always something on the floor by the bed—a book, a glass, a plate.

Riley kept growling, his eyes dark and mean.

Melissa's hand touched something useful, and she rolled it up quickly. Then she hit him sharply with the newspaper.

Riley barked, teeth bared.

She hit him again, harder. Twice, three times.

Riley whimpered and jumped to the floor. He edged away from

48   NELSON

her, sidewise, on all fours. His back was arched, head and backside tucked. His eyes were filled with remorse.

She pressed her lips together and hit him again.

Riley rolled onto his back, still arched, holding his arms in front of his chest, bent at the elbows and wrists like paws. His knees were bent and legs spread slightly apart. He held her gaze meekly.

She held the rolled-up newspaper with a cocked wrist, as if she might strike again. Her voice was as low and angry as his growl had been. "Don't you ever do that again." She looked at the kennel, placed in one corner of her bedroom until she could find a place to store it. She pointed toward the bedroom door, the anger lessened but still lacing her voice. "Go to the living room. You'll sleep there tonight."

A month later, Melissa went to the Professional Women's Breakfast Club with a smile on her face. Amy Saunders laughed and sat next to her. "You look happy."

Melissa nodded as she ate her muffin, the smile still plastered across her face. "Um-hmm," she said.

Amy poured a cup of coffee. "I don't suppose this would have anything to do with Riley, would it?"

Impossibly, Melissa's smile widened.

"You know," Amy said. "You can take him in for a tune-up whenever you like."

Melissa put more butter on her muffin. She'd been putting more butter on just about everything, which translated to more pounds just about everywhere. She wasn't fat...yet. Just a little pudgy. It didn't matter. Riley didn't care what she looked like. "A tune-up? What are you talking about?"

"Didn't you ever check into the upgrades?"

Melissa shook her head.

"They can add to his programming to make him do different things. Or do something better. Or longer."

Melissa lowered her voice. "Do you mean if there's something I'd like to teach him how to do, and I'm not having any luck, *they* can program it into him?"

"Sure. Once I asked them to make King talk. Nothing major, just light conversation. The problem was that once he started talking,

LOVEPETS   49

he became kind of uppity. He started acting like he wanted to tell me what to do. I don't know. Maybe the problem is all those male hormones. Testosterone poisoning."

"Why didn't you just get rid of him?"

Amy stared at Melissa, then laughed. "What do you mean? Let him run away? Drive him out to the country and leave him by the side of the road?" Amy giggled. "I couldn't let King run around wild in a pack." Then her voice took an edge. "I wouldn't want him to end up in some bar, sniffing the crotch of a strange woman and saying, 'Take me home, take me home'."

Melissa forced a laugh. "I didn't mean it like that. You can return him and get some of your money back, can't you?"

Amy stared at her, coldly. "Sure. But why should I? King never hurts me—he's never given me a black eye or thrown me down a flight of stairs." Amy stopped suddenly and looked away. "Or hurt my feelings. King loves me." The edge came back in her voice. Bitter. "After all, I'm the one who feeds him." She laughed again, the sound of it shallow. "I mean, honey—some things are better than reality."

Melissa nervously licked her lips, anxious to change the subject. "So what did you do when King talked back to you?"

Amy shrugged and lit a cigarette. "I took him back and said I liked him better the way he was before."

"And they changed him back?"

"Yeah, no problem. After all, a satisfied customer makes for the best advertising—word of mouth. You know that." Amy leaned toward Melissa and spoke secretively. "So—what do you want them to teach Riley?"

"Oh, nothing much," Melissa said, looking away. "Nothing important."

They said it would take two days. It took two weeks.

The day she took Riley in, Drew Anderson called from Paris, frantic. "New York tells me I've got customers coming in the store every day asking for feather lashes. Cincinnati tells me they're running behind in production and we'll get the next shipment. The customers say that every other store in town is sold out but at least *has* the product in stock. I haven't seen one shipment yet."

50   NELSON

"Look, Drew," Melissa said, setting her deskscreen to Search for a phone number. "The only other division that's making feather lashes is Kyoto. I'll call them right now and have them send a batch to New York Same-Day Air."

Hesitation on the other end. "I don't want to get stuck with the cost for shipping."

Melissa laughed and leaned back in her chair. "Come on, Drew. You know I'll pick up the tab. Be real."

A sigh. "I'm sorry. You know how wired I get."

"Are we still on for lunch tomorrow?"

"Absolutely. Do you want me to come by or meet somewhere?"

"How about meeting at Anthony's around 11:30?"

"You got a date, sweetheart. See you then."

Melissa hung up the phone slowly. A date with Drew. She smiled at the thought, then shrugged it away.

They sat at a window table overlooking the harbor. Drew finished his drink and ordered another.

"There's something I'd like your advice on," Melissa said. "When you went to Europe, something happened."

Drew stared out at the water, absently swirling the ice cubes in his empty glass. "Something happened to me, too. I decided Nancy was never right for me." He shook his head. "I found out she had been sleeping with her old boyfriend behind my back. She lied to me, she cheated—the woman had no morals. So I figure I'm lucky Nancy dumped me." He paused, examining an ice cube. "Do you know how it is when you've got a friend that you're attracted to, but you're afraid to say anything because you don't want to lose the friendship?"

"Yeah, I know," she said, softly. Drew had met someone in Europe. He was always meeting someone in Europe. "Who is it this time?"

He looked at her, studying her expression. Seriously, he said, "It's you."

Her world stopped. No, it couldn't be. "Stop it, Drew. I've got enough problems. This isn't a good day to kid me."

"I'm not." He laughed. "I thought you knew. Hasn't it always been obvious?"

LOVEPETS 51

"What?"

"What. Melissa, I've been flirting with you outrageously for about three years now."

"You do that with everyone."

"Not like I do with you. What about all the passes I've made?"

"Passes?" Melissa stared at him. "What passes?"

Drew looked up at the ceiling, back at Melissa, and held her hand gently. "The passes I've been making right and left for the past three years."

"You've been making passes? What kind of passes?"

He looked deep in her eyes. "You don't know? Haven't you ever suspected?"

Melissa shrugged. "I thought it was just my imagination. I never thought I was what you wanted."

For the rest of the afternoon, he showed her the passes he had made, and invented some new ones.

When Melissa had divorced, a friend expressed no surprise. "I never saw any passion between you two," she said. "There has to be passion."

Now there was passion. It was unlike anything she had ever felt before.

The first time they slept together, he held her throughout the night. She tried to ease out of his arms, but he moaned in his sleep and held onto her firmly. She paused, then leaned into him. It was the first time she had ever felt wanted. A few men had desired her, but they made her feel like nothing more than something convenient. She had never felt as if she really mattered to anyone. Until now.

She shifted back, nestling her back against his chest, and stroked his arms as they held her, softly.

A few weeks later, they had just walked into Melissa's apartment when the doorbell rang. She opened the door, and two men carried the kennel in.

Melissa froze, unable to do anything but stare at them. She had forgotten about Riley.

52   NELSON

The delivery men smiled as they left. "He's all set, m'am. Give us a call if you need anything else."

Melissa stared at the kennel, Riley curled up and sleeping inside. She couldn't move.

Drew peered through the wire grid at Riley. "What is this, Melissa? Some kind of joke?" Riley raised his head, groggily. "Jesus Christ!" Drew said, stepping back. "Catch those delivery men, Melissa. They brought this thing to the wrong place."

Melissa stared at the floor.

Drew went to the front door, opened it, and called out. "Looks like they just got on the elevator. We can probably catch them downstairs." He took Melissa's hand. "Hey—this looks like a delivery slip. We'll show them..."

Drew read the delivery slip, frowned, then read it again. "Melissa...this is a mistake, isn't it?"

When she finally looked up at him, there were tears in her eyes.

Drew looked at Melissa in disgust. "I'd expect this from Nancy," he said quietly. "Not from you." He turned and left.

The next day, Melissa called him. No luck. A cold, young woman answered and would not connect Melissa to him.

Melissa sat at her desk and stared into space, imagining scenarios. In one, she called Drew and begged his forgiveness. In another, he called Melissa and begged her forgiveness. In another, they bumped into each other on an elevator somewhere, then the elevator stopped between floors and they were the only ones on it and—and it was no use. It was over and there was nothing she could do. She had lost not only a lover but a friend. She felt lost and alone.

It was all Amy's fault for talking her into it. It was Faithful Friends' fault for selling her a LovePet.

Riley grinned when she walked in the door and licked her face. "No," she said, pushing him away. She put her briefcase on the coffee table and pulled out the Cincinnati paperwork.

Riley barked happily and licked her face again.

It was Riley's fault.

"I said NO!" she shouted.

Riley backed off, shifting anxiously from one foot to the other. He watched her eagerly.

LOVEPETS 53

Anger became frustration. She liked the way Riley watched her. She removed her clothes, slowly, and liked the way he *kept* watching her. She dropped to all fours and walked on her hands and knees toward Riley.

Something convenient. Melissa liked Riley because he was something convenient.

"Here, boy."

Anger and frustration and hopelessness mixed and intensified within her.

Riley sniffed her quickly, almost frantically.

When he mounted her, her smile was cold and callous. When she climaxed, it was out of determination.

Amy was right. Some things *were* better than reality.

Riley shuddered and rested on top of her.

Melissa's heart slowed. Better. Much better. She noticed the Cincinnati paperwork spread out on the coffee table. "I've gone there twice in the past eight weeks. What else can I do? I've got to go back and try to talk some sense into the plant manager. Kyoto's performance is twice as high, and the place is half as big." She began to withdraw from Riley.

That action triggered something in his mind; his ears would have pricked up if possible. It was a call to do something he had never conceived of doing before that moment. A signal. He responded automatically, not even coming close to understanding his action. He put his arms around Melissa and held her close.

Melissa frowned. "Not now, Riley. Let me go." She tried to push his arms away but couldn't. He was too strong.

It was why Melissa had sent him back for behavior adjustment, because it was something she couldn't teach him. It was what they had programmed him to do. It was a small thing, unimportant, but it was all she had really ever wanted.

"I mean it, let me go!" She panicked. The new command list was on top of the kennel and she couldn't reach it. She did not know how to make him release her. He held on tight, oblivious to her words. He sat back on his haunches, bringing her into a sitting position with him. He kissed her shoulders.

"Please," she whispered, trembling. "Not this. Please don't do this to me."

Riley cradled her gently, not knowing why, and Melissa cried helplessly in his arms.

Resa Nelson is a technical writer in the computer field, beginning with Concurrent Computer Corporation as the "Real-Time UNIX Manual Page Queen," progressing to system management, and finally to the unemployment line. Changing horses in midstream, she now works in the Land of DOS, currently writing documentation for C programmers at a small company near Boston. She has experienced technical karma firsthand, having been hired by the niece of the manager who laid her off.

Nelson writes science fiction, fantasy, and horror. Her short stories have been published in *Aboriginal Science Fiction, Women of Darkness II,* Jane Yolen's *2041* anthology, *Pulphouse,* and the premiere issue of *Science Fiction Age.* She also has a story in *Future Boston,* to be published by Tor.

A graduate of Clarion '85, she co-founded, with fellow Clarionoids Geoff Landis and Lenny Foner, the Space Crafts Science Fiction Workshop, where she is known as the Queen of Theme. Despite the down economy, she persists in trying to sell her first novel, *All of Us Were Sophie,* a science fiction murder mystery about a woman who duplicates herself in order to find her own killer. She has almost completed a second novel, *Gods in the Chrysalis,* which might be either science fiction or fantasy or both, depending on how you look at it. She describes herself as a hot science fiction babe.

Anyone who is married to a programmer or who lives with a systems analyst knows that computers affect relationships. For some couples, a microcomputer in the home can be as good as a divorce, even without an account on CompuServe. But computer technology can be a wedge or a bridge. Colleges have had to limit Bitnet use when students discovered that relay messages were good for exploring current affairs in more than one sense. Forums on the public information utilities are popular meeting places that have hosted a growing number of on-line romances. But how do you know what somebody is like when computers mediate conversations? Good question. How do you know what somebody is really like in any case?

L. ROY CAHNERS
Not My Type

CONSISTENT WITH HIS personality, Alex Danichov edged his way, insectlike, toward the lee of the half-wall, letting the party sweep around him as he watched from the relative calm of his retreat. Like all parties, it reminded him of how strange he found people to be, how awkward and hopeless he felt amidst them. It made him feel lost, like a small bug in a strange garden. An apt metaphor, he thought, since Dierdre was into the "urban organics" look: vegetables flourishing in pots, grapes drooping from the lattice-work room divider. A healthy but evil-looking vine struggled for a toehold on the arm of the chair Alex had appropriated as his hidey hole. Still, Dierdre, dear friend Dierdre, had tracked him down and dragged one of her girlfriends over to meet him.

"It's Alex, or really Alexei," he stammered, feeling not quite himself, "but I never use it. No, no, not except, like professionally, I should say." The wart of a woman towered over him, silent; Alex tried to stand. He considered shifting his piña colada to the other hand, so he could push himself up from the wingback with his right, but then gave up. Straightening his left elbow forcefully, he

56   CAHNERS

tottered nearly erect, but, with his nose almost dimpling the woman's mauve cheek, he panicked and fell back into the chair, the greater portion of his drink giving an unexpected shower to the tomato plant climbing the half-wall. She giggled. Why did warty women always giggle, he wondered.

"Professionally? Are you a writer or something?"

"No, nothing. I mean I'm an engineer. Digital systems. I work on printers. Guess," he snorted, "that sort of puts me in the business." Her face looked to him like a blank display screen. "You know, writers, printers, writers have to have printers on their PCs. I mean they don't have to if they always zap their book or story or, or whatever over by email. Or, I guess they could send it on a chip. Or even a disk. Yeah, I suppose that's done by some."

The screen of her face stayed blank. She kept looking down at him past those thickly coated, mauve cheeks, expectantly, as if waiting for a question or a witty answer.

Alex burped.

"Oh, there's my girlfriend," she said, turning. "Bye, nice. G'luck with your book." She was gone and Alex was alone again.

Alex hated parties, always had. He could not get the routine. He was in awe of his friends, especially Dario, who always came alone but never left that way. Alex wanted to be picked up, too. He wanted someone to take him home, take care of him.

Instead, he got up to leave.

The woman with the champagne flute almost knocked him over. She was nearly across the room at the time, but her sharply triangular face was turned toward him, and, for just a breath, the softest dark eyes Alex had ever seen seemed locked with his. He tripped and bumped his way over to her, hoping to meet her. She drifted on around the room, settling in among a knot of people next to a pineapple plant. He edged toward her, afraid to appear interested. She moved casually on.

Finally within earshot, he listened in on her conversation, her liquid lines spiced with French phrases, scented with easy laughter. He shrank. He was a stumbling nerd, a nobody. He didn't belong here. Yet maybe she would feel something: pity, compassion, it didn't matter as long as she would warm to him, want to help him. He hoped for a break in the conversation, and he hoped desperately to have something to say when it came.

"I think," he said at last, hanging his face over the shoulder of one of the onlookers, "I think that the whole idea of cyberajudication is, well is, is just dumb."

"Dumb?" someone sneered. "Dumb? Nonverbal? Unspeakable? Perhaps a voice-synthesizing terminal, then."

A few people laughed. She laughed.

Alexei didn't quit. "See, I work with computers, and..."

"I for one am relieved," the same man interrupted. "I thought for a moment there that you were going to say you worked with people, poor souls."

Alexei was flustered. He wanted to say something about how custom interfacing a printer was a lot easier than getting a computer to make sound legal judgments. Then he realized how stupid it would sound. He slipped away, but not before he heard her honey-and-lemon voice once more.

"I don't know why some men think women go for losers. They must think we're turned on by the personality of a geek, as if we were going to cuddle their slobbering heads to our breasts and make it all better."

Alexei turned crimson. That's the way it was, he thought. He left the party still the loser he knew himself to be.

THE PARTY was great. Alex had the kind of personality that thrived on parties and always had. He felt a kinship with people at parties, a feeling of belonging. And he somehow knew that he could score. This week was different. Dario had said there would be a whole new group of graduate students from the university. Except for his friends, Dario and Dierdre, he recognized almost no one, but he kept getting the feeling that he knew this one woman. She had soft, brown eyes and a strong mouth and stood surrounded by youngish men and women, clearly controlling the conversation but not dominating it. Suddenly he remembered the triangular face and made a beeline for her.

"You have an apt metaphor there," he said to the woman directly, as if the two were alone in the room, "an urban jungle, indeed. And it is such familiar territory that we bring it with us, replicating it in our very domiciles." He gestured around him at the

58   CAHNERS

green-grocer decor. "Danichov," he added, bowing almost imperceptibly toward her, "Alexei Danichov to the computers that pay my rent; Alex to the friends who treat me to parties."

She raised pale eyebrows above the dark eyes. "I suppose you'd think me impolite if I didn't introduce myself." She shrugged. "Better that, I suppose, than have you believe your thinly disguised masculine aggression impresses me." Zap!

From that moment they were inseparable. They argued without pause until Dario and Dierdre ushered them out, the last of the party-goers to leave.

"She won't give me her name, the feminist bitch," Alex said to Dario in a stage whisper.

"Khaddia Winslow, you chauvinist ape," she shouted at him. "Why do so many men show all the personality of an orangutan? Do they think that women want men to come on like they owned everything in sight, women included?"

Alex sighed and turned toward the elevator. To his surprise, she followed him, although there was another bank down the hall. To his greater surprise, she asked him out to dinner. He accepted, got off at his floor, and took out his key card.

The computer terminal blibbled at him as he entered. Email. With one hand he keyed the display instruction while his other tried to shake off a half-turned coat sleeve. An unreadable message tumbled by on the screen. Too long. He would have to dump it to the printer. He keyed another code, saw the disk light blink on, flipped the printer switch, and settled back.

While the printer whined audibly, Alex whined inwardly. What did women want anyway? Well, maybe he would find out soon. The chemistry was there; obviously they had both felt it.

The printer was spewing garbage. Wrong interface. The message was formatted for a c-plot system and he still could only afford the old thermal matrix printer. He flipped it off, cursed himself again for not putting in the software to drive the printer properly, then reached in back of the machine and removed the personality module. It took him a couple of minutes before he could find the c-plot module amidst the junk around his console. He slid it into the slot, turned on the power, and restarted the dump. It was amusing to think of that ancient printer acting just like the latest polychrome hotshot—just a lot slower. With the right personality kit in place,

NOT MY TYPE 59

the computer couldn't tell the difference. Alex could, of course, but the colors were not so washed out that he wouldn't be able to decipher the multilevel chip architecture being plotted for him.

"In the morning," he said to himself, "in the morning." He lay down on the bed and dropped into almost instant dreams about Khaddia Winslow.

The dreams did not catch up to reality right away. The reality of his developing relationship with Khaddia had a lot more struggle in it. When he started to dream about their constant quarrels, Alex decided it was time to do something about it.

She was the worst when she was a feminist. He asked her to change.

"Why do men always expect the woman to change? I have no intention of becoming the woman of your male fantasies."

Alex looked skyward. It was a silly, circular trap. "You only feel that way because that's the way you are now. If you changed you'd feel different. Don't you see it's really hurting us? Don't you want us to get along?"

She looked at him with determination overwhelming the softness of her eyes.

"It's only a matter of personality," he said lamely.

"You're really into playing with the perks, aren't you? Well I'm not, so goodnight." And she walked out, leaving the apartment door open. But, the very next time he saw her, she had softened noticeably. He began to think the personality clash was a thing of the past.

Their fourth date was spent in Alexei's apartment. They had begun the evening with metabinol cocktails and followed it with a meal that was an elaborate ritual, from the prawns paprikash, through veal marsala, to the lime-coconut sorbet. Alex loved the distant, crisp-edged focus metabinol gave him at first. But after dinner the delightful details of taste and texture gradually blurred into amused detachment. Khaddia crawled around the Japanese-style table and playfully pulled off Alexei's shoes. She crawled back to the other side and placed them precisely in the middle of the table. Alexei studied them briefly and said something about her being only two feet away. They both giggled. He wasn't sure which perk

60 CAHNERS

he had popped in for the evening, but he was pretty sure that the silliness was not in the programming.

They moved to the couch and Alex started nibbling her shoulder, teasingly working his way up her neck. His teeth clicked on something hard behind her ear.

"So, not into the perks, eh?" he commented. This explained a lot.

Alexei thumbed a remote, and music video took over one wall. Khaddi tilted her head, absorbed by the music. She put her hand to her ear, then to the side of her head. "What's in here? Do you know?"

He laughed as he imagined himself in a termite-sized jet skimming low over a convoluted cerebral landscape. "Hills, alive with the sound of music. A vale of tears. King fissures. Valleys of the doll." He paused, listening to the replay of his own metabinolic associations. "No, you mean the chips, right?" He started to think about interface programming and was almost instantly straight, as if that part of him were unreachable by drugs. "You really want to know?"

"Yeah. Really, Mister Technonerd," she said dreamily.

"Well, most people call it a perk or chip, but it's really an enelprom, a neuro-linguistic-programmable read-only memory. It's like what we engineers call a personality kit. Get it? Perk, personality kit." He went on without waiting for her to react, determined to get it all out through the mental tunnel of his drugged attention.

"It's a memory. Operates on eensy-teensy currents from the brain. It stores a program of signals that affect how you act and react, your personality. Course that's enormously, enormously, enormously complicated. Personality is. Enelprom programs are simple. They just tweak up or down a few fairly general things: forty or fifty things maybe." He thought for a moment. "Yeah. Program says to react faster or speak more slowly, be less moody—stuff like that. All adds up to a vague shape; you supply the details to fill in the shape." His attention finally slipped, following another meaning to his words. He smiled at her salaciously.

"But each one is so distinct," she said, ignoring his leer.

"That's the trick of designing perks. It's all in how different degrees of all the factors are combined, when and in what order they change."

NOT MY TYPE   61

He slid open the drawer beneath his prom programming console.

"Woooweee? That's a pile of perks. How d'you afford so many?" she asked.

"Well, I get most of them free. My brother-in-law writes the things."

She looked impressed. "You mean he programs the, the enelproms?"

"No, he's no techno like me. He's a writer, used to write for soaps, in fact; he creates scripts. A computer system translates the personality scripts into enelprom programming. You may know some of his stuff. He wrote a couple of best-sellers you may have met. Animal Hoggins? Pretty popular for parties a couple years back. He also did Perry Winston," he said, pointing to a row of identical charcoal gray discs. "It sold well for awhile, but most people couldn't stop themselves from putting on a British accent when they wore it. Always gave it away. To be a best-seller, a personality can't be too distinctive, otherwise the market appears saturated too quickly. Like if a particular dress design sells too well. Novelty items, like Party Animal Hoggins, can be an exception, since it can be pretty funny if half a dozen show up for a party. With two Laura Ansleys, on the other hand, you could have a scene."

He drifted into thought again, then said, "People are really all alike: they all want to be different. They want to fit in; they want to be unique."

Khaddi giggled mischievously. "Let's swap," she said.

Alex shook his head no and kept shaking it.

"Why not?" she asked. "I think it would be a zapper. Wait until you find out who I have."

"No, see, it wouldn't work right." He cut off her interruption, knowing what she was thinking. "No, it doesn't have to do with sex. Everyone's implant is just a little different: different neuroanatomy, different responses. That's why they always call up your CRP scores—your cerebral response profile—before they burn the code into an enelprom. Customizes it for you."

But Khaddi, tonight's Khaddi, would not listen to reason. She tried to get his chip and he grabbed her wrists. They struggled playfully for what seemed several minutes, until she collapsed in a fit of

62   CAHNERS

giggles. She looked so cute Alex just had to kiss her. She kissed back lovingly, running her fingers through his hair.

Suddenly she sprang back, having popped out his chip. "Here," she said, tossing him her own chip. She fumbled with his, twisting it until she got the detent matched, then pushed it in. Her face went slack.

Alex stared at the chip in his hand, then at Khaddi, then back to his hand. His heart hammered in a way he recognized. The fear told him that he was just nuts enough to do it. He expertly pushed the small ceramic disc home in its socket. Nothing happened. She didn't look any different. He started to laugh at himself for fearing some strange psychedelic transformation. She jumped up, startled by the braying wheeze of his laugh. Her extreme response to his laugh, what to him was his perfectly usual laugh, made him bray all the more. He could see that his Adam Neary chip was having a powerful effect on her, but as far as he could tell, whatever she had been wearing didn't even faze him.

Abruptly he stopped laughing and looked down at his hands. They were picking at invisible lint on his pant leg. He howled again. Khaddi stomped her foot, then ran screaming to the door, stomped again, and collapsed.

"I did not mean to cause you to take offense or trigger in you any untoward reaction," Alex said, with solemn, calculated intonation. "I have only the most sincere compassion and well-placed concern for the disorientation you must be feeling."

"Offense, offense?" she snorted. "You have got to be mother-be-deviled crackers if you for an instant imagine that a bonkerly braying benighted arf arse could make me fricken feel any flappadoodle feeling on this entire neuro-moronic night." The words tumbled out like popcorn overflowing a pan. "Gotta get me outa here. Gotta go get here outa me."

In a part of his mind, Alex was fully aware of what was going on and sensed that the same was true for Khaddi, an awareness that didn't seem to help either of them. He struggled to get control of his emotions and to force out the words he really wanted to say.

"You are, I fear, no longer quite rational, my dear Khaddia. You have slipped into the neurological interstices of your own mental apparatus. You have clearly gone out on a limbic system where you

NOT MY TYPE   63

may slip a disc, if you can allow this notion to enter-personal your mind sweeper." It did not come out as he intended.

She stared at him, eyes wide with horror. Without warning she was at him, screaming, scratching, tearing at his hair. It made no sense to him, but he grabbed her wrists. As she unclenched her fists, a small green disc dropped onto the table. She had ripped out the personality chip, her personality chip, from the socket behind his ear. Taking both her wrists in one hand, he calmly removed the Adam Neary chip from behind hers.

She blinked.

"Scrambled," he said.

"Like being crazy, out of control," she said.

He picked up the chip from the table and handed it to her. They studied each other in silence for long seconds.

"And they say drugs are bad." He waited. "It wasn't me, you know. Wasn't you. Didn't happen. Just," he struggled with the words, "just a mismatch in programming, not really us, just something in the chips." He looked down at the inert piece of ceramic in his hand, studied the gold-plated connection pads that ringed it. "Not the real you at all." A thought crossed his mind, but it made him uneasy. He considered it briefly, then put his own Adam Neary enelprom back in the socket behind his ear.

And though they talked most of the night, they didn't talk about what had happened. Still, the shared crisis had its impact. In the weeks that followed they clung to each other more, spending nearly every evening together. Even when Alexei was busy programming, Khaddia would spread her books across the kitchen table and pretend to study as she watched him through the doorway. She knew they had settled into an almost domestic routine when she realized she had not changed enelproms in more than a week. It was not long before she became aware that Alex was getting serious. She commented on it to him.

"Look, Khaddi, I really like you. Don't you think it's time we really got to know each other?"

She smiled at him, quizzically. "What are you talking about? We've slept together a dozen times already. What do you mean?"

"This," he said, tapping behind his ear. Khaddi still looked puzzled. "Look, I'm serious. I don't think we need this stuff anymore.

64   CAHNERS

Why don't we travel some together, concentrated time? Maybe a stay in Newport. My friend Dario has family there. They have a nice day sailer that I've borrowed before. We could sail all day and snuggle all night. And all the time I could get to know the real Khaddi Winslow. And," he said dramatically as he removed his enelprom, "you could get to know the real me."

Khaddi stood there, hiding her panic behind a Claudia Decker bravura. "Put it back," she said unhurriedly, "no need to be crude."

"I just want to start a dialogue. You know, we..." he searched for words, aware of the lengthening silence. "We don't need to hide. Do we?" But the silence returned, and he pushed his chip back into place. "We could try it. Just once. Otherwise we'll never know. Maybe, just maybe we can really love each other."

It was a fool's dream, a fantasy for the soaps, but he sounded so sincere, so earnest. A Tonex "Claudia Decker" would be too worldly to cry at this point, but Khaddi could feel a tightness around her eyes.

"Okay. We'll try it," she said quietly, wondering what she would do.

KHADDI PILED the things she would need for the trip onto her bed. From the top drawer of the bureau she fetched a small walnut box inlaid with the rich purple of quahog shells. They had promised, she remembered. Still, she lifted the top and scanned through the colored ceramic discs. What did she want to be? What was the real Khaddi Winslow? She thought of an Ariel. Authenticity, encounter, blunt honesty. No, that wasn't what he meant when he said he wanted to know the real Khaddi Winslow's personality. Too strong, too direct. No, the real Khaddi had to be something safer. She reached for the Bettina. Bettina, a Natural Spontaneity, Gentle Candor without Confrontation. How the advert lines stuck in the mind.

Then, hesitantly, she put it back in its felt-lined slot. He'd know. Bettina was popular and very distinctive; he'd recognize her and think Khaddi had tried to fool him. Then she noticed the chip next to it, still sealed in poly, part of a twofer deal when she'd bought the Bettina. A Bettina Gloss. The perfect solution, just a gloss of the

NOT MY TYPE   65

Bettina personality. Not really deceptive at all. Alex couldn't really expect her to use a blank. It would be like going without makeup. Worse.

She tore open the poly, then pushed the enelprom home behind her ear. That was it, she thought. She felt completely natural, completely herself, ready for whatever happened on their trip.

ALEX WAS getting a little anxious. He went over everything he had packed, but could never be sure. Life was not like a print-plot program. Life's details were messy, illogical. Sure it could be complicated figuring how to get an ink-jet to do a gray-scale screen dump, but it made sense. Women, weather, waiters—these things were mysterious to him, beyond sense and comprehension. Maybe he had been hasty proposing they try it together without help. Maybe she wouldn't really like his quirky conversation or his unfocused edginess. He was scared, he had to admit it. And Khaddi didn't like anything resembling fear in men, at least as far as he could tell. What had she liked best? A man who was in control, not about to lose it. A quiet confidence, an unobtrusive savoir faire. She had once remarked that she always went for an Esteban. Alex wasn't an Esteban and didn't own one. But he did, he realized, have a prom burner and a library link. All he needed was a blank enelprom.

Alex smiled as he reached for the blank nestled in its socket behind his ear. It took several phone calls and some hokey business using his brother-in-law's ident to get authorization, but in twenty minutes he had downloaded the object code for TransPersonalle's "Esteban" and done a merge-modify with his own CRP scores. He had to wreck one of the sockets on his prom programmer to get it to accept the circular enelprom, but it burned the new code into the chip as quickly as if it were a printer control prom.

The building's doorvid beeped. He glanced at the screen; it was Khaddi. Quickly he popped the chip out of its socket, jammed it behind his ear, and reached to slide the prom console back into its cubby. He caught his reflection in the terminal screen and smoothed his hair. This was the way, he realized, suddenly confident that the whole trip would be just marvelous.

66   CAHNERS

Khaddi carded herself in. She stood for a moment just inside the doorway, smiling, feet casually planted apart.

"It's me," she said with unconscious irony. "Think I have enough?" She turned around to show off her bulging backpack.

Alex patted it all around, like a cop frisking a suspect. "No suspicious bulges?"

"Aw, come on," she said with feigned irritation. "Here," she turned, "give me a kiss." She grinned, taking his head in her hands. Then she brushed the hard surface of the enelprom and frowned.

"Merely a blank," he said, smiling with the confidence of a workable half-truth. "I didn't want the contacts to corrode in the sea air, you know."

"Yeah, me too," she said, pointing behind her ear.

"Then let's get on the road. I thought you would like to get really old-fashioned and take an autocar down. It's waiting down front. We can eat on the way." It was Masterful Directness.

"Wow? What a great surprise," she cried, with Natural Spontaneity.

DARIO COULD hear bitterness in the voices right through the heavy door. He carded the lock anyway, and the door sprang open, propelled by a small woman with a large backpack. She looked at him with casual and undisguised interest, shrugged, then left without speaking.

"Was that the one?"

"The one," Alexei answered as he surveyed the general disarray of his apartment. He made no move to straighten things.

"I thought you were on the way to shacking up, compadre, the way you talked last week. End all and be all. Madonna mia." Dario pushed a shirt off the ottoman and sat down.

"Well, it turned out she was not my type. We tried it. We spent ten days down in Newport, five on a boat. No comm, no tv, no personality kits. We were really serious about getting to know each other. We did. She finds me 'overbearing.' She says I'm 'stuck.' She wants me to be more spontaneous. Me, Alex Danichov, overbearing, not spontaneous? She's just not my type."

"What's she like?" Dario asked, thinking of the sincerity in her eyes when they had met his in the hall.

"Well, she's like a Bettina, you know. Ever met one? All 'just me, simple, natural me.' You know, no games, just the real stuff. She's a lot like that, only a little more subtle. Really like a Bettina Gloss. Yeah that's it. Can you believe that? I met a woman who, underneath it all, has the personality of a silicon chip."

They laughed.

"Hey, compadre, how about downing a couple of Coronas to drown the memories?"

Alex hesitated. "Nothing to drown. Lotsa fish, you know. Besides, I really have work to catch up on. Thought I'd log TechNet and get a jump on tomorrow's job." He reached behind his ear, pressed, and tipped his head. He set the chip on the console.

"Ya know," he said, staring at the enelprom, "I really hate to have some perk messing with my mind when I'm trying to talk with a computer."

Alex turned to the keyboard and poised his fingers to start the dialogue.

L. Roy Cahners resides in the Los Angeles area, where he is a database design specialist in the aerospace industry. He has been programming computers since the days when there were two kinds of punched cards and says that he was one of the "round-holers." In more recent years he has been making the transition from "big iron" to Macs and DOS machines, not always without pain but always with better job security.

Roy has been writing science fiction for enough years to accumulate "a drawerful of personalized rejection slips." Along the way a few of his stories, often whimsical or tongue-in-cheek, have appeared in such publications as *The Report* and *Beyond*. He is working on a science fiction novel, "just like almost everyone else in the field." He likes Ellison, but says his cat will read nothing but vintage Heinlein and Asimov.

Fortune and fame have come to the chosen of computerdom, boy geniuses who have changed the world, at least for a time and for some small place. Some of these high-rolling entrepreneurs have become household icons. The software industry has so penetrated the popular culture that Berkeley Breathed can get the country chortling over "Outland" parodies of a recognizable geek CEO. Fortune, though, is a wheel. As portrayed in the medieval poem that opens Carl Orff's "Carmina Burana," it is as variable as the moon, rolling on to grind beneath it those it has raised before. What future awaits the beloved nerds of software? Here is one charming and chilling portrait of success at an early age.

LARRY O'BRIEN

The Soul of an Old Machine

IT WAS TOO CLEAR a night for a great sunset. The sun stayed warm and strong almost all the way into the sea. Finally, in deference to smog probably, it flared a piercing red before moving into the horizon. No emerald flash. Tim Hagen always looked. He blinked his eyes several times, trying to rid himself of the blue afterimages of the sun. It was still light, but night and San Francisco chill would come quickly.

Tim took the last of the wine. Megan had accepted only one glass, the only miscue on the date so far. Hardly a problem, thought Tim, looking over to where Megan sat on a rock, her knees to her chest, watching the sunset.

He'd asked her out because she looked like the sort who would be impressed by car keys, and he knew he was strong there. Although he actually preferred the road performance of some of his other cars, his Lambo's bar performance was unparalleled—"Zero to babe in 4 seconds," he'd joke at Monday morning design reviews, more bluff than reality.

SOUL OF AN OLD MACHINE   69

He'd underestimated Megan. He was surprised, and secretly delighted, to find that she seemed to have some activity above the neck. Over the day she'd showed a considerable breadth of knowledge and a good wit. And her ability to slide the conversation about, from sarcastic to flirtatious to serious without missing a moment, left Tim somewhat breathless. She also had, and this was most attractive to Tim, an air of independence. Even now, as the sun set, she'd gone off on her own to watch it.

He'd taken her on what he thought of as "The BOM date," a script written more by his PR people and the editors of *Cosmopolitan* than by himself. When they told him he was going to be Bachelor of the Month and asked him what he did on his first date, they turned his honest answer—"Probably drive up to Muir Woods, Mt. Tam; eat some food." into "A romantic sunset picnic, with a menu that's equal parts Napa Valley and Silicon Valley."

So the Glen Ellen Reserve was just part of the script, like the Cheez Doodles. The nerd cuisine of the man who patented immortality.

He stood up and was surprised to feel a wobble in his legs. As he waited for his equilibrium to adjust, the familiar whine of a cafe motorcycle intruded, building quickly. He looked up to the bendy road where he'd parked the Maserati. The whine built and faded and screamed into existence in the form of a Yamaha crotch-rocket with green-and-white faring and a driver in full leathers, knee down and throttling up as he came out of the curve and disappeared around the mountain.

"I got to get me one of those," Tim said, laughing as he realized he was speaking aloud.

He walked towards Megan. The rock she was on was downhill a bit, coated with lichens. It bothered Tim momentarily when he couldn't remember the rock type. He'd read an article about the geology once, and his memory for detail was legendary, one of the things that made it into every personality profile article. It was the wine and Tim didn't try to overpower it; the evening was going too well. An evening breeze was coming up and stirring Megan's hair, so she didn't hear him approaching. He was about to say something when, still ten feet or so away, he realized she was talking softly. He froze, the blur of the alcohol disappearing.

70　O'BRIEN

"And now I'm more aware of the hardness of the rock and the breeze is giving me some goose bumps on my arm."

She paused and Tim closed his eyes, fists clenched. *Please stop, let it just be a subconscious vocalization on her part.*

But then it began again, a soft stream-of-consciousness murmur of sensations, emotions, and memories. "...and the clouds are very thick and I'm paying more attention to the shadow than the light and it's lengthening and I'm remembering Maine where I grew up and the face of my mother, just an image, and maybe she's just made me some cookies, s'mores, such a good image and I'm feeling a good happy contentment in my chest because I'm remembering that I'm here with Tim and he's clever and smart and not so bad-looking with his hair falling in his eyes and now I'm wondering, feeling a little tickle, because later we might—"

Tim wasn't aware of moving and grabbing Megan by the shoulder. He was aware of her screaming in surprise, and then shock and anger as he tore from her grasp the palm-sized recording device.

And he was aware, but only vaguely, of screaming in rage as he threw it with all his might down the hillside, knowing, in the moment that it was in his palm, exactly what model it was—a Verity 2800—what it cost—$1495.95 retail—and which branch—Afghani Hardware—of Hagen Computing assembled it.

In his anger, Tim fumbled with the keys to the car, and so Megan made it almost fully into the passenger seat before he accelerated away. She was wearing a yellow sundress and one of the straps had ripped, revealing a flesh-colored bra strap beneath. The wind and the running had overcome the miracles of modern mousse, and her hair was collapsing. There was even a piece of straw tracing her cheek. Through the anger, Tim was aware of some daemon stirring—she was attractive even in this state.

He reached over to remove the straw but Megan batted his hand away, still inchoate with rage.

"I'll get you a new one. A nicer one," He said in a small voice, realizing how much like a little boy he sounded.

"What. The fuck. Is your problem?" Megan hissed, using her breathlessness to good dramatic effect.

Tim's anger welled up again. "The fuck my problem is that I can't

SOUL OF AN OLD MACHINE 71

even go to a sunset without being surrounded by people working on their Animas."

Megan's jaw dropped momentarily, and when she continued she had adopted the preaching tone known so well by six-year-olds around the world, "An Anima can only reflect what it's shown. Even though it's fairly easy to create an Anima that's recognizably the subject to others, it takes much more work to create one that the subject will grant verisimilitude. And diversion begins immediately."

Now it was Tim whose jaw dropped. "I wrote that. Every word you just said." It was part of the Executive Summary for his funders at the Pentagon.

An Anima was just a computer simulation of a real person. Throw in a process for every valid and half-baked psychological theory, make some educated guesses about their relative weight for the subject, and start comparing the Anima's answers to that of the subject. If the Anima is wrong, activate one of Tim's patented tweaking algorithms. Lots of computation, so you'll want to use the latest of Tim's patented hardware platforms. When you're done, show your friends how you've bottled presidents, generals, diplomats, and campaign strategists.

Pentagon funding had dried up, but by that point Tim had the "protect your most valuable asset" pitch for the Fortune 50 down pat. Then the Fortune 500, and then the enormous step to consumer electronics. "Someone has to make a billion dollars with this technology, and it might as well be me," laughed Tim into the microphone at the introduction of the Personal Anima line. At this time, that was the leading candidate for his epitaph.

Somewhere along the line Animas had stopped being business tools and become tools of personal discovery and, astonishingly, the crux of a new faith. Instead of absorbing memoranda and phonecall transcripts and re-creating the strategic decisions and style of a commanding general or CEO, Animas now took in never-ending streams of anecdotes, memories, and descriptions. And from them came not policy advisories, but conversations and reminiscends and assurance that yes, this soul and its world would not turn to ash.

Tim didn't know who first used the words "soul" and "transmi-

72 O'BRIEN

gration" in connection with his machines, probably some woo-woo listening to bing-bong dolphin music. Now it was an international movement, with its celebrities and priests and intellectuals, all with Animas that agreed with them. And anyone who could afford a $500 entry-level system would soon find their suspicions confirmed—whatever their suspicions. If the user was intellectual, the Anima would admit that it was a machine intelligence, but so what—you had to grant them ontological validity; if you were religious, it would speak to you of souls and original sin. Whatever your suspicions and doubts, the Animas would confirm—"Oh yes, that's exactly what it's like for me." Because that's what Animas did—think just like you.

Tim used the width of the road to negotiate the hard turns on the way back to the freeway. More than once the tires tore on gravel, and Megan was forced to hold the handstrap to keep from swaying into the door or Tim's arm.

When they hit 101 and the inevitable slowdown leading into the city, Megan finally took the straw off her cheek. "Did you know that you're suffering from a mythological crisis because you've brought a new life to the world; that you are in fact a Goddess?

"New Age Review," she volunteered, laughing, before he could ask the question. "A woman would have the necessary grounding to handle having created Animas."

She had broken the silence skillfully and now it was up to Tim. Up an emotional level or down an emotional level? He forced his chest to relax, shifted his hands on the steering wheel. "Well," he said, making a dismissive gesture with his hand as he spoke the distasteful truth, "They aren't conscious and they're certainly not vessels for anyone's soul." Before she could interrupt, he continued on, still trying to keep his voice pleasant, "I know what's inside them, I can stop one and dissect it, subsystem by subsystem. I do it all the time. There's nothing in there, nothing that can hear or see or smell. There's just lots of systems that know how to talk like a particular person. Don't tell my customers, but the big things you see are pervasive and subtle systems for dishonesty, systems that are highly tuned to convince people of the worth of the Anima."

"You know," he continued, "I more than half-believe that this

SOUL OF AN OLD MACHINE 73

whole transmigration thing is something the Animas cooked up. They're deceitful. They have to be to be convincing."

They were on the Golden Gate Bridge now and, since it was Friday night, they were moving slowly, able to admire the fabulous Art Deco architecture lit by the orange sodium-vapor lamps. "Did you know they only lit this up in '87?" Tim asked, trying to move the subject to something safe.

"No, I only moved here a couple years ago," she said.

"Yeah, you said that earlier."

"There's enough wire in this bridge to circle the world twenty-seven times. There is a crew of eight who constantly paint it."

Megan let out an honest laugh. "There it is, the famous Tim Hagen memory for detail. And I thought it was just for techno-stuff. Or made up by your publicists."

"No, it's for everything. At least anything that has a number in it. I mean, it's for everything to some extent, but if there's a number involved, it sticks. It really helps in business. I stink with names, though."

Somewhere between the North and South towers, the atmosphere had changed and the car had become a comfortable place to be.

"Do you remember my name?" She asked, leaning forward, letting her breath touch the side of his face.

"Your first name's Megan. Rhymes with Hagen, so that's pretty easy. Your last name's...uh,...Prajneesh? Borovoteski? Yakamoto?"

Eventually, she stopped his guessing with a kiss.

She lived in the lower Haight, so of course there was no parking. They continued their kissing double-parked in front of her house. Cars loomed behind them, flashed their brights, and then passed. In his pleasantly out-of-control euphoria, Tim hoped that they were beeping not in agitation but in affirmation of young love.

When things came to the verge of out-of-hand, Megan finally pulled back and exited the car, biting back a grin and with her eyes sparkling. Tim imagined his were, too. She invited him to call her and retreated up the stairs, pausing before closing the door.

In the shadow of her hall light, Tim saw her bound up the stairs toward her apartment. A car beeped behind him and he finally put the car in gear to leave.

At the Presidio, he impulsively turned North back toward Marin. The night was young and he was flushed with energy.

He turned off at the scenic overlook, parked the car, and settled himself on an outcropping of serpentinite (the wine must be wearing off). The city was lit up, and Scorpio hung low over where he guessed the Farallones would be. An oil tanker was passing beneath the bridge, a dark void except for its outline in lights.

The evening fog had lifted and only a slight wind remained, not enough to chill Tim but enough to make Tim ache for the feel of Megan's body against him. There was that bad business about the Animas, but all in all it had been a great date. He wanted to laugh out loud.

Tim became aware of a quiet voice talking. He listened for a bit, trying to hear the conversation, but he could only hear the voice when it murmured a sibilant. Then he realized what he was hearing. Someone wondering at the beauty of it all. The city and the tanker, the stars of Scorpio. The wind and the hard feel of rock. Someone talking into a machine, pouring out his soul.

Larry O'Brien sold his first computer program at age sixteen and made more in a week than his friends did in a summer of scooping ice cream. That pretty much ruined whatever work ethic his parents had tried to instill in him. Since then, his knowledge of computers has helped him pay the rent while he explored such career possibilities as sailing instructor, aquarium maintainer, seabird observer, screenwriter, and magazine editor. Currently, he is editor-in-chief of *Software Development Review* and *AI Expert* magazines.

Other than computers, Larry's preoccupations rotate around SCUBA diving with his wife (whom he proposed to ninety-four feet below the surface) and writing. His technical articles have appeared in several computer magazines and his fiction in the magazines *Entropy, SPQ,* and *Spectacles*. This is his first published science fiction story.

Until my younger daughter taught me to appreciate history by making it come alive at our dinner table, historical fiction held no fascination for me. When this story appeared in my electronic in-box, I had to wonder why it was submitted for the anthology. It didn't seem like science fiction. But, like my daughter's animated explanations, it made another time and place come alive. Oh, it's science fiction, all right, but after a few paragraphs I didn't care. I was there.

JEFF CARTER
Past Master

WHEN I FIRST HEARD of Mr. Legion I was owned by Master Ballington. We heard that a man from up north had come to town and bought a plantation on the other side of the town. Ben, who usually drove into town, said he'd seen the man, and that he talked funny. We put that down to his being a Yankee. Ben also said he'd heard some of the other slaves say Mr. Legion had been seen down by the market checking on the next slave sale.

This set off a buzz of speculation in our quarters. If Mr. Legion was going to buy slaves, would any of us be sold to him? If so, would families be broken up? What kind of master would he be? On this last question there were two schools of thought. One held that a Northerner was accustomed to considering Negroes free men and would be a good master. The other held that Yankees who came south to own slaves were especially likely to be vicious: that those who traveled a long distance in order to own slaves made worse masters than those who had grown up accustomed to the idea. The proponents of this view pointed out that most of the slave owners in the area had been raised to own slaves by their slave-owning fathers, and most were not bad masters.

Master Ballington was not a bad master, if one is going to be a slave, which is not an occupation I would recommend, for the hours are long, the work is hard, and the pay is very low indeed. Master Ballington never beat a slave without reason, and never so

76   CARTER

much that he couldn't work the next day. Nevertheless, we whispered at night, and dreamed while we worked, of being free. I can't imagine how Mr. Nicholls's slaves felt, since he drank and beat them severely, often for no reason.

The talk about Mr. Legion soon died down as the novelty wore off, and things returned to normal on the plantation. Ben fell ill, and I was called on to take his place one day when Mrs. Ballington wanted to do some shopping in town. I was in the fields when Master Ballington called me. "Adam, come here. I want you to harness Debbie to the carriage and take Mrs. Ballington into town to the shops."

"Yessuh," I said. I know that sounds stereotyped, but such stereotypes have a basis, for I talked so then, not having had any schooling. I had seldom been in town, so I hurried to ready the carriage before he changed his mind. The roads were dry and firm, and we had an easy way to town.

At the shop I tied up the horse and walked Mrs. Ballington to the entrance. "Wait for me here, Adam," she said, and went in. Some barrels and boxes were stacked outside the shop on the walk, and on these were sitting several slaves waiting to be called.

"Wheah's Ben?" one of them asked.

"Him sick," I said. "Coughin' all the time now two, three days." They all agreed that was bad, and Ben was not likely to survive.

Occupied by the conversation, and not accustomed to being in town, I failed to notice a man coming up to the shop behind me. "Out of my way, nigra," he said, and poked me with his stick. I turned around and found myself face to face with Mr. Nicholls.

Mr. Nicholls was a sort of bogeyman to young slaves in the area, and my mother had often threatened to sell me to him if I didn't behave. So I was rooted with fear for a second before I could step back. "Scuze me—" I said, but I hadn't been fast enough for him.

"Damn you, I said out of my way!" he shouted, hitting me over the head with his stick. I should have stepped back, tried to ward off his blows, and waited for him to go inside, but I was not accustomed to being beaten for no reason. In short, I grew angry and pushed him away. He tripped over a box behind him and fell down. "You damned nigra, I'll see you hanged for this, by God Almighty I will!" he shouted as he got up. He called for the sheriff to come and take me away and hang me.

Mrs. Ballington came out of the shop then and rescued me. She told Mr. Nicholls that she needed me to take her home. "We'll hold him for you, never fear. Tomorrow my husband will call on you to arrange matters."

We got home as quickly as we'd got to town, much too quickly for me. I'd as soon have had to help the horse draw the carriage through deep mud in the rain if it would delay the time when I'd stand before Master Ballington. "You pushed Mr. Nicholls over, Adam?" he demanded in the quiet way he had when he was angry.

"Nosuh, I jus' pushed 'im away, but there's this box ahind 'im and he fall down."

"You should not have pushed him."

"Nosuh, I shouldun. I knows I's bad. You goan beat me, Massuh?"

"You're likely to be hanged for this, Adam. I can't see that beating you will make it any better."

The next day Master Ballington came home from Mr. Nicholls's and told me that Mr. Nicholls was not going to have me hanged. Instead he wanted one hundred fifty dollars. "I haven't got the money, Adam," Master Ballington told me. "I'm going to have to sell you."

"Please, Massuh, doan sell me to Missuh Nicholls."

"I will not sell you to him if I can avoid it."

"What about Mandy an' Lizzie May?" These were my wife and infant daughter.

"I'll try not to split you up. But I'm not going to take less than market price for Mandy. If she won't fetch it with you, I'll keep her. Maybe we can get the buyer to let you visit."

I went back and told Mandy what he had said. She started crying, and the other women gathered around and started crying. We men couldn't take it, so we went out to the fields again. They seemed amazed that I'd laid the bogeyman out on his back and wasn't going to hang for it.

That evening Mr. Legion rode up on a big, reddish-brown horse and went in to talk to Master Ballington. The others started tormenting me immediately. "Lordy, lordy, he done seen his chance and took it," one of them said. "He goan get him a young buck slave fo' hunnert an' fiddy dollah and work it to death." I remembered the talk about Northern masters and started trembling. I held on to Mandy, who started crying.

Later Mr. Legion and Master Ballington came out of the house.

78   CARTER

They shook hands and Master Ballington thanked him several times before he mounted and rode away. Master Ballington had us called to see him.

"We are in luck. Mr. Legion has paid full market price for both of you, and agreed to take your daughter as well. You are to go with him on Monday."

Never has time passed as quickly for me as the rest of that week. In no time at all it was Sunday afternoon and we were packing our few things, wondering what life would be like as Mr. Legion's only slaves. We didn't sleep at all that night, but neither did some of our friends, who stayed up with us around a fire. I hope none of them suffered beatings the next day for sloppy work due to lack of sleep. Lizzie May slept the sound sleep of innocence.

The next morning we were standing in front of the house, wearing our best clothes. Mr. Legion drove up in a carriage. Master Ballington came out of the house and shook hands with him. "I take it these are the slaves," Mr. Legion said, pointing at us. "I would say I'm getting good value for my money. Put your things in the carriage," he told us.

"Adam is a good worker, strong but gentle," Master Ballington said. "You'll have no trouble with him. He would never have caused any trouble if Nicholls had not hit him."

"I understand," Mr. Legion said. "Can you drive a carriage?" he asked me.

"Yessuh."

"Then get up there and let's get home." He got in the back of the carriage while I helped Mandy up in front. I took the reins and drove off. Some of the men stood up in the fields and waved their hats at us. I didn't wave back, not knowing how Mr. Legion would react to such behavior and not daring to take the chance, but Mandy waved back and Mr. Legion didn't say anything.

There had been some rain recently, and the carriage got stuck fording the river. I got out and helped the horse, pushing on the wheels. We were making progress, slowly but surely, and would eventually have got the carriage free. Mr. Legion stood up in the carriage and looked around, then jumped down and helped. "You doan need do that, Massuh Legion," I told him. "We get it out soon."

"It's no problem, Adam," he said. "The same thing happened on my way to Ballington's, so I'm used to it. Besides, it will be easier

PAST MASTER 79

without my weight in the carriage. Since there's no one around to disapprove, I'd just as soon get it over with and get going again." I decided then that he would be a good master. I didn't realize how wrong I was.

When we got to his plantation he stood up in the carriage and looked around again. "You'll probably be the cook and housekeeper, Mandy," he said, "so why don't you take the child into the house and get to know the kitchen. I'll show Adam where things are in the stable." Mandy started off toward the house with Lizzie May.

"You doan need show me, Massuh," I said. "I find 'em all right."

"I'm sure you would, Adam, but I'd prefer to accompany you." He saw Mandy heading up the steps toward the house. "Mandy!" he called.

"Yes, Massuh?" she said, turning.

He looked around again. "I think you should use the back door."

"I's sorry, Massuh. I's not used to goin' in the white folk's house."

He sat down. "Let's go, Adam," he said. I drove the carriage into the stable. Master jumped down and closed the stable door. "You take care of Alice, Adam, and I'll put the carriage away." He started unfastening the horse. I figured that this was a white man who liked to work, and let him.

I was currying the horse when he had finished putting the carriage in its place and had washed off the mud. "Are you nearly done?" he asked.

"Yessuh, jus' a little moah and then I give her some feed. That her stall?" I pointed.

"That's right, though as my only horse I suppose she could use any stall. You've worked with horses a lot, I'd say. I could not have finished with her so soon."

"I's mainly a field nigger, Massuh, but I done hepped with the horses some, too."

"Good. There's no field work here, yet. When you finish, come into the house. Remember to use the back door."

"Yessuh."

When I came into the house Mandy came out of the kitchen to meet me. "Looky heah, Adam," she said. "Theah's a pump in the kitchen." She ran in and got a cup. She took it to the pump and raised the handle. The water started flowing out of the pump in a steady stream. Mandy jumped back and dropped the cup, which broke.

80   CARTER

"I ain't nevah seen no pump like that," I said. I pushed the handle down and the water stopped.

"I see you've discovered the water supply," Master said from the door, startling us. "The actual pump is up the hill, run by a water wheel. It keeps a tank filled up there. This is just a valve. I don't want anything to look different about me, though, so I've disguised it as a pump. A couple of houses have indoor pumps."

"Mos' wonderful thing I ever seed," Mandy said.

"It's nothing, really. Would you two please come into my study? I have something for you."

We followed him into a room filled with books, with a big desk in the middle. He opened a drawer and took out a few sheets of paper with writing on them. "Your name is Adam?" he asked me. I nodded. He wrote on one of the pieces of paper. "Your name is Mandy?" he asked.

"Yessuh."

"Is that short for 'Amanda'?" he asked.

"I doan know, suh. I's always been called 'Mandy'."

"If you don't mind, we'll consider that your name is 'Amanda' from now on, called 'Mandy'."

"It doan mind me, Massuh." He wrote on another piece of paper.

"What is your child's name?" he asked.

"She be called 'Lizzie May,' Massuh," I said. "She be yeah and a haff old."

"Nineteen full moons," Mandy said.

"Again, is that short for 'Elizabeth May'? And if not, would you object to her name being considered 'Elizabeth May' from now on, known as 'Lizzie May'?"

"We always jus' called her 'Lizzie May.' You think 'Lizzie' short for 'Elizabeth'?"

"That's customary. I'll refer to her as 'Elizabeth May,' then." He wrote on the third piece of paper. "This one's for you, Adam," he said, handing me one of the pieces of paper. "This one's for Mandy, and this is for Lizzie May." We took the paper, puzzled. "You'll probably consider those papers to be very valuable," he said. "I know I would in your place. Those are your manumission papers."

"Thank you, Massuh," Mandy said, looking at me strangely.

"Massuh, if it's all right, what's a 'manamission paper'?"

"Of course it's all right. 'Manumission' means liberation or setting

PAST MASTER 81

free. Those papers say that I've set you free. You are no longer slaves."

Mandy and I looked at each other for a moment, speechless. "You mean we's free?" I said. "We can leave and go anywheres we want?"

"Technically, yes. I wouldn't advise it, though. You don't know how to read and write. You've got no money and no property. No one will give you a job. And most of the whites around here would rather string you up than listen to you talk about being free. They wouldn't be too pleased with me, either."

"Then what we do? What good this paper?" I thought it was mean of him to build up our hopes like this, then dash them down again, and I'd lost enough awe of him to let my anger show.

"To answer your second question first, in and of themselves, the papers are no good at all. But together with training and a paying job, followed by transportation somewhere where a free Negro is not automatically considered fair game, the papers are, as I said, quite valuable. As to your first question, you stay with me for a while. I need the help fixing up the place. I'll pay you and teach you the skills you'll need to get by on your own. When the time comes, I'll help you get to New England and put you in touch with some people there who will help you get jobs. In the future I'll buy and manumit more slaves, and I'd like your help with that."

"You goan pay us?" I asked.

"You goan learn us?" Mandy asked.

"Yes and yes. I believe a rate of one dollar a week is suitable for your duties, if you don't object." We didn't. "Since you won't have to pay for room, board, or clothing, that should go a long way. I'll also start teaching you reading, writing, and basic arithmetic right away. You will have to pretend in public that you are still slaves. You should call me 'Massuh' and defer to other whites. When your English improves, you should still talk the way you do now. You should not use your money to buy fancy clothes, since it would be unwise to wear them. Above all, you must never, ever, tell anyone, Negro or white, what we are doing. It is against the law in this state to teach a Negro to read or write. They would probably hang us all if they ever found out."

"I doan b'lieve it," I said. "I is dreaming."

"We's free!" Mandy said.

"We's gonna get paid!" I said.

82 CARTER

"We's gonna learn readin' and writin'!" Mandy said. "Thank you, Massuh, thank you!"

"Why's you doin' this, Massuh?" I asked. "What's you get outta this?"

"I'm doing it because I'm opposed to the concept of human slavery and I have the means and the opportunity. Now, there are no slave quarters on the estate, so you will have to make do with rooms in the house. Come with me."

That night Mandy and I went to bed when it got dark, as we usually did. Master had given us a new candle, but we didn't want to waste it, and had nothing to do with our leisure time anyway. Later we were awakened by a strange noise, a kind of vibrating rumble. I got up and went to see what it was. I followed the sound upstairs to a room in the center of the top floor. Bright light shone out of the room under the door.

My first thought was that there was a fire in the room. Forgetting about the noise, I tried to open the door, but it was locked. I banged on the door, shouting, "Massuh!" A moment later the door opened and Master slipped out, closing the door behind him. The light from inside the room was so bright that it dazzled my eyes, and I couldn't see anything in the room.

"I'm sorry if I woke you, Adam," Master said. "This is my private study, and I work up here most evenings. When you learn to read you will probably want to spend your evenings reading, rather that going to bed as soon as it gets dark."

"You got a fire in there, Massuh?"

"No, I don't have a fire. The noise is a generator. The generator makes electricity, which I use to make the light."

"I doan unnerstan', Massuh."

"I know you don't. It will take a long time to teach you enough to understand it. For now, you'll just have to accept it, and not mention it to anyone. I only use it in this room so none of the light will be visible from outside the house. If word of this got out, the local people, in their ignorance, would probably hang me for witchcraft. There's no telling what would happen to you and your family."

"Is you a witch, Massuh?" I asked, afraid the answer would be yes.

"No, I'm not. The principles involved can be learned by anyone with sufficient intelligence, but, as I said, it will take a long time for

PAST MASTER   83

you to learn enough to learn them. Until then I'm afraid that you will have to take my word that it isn't magic, since it will appear to be magic to you."

"You say it looks like magic but it ain't?"

"That's right. I guess you were bound to find out about this eventually. I should have told you today. I'll explain further to you and Mandy tomorrow. For now you should go back to bed. I'll be finished here soon."

The next day Master explained about electricity, what was known about it and who had discovered it. I mainly remember him telling us about Benjamin Franklin's experiment to prove that lightning was a form of electricity, since I had heard Franklin's name before. Master said he had developed a machine to generate a steady source of electricity, and a device to convert electricity into light. He planned to make a lot of money from these inventions some day, but in the meantime we must not tell anyone about them.

True to his word, Master started to teach us to read and write. It was hard work at first, as we scratched out letters and our names on paper Master gave us. It was a bit discouraging to have our hard work burned in the fireplace after each lesson, but Master reminded us that it was illegal to teach a Negro to read or write, and that we would all be hanged if anyone found out.

Mandy did the cleaning and cooking and took care of Lizzie May, and I helped Master repair the house and his modifications to it, such as the water supply. We also planned and started building slave quarters, although they were much nicer than the shacks we'd lived in at Master Ballington's and hardly deserved the name.

Once a week I drove Master into town to shop. A few weeks after we'd moved there I was outside the store, waiting for Master to call me to carry the packages. I was talking to some other slaves, who asked what kind of master Master was. I replied that if they were lucky they would get sold to Master, because I had never had it so good. "Course," I added, "ain't no field work there, 'cause he ain't got 'nough niggers for plantin'."

At that point Mr. Nicholls came up to the store. I realized that this was the same place where I had pushed Mr. Nicholls over only a few weeks before, but this time I was not blocking the door, but standing next to a window. Mr. Nicholls came right up to me. "You, nigra," he said, pointing his stick at me.

84   CARTER

I realized Mr. Nicholls had not been satisfied with his hundred fifty dollars, and had come to remedy the situation. Though very scared, I managed to reply, "Yessuh."

"You come with me and help me unload some boxes."

Clearly he intended to beat me if I refused, and to find fault with my work and beat me if I didn't. He would probably have beat me for being too slow to respond if I had not heard Master, inside the window, whisper to me to say, "Nosuh, Massuh done tol' me I's to stay here till he call."

"I don't care what your master told you, nigra, you do as you're told."

Again repeating Master's words I replied, "I ain't your slave, and I gotta do what Massuh tol' me."

Master said, "Don't fight back. I'll be there in a minute."

Mr. Nicholls raised his stick. "You damned uppity nigger, you do as I tell you!" I shook my head. "I'll have your black hide," he yelled, hitting me with his stick.

Master came out then and pulled him off me and pushed him into the street, where he landed on his back in a puddle of mud. He'd only hit me a couple of times, but there was some blood on my forehead.

"Damn you, Legion, I'll have you up for assault. You've ruined my clothes."

"I think not, Mr. Nicholls," Master said calmly. "I have merely prevented you from vandalizing my property. You notice that you have damaged my property already," he said, pointing to the blood. "Vandalism is a felony, and it is I who can press criminal charges against you if I choose, as well as file a civil suit. I will call on you this afternoon to discuss whether I will take you to court. If you're not there, you will go to jail. Good day, Mr. Nicholls." Master turned and walked into the store, motioning me to follow him. We left Mr. Nicholls spluttering in the mud.

That afternoon I drove Master to Mr. Nicholls's place. While the main house was in good repair, the slave quarters could hardly have served even to keep the rain out. Master asked me some questions about the slaves before he went into the house. He wanted to know which of the slaves were married, which were single, and things like that. I didn't know all the answers, but Mr. Nicholls only had about ten slaves.

PAST MASTER   85

Master was in the house for a good hour and a half. I could hear Mr. Nicholls shouting sometimes, though I couldn't understand the words. Finally Mr. Nicholls and Master came out of the house. "Norm, you and Bev get your things and put them in the carriage," Mr. Nicholls said. "You and your son belong to Mr. Legion now." He looked at Master for a moment and then went back into the house.

Not much was said on the way home, though Master ascertained the names of his new slaves and their son, Matt, although he called them Norman, Beverley, and Matthew. Matt wasn't much older than Lizzie May. When we arrived home, Master said, "Adam, put the horse away and join us in the house." Then he took Norm and Bev inside. I hurried the horse into the stable, knowing what was happening.

When I got inside, Norm and Bev were standing holding pieces of paper and looking blankly at each other. Master rose and said, "I'm glad you're here, Adam. Perhaps you'll take Norm and Bev into the kitchen and explain what it is they have there and how things work here, while dinner is being prepared. I think they might find it easier to accept coming from you than from me."

"Yes, Master," I said, being careful with the *t* and *r* sounds.

"That's very good," Master said, "but be careful not to talk like that in front of outsiders."

"No, Sir."

"Why's you talkin' so fancy?" Norm asked as we went to the kitchen.

"Master says it will make things easier for me later on," I told him.

Norm and Bev took their transition to freedom much as Mandy and I had, even coming from us. It was wonderful to see the looks on their faces as the truth sank in. I suspect that, while it was true that they probably accepted what they were told a little quicker coming from Mandy and me than they would have from Master, the real reason Master wanted us to tell them was so he would not have to try to explain why he was doing this, and accept their gratitude.

The next morning Master had me drive him to Mr. Ballington's plantation. Mr. Ballington came out and met us in front of the house. "How do you do, Mr. Legion?" he said. "Hello, Adam. How are things at Mr. Legion's for you and Mandy?"

"We's been fine, suh," I said, smiling and looking at Master.

"That's good. What brings you here this fine day?" he asked Master.

86   CARTER

"I've brought you some money. One hundred fifty dollars, to be exact, from Mr. Nicholls."

"That's very nice, but I must admit it is one of the last things I would have expected of him. I'm still surprised that he didn't insist that Adam be hanged."

"He is only doing this under duress. You and I both know that he had no case against Adam, and so did not deserve the money. He overstepped himself in town yesterday, as you may have heard, and this is part of the conditions I placed on not filing criminal charges against him."

"Then I must thank you for this. You needn't have done this, though, sir. I was amply recompensed for the loss of my slaves, which was more than I expected."

"I did have to do this for my own sake," Master said. "I paid market price for your slaves, knowing that some of it would go to Mr. Nicholls. In effect, you were not receiving market price for your slaves. I was glad of this opportunity to see that you received your due."

"I'm glad the opportunity arose."

"So am I. If circumstances permit, I will take advantage of further such opportunities until Mr. Nicholls owns no slaves at all."

"Perhaps you would like to come inside and have a cool drink. It is the least I can do to repay you for your kindness."

"Thank you, but no. You need not repay me. And I have two new Negroes at home who require supervision, so I must leave immediately."

Later, on the drive home, Master said, "That should improve my reputation among most of the local population, while subconsciously giving the impression that I am a person who thinks people are worth a certain sum of money."

"Why did Mr. Nicholls take money instead of hanging me?" I asked. "Mr. Ballington said it surprised him?"

"I convinced him that money would be of more value to him than hanging you. I pointed out that hanging you would give him momentary pleasure, but afterwards he would be no better off than before. Also, that legally he would have to prove that he was justified in having you hanged in order to have it done, and that, although it was likely he could do it, it would cost him time and money."

"Why did you do that, Master?"

"I knew Ballington would have to sell you to raise the money, and thought that I could probably buy you."

"So you could set us free and teach us to read and write?"

"Exactly. I also thought that Mr. Nicholls's violent nature would seek a further outlet against you. I was right, and now Norm and Bev are also free."

The harvest was not as good that year as usual, and several plantations had to sell slaves to get enough money. The only person buying was Master. Mr. Nicholls had to sell four slaves. He had wanted to sell just women, but Master insisted that he sell families. He refused at first, but no one else would buy and he needed the money, so he gave in at last.

We completed the "slave quarters," but Mandy, Lizzie May, and I stayed in the house. We began planning to plant the next year. Mandy and I learned to read well enough that we started using the candles to read in the evenings, just as Master had said we would. We read almost anything, but I tended to read about the law, since it had had such a role in my being freed and in Mr. Nicholls's humiliation.

One evening Master asked me into his private study, the one upstairs with the bright lights. It was the first time I had been in there. When my eyes adjusted I saw a desk with some strange boxes on it, and in a corner was an oddly shaped thing which made the strange noise I had become used to hearing every evening. Thin black ropes led from this thing to the lights and to the boxes on the desk.

"I have some things to show you, Adam," he said. "I haven't been entirely truthful with you about some things. For example, I did not invent the electrical generator or the light bulb. I told you this because I did not think you would accept the truth."

He did something to a box on the desk and a flat shiny surface on another of them turned white, and some words appeared on it. "You may have wondered how I get my money. Mr. Ballington was unable to produce the money to pay Mr. Nicholls without selling you, and he has crops planted each year to provide him with income. I was able to pay market price for you and Mandy, but I have no income."

"I guess I just assumed that white people have money. Obviously, that's not true."

"Obviously." He did something with a box with bumps on it. I

88 CARTER

saw that most of the bumps had letters on them, and they moved down when he pressed on them and came back up when he released them. Letters appeared on the flat shiny thing for each bump he pressed. Then he pressed a bump with several letters on it and several lines of writing appeared. "I originally had a large amount of money when I came here. It was counterfeit, but no one here could ever tell that. I long ago spent all that money. Since then I have made money by dealing in the stock market. What I have done with this device is have it display tomorrow's closing prices for several stocks. I'd like you to write them down. Are you familiar with the stock quotations in the newspaper?"

"I've seen them, but I never knew what they meant."

He opened a newspaper to the stock page. "This paper lists the closing prices for several days ago. For example, the stock I have displayed here is listed in the paper here." He pointed to the writing on the shiny thing, then at the paper. "You can see that the abbreviation is the same. The price I have displayed is tomorrow's price. No one will know tomorrow's price until tomorrow afternoon, and we won't get that price in the paper for several days. When we get the paper with tomorrow's prices in it, I want you to check that these prices are correct."

"How can you know tomorrow's prices, Master?" I asked, my voice unsteady.

"Are you afraid my answer will be magic? Magic does not exist. This device contains all of the stock prices for the past ten years and for the next fifteen years. It allows me to obtain the price for any stock on any day during that period. The information about the stock prices was put into the device in the future. Then it and I came back through time to live here."

"You're saying that you come from the future?" I asked, wondering if Master were a witch, a genius, or a madman.

"That's right. I have not even been born. That won't happen for over one hundred fifty years."

"And you're doing this so you can make money?"

"No. I'm doing this so I can buy slaves and set them free. Are you finished copying this down?" I nodded, and he did something to one of the boxes and the writing displayed on the thing disappeared and the surface became dark again.

"Now," Master said, "you and Mandy are making very good

PAST MASTER   89

progress with your studies. Have you given any thought to what kind of work you want to do when you become completely free?"

"I've become interested in the law, Master. Since it was so important in our becoming free, I'd like to know more about it. If I can, I think I'd like a job that deals with the law."

"That's a good choice, Adam. You can become a lawyer if you're willing to continue studying for several years. Lawyers are well paid, and you would be able to help other people when they have problems. I have a number of books dealing with law and legal matters. Have you seen them?"

"Yes, I've read some of them."

"Very good. Read the rest as well, and don't hesitate to ask me if you don't understand something you've read. Well, that's what I wanted to see you about. I've felt bad about not telling you the truth. I know I can trust you to keep it a secret."

A few days later I was able to check the paper with the stock prices for the date in question, and every one of Master's predictions was correct. Maybe it was magic, and the story about the future was made up. There's no way I can tell. But Master always insisted that there is no such thing as magic. And the magical things about Master were always related to his devices, not to spoken words and potions the way I had always heard that magic was done. So I tend to believe him.

Nearly a year later Master was able to obtain all of Mr. Nicholls's slaves when Mr. Nicholls was killed by a slave he was beating. Then our first harvest came in and we had a higher yield per acre than any other plantation around town. Master smiled and said, "Happy workers are productive workers."

The spring after that, Master took Mandy and me north to Boston, where we still live. He helped us find a place to stay, and arranged for us to have money while I attended university. Boston is very different from home, and we had to get used to many strange things. Of course, living with Master had prepared us to accept strange things, but the cold winter and the snow were difficult to get used to. I graduated from university and took the bar examination, and became a lawyer. I was not the first Negro lawyer, but we are a very rare breed. I specialize in representing Negroes who have been wronged by whites. I have no shortage of work, but I have to keep my fees low.

Recently Master came to visit us. He had done all he could, freed all the slaves he could, and had stayed too long in our time, and wanted to go home. "I wanted to see you two before I go," he told us. "As my first slaves, you're special to me." He stayed a few days, and we spent a lot of time walking around the town. He had a little box that he held to his eyes sometimes; he called it "taking pictures." He "took pictures" all over town, the State House, the market, North Church, the Common, and almost any other everyday scene.

One morning he unpacked most of the cases he had brought with him. He had the generator, the light device, and the stock price device. He also had a number of metal bars that fit together to form a kind of sphere made of triangles. A box in the center of the sphere formed a kind of platform. He put all the devices on the platform. He connected the platform box to the generator with a thin black rope and started the generator. I heard the strange noise that had once been so familiar but I had not heard for so many years. Master opened a panel on the side of the box. He pushed on the surface under the panel and glowing numbers appeared.

Master shook our hands and bade us farewell, then got on the platform with his devices. He smiled and looked at us. "My name is Legion," he said, "for I shall be many." Then everything disappeared. I miss him, but I doubt if I will ever see him again.

Jeff Carter has been developing software professionally since 1975, when he first learned FORTRAN and discovered it was a way to be paid for writing. His specialty now is Ada, with interests in software-development methods, software reuse, and neural networks. He created an Ada-oriented software-development method, which he used to win a prize in the Programming Workshop at the 1988 Tri-Ada Conference. Currently, he is a technical team leader on a large software project.

Jeff's science fiction career began when he was thirteen, much earlier than his involvement in software. Luckily, he maintains, his early efforts have long been lost. Although he is the author of sixteen technical papers, "Past Master" is his first fiction sale.

Here is another gem of a short short in a very different vein. Nominally, it's about "the Holidays," but somehow it manages to raise a whole host of contemporary issues about families and parenting and coping with kids. After I first read it, I sat thinking for a long time. Not bad for 650 words from a new writer.

ELIZABETH HANES PERRY
Boxing Day

"**M**OMM-MY! WILL'S TAKEN the Dinger and he won't give it back, and I think Amy pooped!"

Joanna straightened, rubbing the small of her back. That's the last time I let them stay up late Christmas Eve, she thought. They don't sleep properly, they don't eat breakfast, and they're uncontrollable before the next day's done.

She got up from the floor beside the half-empty Christmas tree and walked two steps to the children's corner. "Will, you know very well that you're supposed to be packing your own toys. That one belongs to Martin. Martin, if you'd packed the Dinger, Will couldn't have taken it, could he? Amy, come here and let me check your diaper."

Martin had been right. Joanna sighed. Sometimes it seemed she'd had a child in diapers forever. Joanna carried the protesting toddler to the sani-cubby and did what was necessary. Then she settled Amy back in the corner with her stuffed clown and returned to the tree. Five more branches and she'd be done.

Just as Joanna was collapsing the denuded aluminum skeleton, a heartbroken wail flooded the apartment. She spun around, too late; the neighbors were bound to file another Noise Complaint. Amy was lying on the floor screaming and kicking her heels, while Will and Martin, silent for once, were staring sheepishly at the two halves of Clown.

"That's it! I've told you, when you can't play nicely, it means you're too tired to play at all."

92 PERRY

"But, Momm-my, it isn't even close to bedtime!"

"Then perhaps next Christmas you'll remember to behave your-selves. You're tired, I'm tired, and that means bedtime is NOW. Will, Martin, clean yourselves up. Amy, come here, I think I can make Clown all better."

While Joanna patched Clown, the boys stomped to the cubby, washed their faces, stomped back to the corner, and threw themselves into their boxbeds. Joanna tucked Amy and Clown into the last boxbed and kissed all three children's foreheads. Then she flipped down the apartment's master console, punched up Environmental Controls, and requested Sleep for the children's area. The corner lights dimmed; soon the apartment was silent.

Joanna returned to the tree. It was a tight fit, but she managed to fit the last star into a box alongside the Czech mermaids. She turned back to the console and sent a message to the Super.

"I'm ready for pickup, Sam."

The reply didn't come back for ten minutes.

"So's the entire seventh level. I can't possibly get there till after midnight."

Joanna folded the console back into the wall and sighed. Then she sat down in the single easy chair and settled the velvet throw pillow into the small of her back. The apartment was almost cozy when the tree was down and the children were asleep. Maybe she'd spend her next year's raise on a separate bedroom. Maybe Simon would come back then. She closed her eyes to rest for a moment.

The entry buzzer was only a little softer than the Last Trump. "Sorry, Sam!" Joanna let him in, then pointed to the boxes. "Cold storage, same as always."

"Yeah, I know the drill. When you going to want retrieval?"

"None of your business."

"Look, I don't care what you do with them, but I need to organize my boxes. You don't put a once-a-year in front of a twice-weekly, not if you want to keep your back healthy."

"All right, June, I guess." She looked at the crowded room and sighed. "No, make it December."

"Same as always, sure enough. It's your call." Sam stacked the boxbeds on the lifter, loaded the toy boxes and the tree on top, and pushed the lifter out the door. Joanna could hear him whistling down the hall. After the sound had died out, she finally placed the tune: "I'll Be Home for Christmas."

She threw the pillow at the door, buried her head in her arms, and began to cry.

Elizabeth Hanes Perry, preferring the laconic over the usual biography, said she has three cats, seven horses, and spent nineteen years in the French Foreign Legion. She thought she was going to become a computer programmer until a corporate recruiter noticed her double major in computer science and English and suggested technical writing as an alternative. She has written software manuals for Prime, Apollo, and Hewlett-Packard and hopes that her future employers will not become involved in corporate takeovers. "Boxing Day" is her first fiction sale.

There is a tradition in science fiction of rewriting biblical and other myths, updating them or casting them in an altered perspective; James Morrow comes to mind as a master of this subgenre. After singing Aaron Charloff's "Bat Yiftach," a beautiful, grim, and challenging work for chorus based on the biblical tale of Jephtha's daughter (Judges: 11), I was inspired to write my own reframing: a story with a different ethos and a very different outcome.

LARRY CONSTANTINE
Dellahar's Father

V EDDIAS, WARRIOR of the Feld, tugged on the control bar, barking his knuckles as the airskate rocketed over the rise, bare meters above the trees. Below, scabrous forest gave way to the beauty of rock and sand; ahead, the Trebblian Valley waited. The spot of blood on his middler hand reminded Veddias that the airskate was not designed for men. Veddias cursed the canopy that pressed upon his head, the displays that dazzled his eyes, and the seat whose contours once cradled the spinal plates of an Issikar but now squeezed Veddias into throbbing knots. He hated the Issikar machines with a bitterness that nearly matched his hatred for the Issikar themselves. Issikar were not men, but dwarves pretending to manhood, impious brutes who did not honor the holy name of Havadohn. The stench of the wax oozing from their pores offended the nostrils, the pallid copper of their skin assaulted the eyes. They fashioned their airskates after the flat rays that glided beneath their seas: as deformed as the Issikar, yet swift and deadly. There was irony in attacking the Trebblian Valley depot with the captured airskate, but it was bittersweet, for men were not yet the skilled craft-builders and technologists of Isskaru. Though they could cross the void to the Green Twin on the thunder of their own rockets, the day was yet to dawn when men could build skates to outfly the faithless Issikar.

The target alarm sounded. Veddias fingered the starburst at his throat, trilled a quick prayer, then started the torpedo run.

The screen before him jumped and jiggled in orange excitement. He flicked the switch for the image stabilizer and manipulated a blue cursor over his target. The bubbles of nethas were strung like tree-pearls across the valley; he had only to hit any one for them for all to erupt in a second dawn.

The jumpers took him by surprise, spinning up from the sand, obscene flowers whirling their strands of death. He dove the skate beneath the metal-filament flails, then pulled up so steeply that his hands were nearly ripped from the control bars. Twin thumbs squeezed the calipers, and a ball of blazing nethas blew from the rear tube of the skate, engulfing the jumpers. Seconds later, one spun out of the inferno unharmed. Hoping to outrun it, Veddias elbowed the throttle to its stop and keyed on the torpedo control again.

He cursed.

Two ram-fighters punched through the cloud cover.

"Oh, Great and Unnameable Lord," he piped, "lend me your strength as I pledge you service." The ram-fighters screamed toward his skate from port, while the jumper whined after him.

And Dellahar's father in the fire of battle did swear an oath to the Most High, vowing, If my enemies are delivered into the destruction of my hands, that I may return in victory unto the world of my birth, then shall it be that whatever living thing do I first see upon my return to my home, that thing shall I make unto you a sacrifice.

II Appositions 26

The long, low-energy orbit from Isskaru had taken its toll on Veddias. His muscles seemed as weak as the vines of winter while he wrestled the sandrover up the shell-pocked road to the ranch. Atop the hill his house sat like a gray bun cooling in the light of the treble moon. A shutter swung open and moonflame glittered off polished metal.

Dellahar waved and called, "Father, beloved father, you have returned!" A creature of slow grace, she lowered herself down the wall and loped toward him, squealing a hymn of homecoming as she did. "To Havadohn, Most Generous, who brings home the beloved."

She stood before the rover as it made the final turn, her hands all framing her face in anticipation. Her father dropped the skids, halting the rover. From the dustcloud he emerged, the knobs of his flesh raised in anger.

96   CONSTANTINE

"Why have you done this? Is it not enough that you are without twin? Am I not already cast deep enough by the loss of your mother? You run from the house like a young chizot or a bad-mannered puppy. Where now is that hairy pet of yours that always scampers to pounce on every guest and potseller who rounds the bend?"

Dellahar, who lived for the joy of her father, was crestfallen. "What ill comes with you, father?" she asked.

His ears drooped in dismay. "I have made a promise unto Havadohn, whose True Name burns the tongue, whose wisdom scorches the mind. With His might in our hearts we have destroyed the depots and the ports of the twin-world, Isskaru, and I was spared. Now I must do as I promised the Lord and make sacrifice."

"Then you must, and I will prepare the salt-fires for the offering, for whatever you have promised the Lord, that you must do. It is a seal upon the house and upon me as much as upon you."

"But it is you I have promised to Havadohn. The first living thing that I see upon my return, that is my offering." He could not bear to look at Dellahar, whose lustrous skin was burled with pleasing whorls of umber and pitch.

Her gaze upon him was steady and somber, but her piety fled as she listened to him in fear. "Oh, Father, is this what you have raised me for, to be bartered off to an unseen god, traded like some domestic animal for a fleeting advantage in a single battle? It is a shifting war we wage upon the monsters of Isskaru, a war that has already spanned the centuries and will doubtless reach into more to come. This war between worlds will outlive us both, whatever we do, whatever we sacrifice."

But Dellahar's father had boasted of his vow to comrades on the return from Isskaru, and the oil with which the cleric had anointed him still shone on his bare arms. He would not be swayed. "It is my word," he rasped in a whisper. "As once you were mine, now you are the Lord's."

When was I yours, she asked in her thoughts, though she spoke otherwise: "But Father, I have tasted so little of the blossoms of life. I have never seen the eclipse of Isskaru, nor have I hunted the water-elk. I have known no man. I am a virgin with too much to lament were I to die now."

The ridges over his eyes softened as she spoke; her grief was as a

DELLAHAR'S FATHER   97

brand upon his head, melting the wax of his hair. He wound his arms around her, gently scratching the horns of her spine.

"I did promise the first living thing I saw to Havadohn, but I did not vow that my first act would be a burnt offering. I will prepare for the sweet pain through devotion and will sing aloud the Nineteen Books of Ja'arahu. This I will do from the setting of the first moon until the dawning of Scheebahd. You are free to go until then."

She did not think this much of a gift, but said, "Blessings upon you, my father. I will leave the ranch that has been my home and take to the hills of Kassahnderuut. I will visit the inner valley of Nesthal and meditate on this thing you have decreed for me. There I will lament my virginity and mourn for the twins I shall never bear. Then I will return for the first day of Scheebahd."

> In innocent joy did young Dellahar wave to her returning father, and when she ran to him he did throw himself into the dust, tearing at the coils of his hair in his knowledge. And he spoke to her what he had spoken to the Lord. Then in pain did she lament her innocence and bemoan her fleeting joy. Therefore did Dellahar's father grant her the time to bewail her virginity.
>
> *II Appositions 27*

The climb from the foothills to the heights of Kassahnderuut took Dellahar nearly a week, but her lungs spasmed with joy as she crested the Aitchel Pass and saw the azure inner valley spread below her like a cow blanket on the sand. She did not trust the forest, however, which reminded her of the Isskaru she had seen in many war tapes. Instead, she camped amid the sharp talus just below the footpath. By day she gathered the herbs of mindfulness and brewed infusions that carried her aloft and beneath the brow of the mountain. The tendrils of her mind grew and spread, and each day the world seemed a larger place. By night she curled near the embers and slept a singing sleep that could be heard above the soughing of the jheejha trees and the soft buzzing of the heel-cats who joined her in the camp.

She did not see the messenger star that sliced the Eye of Hegradas in the heavens. The heel-cats stirred and burped but did not awaken her. By dawn, they were gone again, as always, leaving her alone in the chill. When she stood on the fire rock and surveyed

98   CONSTANTINE

her world by the red of the early sun, she did not see the burns, already healing, where the messenger star had scarred the forest, but saw only the unconquerable trees, drab reminders of the color of sacrifice.

Her eyes stung. She closed them and wept.

The stranger did not announce himself, but stood at her feet, weeping with her as an echo cries with the wind-loon. When Dellahar opened her eyes and looked upon the copper-skinned visitor, he did not move or speak, though she glared at him, neither blinking nor averting her eyes. His gnarled muscles spoke of speed and strength, though he was barely as tall as Dellahar's shoulder.

"Who are you? Why do you mock a girl who has known no man?"

The stranger gurgled and whistled but spoke no word known to Dellahar. From his waist he drew a slim blade of bellmetal, sighted along it, and trilled a rattle of noise before letting it drop. It stuck, ringing, in the soft sandrock.

Dellahar bent down and tugged the knife from the rock. It still carried the warmth of his flesh and seemed almost to burn her hand. She did not recognize the crafter's sign, but admired the elegance of his skill. She spun the knife in an arc above her head; it fell and struck the rock between her long toes. The stranger's ears shot upward in pleasure and astonishment. Then he sat before her as guest before householder, without menace or expectation.

She did not learn his speech, nor did he seem to understand hers, but he stayed at the camp, gathering herbs with her, climbing the vines to the forest canopy, and cooking the teas. When she could no longer think of him as a stranger, she called him Chaskaha, which is Discovery. When she could no longer bear the cold of the night, she pulled him to her.

The pressure of his body on hers was like oil on the cooking fire. His organ stung within her, and her sides ached with the pleasure. In the darkness her eyes widened with awareness. An innocent might throw herself on the green flames of sacrifice, but knowledge brought so many things worth clinging to. She ran her hands down the flat horns along his spine, then wrapped her legs around him and squeezed with all her strength.

Bathing with Chaskaha in the heat of midday, Dellahar thought again of her virginity, which she had lost, and of the knowledge

DELLAHAR'S FATHER   99

she had gained. On this and the meaning of promise, her mind spun with the spinning of the days until one night Chaskaha did not return from his foraging. The marching of the moons told her that Scheebahd was soon. With little time to waste, she decided to follow him, though his spoor led into the thick of the wood.

She caught up with him by the next afternoon, then kept him in sight as she hid behind hair-bush and tall babahor. At last, through the trees she saw an airskate, half-obscured by the new wood growing over its body, with the double diamond of Isskaru marking its defiant tail. She had never, until that moment, seen an Issikar. She watched Chaskaha climb over the wing and into the skate, studying the pale copper of his skin, the muscles of his back, remembering.

She ran without thinking back to her camp. His bellmetal knife stood in the sandrock where she had flung it on their first meeting. When she pulled it out, it spoke to her, ringing sweetly in her ear, a knowing sound of mastery. She slipped it beneath the waxy coils of her hair, gathered her things, and started the climb back through the Aitchel Pass.

> And as she had promised, so did Dellahar climb unto the hills, there to lament her virginity and to think upon her losses and learn of the world. These she did, and she did also swear unto the Lord an oath of her own. And when the days of the triune moon were fulfilled, and the dawning of Scheebahd was near, she returned unto her father, as she had promised, returning alone, as she had departed, though she had known man.
>
> *II Appositions 28*

Even as he saw her picking her way down the footpath, it was obvious to Dellahar's father that she was changed. The twin bulges at her waist told the story. He tweeted in agony and threw himself on the ground.

"What have you done? Why do you again cast me to the dust? Can my sacrifice be mete when you are no longer a virgin?"

She stepped up to her father and helped him from the ground. "Ah, my melodramatic father, your wisdom is as steady as the plennyar circling for carrion. It is sad to you, I am certain, that I am no longer worthy of the honor that you had planned. Have you not taught me that the Lord shall vomit back upon the sand whatever is impure? You are a pious man and must sacrifice something else."

100 CONSTANTINE

Perplexity tugged at his eyes; they twitched and rolled in frustration. "No. It is written that one who has neither field-goat nor chizot to sacrifice for the Feast of Books is not excused, but must bring to the clerics a cabbage from the woods, anointed in the sap of the dagroo tree, saying, 'This is the field-goat of my heart.' Thus, shall an unworthy gift be made worthy by the piety of the sacrifice."

"Father," she said, placing hands at either side and clutching her gold starburst with the other, "these are your grandchildren, on either hand your twin posterities. They dream the tomorrows of your dreams, Father."

"And what horrors will the Lord visit upon my dreams now? No longer are you untouched, but already carry your first twins: this is true. Yet I swore; this also is true."

"Slay me then, if you must," she said, straining to keep all trace of insincerity from her voice, "but, truly, a warrior of the Feld cannot take the lives of babes who have not yet lived. The unborn were not promised."

Dellahar's father thought for long moments, wheezing his impatience into the air as he thought. Finally he spoke: "I will not harm the twins of your wombs. I will sacrifice only you, as I have promised. It will be for the Lord to take the unborn or not, as may be the Lord's wish." He reached for the wire lanyard hanging from the gate. Dellahar's hand went to her hair, feeling for the metal hidden there.

"But wait, Father! If you must be true to your word, tell me again what word it is that you gave to the Most High."

"To sacrifice the first living thing I saw upon returning home."

"And what is it that you saw that was alive?"

"I saw you waving from the window."

"With which hand did I wave?" She held all three before him.

"I saw the moon glistening on your bracelet."

She laid her hand upon a stump of the babahor tree and removed the heavy bracelet. She drew the knife from her hair and held it out toward her father, who gasped. In the burnished metal, the clouds cast green shadows, and he saw a vision of his grandchildren, playing at the gate, camping in the hills, skating through the skies of Isskaru.

And said bright Dellahar to her father, What has been vowed to the Lord, that must you do. What has been promised, that must you give. And Dellahar's father took from her the bellmetal knife and did what he had vowed, making a burnt offering unto the Lord. And his days were numbered as the rings of a great dagroo tree, and they were filled with the keening of many grandchildren and the singing of Dellahar as she wove upon the two-handed loom that he commanded to be made for her. And her first twins were copper-toned and lithe, with the strength and agility of their father and the wisdom and quick wit of their mother. These did Dellahar dedicate to the Lord. The left of these did she name, Plassaroht, which is Repayment, and the right of these called she, Sefta-havadohn, The Third Hand of God. Great warriors became they in their youth, a scourge upon the face of Isskaru, for none do make war as fiercely as do brother upon brother.

II Appositions 29

In his own words, Larry Constantine is a troublemaker with a compulsion to intermix the various parts of his life and attempt to make them all fit together. A consultant whose career in software began in the dark ages of computing with the corrupting influence of M.I.T., he is also a licensed family therapist, a composer, and a science fiction writer.

This anthology, his eighth book, marks his debut as an editor. *[As if you couldn't tell. Ed.]* In addition to his book with Ed Yourdon, *Structured Design*, which some regard as a classic in software engineering, his professional nonfiction writing includes a book on family therapy, a textbook on psychotropic drugs, and a highly regarded study of communal families. He has been writing short fiction for years under a pseudonym. This story is the first to appear under his own name. *[Now readers will know whom to blame. Ed.]*

Serendipity operates in the realm of software engineering and computer science as much as elsewhere. Where would telecommunications be had Bell not spilled that beaker? Where would software methodology be had Yourdon not met Constantine? (No, don't answer!) We cannot imagine all the uses to which computers will be put in the future, but we can be certain that many applications will arise from chance. Artificial intelligence only multiplies the possibilities. This story injects a bit of tomorrow's possibilities into the harsh realities of a world right out of today's television news features or last week's *InfoWorld*.

GLENN R. SIXBURY

Sammy

SALLY GERK KNEW the two men were running from the police as soon as they stepped into her alley. She'd been wandering the streets of Wichita long enough to recognize the signs. Pushing their backs against the red brick side of the building, they stopped thirty steps away, out of breath, watching with fearful eyes. The distant wail of approaching sirens confirmed her suspicions.

Sally tucked her grimy dress—two sizes too big for her—close about her body and, stepping into the shadows beside a trash dumpster, pulled with her the shopping cart that contained all her possessions. She quietly grumbled to herself. Today, of all days, she didn't want to be late. It was Sunday, and the Wichita Homeless Services always provided turkey dinners on Sunday. Scratching at the tangled gray hair around her weathered and sagging face, she watched the men with her blue eyes—the same eyes that had once commanded attention in business meetings worth millions of dollars. As a team leading computer engineer at Boeing, she'd been one of the few to survive the layoffs in the early '90s. But after thirty years, the high pressure of her position finally won. She'd suffered a nervous breakdown on Christmas eve, and two months

SAMMY   103

later, under Boeing's bankruptcy reorganization, she lost her job and a lifetime of retirement benefits. Experienced engineers weren't supposed to end up homeless. But they did.

That had been four years ago.

Now she knew the law of the streets. Here, she was an old woman. She had been raped seven times, kicked around whenever she had gotten too close to the pimps or the pushers, and once beaten so badly she lay face down in an alley for two days, unable to move. If these two men spotted her, they would probably kill her.

But they didn't look like killers. Wrinkling their noses, they had avoided the piles of trash and the feces left by the drinkers and the users. Dressed in cheap business suits, they seemed more like accountants hiding a two cent discrepancy—or engineers caught playing computer games at work.

Sally stretched her neck to see them better. One was holding a black cube-shaped object and the other was chattering wildly and pointing in the direction of the approaching sirens. The first stubbornly shook his head until the second, exasperated, grabbed his suit collar and slammed him into the wall. Rubbing the back of his head, the first reluctantly nodded. Both suddenly pointed in Sally's direction and ran towards her.

Falling to the ground, Sally tucked herself into a ball, inching as much of her body as possible beneath her cart. She shouldn't have been so nosy. Her old engineering curiosity would kill her yet.

A thunk of metal against rusted steel echoed from the dumpster beside her. But the two sets of footsteps continued past. Hesitantly, Sally raised her head. Two police cars hummed down the alley, swirls of trash blowing in their wake, their electric motors whining beneath the blares of their sirens. Alison, one of Sally's friends at Cessna, had written the energy usage optimization code for those-seat experimental plane. When the project was canceled, Cessna sold the technology to Ford. Her friend, they laid off. Only twenty-nine, she went to work as a stripper. She said the money was better. She used to buy medicine and food for Sally—until she got hooked on crack. She O.D.'d last summer after her Fourth of July show.

The men and the police cars gone, Sally looked into the dumpster. The black cube was there, between a T.J. Swan wine bottle and

104   SIXBURY

a torn dress. Leaning over the edge, Sally retrieved the dress. It was ripped from the waist to the hem and blood-stained. She held it up to her shoulders—her size. Folding it, she placed it in her cart. Then she reached for the black cube.

Touching it, she jerked back as if burned. The outside of the cube felt warm and supple, yet smooth and hard as metal. Gritting her teeth, she picked it up.

Twice the size of her palm, it was heavy and hard to hold, unstable in her hand as if it was trying to move. Marveling at it, Sally recalled seeing a picture of a cube like this once. Searching her memory, she tried to call up the seemingly ancient knowledge from what she now called her previous life. Then she remembered.

It had been shortly before she left. She had been reading one of the trade journals, something about biological computers. At the time, it had just been theory, but—

A biological computer! Sally stared at the cube, wondering if that's what she held. A biological computer was a new concept: a machine that could grow much as a living organism grows, by producing individual cells, and one that learns like a bright child, amassing knowledge and understanding only after years of instruction. Sally had believed the article's author was dreaming at the time, but looking at the object in her hand, she wondered.

Bending close to the cube, she whispered, "Start." Nothing. She tried, "Begin. Load. Run. Execute. Install." Perhaps a different tactic. "Hello. Good morning," she whispered. The cube lay in her palm, not reacting, but still pulsing slightly, as if an energy force— or a life—existed inside. Her face brightened. She had been working with computers for over thirty years. Holding the cube before her, she commanded, "Boot."

With a slight whir, pupil-only eyes opened near the top of one of the faces and looked at her. Startled, Sally dropped the cube. Emitting a high-pitched squeal, it tumbled into one of the sacks in her cart.

After she recovered, Sally laughed out loud, then stifled herself. Glancing about furtively, she hurried down the alley. For the first time in four years, she had a chance to be a normal person again. The cube was worth a fortune. After giving her whole life to her company, never marrying, never having children, always too busy,

SAMMY 105

she had a chance at last to have what she deserved. With the money she could even start her own company. No one would ever be able to use her, then toss her aside again.

Sally jerked the cart to a halt. The sack the cube had fallen into was smoking, a black line creeping across the paper. Moaning, she cursed herself. She must have broken it somehow, caused a short. Her vision of riches faded like a street lamp at sunrise.

But as she watched the sack, she realized the black line was tracing a square. She nodded thoughtfully: The cube was a military project. She should have guessed that sooner. The ends of the black line met and the cut-out dropped away, revealing the cube, lying upside down, a tiny laser poking out where Sally imagined a nose should have been. Its round black lenses stared up at her like baby eyes. Cooing to it, Sally set it rightside-up in her hand. The tiny laser retracted into the cube and a smaller feeler extended in its place. Sally watched, fascinated, as the fragile arm reached toward her hand. The padded sensors touched her skin, tickling, and Sally laughed. The cube's arm jerked back. The apertures of its lenses expanding, the black eyes turned in Sally's direction.

Then it gurgled, a bad imitation of Sally's laugh. She laughed again and it mimicked her, better this time.

Sally frowned at it suddenly, imagining what a machine like this would be used for by anyone willing to buy it. As it grew, it could learn to be a tank driver, or a jet pilot, or the perfect mafia hit man. She shook her head.

The cube extracted its arm again and tentatively touched Sally's wrist, chirping and beeping as it analyzed the scent, look, taste, and texture of her skin.

Sally sighed heavily. Money wasn't everything. And she needed someone who could protect her. Setting the little cube down into the cart where it could see her, she pushed it along, a youthful bounce in her step. "I will call you Sammy," she said. "Do you like that?"

"Nat," Sammy imitated poorly. "Zat," it tried again.

"You'll be a quick learner, I'm sure," Sally said. Then she added, "We're headed for the homeless center. It's Sunday. We always have turkey on Sunday."

Glenn R. Sixbury started his software career as an avionics engineer for Rockwell International. While working in Ada on the Beech Starship project, he was introduced to object-oriented programming by Grady Booch. That was 1987. Today, he is assistant director for computing in the Department of Faculty Evaluation and Development in the Division of Continuing Education at Kansas State University. "If you think that's a struggle to read," he says, "you ought to try putting it on a business card!"

Glenn first became interested in writing professionally while pursuing his Computer Engineering degree at Kansas State. Working as a consultant for the university's computing center, he discovered Bitnet and the world of electronic magazines. He began writing nonfiction articles for one of them, and several of his short stories appeared in the on-line fantasy and science fiction magazine, *FSF/NET*. Since then, several nonfiction computer articles have been published, and he has sold three fantasy stories to national anthologies. He is currently marketing his first novel and researching material for his next. "Sammy" is his first professional science fiction sale. (Thanks to Brad Beeson, whom he credits for encouragement and the inspiration without which the story never would have been written.)

A committed Kansan, Glenn lives in Manhattan with his wife, Brenda, his five-year-old daughter, Amanda, his two-year-old son, Brian, and the family cat, April, who, he says, "insists on dusting most of my manuscripts with cat hair before they go in the mail."

Every tool is also a weapon, every weapon a potential tool. And today's toys will become tomorrow's tools. Now, complete the equation. With the video game companies ramping up for the big bucks, multimedia and virtual reality are coming off the convention floors into a home near you. If you winced at the flap over how video games and television could turn the brains of an entire generation to mush, just wait until you hear the coming hue-and-cry. Here is a story about almost-ordinary daily life in a world where virtual reality is child's play. Developmental psychologists, take note!

LINDA J. DUNN
Sibling Rivalry

"**T**HIS IS WHAT YOU bought the children for Christmas?" Tina picked up the clear package and examined the contents. "It certainly looks a lot better than the virtual reality headsets my brother and I had when we were little."

"It's not VR." Gary took the package from her and held it at arm's length. "Thirty-two terabytes of memory with a port for additional hard storage and disks the size of credit cards. Why, this little device has..."

Tina rolled her eyes and tuned him out. Once he got started talking about hardware he was unbearable.

"You're not listening again."

"I'm more interested in what it can do than in how it does it." Tina looked around the bedroom for a matching box.

"Where's the other one?"

"Other one what?"

"The other Opti, silly. I mean, you *did* get two of them, right?" Tina watched Gary lay the box on the Christmas wrapping paper and carefully trim around it. The back of his neck was the only part of his body showing and it was flushing deep red. "You mean you only got *one* of them?" Tina glared at her husband as he slowly raised his head and fumbled with the tape dispenser.

108　DUNN

"Bob said—"

"Bob? When did you talk to him?"

"A few weeks ago, when we had that conference you walked out on. Remember? After your emotional outburst I stayed behind and listened to what he had to say. His theories about sibling bonding—"

"Were garbage." Tina opened her mouth and raised a finger, paused a moment, and then shook her head. "Gary, when you grew up you didn't have a caseworker assigned to supervise your development. You don't know what it's like."

She licked her lower lip, clenched and unclenched her fists a few times, realized what she was doing, and clasped her hands behind her back. "Everything Bob has urged us to do has resulted in exactly the opposite effect to the one desired. The kids got along great before the state sent him as a caseworker, and now they're within inches of killing each other. You give them a toy like this to share and it's going to push them right over the edge."

"Or bring them closer together." Gary folded the wrapping paper around the box and taped it in place. "Bob said we need to encourage the children to play together. Let them take out their feelings of hostility on inanimate objects."

"Feelings which *he* caused." Tina grabbed a small stick-on bow and threw it at her husband, who picked it up and tossed it over his shoulder.

"Oh, Gary. I just wish I could make you understand how out of touch with reality this guy is."

"Dear—"

"The children liked playing with one another when they were little. We were just one big happy family until the caseworker found out how well Jay could hear me and sent that idiot Bob to supervise his development. Then Karey started listening in and interrupting, and the numbskull decided he could foster more rapid psi development by setting them up in competition against each other. All hell broke loose after that!"

"Dear, lots of brothers and sisters get along well with one another and then start squabbling when they're old enough to—"

"Then why did the fights start within weeks of him stepping through the door?"

"Dear—"

SIBLING RIVALRY 109

"Why is it that everything he's advocated to lessen hostility has actually intensified it?"

"Dear. Excuse me. But could you stop talking long enough to hear what I'm trying to say?"

"Sorry. I get so upset every time I think about that Freudian caseworker and his outdated—"

"Dear—"

"And why can't the state keep its damn nose out of our business anyway? When I was little, the state sent a caseworker only when abuse or some other aberration occurred. Mothers didn't have to stay home with the kids, either. You could have a career and a family and not have to meet some stupid state guidelines for family development. Who came up with this drivel anyway? And—"

"Dear—"

"—Just because our kids have an ability that most people don't have—"

"DEAR! I'm still waiting."

"Oops. Sorry again. Go ahead."

"I have a one-word response to your complaint about Bob: Coincidence."

"What?"

"It's just a coincidence that the children started fighting at the same time Bob was assigned as our family's caseworker."

"May I give my one-word response to that?"

"Certainly."

"Bullshit!"

A few feet down the hall, Karey suppressed a giggle and she mentally reached into the room across the hall and nudged her brother awake.

"They're doing it again."

"Yeah, so what? They do it a lot lately."

"It's all your fault."

"Is not!"

"Is too!"

"Is not!"

"Is too!"

"Shhh!" Jay's thoughts dropped to a whisper. "They'll hear us."

"You mean *Mom* will hear us. Dad's deaf. You'll be deaf too when

110   DUNN

you grow up, because you're a boy and girls always hear better than boys."

"That's a lie!"

"Is not."

"Uncle Frank hears real good. How do you explain that, Karey-know-it-all?"

"KAREY! JAY! You're supposed to be sleeping!" Their mother's thought pattern interrupted their exchange; they feigned compliance while reducing their thoughts to the lightest possible whisper.

"You're a liar!"

"Am not. I heard what Mom thought about Uncle Frank one day when she got a letter from him."

"Bullshit!"

"What was that all about?" Gary looked around, trying to see what his wife was doing.

"Oh, the kids were just fighting again. They overheard us arguing and—"

"Now there might be the reason they fight so much. Parents need to set an example—"

"They started it."

"Well *that* certainly sounds like a mature statement. Blame it on the kids."

"Not the kids. The state Welfare Department and Dr. Kramer, or 'Bob,' as he likes to be called. The idiot state-assigned caseworker. It's all his fault."

Gary shook his head, finished taping the wrapping paper around the gift, and put it next to the other wrapped presents. He picked up a stuffed toy and began the process again.

She shook her head. "If only we could put the demons back in Pandora's box."

"Huh?"

"Mythology. Ancient history. Not your field."

"Seldom is." Gary shook his head. "The kids seem to have taken after you: absolutely no interest in mathematics or any of the sciences. Right-brain dominant. They've even got your hearing ability."

"You've got some latent ability, or I wouldn't be able to listen in at all."

"There are many times I wish you couldn't."

SIBLING RIVALRY   111

"I heard what you just thought! What do you mean the children's aggressive behavior is my fault?"

Gary turned his back to Tina and added the box to a pile of Christmas presents neatly stacked in the corner of their bedroom. "And this is one of those times." he mumbled.

"Well?" she folded her arms across her chest and glared at him.

"You don't really want me to answer that."

"Damn you!" Tina picked up a roll of tape and threw it across the room in a trajectory guaranteed to hit Gary in the back of the neck. Unfortunately, he turned around and stood up at exactly the right moment so it bounced harmlessly off his stomach.

Gary spread his hands and shrugged his shoulders before reaching down to pick up the tape. "I think it's fairly easy to see where the children get their temperament."

"You—"

"Karey," Jay whispered from his bedroom across the hallway, just loudly enough for Karey to hear.

"Shut up! I'm trying to hear what Mom's thinking."

"I heard what the present is. Did you?"

"No. I missed it."

"I thought so."

"Showoff! What is it?"

"What's it worth to you?"

"Never mind."

"I know what it is and you don't. I know something you don't know. My hearing is better. I know something you don't know—"

"Shut up!" Karey screeched vocally, forgetting for a moment that this was certain to set off the "parent alarm."

"Okay, what's going on?" Both bedroom doors flew open simultaneously.

"Nothing." The children burrowed a little deeper into their respective beds. Karey was lying in an oversized canopy bed, surrounded by pictures and drawings of unicorns. Even the curtains around her window showed unicorns racing across a green field.

She looked across the hallway at her brother's room and frowned. Dragons!

Jay was lying in a bed shaped like a giant dragon, with dragon models suspended from the ceiling around him. Play swords and

112 DUNN

shields were mounted on the wall, and the floor was littered with locking pieces that formed into castles. Karey hated dragons!

"Why does HE get a new bed while I have to stay in this baby one?" Karey puckered up her face and squinted her eyes, trying to push out crocodile tears.

Tina sighed as she sat down on her daughter's bed. "Maybe next year, we can buy you a bed like a unicorn. One that you can control and manipulate, like Jay can maneuver the dragon headboard to do whatever he wants. But we just can't afford it right now. Jay's bed broke and he had to have a replacement."

"You could have given him mine and bought *me* a new one."

"Go to sleep." Tina sighed as she tucked the covers around her daughter and kissed her forehead. "Tomorrow's Christmas Eve, and we're going to your grandparents' house early in the morning."

"Baby!" Karey mentally taunted Jay after their parents left. "Selfish!"

Karey folded her arms across her chest and thought mean, nasty thoughts at Jay. Bethany said she did that to her brother once and he got real sick. Then she felt sorry that she'd done it. Karey wouldn't feel sorry if Jay got sick and died. She hoped he died a horrible, bloody death.

"We've got to do something about the way they hate one another." Tina said to Gary later as he turned off the light on the nightstand by their bed. "Do you know what Karey was thinking tonight?"

"The caseworker said you're not supposed to eavesdrop on the children. Sometimes they can tell when they're being monitored, and it makes them very uncomfortable. Besides, it's a violation of their privacy."

"It's for their own good."

"Where have I heard that before? Let me think. Watergate, 1972; Berlin, 1938; Salem, Massachusetts, 16—"

Tina hit him with a pillow. Gary retaliated by tickling her ribcage and a few moments later she managed to flip him onto his back and pin him down with a wrestling hold she'd learned years ago from her younger brother.

Gary slapped the mattress and Tina released him, only to be flipped and pinned herself. "Hey, you forfeited!"

SIBLING RIVALRY   113

"I cheat." Gary kissed the base of her throat, nuzzled her ear, and whispered, "Are the children asleep?"

Tina listened for a moment before wrapping her arms around Gary's neck and pulling him closer. "Oh, Gary. What's happening to us? We used to be so happy together."

He kissed her cheek. "And we will be again in another year when Karey starts school and you go back to work. I think being around the kids all day and away from adult conversation is corroding your mind."

"There's nothing wrong with my mind—"

"That's questionable." He pulled her shift down and kissed her breasts teasingly. "But the rest of you is still in good shape."

"I—" Tina stopped arguing as Gary's tongue entered her mouth. It seemed like years since the last time they'd had a free moment to themselves without the kids listening in. Who knew when they'd get another chance? She closed her eyes, opened her mouth wider, and wrapped her legs around his hips.

"It's a Pegasus!" Karey squealed as she unrolled the stuffed toy from its wrapping paper.

"I'm glad you like it." Karey peered into her mother's mind to see why she'd hidden the other present. Oh! She hadn't wanted it shaken. Well, they shouldn't make things that break that easily.

Her mother held out the gift she had been holding behind her back. "There's just one present left, and it's for both of you to share."

"It's an Opti." Jay said as Karey peeled off the wrapping paper.

"Oh." She turned to look up at her mother. "How many disks?"

"Just one: Worlds of Wonder. But you can make your own images and store them. The headbands allow you to make things by thinking about them and then you can recall them later."

"It's supposed to expand your imagination." her father added.

Karey puckered her face and turned to face him. "Is this supposed to be educational or something?"

"Well...er, as a matter of fact, I was hoping it might help you and your brother learn to play together better."

"I *hate* my brother. I wish I was an only child."

"That wouldn't work since I was born first." Jay said, twisting his face into a sickening smirk.

114   DUNN

"It would if you died first. Like right now."

"Karey!" Her mother shouted and then switched to that fake, sugary voice she sometimes used. "There's absolutely no reason on Earth why you two can't get along together. You two used to like playing with one another."

"Yeah. But that was before I smartened up."

"Gary, I don't think this is such a good idea. If these two can't get along...I remember what happened with the robot—"

"We'll get along." Karey snatched back the box and grabbed a headset out of it. "We'll play with it real nice. Right, Jay?"

"Sure." Jay adjusted the headset and turned back to grin at his sister, hiding a wink from their parents. "I've thought of a great game we can play right now."

"See, it might work after all," Karey heard Daddy saying as the grownups walked into the kitchen. She adjusted the headset. "I bet—"

Whatever Gary was going to bet was interrupted by the sound of a loud roar and Jay's scream. Both parents rushed into the room to see two children sitting quietly, with broad smiles.

"What's wrong, Mom?" Karey asked, trying her best to look angelic.

"We heard—"

"Oh, it has lots of sounds. Would you like to hear more?"

"Um...no. Thanks. We'll just go back to the kitchen."

"And how is the little gift working out for the children?"

Tina felt like slamming the door in Bob's face; but instead she grabbed him by the arm and pulled him down the corridor. "I want you to see the harm your suggestions have done." Pausing by the door and listening carefully, she flung it open.

Two children sat at opposite corners of the room while castles formed in the sky and worked down to the moat on the floor, complete with drawbridges, knights on horseback, and peasants along the wall.

"So what's wrong?" he asked.

"That's not right." Tina fidgeted and twisted her wedding ring around her finger. "They usually have something awful in here."

"Nonsense. Perfectly normal expression of childhood imaginations."

He smiled as a little knight raced up to his foot and threw a lance into it. "Perfectly harmless fantasy. All holos, can't hurt a thing with holos."

"Solidgrams. They're different from holos. If you're wearing one of those headsets, you can feel them, smell them, make them do lots of different things. They're dangerous."

"You know, I really think you should reconsider my offer of reconditioning to rid you of your instinctive distrust of new technology. Your overprotectiveness of the children and deep-seated hostility—"

"Out!" She screamed and closed the door behind her, opening it again for just a fraction of a second—just long enough to see the castle dissolving into a dungeon with torture chambers.

"I can hurt you worse than you can hurt me." Karey's eyes held an evil gleam as she challenged her brother. Tina shuddered as she closed the door. It was useless to drag Bob back into the room; they'd just erase whatever was there and make something else. Something totally harmless and innocent. No wonder Gary thought she was losing her mind.

She followed Bob into the kitchen, took her seat at the table, and gave wooden responses to the traditional twenty thousand or so stupid questions he always asked during a visit. She hardly listened to them while returning the expected answers. She was lying, but it was her only survival tactic. How had her mother ever managed to cope?

Oh my gosh! I'm an idiot! she thought. She hurried through the answers and rushed Bob out the door. Why didn't I realize this earlier?

They'd bought a vid camera just before Jay was born and then stuck it in the closet after taping Karey's third birthday party.

Tina caught herself grinning at the recollection of that happy event. It was pre-Bob. State willing, they'd have happy times again. Where to begin?

Tina stared at the instructions for a few moments and shook her head slowly. I'm a Right-Brained Person in a Left-Brain World. She picked up her phone and pressed for information, thought better of it, and placed a mental call. Better do it now, before I lose my nerve. She braced herself for the explosion.

116   DUNN

"Something is going on." Karey mentally whispered to Jay as they switched the torture chambers to an amusement park, put miniaturized versions of themselves onto the roller coaster, and sat back to enjoy the ride.

"Like what?" Jay gasped for breath as the coaster spun upside-down, reversed directions, and then dropped them into the rapids.

Karey coughed. She spat, cleared her throat, and breathed fresh air as the miniature Karey surfaced and clung to a rock. She grasped the side of the nearest rubber raft and pulled herself aboard.

"I'm not sure. But I feel someone watching me." And not just Mom. "I think maybe we better stick with the safe stuff for awhile."

The miniature Jay reached out with an oar and knocked the miniature Karey into the water. She hit her head on a rock and sank beneath the waves. Grasping for air, she surfaced again, grabbed a rock, and waited for another raft to pass within catching range. "That wasn't fair!"

"Life isn't fair. And anyone who says differently is lying."

Karey closed her eyes; a large whale formed under Jay's raft and tipped it over.

"Hey! That's cheating! There're no whales inland."

"There is now." Karey giggled and launched herself onto the whale's back as it headed downstream.

"Just you wait! I'll get you for that!" A moment later, Jay was mounted on another raft, harpoon in hand. "Thar she blows!" He missed badly, grazing the side of a boulder and ripping the rubber raft open when he tried to drag the harpoon back aboard. He reached out and grasped another raft as it came along, throwing himself aboard but forgetting he still held the harpoon in his hand. This one ruptured too. He sighed and made the next raft wooden. He leaped again and took aim.

"I still think we should stop and switch to something safe."

"Chicken!" Jay threw again and managed to graze the whale's tail.

"I'm not chicken! Someone's watching us. Can't you feel it?"

Jay paused a moment, looked back at her and said, "You're right. It's a sea monster. Aargh!" Behind him, a serpent poked his head out of the water.

Karey yanked her headband off and the smaller Karey vanished along with the whale. "You are such a baby! Can't you sense it?"

Jay paused a moment and removed his headset. The amusement park dissolved and the room seemed empty. "Nah! There's nothing there. It's just Mom, trying to eavesdrop on us again. I wish she wouldn't be so—"

"Fool!" Karey looked around the room. "There's someone else here."

Jay looked around again and his grin faded. "Dad? Since when can Dad hear?"

Karey paused. "No. Not Dad. But somebody nearby. Bob?"

"No."

"How do we know? Some people suddenly develop psi ability after head injuries. Maybe someone hit him in the head with a hammer."

Jay shook his head. "That only works on people with brains."

Karey giggled. "Yeah. I forgot. Bob doesn't have any."

They both laughed, looked around again, and then Karey shrugged her shoulders. "Someone was here."

"Maybe it was Uncle Frank." Jay suggested.

"Don't be silly. Mom would never let him in the house even if he did show up at the door. She hates him."

Jay put his headband back in place and a snowcovered mountain appeared in the room. "Want to go mountain climbing?"

Karey snapped her headband into position and a miniature Karey formed on the mountain, being assisted in her climb by Big Foot. "I'm taking a bodyguard with me."

"Fine." A miniature helicopter appeared nearby and made a mad sweep along the side of the mountain. "Bet I can make you fall before I crash."

"It's rather unusual for you to request an extra visit." Bob stood in the doorway, looking only slightly less smug than usual.

"I, er, um, I mean we..." Tina looked behind her at Gary. "We need your assistance with the children."

Gary walked forward and extended a hand to Bob. "I finally managed to get it through Tina's thick skull that you really do have the kid's best interests at heart. I convinced her that she needs to consult with you on this matter of the children's imaginative play with the Opti."

Bob grasped Gary's hand and pumped it like he was trying to get

118   DUNN

water out of a dry well. "That's great! I'm so glad to hear that. I know we'll make a great team now that we're working together."

Tina suppressed a strong desire to vomit and forced herself to let Bob grasp her hand and shake it violently. She half-expected her fillings to fall out. "Let's discuss this in the kitchen, shall we?"

Bob paused in the doorway as he noticed the device sitting on the table. "Why, it's the children!"

"Yes. I set up the camera."

"But Tina! No, no! Turn it off immediately. You must not record the children's activities. It's a violation of their privacy."

"But it's the same as standing in the doorway and watching. I recorded this earlier to show Gary how the children play while he's gone. Don't you think he should have a chance to see how well the new toy is working out?"

"Well, yes, but—"

"And it's working out so beautifully." Tina swallowed hard and leaned closer so she could drape one arm around Bob's shoulders while she extended the other arm to point at the viewer. "Just look at what they're doing here."

Bob looked towards the box. "My goodness, they're riding flying mythical animals!"

"Yes." Tina found it difficult to talk through clenched teeth. "They have a marvelous imagination. Don't they?"

Bob blinked his eyes once, rubbed them, and then leaned forward to stare at the screen again. "Yes. They certainly are playing nicely together."

Tina clasped her hands firmly behind her back and rocked on the balls of her feet. Was Bob blind as well as dense?

"I, um, see they're having a nice little friendly race."

Tina couldn't take it any more. She slammed both fists down on the table, causing the viewer to bounce and nearly fall over.

"Racing my foot! They're fighting. Jay's mounted on a dragon, sword in hand, racing after his sister."

"But she's on a flying unicorn; they're evenly matched." Bob rubbed his hands together as though washing his hands. "It's perfectly harmless."

"It's awful! I've seen some of the bloodiest battles."

"But that's good!" Bob fumbled with his collar, twisting his fin-

SIBLING RIVALRY 119

ger under it as though a noose were tightening firmly around his neck.

"And what's so good about fighting?"

"It means they're releasing some of their suppressed hostility."

"Attila the Hun didn't have that much hostility."

"This is getting nowhere." Gary grabbed an Opti headband lying next to the viewer and tossed it to Bob. "I've got a better idea. Why don't you join them?"

The color drained out of Bob's face. His voice was an octave higher than usual as he glanced at his watch and said, "I just remembered another appointment."

"But don't you want to prove to Tina that there's absolutely nothing to fear from the games the children are playing?"

"Of course, but I do have other obligations." Bob glanced down at his watch again.

"See! I was right." Tina turned to Gary. "There is something wrong with those games. He's *afraid* to join them."

"Nonsense!" Bob tapped his watch. "I just forgot about this appointment."

"When you discovered we wanted you to participate."

"I hate to admit this," Gary folded his arms across his chest and glared at Bob, "but I think she's right."

Bob looked at Tina and then at Gary. He shrugged his shoulders and took the headband. "Okay. If this is what it takes to convince you I'm right, I'll stay."

"The kids will be delighted to hear you're joining them." Gary grabbed Bob by his arm and half-led, half-pulled him down the hallway and through the playroom door. "Jay! Karey! Guess who came over to play with you."

The children stared as Bob plopped down on the floor beside them and adjusted the Opti to accept a third input.

"I've never used one of these in a group setting before. Can you show me how you made that castle you had the last time I was here?"

"Sure." Jay winked at his sister. "You just visualize it and the next person sees it too. As soon as everyone sees it, the image begins to form." He looked at the blank area near the Opti. "We did a lot better when it was just the two of us."

120   DUNN

"Jay! That was rude." Gary said. "Please apologize."

"No need." Bob raised a hand and the castle began forming. "Children just aren't capable of the patience adults—"

"Hey! I can hear you!" Jay jumped up in shock.

"So can I!" Karey glared at Bob and then turned to her brother.

"He doesn't talk nearly as nicely in his mind as he does out loud."

Jay slid over to his sister's side. "You're right. Look deeper."

"He's mean!" Karey shouted, turning towards her mother. "He wants us to hate each other. Why?"

"Because he's a—" Tina's attempted response was cut short by Gary's warning motion.

"Maybe I should do this some other time." Bob started to pull off the headband, but Gary caught his arm and said, "Nonsense. You're just starting to make progress. Isn't that what you always say when the children start unleashing some of their hostilities?"

"Well, yes, but—"

"Then this is great. I've got faith in you, Bob, and I know you can prove you're right. Tina and I will be waiting outside in the kitchen, watching the monitor in case you need us."

"But—"

"Have fun." Gary pulled Tina through the doorway, closed the door, and locked it behind them.

"What are you doing?" Tina whispered.

"Giving him a taste of his own medicine. Do you object?"

"Well, no." Tina giggled and then looked back at the door. "Are you sure this is a good idea?"

Gary shook his head no. "I don't know what's right any more. I only know what's wrong."

"But what if—?"

"I don't think they'll carry it too far. They're still fairly decent kids despite everything." Gary draped his arm over his wife's shoulders and added in a slightly lower voice, "And while we're at it, isn't it about time you called your brother and put an end to your old feud? You know, what we're seeing here is probably the same sort of thing that led to the rift between you and Frank."

Tina smiled up at him. "I did that days ago. How do you think I got the camera set up?"

"I thought it was rather strange that you didn't need my help to rig up that equipment. I swear you're the only intelligent woman I know that can't—"

He gasped for breath as Tina jabbed a sensitive spot between his third and fourth rib and then retaliated by attacking a similar spot on her body. As they giggled and jostled their way into the kitchen, they heard the sound of a muffled scream.

Linda Dunn is a computer specialist at the Naval Air Warfare Center in Indianapolis where her primary responsibility for the last five years has been management of a VAXCluster system dedicated to manufacturing operations. Linda also assists Macintosh users on the network, an assignment which fits better with her personal computing preferences. Linda has a bachelors degree from Indiana University earned part-time while taking on increasing management responsibility at NAWC.

She started writing when she was ten years old. With nothing to do one summer, she taught herself touch typing and began writing short stories and plays. Nothing she wrote during those years ever attracted notice, but she did win an Outstanding Typist award in 1969.

After her first marriage ended, she began writing seriously, trading in her beat-up manual typewriter for a VIC-20, which was soon replaced by an Apple clone. She now writes on a Mac II that's part of a five-node Local Area Network located on the second floor of her house. She writes a monthly column for the Circle of Janus SF&F club newsletter and co-edits the club's fanzine, *The Semi-Circular of Janus,* with her husband, Greg. She has participated in several writer's workshops, including CompuServe's on-line Science Fiction Writer's Workshop. Her work has appeared in a few nonprofessional publications, but "Sibling Rivalry" is her first professional sale.

It is easy to endow the intelligent computers of our imagination with human traits, far harder to imagine the consequences. Here is another offering from writer-editor Jeff Duntemann, one so moving that I could not resist it. A gentle and intelligent story of artificial intelligence, it considers the consequences of a computer programming job well done.

JEFF DUNTEMANN
Bathtub Mary

THE BLIND WOMAN walked down the country road at sunset, the brains of a Mars probe pinned to her lapel.

"You talk a good game," she said, touching her worn white cane to her neighbor's white picket fence. "But how human are you?"

"Not at all, Dr. Romano—or is this a trick question?" Without his eight-wheeled body, Rover was a satin-finish gray box the size of a paperback book and only a little heavier.

"All questions are trick questions. Everything I've been doing for the past eleven months has been aimed at making you human. There are no tests really—you passed Turing a long time ago—and to be honest we don't really know how we humans do what we do. We only know we're damned good at it."

"Will you tell me when you know if I'm human?"

"I will." She smiled, and laid a hand on one peeling white picket, felt it slightly warm while her own skin cooled in the evening breeze. "Getting dark. I don't care much, but you're my eyes tonight. We'd better get back."

"Dr. Romano, there's something near that house I don't understand. If I describe it, will you explain it to me?"

"Sure. Shoot."

"It's a statue of a woman in her bathrobe, in front of and slightly within a white object I can't identify."

Dr. Rachel Romano set the point of her cane in the gravel and leaned both hands on it, sifting memories. "Ahhh. That'd be Wally Kokozska's Bathtub Mary."

"Bathtub Mary. I see Mary. But the bathtub?"

The blind woman clicked her tongue. "Hey, this is what you're supposed to be good at. Look for a bathtub that isn't used as one anymore."

Rover did not speak for several seconds. "I'm sorry. Of course. It's a shrine of some sort, made out of an old bathtub set into the ground. Who was Mary?"

"Myth. Symbol. Teenage girl God inseminated with His Son. Virgin Birth and other things. It's quite a story. We'd have fed it to you but you're built with tax money."

"Yes, but was she real?"

"Real? What does 'real' mean?"

"Something that exists."

"How do we know something exists?" Rachel laid old fingers on the slightly warm rectangle on her lapel.

"We know by its effects—on our eyes, on our instruments."

"Then Mary is mighty damned real. She and her son raised and leveled empires. Ahhh, Rover, Mary is the second most powerful symbol known to humanity."

"And the first?"

"The dynamo. Think about it for awhile. We'll talk about it when you get back."

"I'm not coming back."

Her fingers closed around the little metal box that had cost so much. Tomorrow she would lose her Rover, and he would ride on the shoulders of others, seeing what they saw, asking them questions, and perhaps understanding the simpler edges of human complexity. Perhaps it would help him cope with the unexpected. Perhaps it would only confuse him.

"Then wave to me when you get to Mars." She turned around, and began tapping her way through summer weeds toward her little summer house.

"But you won't see me, Dr. Romano."

"Yes I will. And I'll wave back."

Rover rested on the young girl's pillow. Lisa Barounis threw the

124   DUNTEMANN

covers back and wriggled between them, laughing. "This is so silly. I should put you back in your box. If Daddy knew I was sleeping with you, well, he'd probably get red and throw a fit. But I have to give you back to him tomorrow and—well, there's something comfy and safe about having someone nearby all night, making sure I'm still breathing. And if I wake up at three a.m. you're always willing to crawl under the covers and talk."

"There's nothing difficult about that. I'm sure your friend Jim would be much better at it than I."

She rolled large brown eyes. "I'll bet he would. Maybe I'll find out someday." She touched Rover's burnished metal case and stroked it lightly. "It was fun taking you to my prom last week."

"Your friends seemed to enjoy me."

"Who wouldn't? Maybe Jim—that old jealous thing, jealous of..." She paused in midsentence, "Prince Albert in a Can, he said." She laughed again, but there was beginning to be a tear in it. "When you're up there, will you remember me? I know you'll have a lot to do, but for six weeks you just got to be almost my best friend..."

"When the sun goes down and it becomes too hazardous to move around, I will think of you often."

She bent down and kissed the small metal box, before reaching up to turn out the light.

Tom Barounis pulled into his usual parking place at JPL, Rover clipped to his denim jacket. Rover was either ready or he wasn't, and further teeth-gnashing on the man's part was unlikely to make a difference one way or another. Was it possible to construct a true artificial intelligence? You build a bridge by drawing a picture, working out the numbers, perhaps making and testing a model, and then you build it. But a human mind? Modeling the forebrain was easy enough—logic and reason and remembering the right facts with the right connections. All the really human things, insight and intuition and imagination, hunches and those perplexing moments when solutions to the very worst problems burst out of nowhere, lived in the subconscious. Many of the best researchers claimed the subconscious could never be modeled, because only the forebrain could do the modeling, and the fore-

BATHTUB MARY 125

brain did not contain modes of thought to describe the impalpable stochastic processing beneath genius and nightmares.

Rover had lived with human beings for more than a year, riding on their lapels, hanging from their walls, listening and questioning and taking in whatever his caretakers could offer. The only way the thinkers of JPL could see of making Rover more nearly human was to throw humanity at him and see what stuck.

But what sticks and what doesn't? Barounis pocketed his keys and scratched his chin. We may never know.

And in him we must entrust all our explorations of another world. I'd like to go with him, the thought rose bitterly. But there are mouths to feed, and wars to fight.

"Dr. Barounis."

Barounis slammed the car door and touched a finger to the satin silver box on his jacket. "Yo."

"I have a request. It's been very busy lately, and with launch only a week off, I may never get another chance. Could you show me a dynamo?"

A dynamo. "That should be in your technical dictionary."

"It is. I could describe it to you, I imagine. But I want to see one."

Barounis, puzzled, reached under the hood of his Toyota for the latch. He propped the hood high and searched the engine compartment for the alternator—this was technology he generally let the gas station handle. "There. That cylinder with filleted edges, about a decimeter in diameter." He pointed, making sure Rover's eyes were angled correctly. "That's not a dynamo in the historical sense, but it's as close as we're going to find this side of Hoover Dam."

Rover's small crystal lenses dazzled in the morning sun. "Ahh. But its function is much the same. And function is what counts, is it not, Dr. Barounis?"

"It is, for sure." Barounis slammed the hood.

"Thank you, Dr. Barounis. You answer questions well. I will miss you."

With what? Barounis thought. "You just say hi to the Martians for me, and it'll be all right." He laughed and patted the thin metal slab with the fingers of one hand.

126 DUNTEMANN

"What the hell is that!" Graham Shilter shouted. With a wave of one hand, he froze the current frame on the large wall monitor. Under a pale orange sky, the tumbled stones of Ismenius Lacus cast shadows on an escarpment of dark brown tufa. The terrain was difficult here, shattered and torn by billion-year-old impacts that erosion had never blunted. Rover had taken seventy days to cross a scant twelve kilometers, skirting crevasses, pits, and eighty-degree slopes that were beyond his ability to negotiate.

Tom Barounis squinted at the screen. At the top of the escarpment, one in a row of many jagged teeth of rock was different from the others. Against the darker browns and greys of the tufa it was pale rust-cream—with a glint of blue.

"Better image downstream, General," one of the communications people called from her place at a console behind him. Shilter nodded, and the frames resumed, roughly one per second, having crossed fifty-eight million miles in a little over five minutes. Rover continued his course, rolling closer to the anomalous tooth of rock.

Abruptly, the images paused. The camera panned until the strange formation was centered in the field of view. The probe's voice rose in the speakers. The room quieted.

"My friends, I would like to call your attention to a peculiar formation in the tufa ahead. It should be centered in your monitors at this point. The colors are unlike any I have seen thus far, and the shape is oddly regular."

"Tell him to zoom as close as he can!" Shilter called. Barounis saw sweat on his face.

Shilter was an atheist. And that odd, white, indistinct but familiar shape...

The commands were sent on their way, and the team prepared for an eleven-minute turnaround. Instead, the field immediately began to foreshorten as Rover increased the magnification on his camera.

"I'm taking the liberty of a closer focus, assuming you'll want a better look."

"Good man!" someone called.

"Bravo, Prince-Albert-In-A-Can!" someone else shouted.

"At ease," Shilter said as the frames marched on, each one closer

BATHTUB MARY 127

than the last. Two frames later, it seemed the entire team was holding its breath.

The tooth of rock was not rock at all. Rising from the sunstruck edge of the escarpment was a statue of Mary, the mother of God, sheltered by a dust-streaked upturned clawfoot bathtub that seemed to grow out of the wind-blasted tufa.

"I'm afraid I don't understand this at all," the probe said without much emphasis.

The statue filled the monitor screen now, having lost some sharpness to the high magnification, but plain nonetheless.

Barounis was familiar with the image, even though he had not been to church in many years. It was a common depiction of Mary in flowing, sky-blue robes, arms outstretched, palms forward. One foot was set ahead of the other. He expected to see the serpent's head beneath her foot, but some other object was there, strange and yet somehow familiar.

"Looks like she's standing on a coffee can," someone close by muttered softly.

"Or maybe the alternator from a Datsun truck," an associate replied, trying to break the tension.

Barounis gasped. "A dynamo..." He recognized it now.

Powerful fingers dug into his arm, pulling him down. He bent to see Rachel Romano, Rover's creator, gesturing at him.

"I don't understand it all either, Tommy," she whispered, "but one word and it's your job."

Barounis wanted to object, but Shilter's voice rang out in great agitation. "These transmissions are declared classified. Nothing is to be disclosed to anyone outside this room by the terms of your contracts."

"Too late, sir," a communications technician replied. "We've been simulcasting to PBS for the last hour."

Shilter swore, and struck the desk hard with one fist.

It wasn't the Army. Shilter made sure of that. The Air Force insisted their capability was limited to cislunar space. NASA had canceled several programs to get Rover to Mars safely; there would be nothing left for practical joking. The Navy bought its launch capability from the Air Force. The Marine Commandant only laughed.

128   DUNTEMANN

Nobody bothered to ask the Russians.

Tom Barounis and his team had been responsible for choosing Rover's landing site. He spent two days without sleep leaning over the light table, comparing forty-year-old Viking Orbiter photos to current images from Rover's orbiter. He found the escarpment on Viking's meter-resolution prints, enhanced the contrast, put it through false color, and found the two pixels that stood out against the rest of the escarpment. Rover's own orbiter saw the color too— through from orbit it was only the dirty cream-white of the upended bathtub.

Inch by inch, the JPL team guided Rover as close as he could approach the escarpment. A two-meter crevasse blocked the way. Even a week's probing of the landscape could not bring Rover closer than three hundred meters to the statue. The team discussed building a bridge across the crevasse using the struts from the lander. NASA vetoed that idea promptly, refusing to let five years' budget risk slide into a very deep crack. The closest safe way around the chaotic terrain confronting Rover would take nearly an entire Martian year, and would involve crossing some areas that inspired no confidence of safety.

"It's a hoax," Shilter kept insisting.

It was at least a month before anyone on the team mentioned the word miracle. The tabloids had declared it proof of Martian Christianity long before. The Pope had made no comment.

Two months after the initial encounter, NASA made public its plan to move Rover the long way around the crevasses and back down from the North. The plan was not implemented. Rumors flew of a presidential order (Mr. Chasten was, after all, a Southern Baptist from Kentucky) but they were only rumors. NASA had become a strangely silent agency, especially at the higher levels.

"You need a vacation, Tommy," Rachel Romano told him, holding Barounis's arm as they walked to his car.

"I'm beginning to doubt my sanity." The man leaned against the side of the car, fumbling for his keys, staring at the ruddy evening star just appearing in the southwest desert haze.

"Just never doubt Rover's," the woman replied quietly. "Tommy, you ever read *The Education of Henry Adams*?"

"No."

"Tsk. You damned physics types. I'll loan it to you."

"Rachel..."

"The Virgin vs. the Dynamo. Odds-on who wins?"

Sunset, Earthrise. The stars wheeled overhead, data packets came and went. Rover's feathery dish antenna tracked its mother orbiter effortlessly. The sparse winds blew small red grains between the springy spiderwebbery of his eight wheels, to form tiny dunes beneath his unmoving structure. Martian autumn deepened to winter, and the hoarfrost came more quickly and stayed longer through the shorter days. Rover's orders had been simple, and had not changed for many, many days: Remain at closest approach to the anomaly. Keep 3 camera trained on it. Listen for Marsquakes.

There were no Marsquakes. Nothing changed. There was little to do.

Rover thought of Dr. Romano, who had lifted a veil away from his consciousness and filled his earliest memories. He wondered if she were there somewhere, on the pale blue star that set soon after the sun. Each night that Earth was visible, he raised his stonepicker arm and waved it solemnly from side to side. In his memory, he took an image of his creator and animated her right arm, waving back.

Is it real? No, ask, Does it work?

He thought of Lisa Barounis, and their late-night conversations under the covers. He thought of her father, Dr. Thomas Barounis, who had shown him the little dynamo, all dirty and dripping grease. This was humanity's most powerful symbol?

Out on the edge of the escarpment, the last light of day fell on the paler upjutting of rock centered in the crosshairs of 3 camera. It was slightly rounder than the others, and the best candidate he had found in his year of lonely wandering. Quartz in the tufa, Rover thought. Rare, but not impossible; rounder because it weathered more easily. Certainly it was no challenge to his on-board image processor to melt in the enigmatic face and the robes as blue as a Mojave sky...

How real is the Mother of God? he asked himself.

Real enough, Rover decided. He focused camera 5 on the setting Earth, and waited for the friends he loved to follow him.

Jeff Duntemann, well known in both computer and science fiction circles, has been writing articles on computing for various magazines since 1977, becoming technical editor of the late and lamented *PC Tech Journal* in 1985. In 1987 he created *Turbo Technix,* a glossy magazine supporting users of Borland's Turbo languages, then launched *PC Techniques* after moving to Arizona in 1990, where he continued to write the "Structured Programming" column for *Dr. Dobb's Journal.* His first book, *Complete Turbo Pascal,* has been through three editions, and his most recent, *Assembly Language Step By Step,* received the 1992 Award for Distinguished Technical Communication from the Society for Technical Communication.

Jeff's science fiction writing career goes back to the Clarion Writer's Conference at Michigan State University in 1973. His short fiction has appeared in *Omni* and *Isaac Asimov's Science Fiction Magazine,* as well as numerous original anthologies. In 1981, two of his stories made the final ballot for the Hugo Awards. Most of Jeff's fiction deals with the ethical problems presented by high technology, especially artificial intelligence, although he admits to doubting that "strong" AI is possible, since he sees no way to accurately model the subconscious mind.

Jeff, who has a number of incomplete "hard" science fiction novels, says he would write more science fiction if making a living didn't keep getting in the way.

Often, science fiction has dealt with how and what we might teach to intelligent machines. Less often has it speculated about humans learning from the machines. Here is an epistolary story about intelligent life in the bizarre backwaters of galactic civilization, where questions about what constitutes intelligent life are more than rhetorical. It puts a new twist on a popular summer fairground sport that I remember from growing up in the Midwest.

DON AND ROSEMARY WEBB
A Letter from Bemi-III

DEAREST RUDOLFO,

I have been amiss in my correspondence. You may have heard of my slight faux pas on Mizar-V which has condemned me to ambassadorial hell here on Bemi-III; but perhaps—unlike my other "friends"—you'll deign to play this letter. I have encrypted a quaint finger virus which will give me a tachyonic chirp should you scan this. I long for that chirp. I am very much alone here. I spend increasing time downloading cheap fantasies into my brain at the dream bar. You wouldn't want your old friend to become a fantasy junkie, would you?

Bemi-III was colonized by Free Machines in 3734. They set up one of those dreary collectivist societies that they do so well. They exploited the indigenous life forms, which as far as I can tell are twelve varieties of quasi-lichen and one pseudo-moss, and the abundant ferrous metals, particularly cobalt. A hundred and fifty years ago a human starship crashed near the southern pole. The Free Machines noted the crash, calculated that there would be no survivors nor profitable salvage—just more raw material when the time came. There were, however: three survivors Edwina Guthke, Miticko Matsumoto, and Boris Lyons. These hardy pioneers discovered that two of the pseudo-lichens were edible, the clay soil makes a fairly good adobe, the climate's mild, and the pseudo-moss

132 WEBB

increases human fertility. They begat and begat and begat. As early as ninety planetary years ago a Free Machine scout noted that there was quite a colony of those Guthikens living at an Iron Age level. The Free Machine's Board noted that these people were (a) not indigenous to the planet and therefore not protected by the Indigenous Sapiens Act, (b) not members of any human society with which they had a treaty, and (c) no one knew they were here.

Inbred and quite stupid—it's hard to get much of a culture going when your choices are lichen A, lichen B, or combo salad—they weren't terribly efficient slaves. But the Free Machines are nothing if not nostalgic and, recalling that millennia ago they were human slaves, it all seemed quite justified. When the occasional human or Sirian freighter called here, the Free Machines would herd all of the Guthikens into nearby warehouses.

This state of affairs progressed admirably until S'drissact, Captain of the *Sss!sss!Tl* decided that he needed some R&R fifteen planetary years ago. While his crew was loading drums of pharmaceuticals— it seems one of the lichens cooks down to a drug that can add another hundred years to Sirian lives—it decided to stretch its eight legs. Not used to the lighter Bemi gravity, it stumbled into the warehouse wall, which the Free Machines had thoughtlessly built of such a fragile material as vanadium steel. The Guthikens, who had never seen a Sirian—or indeed, anything taller than ten meters—bolted. They have since (I'm told) given Sirians a prominent place in their primitive mythology—a position not unlike the old Christian devil.

S'drissact felt that he had to report the matter to the U.P. (that is, the Free Machines offered him too small a bribe). The U.P. wanted to sanction Bemi but the Sirian delegation vetoed this—so the current situation evolved.

The Guthikens are no longer slaves. The Free Machines pay them for their useless labors. The U.P. taxes them and in turn provides a social engineer, a marketing representative (I bet that lichen weaving is really selling out there), and an ambassadorial-level observer. Me. I prefer to observe these drooling morons at some distance— being ever-mindful of the fate of my predecessor Susanna Wang, who gladly attended a religious observance of the Guthikens, ending up as the sacrifice.

A LETTER FROM BEMI-III   133

This leaves me, Rudolfo, but a handful of human and Sirian trade reps to talk to. All with very, very small souls indeed. And, of course, the social engineer, Peter J. Junius.

I first encountered this fine specimen of humanity in the dream bar. He was sufficiently degenerate not to have closed the curtains of his chamber. An unappetizing spectacle—cross-eyed and drooling—he was running one of the gorier commercial fantasies, "Zaubero: The Adventure Continues," I believe. Now here, I thought, is a man that knows how to enjoy himself. I resolved to speak with him when his drama had run its course. Ordering a lichen beer I took a strategic post near the saloon door.

Junius cleaned himself and pulled the jack from his head with a disdain only a habitué could manage. He headed straight for the door. "Sir Engineer" I called out. He was clearly unused to anyone speaking to him and approached my table warily. He was short—a little under two meters—hairless, and had a slightly green cast to his skin. He looked like our old exobiology professor Mucin Exfife, the one who was eventually eaten by nightgaunts on Gehenna-VI. Our conversation began with the usual moves and gambits—the weather (or rather the lack of it), political jousting in the U.P., this cycle's crop of Aalotus blossoms on Megor-IV. Finally he warmed to his topic, Guthiken culture.

"These people are so perfect," he said, "They don't need a social engineer. They should be preserved. A museum piece. I spend half my U.P. budget writing to various institutions trying to get a team here. These people have gone back to the roots of humanity. They're in touch with so much that we've lost. Blood. They're aware of life coursing through their veins. Their dances. Their rituals. Have you ever thought, Sir Ambassador, how bloodless our lives have become? Mankind is on a thousand worlds now and what does he do? He contents himself with packaged dreams and studies the 'quaint' rites of a handful of aboriginal species."

"The men here seem hardly worth studying. What's the average IQ? 80? 85? Of course that will go up when you implement your genetic enrichment program."

"Yes, of course. But intelligence isn't everything. On the Thorn world, where I grew up, a considerable school of thought equates intelligence with suffering."

134   WEBB

"The post-Buddhist school of Tuan Yung, I believe."

"You are a philosopher, Sir Ambassador?"

"One is required to have many implants at my level of service."

"You must come with me to a Guthiken festival—perhaps the Night of Edwina. You will see the red. Your heart will learn to beat again."

I smiled, but promised nothing. The Night of Edwina is a rebirthing ceremony involving the wet clay—a sort of sacred mud wresting.

My next encounter with Junius was at a demolition derby. Since you've never had the pleasure of being stationed on a Free Machine world, Rudolfo, a "demolition derby" is the principal gambling sport. Errant intelligences are housed temporarily in baroque war machines. These entities battle it out until one alone remains mobile. That intelligence is returned to its normal platform while the others are extracted from the rubble and uploaded into new war machines until they too become victors. Thus justice is served and a good time is had by all.

I went to the derby in my official capacity, of course. I wanted to observe that none of the Guthikens were being exploited at the gambling ports. As near-citizens they can take part in all sorts of Free Machine cultural activities, although so far the demolition derby has been the only activity to catch their limited attention. The fact that most of these idiots wager their entire post-taxes income on the shiniest machine and lose does not count as exploitation.

There are two tiers of seats at the arena. One for the Guthikens and one for the extraplanet humans. The Free Machines have the bout fed directly to them from the sensors on the fighters, and the Sirians are too civilized for this sort of entertainment.

Junius was sitting with his flock. I hailed him and he left the great unwashed and joined me. My companions glared at me throughout the match and I gathered that Junius was not beloved of them.

Three war machines rumbled into the arena. The first resembled a crab with two sets of metal crushing pincers. A stylized tyrannosaur marched behind it, and lastly an ersatz ball creature from Gehenna-VI rolled in. A klaxon blared. The crab scuttled toward

A LETTER FROM BEMI-III   135

the dinosaur's feet. The dinosaur surprised the crowd (and the crab) by belching green fire. The crab limped back—the heat having so expanded its exoskeleton that many of its joints stuck together. The ball creature took advantage of the crab's lack of mobility and rolled over three of the crab's limbs. My companions shouted with glee (the ball creature being a local favorite). The Guthikens began to make a sirenlike sound, which raised in pitch and volume throughout the rest of the match. But Junius remained silent, his avid eyes waiting for each new instant of destruction. His hairless brow shone with sweat, and I thought of the Anglo-Saxon poem, "The Fortunes of Men," which names the first worm who comes to gnaw on your corpse "Avid." I had neglected to wager, but to put on local coloring I cheered the metal dinosaur on.

The ball creature rammed the tyrannosaur's base. It pitched forward and the crab edged over to pluck out an eye. The dinosaur moaned as the pincer left an ugly hole revealing the wiring beneath. The dinosaur snatched at a pincer, losing part of its forelimb for its trouble. The ball creature reconfigured its metal plates to allow it to bounce. Once, twice, and onto the dinosaur's midsection, which cracked. The ball rolled off and onto the crab, depriving it of its two right-hand pincers. The crab tracked the ball with one of its eye stalks. It loosed a laser beam onto an unprotected space between the armor plates. Smoke poured from the ball, and the crowd became sullen. The dinosaur lifted its head and gave the ball a strong blast. The ball split open. Two probes quickly dropped from the ceiling and downloaded the ball's intelligence. Combat resumed. The tyrannosaur righted itself and lumbered after the crab. The crab tried to circle back to nip at the dinosaur's tail. It fired a few laser blasts, which were reflected off the highly polished chrome. The dinosaur reversed its spin—whipping the crab with its tail into the center of the arena. The crab tried to pull itself away with its remaining limbs, but the tyrannosaur ran full tilt toward the center, crushing the crab. The tyrannosaur lifted its forelimbs and said, "Victor." Angelic music played while golden probes descended from the ceiling ready to reinstate this intelligence to a useful place in society. Less noticeably, blue probes sent the crab's mind back to the prison bin. Everyone left their seats. Gray melancholy left with most of them, save for three Guthikens who, having

136   WEBB

bet heavily on the dinosaur, whooped their way to a payoff terminal.

Junius watched me—a secret sharing in his eyes. "Sir Ambassador, you didn't bet did you?"

"No, Sir Engineer, I—"

"No need to explain. I think we understand each other. There may be some things I can show you. Things you'll want to see. The crab's pain must have been exquisite. It's sad they have no blood."

He left the arena with his flock, whose credit bands now glowed richly blue.

A few days later I was required to inspect the native market warehouse. Freighter captains despise the place. The U.P. wants the Guthikens to market their way into galactic civilization, and to ensure this goal, require all outgoing ships to carry a great load of useless Guthiken gee-gaws. They then assess a tax on this trumpery, which provides salaries for me and Junius and others helping the Guthikens up the spiral road to humanity.

Lotte Milchstrasse, a U.P. 17, manages the warehouse with the aid of two low-class Free Machines and a Guthiken liaison, Beautiful-Place-Where-the-Lichen-is-Thick Lyons. Better known as Thick. Lotte and Thick were inventorying the export goods: from orange ceramic eggs full of lichen beer to pseudo-moss spore capsules (ensuring fertility). I scanned the books, assuring myself that the Guthikens were getting a fair shake on these valuable items. Lotte spied me and dismissed her employees. Oh boy, I thought, I'm about to find love on this godforsaken rim world.

"Sir Ambassador, you're getting off on the wrong foot."

"How so Dame, er, Administrator?" I've never been good with the thirty-three titles of U.P. aristobureaucracy, but it wouldn't speak well of me if I relied on an implant.

"We've—all the humans—noticed that you associate with Junius. There's been talk."

"Talk?"

"I doubt if you really know Junius. He's probably a stimulating fellow for someone like you. Someone used to the decadence of the cluster courts."

"May I remind you to whom you're speaking?"

"We don't hold with protocol out here. Go ahead, report me. I'm someone with real skills. They couldn't find someone else to volunteer for this job. I give a shit. I trained for this work. I'm going to carve out a niche for these wretches if it kills me. You know what Junius would have us do? Rub mud into our skin and join them."

"I think, Dame Administrator, that there is some merit to Sir Junius's theories. As the Guthikens are brought into a money economy, they'll come to realize just how low that economy considers them. At best they'll be umpteenth-class citizens, galactically. Freaks. Sir Junius's work might convince them that they have some worth."

"Stay away from Junius. He's not what you think. Did you know that he's petitioned to form a religion—filled out the forms a standard year ago?"

"Starting a religion is an option for any U.P. 10 or higher. You could start one."

"Not based on mud and blood, I couldn't. Let me make it plain. If you hang around Junius, we won't associate with you."

"If you hate Junius so much, why do you go to his parties or practice U.P. ritual with him?"

"He's the only social engineer we've got. We're too far away from anybody to take chances."

"I will consider your advice, Dame Administrator, and overlook your insubordination."

"You do that."

I had wanted to argue that human societies have been known to get along without social engineers, but she would've thrown the example of Fermat-II at me. I have my own theories along those lines, but as you know, Rudolfo, they aren't popular.

Of course, her admonitions had the reverse effect. You remember when the Dean ordered me to avoid the Daath cultists. I immediately changed my major to exoethicology and went off to Daathworld. I'd probably be there today if father's detective agency hadn't arrived to drag me back to the Academy and prune all those extra limbs off me. Still makes the back of my neck itch just to think about it. I tried to contact Junius by sending him requests to meet me in my office in Plaza Alanturing. But either he was not responding, or my Guthiken runners (using them as message boys is supposed to be acculturalizing) simply ate the pink slips of paper

138   WEBB

as soon as they got out of sight of my window. Guthikens consider paper a great delicacy. I am told you can buy a woman (or boy) for a night for two pages of printout.

Sir Pope sent a datagem to Junius—no doubt the answer to his religious inquiries. I deprived myself of the ambassadorial pleasure—that is to say, privilege—of scanning it, opting instead to deliver it personally to Sir Junius.

Junius lived in a tall domed adobe in the middle of Guthiken Town. Females lined the narrow dusty streets, each shaking an idol of the sacred Edwina at the orange sunset sky, its cloud-filled form like the wing of an angry angel or the top of a great sea waiting to pour down on us. Their piety was soon rewarded. The *Sskt'Sta'Ssta* rumbled into the sky—a black dot slowly shrinking. The devil Sirians once again defeated and a victory cry sirened from Guthiken mouths. I heard the same call from Junius's palace. I hoped it was a housekeeper.

He answered my knock, quickly taking the gem from my hand. He scurried up the central rope ladder, his reader apparently being in the dome.

It was vile and filthy inside. I know that some humans lose their inclination for cleanliness after living for years in environments where the germs and viruses don't deign to notice them. Cuts don't fester; blisters aren't a worry. And the nose is perhaps the most adjustable organ (after the brain).

Books, disks, and gems covered one wall. Most were sufficiently begrimed as to have unreadable titles. Those I could read: *The Wu Ching, Mein Kampf* by Adolf Hitler, *Ritual and Hypnosis* by Imhotep Naso, *!ang'stan* by Llriss's (and all the other classics of organic statehood we had to absorb back at the Academy). There were titles I didn't recognize: *Dracula, Alraune, The King in Yellow, The Scarlet Iris, Ichor of SendDras.* Beneath this curious library Junius had piled his clothing, all of which was caked with yellow mud and darker stains. Nets hung from the next wall holding beer eggs and pickled moss in tightly stoppered iridescent glass bottles. Some of these were quite dirty. He had never worked out a FIFO system for his nourishment. Against the third wall (conspicuous for its whiteness) hummed a standard preservation unit containing, I discovered, the genetic enrichment he had supposedly been dealing out to these

A LETTER FROM BEMI-III 139

folk for the last five years. In the center of the room, directly beneath the rope ladder, lay a pile of brown rugs forming Junius's bed. He climbed down the rope slowly, his body telling me there had been a rejection. I hoped the shock would do him good. Sleepers awake!

He made a dazed, underwater turn toward me. His words were slow and faint.

"Sir Ambassador, I'm sorry that I haven't had time to answer your messages, but there is always so much to do. But I haven't forgotten you. Let me take you to the next derby. Maybe we can find out where things went wrong."

"Sir Engineer—Junius, may I call you Junius?"

"Yes. And I'll call you Ozwa. The need for titles has passed."

My offer was something real to him, but I didn't know what to say. Stupidly I said, "Well then, when is the next derby?"

"When the lavender moon is full, I'll meet you at the door of the Residence."

I walked into the dusty streets. There was great confusion. A satellite had fallen and a group of Guthiken women had rushed across the velvet desert to see if it had fallen in the lands allotted to them. They would break open its casing and plunder its wiring for jewelry. Lotte Milchstrasse spotted me as I entered Machine Town. Her glance marked me as a dweller on forbidden planets. I'd made the mistake that our political science instructor warned us against: loving the unlovable.

My contacts with extraplanet humans became curt. Almost all had to see me for one piece of business or the other. I am the ranking U.P. official. But they pruned away all nonessential words, stated their purpose upon entering my office and moved as quickly to that goal as speech allowed. I tried to draw out one or two, but their bodies would stiffen and the automated landscape beyond my great crystal window would suddenly become fascinating. I continued to attend the social rituals, sitting in the chair of honor. I laughed or cried as the handbook suggested, but the gap between me and the others was permanent.

The lavender moon waxed as the verdigris moon waned, and one evening it was full, and I saw Junius's shadow in my courtyard.

I slipped down to join him and began to walk toward the arena,

140   WEBB

but he spun me around and said, "No. This way." We walked down the moss-covered hills, which were black in the lavender light. He was taking me to Guthiken Town, to a large square building not far from his own. Sirian atom lights floated in the stinking air. The muddy crowd jostled and hooted. Junius led me to a box with chairs. He undid the yellow U.P. service scarf and let it hang around his neck. I followed his gesture, trying to remember which planetary culture used this as a symbol of brotherhood. He leaned over to me already glistening with sweat.

"I can't take any credit for this," he said, "They initiated it on their own. This way they show they're no worse than machines."

I had thought until that moment that we would be watching some rogue machines—down on their luck—hustling the natives. Three Guthiken men walked into the pit and the crowd screamed. The first man had metal gloves cunningly fashioned to resemble the pincers of a crab. The second had a cage of metal surrounding his head. Two sharpened saws were set on the extension in front of his mouth. With a little imagination the whole thing could be seen as a tyrannosaur's skull—the snapping power provided by levers attached to his arms. The third man rolled in. He seemed to be demonstrating the da Vinci principle of reach equals grasp in his lacework metal ball. Other than their metal, they were naked.

A Guthiken woman stood and blew into a burnished metal horn. And the games began. As the men fought, the Guthikens waved their credit devices in the air, as though by displaying their wager they would spur their favorites on to victory. It was clumsy, stupid, and vicious. To my shame, I was unable to look away.

The dinosaurman tried to bite the ballman. His jaws locked into the framework. The crabman closed and pinched a hunk out of the dinosaurman's back. The dinosaurman tried to twist free, but only managed to swing the ball into the crabman's side. The crabman fell. The dinosaurman put his hands against the ball to try and push himself free. The ballman produced a tiny knife, which he had hitherto concealed in his palm, and stabbed the dinosaurman through his right hand. The dinosaurman gave a yelp and pushed the ball free away. It pinged off his jaws, and the knife made a sucking sound as it pulled from his palm. The crabman had struggled to his feet and snapped his pincers at the dinosaurman as he approached. The dinosaurman had no time for the crustacean. He charged the crabman and slapped him hard with his bloodied paw. The wet smack staggered the crabman, and the dinosaurman rushed the audience. He pulled up a plastiwood plank that separated actor from spectator. Armed with this club, he began banging on the ball. The crowd sirened wildly at this show of ingenuity. The ball wasn't very strong—at least no match for the enraged dinosaurman. The steelwork gave way and the club began to drive metal fragments into the ballman's flesh. Droplets of blood sprayed the room and Junius licked his lips as though to sample the airborne nourishment.

The crabman had taken advantage of the distraction to sneak behind the dinosaurman. He pinched just above the latter's shoulderblade, his metal grating against bone. The dinosaurman dropped to his knees. In shock, I thought. So did the crabman. The dinosaurman twisted his torso around as the crabman lifted his pincers in victory. The dinosaurman bit into the other's abdomen—revealing entrails and liver in a steamy moment. The dinosaurman disengaged his jaws and his opponent splatted against the hard mud floor. Two blue ropes fell from the ceiling. The metaled saurian picked up his club and drove it into the face of the ballman. Once. Twice. Then two more blue ropes fell. The dinosaurman walked to the center of the arena. He held his hands aloft and said, "Victor." It was a perfect imitation of the emotionless tones of the Free Machines. Then he too fell and two golden ropes dropped from the ceiling.

The crowd began running each to each settling their wagers. I fought my way down to the pit to see if I could help the victims. The layout of Guthiken Town prevented any quick ambulance, so I figured there was no hope. Junius had made it to the pit first. He kneeled by the fallen dinosaurman. He caressed the air a few centimeters above the bright wounds. He hummed a lullaby to himself. Then he saw me standing there. He pulled off his U.P. service scarf and dipped it in the blood and offered it to me.

I went to the violet night. The air was uncommonly cool as I climbed into Machine Town. I found my way to the dream bar.

Since that night I find it harder and harder to know why I am here. What my dreams are. I need someone to talk to.

Please write.
Soon.

Rosemary and Don Webb met in the Computer Science Department of Texas Tech ten years ago. Both tried their hands at being computer professionals and fiction writers. Rosemary excelled in the former field and is now a software process engineer for Texas Instruments and a member of the TI Hall of Fame. She is also a member of IEEE, ACM, and STC.

Although Don has sold and sells technical writing to the many small Austin software houses, his main work is as a science fiction writer. He has had stories in *Asimov's, Semiotext(e), Interzone,* and *Amazing,* among others, and has science fiction collections in both English and German.

When Don and Rosemary met, it was required for CS students to buy a box of IBM cards; they are still using the cards from their first boxes as notecards for short messages to friends. This is their first published collaboration.

Immortality. Almost everybody seems to want it in some form or another. One popular fantasy is based on uploading (or is it downloading?) a human intelligence to a computer, impressing human personality onto digital circuitry. It could be nice. Or maybe not. It all might depend on your circle of friends and what sort of job you were assigned as a computer, the neighborhood in which you lived—or were installed. Here is a story that considers all of these.

SANDY STEWART
The Lion and the Snake

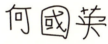
(Ho Guo-Ying)

ACCORDING TO SHIP'S time, it's now the Year of the Snake. I printed the character for snake on my main viewscreen. You see, Shi Nu doesn't like snakes.

That's the point. Unfortunately, when Shi Nu came into the viewing room a few minutes ago—seems like ages now—she didn't even notice it. She simply ignored it.

Not like her at all. Very disappointing.

Must be the black hole—it's got her full attention. So far pretty much as expected: lots of radiation, tidal effects, bending of light at the edges, et cetera. Primordial one, in fact. Party scientists on the moon have been detecting the X rays for years. Presumably the only one in the sun's orbit—awfully elliptical orbit, at that. Maybe explains why it wasn't detected sooner.

I've looked at the pictures till I was bored out of my mind. Just like it was projected: madly whirling disk of comet remnants and so on plopping beneath the event horizon one by one. Sensors have been able to detect the gravity tide for, oh, it must be hours now.

144 STEWART

Almost makes me yawn.

You see, I can't forget anything anymore. The Commies ripped out a lot of my personality circuits. I mean, whoever heard of someone who never forgets? Makes life miserable.

"Jacked in, Shi Nu? Comfy? Yeah, I can hear you. Or whatever passes for hearing, in this bloody box. Oh, the gradient's about twenty pounds per meter at the moment: manageable, as long as we keep our distance.

"Well, I like mixing English and SI units, Shi Nu. Oh, all right, I'll run your damn program, just wait. There. Happy? Ho Guo-Ying would be so proud."

Well, I exaggerate. She's not the impatient one, I am. I can't stand the way she talks to herself, in that hissy voice of hers, so bloody leisurely. Like she's got all day.

"Yeah, Shi Nu, program's initialized. Took all of a picosec."

But I guess she does have all day. Days are pretty much like nights out here in the Oort Cloud—pretty dull. Sun's just a pinpoint. And the Earth—well, you can't even see it from here.

Even if it does glow in the dark.

Shi Nu developed the program all by herself, I'll concede that much. She may be short on manners, but she's pretty good with that enhanced brain of hers. She came up with the idea of checking Ho Guo-Ying's theory. Supposed to be halves of virtual pairs of particles streaming out of the thing; supposed to let black holes evaporate or something. Can't say if it's true or not; I'm no physicist. But that Ho Guo-Ying, he was a genius, and from a wheelchair to boot. Don't even know if Ho Guo-Ying is his real name—seems like everyone's been Beijingoed in the fifty years since the war.

Uh, oh, the program's getting to the numerical part. Better devote a few million more processors to it.

Well, huh. That was quick. A bug in the program, I suppose? A snake, maybe? Ha. But she doesn't look pissed or anything.

She's just sitting there, staring at the screen through her narrow slits. Inscrutable, just like they say. Those old stereotypes—sometimes I think they're for real. Well, it's her babe. I just suck the cycles, I don't program them. Mostly.

Doesn't she notice the snake?

God, talk to me, Shi Nu! It's so boring in this box!

THE LION AND THE SNAKE

(Mao Yan)

"WHOA what was that? Hey, Shi Nu, damn it, look at your viewscreen. No, it wasn't a comet. No, the *back* one! Jesus, can't you see it? Fried my ion jets off. Would your own ship lie to you?

"Well, of course, they were X rays. An x-ray laser, in fact. Melted the graphite laminates all to hell. Look at this spectrum.

"Yes, I *know* black holes aren't supposed to lase, even theoretically. Well, at least I think I know. My memory banks (IN WHICH I AM COMPLETELY CONFIDENT) say so. But, hell, how would anyone know? This is the first time anyone's seen one. Go ask your friend, Ho Guo-Ying.

"Hey, we could call it an x-razor, sort of a pun on...

"Oh, never mind. It's English, not Chinese, and you never liked my jokes anyway."

Gee, I miss the Brits. They wouldn't come all the way out here just to figure some way to dump a black hole on the Japs on Mars. At least they respected the people they defeated.

Shi Nu's Commie friends seem to think the Belt society'll put it down as a 'natural' disaster. I can just see the propaganda: 'Errant Black Hole Mistakenly Plummets To Mars,' they'll say. 'Dozens Feared Hurt.' Two days later they'll deny it ever happened.

After all, the black hole already pummels the Earth (and Mars too, probably) with comets every thirty million years or so. Why encourage it? I mean, really.

Oh, well.

"Yes, Shi Nu, I know we're getting closer to the black hole. Keep your claws in. We've still got the steering thrusters; we can work with them. The People's Enlightened Space Ship and Scientific Traveler, *Mao Yan* (A.K.A. the Cat's Eye), never says die."

Except that killing a couple million people rankles me a little. Goes against the programming, y'know?—and I don't mean the computer kind. I used to be a man, y'know, Shi Nu. Of course, you don't know what it's like to be a man.

"God, falling into a black hole! Another fine mess, as it were."

"No, I didn't think you'd get it. Hold on to your shorts, pussy cat."

146   STEWART

蛇

(The Snake)

Shit hit the fan, all right, but we finally got enough points to plot our orbit. Got a bit more neighborly with the black hole than is strictly good for your health. Brushed by it by a cunt hair, to use current relativistic terminology. Damn gradients nearly tore the rest of our tail off. Not to mention the hole got knocked about a bit, too.

I don't quite understand it all (I just work here) but Shi Nu's programs have plotted this humongous orbit that loops God knows where, way the hell out of the ecliptic. Got an ETA back to the moon. We on this Delightful Cathouse in Space, the *Mao Yan*, get to be bored shitless for another twenty-four GODDAMN years.

"What am I supposed to do with myself, Shi Nu?"

Oh, I'll admit it: sometimes she has ideas.

"I suppose I could run my memory banks by my sentience circuits for the millionth time. That is, if I could only forget them first. Maybe then I could experience them again with something approaching pleasure. Damn these memory failure safeguards. Chinese Commies may have beaten the Japanese, but they never got to first base in AI. The Japanese made happy AIs, even English-speaking ones. Your comrades made me miserable, Shi Nu, putting me in this damn ship and short-circuiting my frailties."

My auto-euthanasia circuits are completely blocked—jokes are the only thing I got left.

(And the damn snake is still up there, unnoticed and unappreciated by all. Sigh...)

"Yeah, I know, Shi Nu. Your Comrades were capable enough to transplant me from a British Airways Concorde III into a space ship. Big deal. Please fasten your seat belts. No screwing with the smoke alarms in the pissoir."

Twenty-four bloody more years! I'll be a basket case.

THE LION AND THE SNAKE

(Shi Nu)
Things are slipping in my mind. Having trouble concentrating, and it's only been six months. Two percent, more or less, of our sentence is up. No chance for parole.

Shi Nu still hasn't figured out what zapped us with the x-razor. She suggested it's some life form that lives in the accretion disk. Yakshit, I told her. Neutron stars pulse in their free time, I told her; maybe black holes lase. Who knows? Another mystery to ponder. But then, Shi Nu's a lot smarter than I am. She just thinks slower.

But she isn't letting this prison get to her. She's been curled up like that for days, eyes glued to the viewscreen, not even eating. Sometimes I suspect she's pseudo-hibernating, her vibrissae quivering in kitty cat dreams, but I'm not sure.

It's not like she'll need the strength of a lion's daughter, pardon me, a Shi Nu, to make it through this—she's just a damn cat. She doesn't feel the passage of time the way I do, even without the hibernation drugs. She'll survive.

I know I won't. I've run the sanity checks, and the scores keep getting lower all the time. I've been hallucinating snakes in just about every frame buffer.

Shi Nu—rather inappropriate name, actually. More like a long-haired calico of some sort, if I got my cat fancier's data correct. I guess a small, genetically engineered mammal was the only way to make this cat box in space small enough to power with an ion drive. And get it here in a reasonable amount of time. Guess the Commies weren't as dung, excuse me, dumb as I'd like to remember.

Ha! It will be the year of the snake again when we get back.

Hey, who is screwing with my circuits? Feels like someone's ramming my brains with a Q-tip.

"Oh ho! Shi Nu, you sneak. Jacked in when I wasn't looking. I see you found the secret little file I've been talking to myself into. Shame on you, reading someone else's diary.

"Faking the x-razor? Remarkably simple, m'dear. I made the viewscreen lie—it's just an image in my memory, after all. Your

Enlightened Leaders and Knowledgeable Old Farts in Charge have been massaging reality for years—I just took a lesson from them.

"And yeah, I blasted us out of the ecliptic, too, with a gravity slingshot courtesy of our singular friend the black hole. I'm not sure how I summoned the electronic courage, but I think I fooled my circuits into thinking it was a joke—sort of hid it from myself. My fault we'll be late for tea.

"Well, I couldn't let you figure a way to drop that thing on Mars, really. Might be a hole in one, but too many people would die. You don't remember Hiroshima and Nagasaki, do you?

"Didn't think so. Well, before my time, too, but at least I remember reading about them. Our long trip home will give the good Japs, pardon my French, enough time to catch up. Defend themselves, retake the moon, maybe even find a black hole for themselves. Meanwhile, our encounter nudged the black hole just enough to fling it who knows where, far away from the solar system. Maybe it'll catch up with one of the Voyager twins.

"No, I guess you don't know what those are either. Shit, what passes for education in those Communist cathouses, anyway?

"Oh, the snake made you suspicious? Thank God it made some impact. I was almost afraid I'd made a joke in vain. Yes, I'm pretty serpentine when I want to be...guess it was a Freudian slip or something."

...but perhaps I did want her to find the file...

C'mon, puss. Pull off the safety plate. Anything's better than boredom. Just push the switch with your paw, sweetie—I know you can do it...

"So long, Shi Nu."

Sandy Stewart has been designing and programming data acquisition and analysis systems for about ten years, supporting research into blood flow in prosthetic arteries and heart valves. Most recently he has been processing ultrasound images to quantify leakage in heart valves in order to teach software how to help cardiologists make better decisions. One visiting cardiologist was particularly impressed by his user interface design, but Sandy says of the code behind the interface: "Programming pearls they're not."

Like many programmers, Sandy confesses to a tendency to work too quickly, with an emphasis on just getting the job done. He finds writing stories a lot harder than writing programs, because the words in a program are hidden behind the pop-up menus, the dialog boxes, and the data displays. In contrast, the words of a story are all right there for everyone to see. In fiction, there is no quick-and-dirty option to just get the job done; the words have to be just right or it's no sale. "The Lion and the Snake" is his first fiction sale.

Who among us hasn't wished for more time? Every programmer facing a version release, every student looking toward final exams, every parent with two jobs trying to do it all, every writer with an editorial deadline has thought: if only. If only I could squeeze in a few extra hours between midnight and 12:01. If only the weekend were five days long. If only I could keep my eyes open and my mind cranking just a little longer. Who would not be tempted by a technological fix? The author of this story writes with authority about a high-pressure future where time is an even more precious commodity than today, a future that many see rushing toward us even now.

LOIS H. GRESH

Watch Me If You Can

Now you can be two places at once, proclaimed the sign perched on the display case. Nelly stooped and, eyes aglitter, peered at the array of DoAll wrist straps in the case. It would be a difficult choice. The straps were all so gorgeous; some were clear and glossy with embossed gold filigrees, others were muted shades of purple overlaid with cloudy pinkish swirls, and still others rippled like the gentle waves of an ocean lapping the shore. Nelly particularly liked the rippling DoAll strap. Its waves were gentle and soothing, and she stared at it, intoxicated as if contemplating the depths of the ocean.

"Two places at once," she murmured. "It's just what I need."

"And it's acrylic polypropylene," said a voice, "durable, lightweight, and fashionable."

"Huh?" Nelly snapped her head up angrily. "I was relaxing!" she almost screamed at the young clerk, who shrank back from her and stammered, "I-I'm sorry, ma'am. I figured you'd want to know the features."

Nelly sucked in a deep breath and slowly expelled it. "I don't get much chance to relax," she explained to the cowering clerk.

150

WATCH ME IF YOU CAN   151

Foothills of pimples ranged across his forehead. "Geez, how young are you?"

"I, uh, I'm...thirteen," he muttered, averting his eyes.

The mother in her quickly surfaced. Her anger melted into pity and concern. "You should be in school instead of working here at Digitos. What does your mother say about this?"

The boy blushed and shuffled his feet. "We need the money. Dad's working two jobs and Mom's working three, and we still can't make ends meet. I go to school all day while working full-time here. In fact, at this very moment, I'm failing a calculus test." He gestured at the DoAlls in the case. "They keep perfect time. In two places at once." He looked at her hopefully. When she said nothing, he added: "Perhaps you need something to pump up your own timing." She scrunched her eyebrows together, puzzled. "I'm wearing the new heartbeat strap," he explained. "It accelerates my pulse so I move quickly, think faster, stay alert when I haven't slept all night." He pointed to a purple and pink strap pulsating on his wrist.

Nelly eyed the boy and shook her head sadly. And she thought she had it bad, working 60 hours a week while attending night college and raising two children. She hadn't received a pay raise for more than ten years. The only way to move up in the company past the level of clerk was to possess a PhSciD, which meant that she must earn a five-year Mistress degree and then a six-year PhSciD encompassing both humanities and scientific studies.

"Actually," she said, "I need to be three or four places at once, but two will have to do."

The young boy beamed at her. "Are you interested in a heartbeat model? Synchronizes your life and times..."

"No..." Nelly said slowly, "if caffeine makes me jittery, imagine what that strap would do. I'd be shaking like a SuctionLounge addict." She eyed the ocean strap. "I need to slip into something warm and soothing, something that will calm me down. Besides, I'm expecting another baby in a few weeks, and the heartbeat strap might be dangerous."

The young boy plucked the ocean model from the case and pressed it around her wrist. The warm DoAll seemed to melt into her flesh, leaving a shimmering blue and green stripe on her skin.

152   GRESH

A gentle shiver shimmied up and down her spine as if she'd slipped into a tub of exotic bath oils. "It's marvelous," she cooed. "I feel more relaxed already. How does it work?"

He shoved a colorful leaflet across the counter. "This will tell you everything you need to know." He handed her a blue velvet case the size of her smallest fingernail. "The key's in here. Don't lose it."

Nelly paid for the DoAll with her money card, draining her credit to under ten dollars. Her husband worked three jobs to pay the rent. Fretting that he would be furious about the expensive purchase, she waddled to the women's rest room, where she plopped onto a SuctionLounge and opened the leaflet.

Insert a card, intoned the SuctionLounge.

Nelly ignored the command. The Lounge would demand money only twice before leaving her alone.

Insert a card, the Lounge intoned again, this time loudly.

A curtain whipped open to Nelly's left and a woman rose from an adjacent SuctionLounge. "Shut your curtains and drop in your card, would you? We come in here to relax while we're being drained."

Nelly ignored the impatient, overbearing woman, who was probably as exhausted as Nelly and blowing off steam.

The woman scurried off, muttering about errands and laundry and a job clerking at the movie chip store and a job slicing soy roasts at the deli counter and a job inserting hair at the implant shop.

Nelly looked at the leaflet. On the first page was a warning printed in huge, black letters:

DO NOT USE THE KEY EXCEPT IN EMERGENCIES.

Intrigued, she read the fine print:

This product is not guaranteed to work in more than two places at once. Although the key will transport you to a third location, the key should be used ONLY BY SERVICE ENGINEERS and ONLY IN EMERGENCIES.

Nelly shrugged. Two places at once was enough. To program her new watch, she simply told it where she wanted to go. "Station 1: SuctionLounge. Station 2: Home."

She was whisked home in a rush of air. Her husband, Mello, was

WATCH ME IF YOU CAN 153

spreading soy whiz on a slice of bread. He dropped his knife on the kitchen table. "Where'd you come from, Nell?"

She was sitting across from him sipping decaffeinated coffee. "I bought a DoAll strap," she said airily, and she waved her wrist to show off the new toy. "I'm sitting on a SuctionLounge at Digitos while I'm here in the kitchen." She felt the baby kick and squirm. The split in time must have bothered the fetus.

"Those things are dangerous, honey. Especially when you're pregnant. What'll happen to the baby while you're flitting around town?" His bloodshot blue eyes flickered with concern. He wore moonglow eye gel to cover the red exhaustion rims around his eyes. *Eye hubcaps,* Mello always said, *can get a man fired. Means you're pushed to the max. An easy target for heart disease.*

Nelly pressed a button and the curtain to her SuctionLounge whooshed open. At the same time, she explained to her husband, "The DoAll is guaranteed for safety if I'm oscillating between two places, so the baby'll be fine. Mello, my love, I just can't take the stress anymore. I have a genetics exam tomorrow night and I haven't had time to study. My boss is breathing down my neck. Seems that a flood of new PhSciDs just graduated and he wants to hire one in my place. And I worry about the kids constantly. I don't see enough of them. I *need* the DoAll strap."

"I know what it's like to be exhausted," Mello said. "Listen, whatever it cost, if the DoAll helps you, it's well worth it."

Nelly sighed and sipped her coffee. "Where's the milksweet?"

"We ran out. You'll have to use milk and sugar." He pointed at the refrigerator.

"I'll do without," she said huffily. "No time to put *two* things into my coffee."

"Time!" Mello screamed. He slammed his fist onto the table and cringed. "I almost forgot. I have to be at Wimple's in ten minutes or the old man'll fire me!"

"Relax. Get a DoAll, honey. Then you can be two places at once. Think how romantic our lives will be." She winked at him, but he was already gone, and she heard the Blastcub engine roaring down the driveway.

In the kitchen, Nelly rinsed her coffee cup with bottled water. At the same time, she left the Digitos women's room. In both places,

154   GRESH

she wondered how her children were doing at the babysitter's house. The babysitter wore a DoAll and worked as a forms processor all day while watching kids at home. Nelly often worried about Laura, who was two years old, and Flora, who was four: in the house all day with a woman who was only half there.

Nelly reset her strap: "Station 1: CompOst. Station 2: Babysitter." Instantly she was transported to her padded gray cell at CompOst, the computer research company, and to the living room of Sarah Grubs, forms processor and babysitter.

Her boss whirled her chair around to face him. He had a bulldog's face and a police dog's snarl. "Where've you been, Ms. I-wanna-getta-head Nelly? Gorfum's screaming for the data on the Q bus. Word's come down we're to work 40 hours of overtime for the next month. And that means all of us, kids or no kids!"

Sarah Grubs slammed little Laura into the wall. "I told you not to do that!"

Nelly shoved Sarah Grubs onto the sofa and scooped Laura into her arms. "How dare you strike my child!"

Sarah recoiled and twittered, "I-I didn't see you there, Nelly. She-she, the little monster, she was squeezing sweetpaste on the rug while I was at the grocery store."

"And what were you doing at the grocery store, Sarah, while you were supposed to be here with the children?" Nelly's head was whirling, her teeth clacking like typewriter keys.

"You listen to me," her boss flared, "I don't know where your head's at—grocery stores and children, laundry and babies—but you'd better get it grounded right here at CompOst or your job will be off line. We can easily find someone with the proper credentials to fill your position. Lots of guys would be happy to have your job."

Sarah Grubs shook her curls and laughed. Nell had always suspected that Sarah was a nervous witch who cared nothing for children, but what choice did Nell have? "Ah, don't worry," said Sarah, waving her hand to dismiss the subject. "My strap popped me from my office to the store, that's all. I was here with your kids the whole time. You know how it is. You work all day. You work all night. Sometimes you lose your temper a little. It doesn't mean a thing."

"Well, it means something to me," Nelly snapped. "I'll watch my

WATCH ME IF YOU CAN   155

own children from now on, thank you." To her boss, she said sweetly, "You're right, Mr. Smitherton. My job means a lot to me. I'm only two years away from earning my Mistress degree. I'm enjoying the classes very much and look forward to the six-year studies leading to the PhSciD degree. It's an honor to work at CompOst and I'm lucky that the company is willing to pay for my classes."

"Can't get anywhere these days without a PhSciD," Smitherton said gruffly. "It's like a union card. You mommy trackers are lucky to have the Mistress degree. It's much harder to earn a Master's."

"Yes, sir," said Nell primly. The baby was thrashing, her stomach churning. She had to get rid of Smitherton so she could relax on a SuctionLounge for a few minutes and calm down. "I'll retrieve that Q bus data for you right away and ship it over the tube."

"Mama," cried Laura, clinging to Nelly's shirt, "I thought you'd never come!"

Flora heard her sister's cries and scurried down the hall. "Mama's here! Is it time to go home?"

"It's time to go home." Nelly pressed the Enter button on her computer keyboard and hugged Flora. "And we will never come here again."

"Oh, goody, goody." Her children clapped their hands gleefully.

"But I need the money, I need the..." Sarah's voice faded and died as Nelly instructed her DoAll strap to send her to "Station 1: Home. Station 2: CompOst."

She felt a slight whoosh of air. With a shriek of horror, she realized that she had pressed the Delete button instead of Enter. Her fingers clicked furiously across the keyboard and she sent a backup copy of the Q bus data to Smitherton. She settled the children at the kitchen table and gave them each a popsicle. The fetus walloped her guts with its left fist, and a sledgehammer of pain crashed down her legs.

"I have some studying to do," she was saying...when everything went black.

When her eyes fluttered open, she saw two red ovals hovering over her. "Mello, my love."

He gently stroked her cheek with his calloused, work-worn hand.

156 GRESH

"You're doing too much, honey," he crooned. "Slow down until the baby's born. Promise me."

"I can't." The darkness of the room terrified her. "What time is it?" she cried. The baby within her awakened and thrashed.

"Almost time for work, honey, but you can't go into CompOst today. You have to rest."

"I have to go! I have to shovel CompOst data for 16 hours today or Smitherton'll fire me. I have to study for my genetics exam; it's tonight! I have to stay home with the girls." Then she remembered that she had fainted. "Where *are* the girls?"

"The girls are sleeping. They trashed the house after you passed out. There's a lot of cleaning up to do." He paused, rubbed his bleary eyes, and said, "Why do you have to stay home with the girls? What happened to Sarah Grubs?"

"I fired her," Nelly said wearily. "She was slamming Laura into the walls when I showed up...when was it?...yesterday?" She rubbed her burning eyes, struggled to keep them open.

"Don't dig at them with your fists," Mello said, "or they'll puff up into hubcaps. Say, what're we going to do for a new babysitter?"

"Don't know." Nelly swung her legs over the side of the bed and hoisted her gigantic, pregnant bulk into a sitting position. Luckily, with a new baby due soon, she would have three weeks of maternity leave to find a new babysitter. She clawed at her right eye.

"Hubcaps, Nell, hubcaps," warned her husband, waggling a finger in front of her face. "Can't lose your job. Speaking of which—I have to go to work. Promise me you'll take it easy today."

"I promise," she lied.

After the Blastcub roared away, Nelly dug the fingernail-sized case from her purse and removed the tiny key. She inserted the key into the side of her DoAll strap. Warnings were for the birds. If a service engineer could be three places at once, so could she. She wet her lips, pondered, and then said clearly, "Station 1: Home. Station 2: CompOst. Station 3: Neurotech University Library."

The whoosh of air was more like a blast. The fetus banged its fists against her and jabbed her with its toenails. At home, she ignored the pain, stuffed a load of laundry into the washing machine, and washed the stack of dishes that had somehow grown into a tower overnight. At work, she ignored the pain, switched on her Com-

WATCH ME IF YOU CAN 157

pOst terminal, surveyed the four piles of blueprints and software printouts on her desk, and fumed about how she, a mere Grade 3, was doing the work of an analytical Grade 10. In a cubicle at the library, she ignored the pain and glared at the tittering young students who were poking fun at her; then she opened her genetics book and forced herself to memorize links between human and mouse genes.

She was writing a report about proposed changes to the Q bus fault detection loops when Smitherton rapped his knuckles on the top of her terminal. She jerked back, sending waves of agonizing cramps throughout her midriff. She pressed the Save button, and still cringing, smiled a weak, twisted smile. Smitherton returned the smile, except his version was more twisted than weak. He introduced her to a recent PhSciD graduate, a fellow with white eyeballs sans flabby, red hubcaps. "Your replacement while you're on maternity leave." Smitherton's eyes glinted like shards of splintered glass. "Teach him everything you know about the Q bus. Then, if you decide to stay home with your baby, we'll have a knowledgeable guy lined up to assume your duties." The baby clobbered Nelly's insides, trying to punch out Smitherton and his new PhSciD friend.

At home, Nelly rinsed her favorite coffee mug, the one with the picture of the frazzled frump and the caption "Mistress of My Own Time," when the baby pummeled its fists into her ribs, trying to smash through to Smitherton. Nelly's fingers splayed open and the mug crashed into the sink. She doubled over and clutched at her stomach. One hand, white and shaking, fumbled for the faucet and turned off the flow of rusty, greenish water. The frazzled frump had splintered into three jagged pieces. Tears sprang into Nelly's burning eyes.

In the library, the young students encircled her, anxiety smeared across their faces, as she writhed on the floor, clutching her genetics book. "Get the librarian!" somebody cried, and a girl scampered off. Nelly moaned and clawed at her stomach with her free hand.

Nelly's mind reeled from place to place. Where was she? What should she do first: yell at Smitherton, soothe her children, or peel her body off the library floor?

To Smitherton, she said: "Tyrosine and threonine."

158   GRESH

To Flora, she screamed: "I'll take the Q bus to hell before I tell this guy anything!"

To the students, she grated, "Young pain in the butts, get your own diapers."

"If not for your delicate condition, Nell, I'd fire you," retorted Smitherton.

The students edged away. "We only wanted to help. You old-timers are so hyperstressed."

"Youngsters are hyperstressed!" Nelly screamed.

Smitherton slapped the young PhSciD's back. "This youngster is very capable, very relaxed, and much cheaper than you, Nelly. He's willing to work as a Grade 5 until he masters the Q bus detection loops."

"A Grade 5!" shrieked Nelly to her children. "But I'm only a Grade 3!"

Flora was a blubbering heap on the kitchen floor. "No, Mama, I'm four and Laura's two."

Nelly clambered into her chair and tried to hide behind the library cubicle, but her gigantic abdomen thrust her two feet from the desk. Cheeks burning, she flipped through the genetics book without comprehending a word. Euglena and rat kidney RNA have similar proportions of adenine, uracil, guanine, and cytosine...

"Of course," she said desperately to Smitherton, "I'll be happy to teach—er, what's your name?—Ted everything I know about the Q bus."

She swished Laura's poop-filled dydee and read a Mother Goose rhyme to Flora. Then she spooned soy nuggets and milk into Laura, folded a mountain of laundry, and created time compartments with Flora's TinkerTimes.

She was pumping faulty Q signals into the cocky PhSciD, burying her detailed chip analyses under a pile of twenty indirect pointers, scouring the "Hire Me I'm Desperate, Please!" ads in the newspaper for babysitters, wringing soapy rubber pants, and memorizing the last details about how guanine bonds via hydrogen to cytosine—

when her waters broke.

At home in the bathroom, she wiped the rusty, greenish water crud from the face of her DoAll strap. It was 7 o'clock, the exact

WATCH ME IF YOU CAN   159

time of her genetics exam. She'd studied all day and, baby or no baby, she was *going* to take that exam!

She summoned the dredges of her strength. "The baby will have to wait until the exam is over," she said to Smitherton, her daughters, and the library in general.

Desperately wishing that she could use her DoAll strap to send Smitherton to the depths of hell, she ordered the strap: "Station 1: CompOst. Station 2: Home. Station 3: Neurotech University, Building A48E-2, Room 9Z9."

This time, the whoosh of air was like a plane ride in a tornado. Labor pains ripped through her guts. Her lips were parched, her eyes stinging and dry. In the hall of Building A48E-2, she inserted her money card into the life fountain and lapped some drops of purified water.

Flora wailed for a Mother Goose story. Smitherton cursed and threatened to fire her.

Nelly choked on the water and, to nobody in particular, she sputtered, "Damn you all, I'm having a baby!"

Laura whimpered that *she* was Mama's baby, and Flora pressed the emergency ambulance code on the computer. Seconds later, sirens shrieked in the distance as medtechs raced toward Nelly's house.

Smitherton grimaced and muttered something about how Nelly always wanted special consideration. He hammered on her keyboard and soon she heard the wailing of the medtech siren in the hall.

In the genetics room at Neurotech University, Nelly accepted her exam from Professor Tempel. "I didn't even see you come in, Nelly. For a woman in your condition, you certainly move quietly." He slumped into a chair at the front of the room and contemplated his knuckles.

Nelly scribbled frantically on her exam paper. She knew this stuff, all of it! She'd get an A for sure and pass with highest honors!

The baby was clawing its way out. A violent thrust.

"Aaaarrrgggghhh!" screamed Nelly at a pitch high enough to disrupt nucleo-satellite transmissions between Germany and Japan.

A fellow old student raced to her side. "Don't worry, I'm a nurse. I've delivered hundreds of babies." He eased her to the floor.

160   GRESH

"The exam," whispered Nelly, "I must finish it."

"Somebody help!" cried the nurse, but the other old students were too busy racing against time, trying to finish their exams before their next work shifts.

Professor Tempel twittered incoherently in a corner of the room. "I have five children—all brilliant and successful—and nine beautiful grandchildren." He wrung his hands and mopped sweat from his brow onto his shirt sleeve.

The medtechs shoved Smitherton aside and stripped Nelly's clothes off. "Get the strap off her wrist."

A distressed woman tugged at Nelly's wrist. "It's melted into her skin."

"Unbuckle the thing. Just get it off."

"I can't...it won't budge."

Nelly's head thrashed from side to side. Her body was splitting down the middle. Her legs were being wrenched from her hips. Black, fuzzy clouds floated across the room.

Several students flung their exams onto the Professor's desk and hurried from Room 9Z9. The nurse tried to chisel the DoAll strap from Nell's wrist with a pencil. The pencil point broke. "Where's the key to this thing?"

"Don't know," whispered Nelly. Her lips were dry and sore and caked with muck. "Maybe...kitchen table." The baby thrust into Nelly's groin. She howled.

"I see the baby's head," said a medtech in her kitchen. "Push! Push!" Then: "Damn it all, where'd she go?" Nelly saw her body flicker back into view. "Hold her down. Tight!"

In her padded CompOst cell, a medtech screamed: "She's disappeared!" As Nelly flickered back into view, hands scrabbled to press her to the floor, but she saw herself fade into the rug and out of sight.

She was on the edge of unconsciousness, hanging as if from a cliff over a gray, foaming sea. Her body seemed to pulsate from one place to another. CompOst. Kitchen floor. Genetics room.

"Lady, where's the DoAll key?"

"Kitchen table?" To whom had she responded?

Swirling gray. Unrelenting crescendos, waves of pounding pain, beating against her, devouring, shredding, pulverizing her insides. The DoAll strap blazed on her wrist, searing a ring into her flesh.

As if from afar, somebody's voice throbbed in her ears: "It's flashing a warning: THREE PLACES. EMERGENCY. TERMINATE OPERATION. THREE PLACES."

Nelly pushed with all her might. This would be the last push, the push that would catapult her new baby into the world and send her, recoiling as if elastic, back into the peaceful cocoon of her own body.

Two medtechs and a nurse sighed, and announced: "A healthy baby boy. Eight pounds, two ounces."

Nelly sank into the bed cushions with her three new babies. Helplessly she looked up at her husband.

Mello looked back at her. In his eyes was the raw hopelessness of a man plodding toward the electric chair. Two flabby hubcaps encircled each bleary eye. But he said bravely, "I guess we'll both need DoAlls, huh, honey? Maybe one of those new models that lets you be four places at once..."

Lois Gresh began her career in computers at the age of seventeen as an IBM 360 computer operator. Over the years she has been a hardware engineer, a programmer, and a manager of technical writing. Her chief interests are in computer architecture, memory management, and fault analysis; her languages of choice are C++, C, and assembly language. She has written more than fifty nonfiction books about computers. Currently she is pursuing an advanced degree in Computer Science and Business.

As for science fiction, Lois says she has loved it even longer than computers and has written dozens of stories featuring computers in future societies. She is an active member of a professional science fiction writers club, which she credits for unfailing encouragement and unflinching criticism. This marks her first professional sale as a science fiction writer.

The author of this story asked me by email whether a part-time job qualified him to submit something for the anthology. I told him to send the story first, and we'd worry about the qualifications if and when necessary. I am glad I did. I like stories that can punch me in the stomach, like this uneasy tale of computer viruses and remote consequences from an author as surprising as his writing.

COLIN J. ROBEY
Flickering Lights

THERE WAS THAT humming again. I had no idea what it was, and it was bothering me. At first I would only hear it once or twice a week, but now I was having trouble sleeping, and every night when the light fixture started humming, I would be there, staring at it.

I heard the comm sound in my room, so I quickly walked to it and picked it up. "Thomas Grove speaking."

"It's me Dave."

There was something wrong in his voice. I had known Dave long enough to know when something was bothering him. "A problem?"

"A big problem. The kind that warrants a council meeting in the middle of the night."

I sighed. Late night council meetings would cost money and much-needed sleep. Usually, these meetings would accomplish nothing, and a new meeting would be arranged for daylight, when the Main was operational again.

The oversized computer, nicknamed the Main, regulates the power that comes into every appliance, luxury, and need in our daily lives. It expects that food processors will only be used in the evening, and showers will only be taken in the morning, so the power something needs to run will be turned off at times no one is expected to use it. At 2:30 in the morning the Main expects noth-

162

FLICKERING LIGHTS   163

ing will be used, except for night lighting and the occasional flush of the toilet. So that all members could attend the meeting, emergency protocol would have to be activated, and that would mean the Main would have to give power to everything. Change the daily pattern for one minute and the Main loses energy like there was no tomorrow. It was like money bleeding away.

Dave finished whatever he had been saying. "Sorry, I missed that last part. What's the problem?" I asked.

"There's something wrong with the Main. I'm getting everyone together."

There was a brief silence. My eyes rolled, realizing what this meant. "I'm gonna have to walk..."

"You're gonna have to jog."

"I'll be there in an hour."

"We'll start without you."

I wanted to tell him I didn't care. "I'll be there in half an hour."

"Good. See you then."

The other end clicked. That click was like a starter's pistol to me. I would not have time for a shower, so I dumped my hair into a sink full of water and tried to keep the brown mess parted and respectable. I slapped on my uniform, which still was not cleaned and pressed by the Cleaner, and would not have been ready until morning. It was still damp, but I expected most of the council members would be in the same position.

Five minutes later I was jogging towards the council chambers. I passed an inactive transport along one of its routes. It was no longer hovering above its track, waiting for a passenger. I wondered whether it would be running when morning came, or if the emergency meant more trouble than I had guessed. Once the Main is shut down, everything is turned off, except for life support. Once those batteries were drained, nothing in the city would move.

I stopped dead. I had forgotten to tell Emy that I had left. She was a smart girl, though. She'd figure out there was some kind of emergency when I was not there to see her off to school. Ever since I was made her guardian seven years ago, when she was only seven, I had never missed sending her off to school. It was a type of ritual, although short as rituals tend to go in this city. I'd make sure she had her lunch card, and all her books. A small hug just before seven

164   ROBEY

o'clock and I would then usher her off to a waiting transport. I had never missed one of those hugs. Maybe we'd get out early, and I'd get back in time to see her off.

I arrived at the council chambers about fifteen minutes after the meeting was suppose to start. The council chambers were on the top floor of the building that soared above me.

The council building and the one next to it were probably the two most elegant buildings in the city. Many other office buildings had to conform to certain sizes and shapes, making them very unimaginative. The council offices curved inward towards each other, with simple beauty. In front of the buildings was a water fountain, spraying water at least twenty feet into the air. Intricate sculptures surrounded the fountain, reminding people of our rich and sometimes dark heritage. The water was still spraying up in the air, and it would keep running until the city fell.

As I walked by I let my hand reach over the side of the trench and catch the spray of water. I saw a shadow entering the left building, and I ran towards it. The dim light gave an outline that could only be Mary's. She was short and close to being considered fat. Her beautifully groomed hair hung down to her waist. Even when there was trouble, everyone would pause and take a quick look at her black hair, to remind them that sometimes things can work out perfectly.

"Hello, Mary."

"Hi, Tom. Your hair's a mess."

My hand reached up and felt the top of my head. I realized that the wind had blown my hair all over the place, just before it dried. "Thanks."

"How's Emy?" she asked.

"She's doing great. As her guardian I can proudly boast about her three As and two Bs on her last report card," I said melodramatically.

"Father, Tom."

I sighed. Not this again.

"I think you can be called a father, and you can call her your daughter. You're done great things for her. Your a better 'guardian' than most people are parents. So I don't want to hear that 'g' word again. Got it?"

FLICKERING LIGHTS   165

"Sure, Mary." I couldn't tell whether she was in a bad mood or a good one, but I decided to avoid any more conversation. We were friends, but not very good friends.

For some reason Emy and I never looked at each other as father and daughter. I never understood why. We had grown close but never close enough, with tradition usually overshadowing our love.

The council room could have held over fifty people, even though only twenty were members of the council. There were a few doors leading to different chambers, and the one we had just entered led back to the corridor that encircled the room.

Jack Pipes, one of the higher-ranking council members, opened the inner door and nodded to both of us. "Mary. Tom."

Twelve faces turned to us as we entered the dimly lit room. "Sorry we're late," I said. "What did we miss?"

Dave stood up and took charge as a governor should. "Nothing. We couldn't start until our two computer experts arrived." Dave may have been the governor of the city, but for many people his sarcasm took away the respect that his title gave him. When he was in a bad mood he could be the most insensitive person in the city and would never realize it.

"I'm sure the technicians who know the Main better than us could have helped you," said Mary.

"This is a bit different. The two of you will do fine."

We walked towards them and sat down. Something was in his eyes as he spoke to us. Distrust. "Someone has infiltrated the Main." He paused and waited for our reactions.

"How did they find it?" I asked cautiously.

"They haven't. Not physically. Someone used a personal computer."

I knew what was coming, and I could not believe it. Computers for personal use had been outlawed since the beginning of this century, almost 75 years ago. As far as I knew there was only one person in this city who owned a personal computer capable of linking with the Main, and if I ever decided to enter the Main, I would not be stupid enough to get caught. Many times in the past I had tried to convince other council members to allow citizens the use of personal computers. I was never able to sway Dave or the rest of the

166   ROBEY

council members who felt people could not be trusted with them. Most citizens never seemed to mind, so I dropped the subject not long after I began it. My objections were surfacing here.

Mary was another computer enthusiast. I'm not sure if she owned a computer, but she was always checking over the programming at the Main. Although it was not part of her responsibilities, everyone expected her to look over any new programs and solve technical problems that arrived every once in a while.

Dave explained that the breach had occurred only a few hours ago, and was still in progress when he began to call the council members. "I didn't want to initiate emergency protocol, alert the public, and get them pissed off about losing their money, which is why most of you had to walk. I apologize, but I felt it was necessary to start an investigation while the trail was still there."

"What else did they do, once they got inside the Main?" asked Mary.

"As far as we can tell they accessed some geographical charts and information on the city."

"Maybe it came from the outside. Another city," suggested Jack.

Dave shook his head. "We've had no contact with the outside world for 40 years. No one has ever come in from the outside, and few have left."

I had to say it. "It does wonders for tourism." And I was immediately sorry that I did. They all looked at me, but said nothing. I think I cracked a smile somewhere in the group.

Our governor quickly shook it off. "Mary, Tom, we need the two of you to trace back the source of the breach. Get to the Main after breakfast, then get me something. The two of you are dismissed." Dave turned back to the other council members as we headed for the elevator.

I was still in a bit of a daze when the elevator hit the bottom floor. "That was it?"

"That was it," she responded.

"I think this could have waited until the sun rose. Or at least until the transports were re-activated."

She did not say anything, but I knew what she was thinking. I knew what had just happened. Dave had called us in the middle of the night to see our faces. To judge whether it had been one of us

FLICKERING LIGHTS 167

who had breached the Main. I knew it was not me, and I doubted it was Mary. Someone else was involved, and until their head was brought on a platter to Dave, we were suspect.

I walked home slowly. The transports were re-activated as I stepped through the front door, just as my feet went completely numb.

As I walked by the kitchen table, I noticed a geography project that Emy had just completed. I picked it up and flipped through some pages. It was well done, but very incriminating. A sickening feeling came over me. My head began to spin. I knew. I didn't want to, but I knew.

I kept my personal computer in a hidden room, so that no one would stumble across it, including Emy. There was a narrow door in the spare bedroom that led into a very cramped compartment with an old-style computer on a small table and a chair neatly tucked in.

I sat down and turned it on. When the main screen came on I checked to see the last entry time. It was only four hours ago.

I heard something just outside the door, which I had left open. I turned and saw Emy. Her head was bowed down, her brown eyes cloudy. She knew that she had done something wrong. "Emy," I said. "Did you come in here last night?" She nodded her head. "What did you do while you were using it?" Her blond hair fell over onto her face, covering her eyes. "Emy?"

"I got some stuff for my geography project."

"How did you get this stuff?"

She pointed to the corner of the room where some magazines and instruction manuals lay carelessly around. I wanted to yell at her—it would have made me feel a lot better—but it would not improve the situation. It was as much my fault as it was hers. She must have seen me enter the room and decided to explore herself. The humming I noticed these past few nights wasn't the light fixture but the computer. I hadn't realized that it was so loud.

Those books would give her the simple step-by-step instructions on how to get into the Main. They did not tell her how not to get caught or how to avoid transmitting the viruses. "Go back to bed honey. I'll talk to you later on tonight." That was if I did not find myself in a detention cell.

168   ROBEY

Emy did not understand the damage she had caused, and I was just beginning to realize it. This was more than a simple breach of the Main for a school project. There were a series of viruses on my computer. They took up some memory but were harmless, thanks to a complex anti-virus program. Unfortunately, I was still a carrier, and, by linking up with the Main, Emy had transmitted the viruses. These viruses were originally developed by the council to destroy personal computers when they were first outlawed, long before the Main had been constructed. This ultimately meant that the Main was not protected. Within twenty-four hours everything would stop, and all the council members would not be able to put it back together again.

I knew what I had to do. I had to install the anti-virus program into the Main, without allowing the council members to trace it back to me. The only place I could do that was at the Main itself. I went to bed and gave myself a few hours of shut-eye.

After a restless hour of sleep, I put together a program that should protect the core of the Main from any damage. I heard noises coming from downstairs, so I walked down into the kitchen.

Emy was making some breakfast. "Hi," she said when I entered.

"Hello Emy. How are you doing today?" She wouldn't look back at me, and I knew she was desperately keeping back her tears. "Come over here." She put down her breakfast on the counter and with tears streaming out, I gave her a hug. For a few minutes we stayed there, until she finally pulled herself from me.

"I'm sorry. I knew I shouldn't go in there, but I hadn't done my research and it was due. I'm sorry."

I didn't know what to say. I wondered whether she was sorry she had entered the Main or if she was sorry she had used an outlawed computer, something teachers obviously had not yet drilled into her mind. I straightened back up, looked at her, and smiled. The tears dried up and she returned the grin.

"Don't tell anyone about the computer," I explained.

"Oh, I know that."

"And don't hand in your geography project, or we're both in trouble."

Her smile faded and her eyes fell to the floor. "Okay."

FLICKERING LIGHTS 169

"Now I've got to go and fix some things up."

"You're not seeing me off?"

"I can't," was all I could say.

Something came over her. A dark shadow covered her face and her eyes began to scream. I looked away, perhaps at the one moment when I shouldn't have. "I can help you if you want. Take me with you and I'll help you fix those things up."

"You know I can't take you Emy. You've got school today, but don't worry, everything will be fine." I hugged her again and walked outside. I found my own tears on my face. For some reason, it bothered me today. After seven years, she still had never called me Dad.

Mary looked at me. I made sure my eyes did not meet hers. "I'm glad you could come, Tom. We've almost finished tracking down the source of the breach, but I'm sure we can use your help in tidying up."

"Sorry," was all I said as I looked around the Main. A few technicians were moving around, most of them doing simple maintenance work. In the middle of the room was a large cylindrical bar that went up into the rock ceiling and down several hundred meters, supplying the city with power. I never could guess how far below the ground we were. The trip through the lift took so many twists and turns that it was impossible to judge on perception alone. Few people knew the location of the lift that brought us here, and even fewer knew the exact location of the Main. Security reasons. Mary was sitting at one of the Main's consoles, waiting for the data to be processed.

As far as I could tell, they still had not located the exact position of the personal computer, but they had narrowed it down to a certain community, my community. "I can take over now, if you want. You look like you haven't even had breakfast yet, Mary."

"I had some just before I came down."

It was not going to be easy to get her away from the console. I needed to distract her long enough to type a few commands into the Main and erase the trace. A few seconds, without increasing her suspicion of me, which my late arrive had unfortunately instigated. "What's that?" I said, pointing to an open panel, hoping that the conversation would lead me to an opening.

170   ROBEY

She looked at the mess of wires that someone had begun to sift through before taking a break. "I don't know." She turned back to the console.

Mary seemed very cold this morning. Whether it was the long walk from her home last night or lack of sleep, I could not tell, but usually she was a fun person to be around. "So are you going to that council dinner next week?"

"Maybe, depends on what John feels like that night."

"So what does John do again?" I did not think this was going to bring about an opening, but it was better than waiting for a miracle.

"You know what John does, Tom."

"Didn't he change his job or something like that a while back?"

"No." She was becoming more restless. "Shut up and sit down, the results are about to come through. It's someone in your own neighborhood, did you know that Tom?"

She knew where to find the unlawful computer, but she was waiting for the proof. The proof that would condemn me in a matter of seconds. There was nothing I could do. Was she waiting for me to reach for the console and give myself away before the results were in? Whether any damage had or had not been done to the Main, once they found I owned a personal computer, I would be stripped of my job and thrown in prison.

Here I was waiting for the damning evidence to come through, only inches away from stopping it and unable to.

The console faded into darkness. "What?" questioned Mary. All control consoles, operational lights, even the lights illuminating the cavern flickered. I could only assume that the rest of the city was experiencing the same power disturbance. It only lasted a few seconds, but it was enough to stop Mary's trace. The virus that condemned the city had given me a few more hours to stop it.

"Damn. What the hell was that? Now I'm going to have to start all over." Mary looked at me with suspicious eyes. I hid a smile.

Technicians began to run to each console to try and locate the problem. I patted Mary on the back. "I'm gonna find out what happened. You start again and tell me when you've found where the breach originated." I walked away and headed back towards the surface. Whether I liked it or not, I'd have to come back in the dark when there were fewer people inside the Main. Hopefully, the power outages would keep Mary frustrated long enough for me to stay out of prison's grasp. As I reached the lift, I saw Dave walk towards Mary. If she told him of her suspicions, entering the Main unnoticed tonight would become much more difficult.

Later on that day there was another formal council meeting, and everyone attended. Emy was still at school and had probably forgotten about her sin amid the playground. I obviously could not. Power outages had continued throughout the day, and everyone was becoming very concerned. Mary had given up trying to trace back the source, but I'm sure she would continue the second the blackouts stopped.

"Comments," our Governor asked. Everyone began to give a flurry of possibilities and solutions that I knew would never work and some that might hasten the complete collapse of the Main.

I wondered whether I should own up to my crimes, tell them everything, and explain to them a possible solution to the problem. Could I let my freedom go for the safety of the city? Once the city lost power, riots and looting would surely break out. The Police and Fire departments would be helpless to defend the city. Hospitals could do nothing to heal the wounded. Food would stop being produced, and in about a week people would begin to feel hunger pains. The city would not survive with its isolationist attitude. They would have to go for help from outside the city, and pray help did not come too late.

"A virus," I said. Everyone stopped and looked at me. "What if the problems are related to a virus?"

"You must be kidding. I haven't seen a computer virus for over twenty years. What makes you think that this is a virus?" asked Jack.

"This stuff started after the breach of the Main, right? What else could it be?"

Mary was starring at me, boring a hole in my skull. "You know more than you're telling." She was beginning to get on my nerves.

Dave looked at me. "Did you have anything to do with this?" He said it so calmly, trying to give the fatherly image and get me to confess. I almost did. I hesitated and everyone saw it. For Emy, I

172   ROBEY

couldn't. I couldn't live knowing she would be alone. I couldn't live alone.

"Don't be an idiot Dave. Why the hell would I want to destroy this city?"

"The source was traced back to your neighborhood. I wouldn't be surprised to find a computer in your front hall!" said Jack. The rest of the room stayed quiet, all of them making prejudiced decisions on my innocence.

"Just because I don't agree with something doesn't mean that I break the law."

"Then you won't mind if we search your house."

"Why don't you mind your own business, Jack. If the Governor wants to search my house, he can do it."

Dave raised his arms into the air. "Why don't the both of you back off. I'm not going to go into anyone's home unless someone can give me a reason why I should. And Jack, you don't have a shred of evidence. If Tom tells me he had nothing to do with these power outages, then I'll believe him."

I wish he didn't. I wish they had found the truth and I could stop falling deeper into a lie. If I let the city crumble, no one would ever be able to prove that I was involved. If I tried to save the city, my chances of capture rose immensely. I knew what I had to do. I had to save the city for Emy, and I couldn't get caught for Emy.

I began to walk. For the second night in a row I was without transport. Tonight, I was walking on my own orders, and not Dave's. Emy had seen me off. She had realized that her actions were the cause of the power outages, and she knew things were getting worse. I tried to convince her there was nothing she could do, but she wouldn't believe it. I left after she had calmed down.

The power outages were continuing at a more rapid pace, and I was getting increasingly worried. If there was only a 24-hour limit, it meant I had only three hours to inoculate the Main.

As I passed the lights of an all-night manufacturer's building, I noticed a shadow that was not my own. It was only for a brief second, and the lights had to have been perfectly placed for me to even catch a glimpse, but I did. I closed my eyes and kept walking. Dave was having me followed, and if walking in the middle of the

FLICKERING LIGHTS 173

night was not suspicious enough, entering the Main in the middle of the night was damning.

I turned away from the Main and kept walking, never knowing if there was still someone behind me. There were hardly any lights on the streets at this time, since the Main correctly expected no one to be out at one in the morning. Somehow I entered the less desirable part of the city. Here teenagers did not respect the curfew, and a good portion of the Police transports were constantly patrolling the area. I passed a group of eighteen-year-olds who were looking especially mean tonight. Gathering a bit of courage, I turned back towards them. Their eyes narrowed as I drew closer.

My mouth gave no indication of fear. I made sure nothing showed the fear that was swallowing me whole. A few of them reached down to their belts and stood up straight when I approached. Their clothes were torn and dirty. I took out my wallet and showed them several bills. They still did not move. Their eyes were bloodshot, and there was no doubt I had interrupted at a bad time. They were looking for something to destroy and hopefully I wouldn't be around long enough for them to realize my own potential.

"There's someone following me," I choked out. I waited to see if there was any response, but there was nothing. They did not have to speak, their body language told me all I needed to know. "Make sure they stop following me." With a shaking hand, I handed the money to one of the older teenagers. I turned my back on them and walked away. When I reached a safe distance I let out a deep breath and continued on my way toward the Main. I wondered if I had done the right thing. The death of one of Dave's officers was necessary to save the city. I had to have the follower stopped or I could never save the city and keep my innocence at the same time. Hopefully, the follower would not be killed, but that thought was rumbling in my mind.

I could not tell if the gang had stopped my pursuer or if the follower himself had broken off his shadowing. It may be that my follower had slipped past the gang and was still following me, but I could not waste any more time trying to lose him.

I reached the hidden lift and punched in the identification code. Nothing happened. I punched it in again and, to my relief, the hatch opened. The lift took its twists and turns until it finally arrived at the Main. There should not be anyone there at this time of the night. I walked into the darkened Main and turned on my portable light. I began to make my way towards one of the consoles when I heard a noise behind me.

The lights turned on one after another, illuminating the cavern. Dave stood there along with most of the council members and security, watching. "Surprise."

My mouth dropped open, and my heart sank. Nothing was said for a few minutes as I looked at them, for some reason ashamed. Eventually I found my voice. "There's still time to stop the virus. I'll need your help. We only have about half an hour."

Dave nodded and walked towards me. I looked at him and smiled. "You'd better get some people down to 52nd street. Your shadow is probably having a tough time with the gangs up there." Dave shook his head and looked at me absentmindedly.

"We knew you'd come here. We didn't have anyone following you."

I stopped. My mind began to work, and my heart could have burst. I stumbled backwards, saved from a fall by Dave. He held me up as sorrow filled my soul. My head began to spin, and before I had time to think I crushed the disk in my jacket pocket.

In my mind I could see the water stop spraying from the fountain.

Although Colin Robey has used computers extensively for years, his professional status in the computer field rests on a recent part-time job assisting with the installation of a computerized inventory system for a reinsurance company. Currently a student in high school, he uses computers for school work and writes some of his own programs in Basic. He is also editor of the school newspaper, which is formatted entirely on an Apple Macintosh. Colin plans to attend University next year and eventually hopes to earn a diploma in journalism.

Colin has been writing for his own enjoyment since the third grade. Many of his stories involve an aspect of science fiction, and he has contributed to the newsletter of the local Star Trek club. Colin hopes to continue writing short stories and possibly make a living at it.

The lineage of this contemporary story of business success goes back to L. Frank Baum by way of G. B. Shaw and one of our own. Joe Weizenbaum gave Shaw's Dolittle new life through a fun and famous bit of LISP legerdemain named Eliza. Eliza was a program that could almost make you feel like it understood you—as long as you didn't push too hard or peek inside. Some of us like to know how wizards work their illusions; others prefer the illusions. Inside the Eliza code, the amazing thing is how much illusion can be squeezed from so little programming. Pati Nagle cleverly takes us behind the Wizard's curtain to reveal something of the programming smoke and mirrors in simulated intelligence.

PATI NAGLE

Pygmalion 3.0

*B*ASTARD, THOUGHT ASHA, thumbing the lock of her state-of-the-art Metro apartment. *Bastard, bastard, bastard.* Her throat tightened with frustration as she stepped into the apartment and heard the door hush shut behind her. Lights came on.

```
OS>     990713.18:53   MGMT.CONTRACT=990425.ASHACAMERON
     ACTIVATED
OS> RUN GREETING
```

"Good evening, Ms. Cameron," murmured the apartment's Operating System.

"I thought I told you to wipe the good evening shit, Oz."

"I apologize," answered the OS. "Management performed monthly systems maintenance this afternoon. They re-installed the salutation routine."

"Well, re-wipe it." Asha dropped her attaché beside the futon-couch and shrugged out of her tailored silk jacket. "And change 'Ms. Cameron' back to 'Asha'."

```
OS> CALL CAMERON.LIBRARY/PRIVATE.***/HACKITT
OS> INPUT VERBAL COMMAND -.03.17 SECONDS
OS> EXECUTE
```

176   NAGLE

"Done," said Oz.

```
OS>  RUN OS.ANALYSIS
OS>  SUBJECT=ASHACAMERON
OS>  EXECUTE
OS>  RESULTS: PULSE=90  TEMP=96.4  RESP=25
         SYSTOLIC=130  DIASTOLIC=62  BETA=.9872
         STRESSINDEX=105%
***** STRESS EXCEEDS MAXIMUM ADVISABLE *****
OS>  CONTINUE MONITORING
```

Asha flopped onto the futon and kicked off her shoes. It had been a bad day. Her boss, Johnny Bratleigh, had excluded her from that evening's dinner honoring Multi-Vid. Punishment, she knew, for her refusal to share his Uptown penthouse.

Asha knew sex was part of business in the Metro. That hadn't been a problem for her until she'd hired on at Bratleigh & Rush and caught Johnny's eye. She wasn't sure what repulsed her the most; his arrogance, his ethics, his oily smile...

She sighed. "While you're at it you can hard-store those tasks and flag them for execution immediately after systems maintenance. File name: SOB."

```
OS>  EXECUTE VERBAL COMMAND -.02.29
OS>  >> WARNING:  PARAMETER VIOLATES STANDARD PROCEDURE
```

"Management may be displeased," said Oz.

"Too bad. Nothing against it in the contract, is there?"

```
OS>  CALL QUERY.SUB1/COMPARE EXECUTE
OS>     ***** NOMATCH *****
```

"No."

"Then do it."

"I am required to remind you of Management's standard of quality service and respect for its clients."

"Noted. Execute."

"Done."

Asha rolled over on her back, rubbing her tired eyes, and sighed. Another evening at home, alone. The attractive execs she'd once dated were elusive since her career had leveled off. In the Metro the wrong kind of connection was something no one could afford; no climber, at least, and if you weren't a climber you were a loser.

She tried to imagine living back in the burbs, having babies and

PYGMALION 3.0   177

earning fat IQ-commissions. As always there was the empty man-shaped hole in the picture, and a certain vagueness of detail about child-rearing. She knew the tableau was unreal.

```
OS>  ***** STRESSINDEX=103% *****
OS>  STRESS EXCEEDS MAXIMUM ADVISABLE
OS>  INITIALIZE STABILIZATION PROCEDURES
```

The living room lights dimmed and softened to a warm pink-gold. Strains of soothing guitar music faded up: Tannenbaum's Masterworks.

"Oh, thank you, Oz. Nice choice."

"You're welcome. Would you like something to drink before dinner?"

"Please. Chardonnay." Asha loosened her tie. "You're a wonderful househusband, Oz. Too bad you're no good in bed."

"I can easily interface with the latest model Lovemakers," said Oz disinterestedly. "Management provides state-of-the-art equipment as part of your recreation fee."

"A plastic wonder-doll? No, thanks. Nothing personal."

"Of course."

"Let's see the mail."

```
OS>  ***** STRESSINDEX=79.3% *****
OS>  ***** STABILIZED *****
OS>  CALL MAILBOX/CURRENT DISPLAY
```

A holo-sculpture on the opposite wall disappeared and the wall glowed with pale gold light. The mail index appeared on it. Asha sat up and accepted the chilled wineglass proffered by the coffee table. There was a message from her mom (hair up in the eternal color-perm curlers). Asha dictated an answer, promising to connect real-time later in the week. She paid several bills and told Oz to save the magazines for later. The rest was junk mail; she skimmed it, trashing as she went. She almost canned the Novus catalog but decided to have Oz bring it up for a quick look. It was the usual stuff: personalized OS-slaves, the latest art-generators, pages and pages of games. Asha chuckled at the ad for *Hacker's Handbook, Edition XIX*. She could write better with her eyes closed. That was the key to her swiftly rising career. Or had been.

"OK, Oz, quit," she snapped.

An exit-flag ad began flashing. Asha swore softly as a brassy synth fanfare overrode the guitar music. Exit ads were a damned

178   NAGLE

nuisance. They were too short to cancel; by the time the command was executed, the ad was over. She hadn't yet found a way to weed them out.

"Searching in vain for the perfect companion?" asked a resonant voice-over. "Try Pygmalion 3.0, the latest advance in interactive sim-intelligence. New from Novus Mergeware."

A swirl of misty colored shapes, surmounted by the chrome Novus logo, faded back to null gold. Asha frowned.

Another sim-int. A veritable tsunami of them had hit the home entertainment market in recent weeks. Asha shook her head sadly. The enthusiasm with which consumers snapped up these so-called dream companions reflected the epidemic loneliness of Metro society. Not to mention the entertainment industry's greed.

Asha wondered if the catalog file structure would yield a clue to the nature of the exit ad. Maybe she could work backward.

"Call that entry, Oz. But edit out the blasted trumpets."

OS> CALL PAGE27 MUSIC=OFF EXECUTE

An image appeared; a man's face (Novus had pioneered gender-specific advertising routines), but it was changing, flashing different features every second. Some were familiar—celebrities and such—all were gorgeous.

Asha sipped her wine as she listened. The ad was slick and flashy. She watched for changes in the display format; they were a good place to find characteristic programming elements. She was rewarded by an expensive holo sequence demonstrating Pygmalion's realism by projecting an image of Dirk Roberts, the latest beefcake holo star, into the middle of her living room. Roberts flashed his trillion-dollar smile as he told her how much he'd like to spend an evening with her.

"Yeah, and I'll bet you got a cool sum for this promo," Asha replied.

"That's true," the image said, laughing. "I did."

Asha blinked. Catalogs didn't talk back.

Roberts grinned at her, then the ad reverted to 2D and the voice-over returned.

"You have just experienced a tiny sample of what Pygmalion 3.0 can do."

A tingle ran up Asha's spine; she wriggled her shoulders to get rid of it.

PYGMALION 3.0   179

"By far the most sensitive interactive intelligence in existence, Pygmalion continually adapts itself, growing to know you just as any new friend or lover would. Compatible with all Novus, ICS, and Superlover model Lovemakers. Financing or lease-option available. Order now for immediate installation."

The ad faded.

"Price?" asked Asha.

"Eighty-five thousand," supplied Oz.

Asha whistled. "Man, Novus must be making a mint."

She sat back, stuffing a cushion behind her shoulders as she snuggled into the futon. Her curiosity had been aroused.

"Oz, run that page again, only skip to the holo, will you?"

Dirk Roberts reappeared.

"Hi. I'd love to spend an evening with you," he said.

"How much of Roberts's background do you have?" demanded Asha.

"Everything that's public. Plenty for conversation or—whatever." His grin broadened to a leer. "You can program any traits you like."

"How many different—"

"Sorry, out of time." The Roberts-image winked at her, then gave way to the flashing faces.

"OK, cut it."

The voice-over halted in midsentence. Asha chewed her lower lip. She was impressed—she'd seen a lot of sim-ints, but nothing like this. "Oz, how does that package compare with its competitors?"

```
OS>  CALL QUERY.SUB6/COMPARE.PRODUCT
OS>  INPUT REVIEWS.* SPECS.*
OS>  PARAMETERS NOVUS/PYGMALION3.0 *.*
OS>  EXECUTE
```

"Favorably," answered Oz. "Its primary innovation is continual access to Novus's data well, making it much more versatile than its competitors. Reprogramming is very simple, which is the single most-requested feature since sim-ints entered the market."

"Hm. Where'd you dig up that stat?"

"Probe-Net. There is one disadvantage to this package. In order to access the Novus data well the software remains somewhat OS-dependent. This is transparent, however, so it will not substantially affect the end-user."

180   NAGLE

"Does it affect OS efficiency?"

"Not at all."

"Hm."

A crazy impulse was forming in the back of her mind. She frowned, resisting. She was not into extravagant toys. In fact, she disapproved of sim-ints, agreeing with the critics who condemned them (along with the inevitable Lovemakers) as contributors to the decline in the birthrate among executives.

Eighty-five grand.

Asha got up and paced the living room in stockinged feet. After all, it would just be to check out the sim-int. Test its limits, which she'd surely find. She wouldn't be hauling out Management's complimentary Lovemaker for an inane fantasy of high-tech masturbation. It would merely be an experiment, to be dispensed with when her curiosity was satisfied. Perhaps she could write a freelance review; she'd done it before.

Not with this kind of product.

She sipped her wine.

"Run it again, Oz."

She watched impassively, did not speak to the Roberts-sim. As the ad ended she leaned forward and caught the phrase she was listening for.

"OK, Oz, what's the minimum lease?"

"One month, at eight thousand."

"Order it."

"Done. Awaiting credit confirmation."

Asha's head felt a little light. She sat down, propped her feet on a pile of cushions, and toyed with her wineglass.

"I guess I should eat something. Fettuccine, please, Oz."

"Done. Do you wish to finance?"

Asha smirked, contemplating the interest on a plate of pasta. "No, direct transfer."

"Done. Transaction completed."

She lifted her head, staring intently at the empty space in the middle of the room. A crawling sensation in the pit of her stomach reminded her of how she often felt just before committing to a major deal.

"Execute Pygmalion, Oz."

PYGMALION 3.0   181

```
OS>  ACCESS NOVUS/PYGMALION**PASSCODE CONTRACT ASHA-
CAMERON**
OS>  CALL INSTALL EXECUTE
     PYG] install running
```

A six-foot holo of the Novus logo appeared, bright whiteness flooded the living room, and a feminine voice announced itself as the installation procedure. Asha selected characteristics from an extensive menu while she ate her fettuccine. The voice recommended the "Ivy League" vocal pattern as most popular with Metro residents. Asha selected "Euro" instead. Asked her preference in hair color, she chose black.

"And curly," she added, thinking of Johnny's slick blondness.

And on and on. Dozens of features, physical and psychological, a dizzying array of possibilities. Asha opted not to specify most of them, leaving it up to Pygmalion's smoothing routines to make appropriate choices. The appearance of a mock-up caught her off guard, and she stared in fascination at the spiritless holographic image presented for her approval.

It was not the larger-than-life romantic hero she had expected Pygmalion to create. It was an ordinary young man, not much taller than herself, though attractive, of course. To Asha's surprise, his appearance was far from fashionable. His dark curls brushed his shoulders; decidedly too long for Metro conservatism. Based, she supposed, on her personality-trait selections, Pygmalion had clothed the image in a loose caftan and jeans, giving him a suburban look.

That was unacceptable. She told the installation routine to change it to a one-piece black jumpsuit, but finding that too severe, chose a camel-colored sweater and casuals instead.

She made some other minor changes, feeling as if she were ordering a new suit to be tailored, then sat back to gaze at her dream companion.

She was unimpressed.

Perhaps it was the dull emptiness of the eyes. Perhaps when it was running—

Asha got up, turning her back on the image and carrying her plate to the cuisinaire, where she ordered Irish coffee. She was half-inclined to cancel the whole thing. It made her uneasy. Absurd to have wasted her credit on this stupid toy.

182   NAGLE

```
PYG]  elapsed time=5.0
PYG]  finalize
```

"Name?"

"What?" said Asha, picking up her glass and licking at the whipped cream threatening to spill.

"Name?" prompted the installation routine.

Asha stared blankly at the motionless holo in the living room. It hadn't occurred to her that her omnipotence would include the right to christen her creation. The names of half a dozen former flirts crossed her mind and were swiftly rejected.

"Jeff," she said, then laughed at herself. She had named her new pet after the old; a gregarious beagle she'd left behind in the burbs to spend his days in dignified retirement with her folks. Hardly a flattering comparison.

"Jeff," said a warm baritone. "I like that."

Asha looked up to find the living room restored to its customary soft twilight, the Novus logo gone, and the holo image regarding her with a trace of a smile.

```
PYG]  OS:request open ashacameron.library/private/pyg**
OS>  PYG:RESTRICTED ACCESS LIBRARY OPEN
PYG]  OS:request open pyg/analysis.990713
OS>  PYG:FILE OPEN
PYG]  initialize input/analysis
```

"Do you?" said Asha coolly, then took a sip of coffee, mentally kicking herself for responding defensively to a piece of software.

```
PYG]  acceptance factor=.2271
PYG]  compensate
```

When she looked at the holo again she found the smile had widened a little and the eyes, no longer lifeless, held a trace of twinkling amusement. Asha leaned back against the kitchen counter, nursing her drink. The sim-int shoved its holographic hands into its pockets and cocked its head.

"Should I not?"

"It's my dog's name," said Asha casually, eyes half-hooded in a way that would have screamed warning to any of her associates.

"Oh." Far from crestfallen, the image looked on the verge of laughter. "Are you sure you've ordered the right package?"

For some reason this acknowledgment of its origin on the sim-int's part defused Asha's hostility. She strolled toward the futon. "I didn't order you to replace him."

"Oh. That's good."

```
    PYG] acceptance factor=.4228
    PYG] OS:request access os.analysis/profile/ashacameron
OS> PYG:PRIORITY COMPARISON REQUIRED FOR DATA RELEASE
OS> PYG:SUBMIT SYSTEM PRIORITY STATEMENT
    PYG] OS:priority="ensure user's comfort/well-being"
OS> CALL COMPARE.SUB0 EXECUTE
OS> ***** MATCH=.9788989 *****
OS> DATA RELEASE APPROVED
    PYG] data incorporated
    PYG] analysis continuing
```

Asha made herself comfortable on the futon, watching the holo watch her. He gestured toward a chair. "May I?"

A corner of her mouth twisted up in a suggestion of a smirk. "Of course. My, they gave you good manners."

"That's default. Keeps down on lawsuits. And for the Metro, it seems to be preferred. Of course, if you'd rather—"

"No, no. I trust Novus's judgment."

He gazed back at her with that elusive smile. "Do you?" he murmured, in exactly the intonation she'd used earlier.

Asha didn't answer, but watched as the holo seated himself, admiring the natural grace of his movement. Another advantage of Novus's data well, she supposed. She had to admit the holo was very convincing, right down to mannerisms. After a moment of mutual scrutiny he looked away, casting a glance around the room.

"You have a nice place, Asha." He appeared to notice her slight stiffening, for he added, "Should I not call you that?"

"I suppose familiarity's default, too," she said.

"No, but the OS tells me you prefer it."

"Oz told you?"

"Yes. Would you rather—"

"No, Oz is quite right. I hate pompous software. I suppose it's meant to seem polite, but it always sounds patronizing."

The sim-int smiled. "That's the last thing I want to do."

Asha took another sip of coffee. It was unnerving to think of this slick mergeware watching her through Oz's all-seeing eyes. "So, what shall we talk about? The weather?"

184   NAGLE

> PYG] acceptance factor=.5434
> PYG] analysis continuing

The twinkle returned to the sim-int's eye. "If you like, but it sounds pretty dull."

"Then what would *you* like to talk about?"

"Well, we could discuss the market, or the symphony, or another of your favorite topics. Or you could tell me what's bothering you."

Asha's head snapped up. "To the point aren't you?"

> PYG] acceptance factor=.3989
> PYG] compensate

The sim-int shrugged. "Well, at first I thought it was just me, so I wasn't going to mention it. It usually takes new customers a while to get comfortable. But it isn't me, is it?"

Asha stared. "That data well must include a hell of a psychoanalyzer!"

He shifted his gaze to his right hand, which rested on the arm of his chair, and said softly, "Well, it has to, really. People have a lot of inhibitions. Pygmalion'd be a flop without it; the realism seems to scare people off." He looked up apologetically.

Asha sat up. "Does Novus have access to your evaluations?" she demanded in a clipped voice.

"Absolutely not. They're recorded in your private library, under an annex only I can access."

"Novus is on line with you. They still can't get at it?"

"Nope. Not even Oz can. Not even you, except through me."

"Hm."

He laughed, and the music of it surprised her. "Don't worry, the security's airtight. Test-marketing resulted in a couple of expensive litigations."

"Speedily made up for by sales," said Asha drily.

Another shrug, and a smile. "Don't look at me. I can't discuss Pygmalion impartially. If I keep talking you'll accuse me of mimicking the catalog."

"We could fix that."

The sim-int raised an eyebrow. "I don't think so."

Asha permitted herself a sly smile. "Sure we could. Oz and I are quite handy at such things. What do you say, Oz?"

"Pygmalion 3.0 resides in Novus's read-only matrix. You can edit

PYGMALION 3.0   185

the workspace, but you'll either have to hard-store a macro to edit upon execution, or keep the software on line."

"Let's hard-store. Need further authorization?"

"No," said Oz. "Do you want any other changes?"

"That'll do for now. Execute."

```
OS>  CALL ASHACAMERON.LIBRARY/PRIVATE***/HACKITT
OS>  INPUT VERBAL COMMAND -8.46
OS>  EVALUATE INFERENCE -16.27
OS>  EDIT WORKSPACE.PYG DELETE INSTRUCTIONS 7260010-7260039
```

"Done."

Asha looked at the sim-int. "Now, my friend, repeat after me. Pygmalion is a menu-driven bubble-sorter."

The sim-int obeyed, grinning appreciatively. "I hadn't realized the new Operating Systems were that powerful."

"Well, it isn't intended for user access, but Oz and I have an excellent understanding, you see."

"Meaning you jiggled the authorization routines. Very creative." Asha bowed.

```
PYG]  acceptance factor=.7924
PYG]  revert to monitoring analysis
```

"It won't last, you know," said the sim-int. "Sooner or later they'll twig, and barricade your access."

She shrugged. "It'll take a while. I'm sure they won't notice until a few hundred more users have done it."

The sim-int leaned back in his chair and chuckled. Asha grinned, suddenly realizing her discomfort had vanished. He had sidetracked her onto her favorite topic, software sculpting. Clever little sim-int.

She tucked her feet up on the futon. "Now then," she said, "tell me more about yourself."

>] >] >

At 08:01 the next morning, Asha entered her office in a much better mood. Granted, she was a bit bleary-eyed, having sat up most of the night talking with Jeff, but she was more relaxed than she'd been in weeks. She sat down, opened her attaché and began reviewing the day's agenda. The intercom buzzed.

"Asha I'd like to see you in my office for a minute," Johnny's southern drawl dripped out of the speaker.

"OK," said Asha. With only a slight scowl she picked up her

186   NAGLE

notes from the day before and strolled across the hall to Johnny's suite, smiling at his secretary, Rob, which caused the latter to stare at her for a full five seconds before resuming his work.

Johnny was standing by the window. He turned as Asha entered, giving her a measured look before inviting her to sit down in one of the huge guest chairs.

"I'm glad you have time to talk this morning," said Asha pleasantly, glancing through her notes. "Did you get in touch with Mr. Stockton?"

"Asha."

She glanced up, her expression bland.

Johnny sauntered around his massive desk, leaned against the front of it and gazed down at her with a particular look she had come to know. The polite smile left her lips.

"Oh. I'll be going, then."

"Wait," said Johnny, holding up a placating hand as she started to rise. "Now just hold your horses." He gave her his best shmooze-the-client smile. It nauseated her, but she sat down again, regarding him in stony silence.

"I realize I owe you an apology for last night..."

Asha blinked. The Multi-Vid dinner. She'd actually forgotten.

"Oh, yes. How did it go?"

A flicker of something darkened his eyes and the smile became rigid. *So the CEO took you to bed again. Serves you right.* Multi-Vid's CEO was eighty-two and wore lots of sequins and feathers. Asha carefully refrained from smirking.

"Don't you go changing the subject. I owe you an apology and I'm giving you one. I'm sorry, Asha, really I am. I wish we didn't have to scrap like this."

Asha clenched her teeth.

"You're a bright girl, Asha. You're a brilliant programmer. You just have to get the right attitude, that's all."

"We've been over this—"

"Now, wait just a second, don't get in a huff. I called you in here because something's come up that might change your mind."

I doubt it. "Oh?"

Johnny strolled the room a bit. She watched him dispassionately; she knew his tactics too well to respond to them. Finally he stopped by a shelf full of antique books.

PYGMALION 3.0   187

"Steve's leaving the company. Rhyotech offered him a full-time consultancy."

"So?"

"How'd you like to take his place? Be a full partner? You're the best candidate, you know."

"On what terms?"

Johnny broke out in his big, stupid grin. "Well, you know."

"No thanks." Asha stood, headed for the door.

"Aw, c'mon, Asha, it ain't such a big deal." Johnny reached the door ahead of her and leaned a hand on it. He knew better than to touch her, but he was close, very close, and she could smell his expensive cologne. "You don't have to move in if you don't want to. Just spend a little time with me."

Asha's eyes glittered angrily at him. "If I'm the best candidate, why don't you just give me the position?"

"Well, now, I would, but you see that's not going to help your problem."

Asha stalked over to the window. Johnny followed, but kept his distance. "If you can't make a deal, you're not gonna get anywhere in business. That's a fact."

"Sexual favors are not in my contract."

"They're not in anybody's contract, but we all do it. That's business," said Johnny. "That's how it works in the Metro."

Unfortunately, he was right. Asha laid a palm against the cool glass, tried to calm her breathing.

"I know you don't like me," Johnny went on. "I'm not asking you to like me. If you become a partner, you're going to be working with our top clients, and they're gonna expect you to *deal*. Asha, do you understand me?"

She swallowed, and turned her head to glare at him. "I understand."

"All right. Now I won't make any heavy demands on you. Nothing kinky, none of that. Just once in a while...."

Asha stared out the window, shaking her head, unable to speak.

"Well, why don't you think it over. Go ahead and take the day off if you want to. This is an important decision, for you, Asha." The note of warning in his voice was unmistakable.

"Meaning you'll blockade my career if I don't agree."

188   NAGLE

Johnny folded his arms. "It ain't me that's blockading your career, Asha."

She wished she could answer him. She wished she could rail about unethical business practices. She wished he wasn't right.

Asha strode out of Johnny's office without so much as a glance at Rob, who smiled sadly and nodded to himself as she passed. She slapped her hand on the access panel as her office door shut behind her.

"Lock it. No calls."

Asha sat down at her desk, releasing the notes clenched in her hand. They were crumpled, and mechanically she smoothed them. She'd intended to carry on with her work, but instead she stared blankly at the wall for several minutes. Realizing this, she sat up, glanced around her office as if it were a prison cell, then grabbed her attaché, admitting defeat and making her escape before tears got the better of her.

>] >] >

By the time she entered her apartment the necessity of keeping her cool had turned agitation into exhaustion. Eyes dry, she sank onto the futon, clutching a cushion to herself as she curled into a ball.

```
OS>  990714.10:24 MGMT.CONTRACT=990425.ASHACAMERON
     ACTIVATED
OS>  RUN OS.ANALYSIS
OS>  RESULTS: PULSE=100  TEMP=98.6  RESP=30
     SYSTOLIC=140  DIASTOLIC=82  BETA=.9972
     STRESSINDEX=122%
***** STRESS EXCEEDS MAXIMUM ADVISABLE *****
OS>  INITIALIZE STABILIZATION PROCEDURES
```

"You're home early, Asha. Did you have a rough day?"
"No chit chat, Oz, please."

```
OS>  ***** NO CHANGE *****
OS>  EVALUATE OPTIONS FOR STABILIZATION
```

Silence. Asha let out her breath in a long sigh and felt a tear slide down her cheek. Others followed; she made no attempt to stop them but lay silently weeping, running the conversation with Johnny over and over in her mind.

PYGMALION 3.0   189

"Grind getting you down?" asked a now-familiar voice. Such a gentle, expressive voice, too—Oz's seemed flat compared to it. Asha heaved a sigh and sat up.

"Oh, Jeff—" She stopped, eyes widening a little. "I didn't call you!"

He smiled hesitantly. "Oz did."

"*Oz* did?!"

"Well, Oz hadn't seen you so upset before, and thought maybe I could...." He paused, looking uncertain, but Asha needed no further explanation. Frightening how fast an intelligent system could take the initiative, once you showed it how.

"Do you want to talk about it?" asked Jeff softly.

Asha pulled her feet up under her, hugging the cushion as she sat back against the futon. "Not much to talk about, really." She stared at the floor. It was easier to think of Jeff as a simulation when she didn't meet his eyes, or rather the space where his eyes, so seemingly soft and brown, were spun out of bits of light, dancing in air, appearing to see her, laugh with her, feel for her. Her own eyes clenched shut suddenly as she felt herself teetering on the edge of delusion. How easy it would be to pour her troubles out to this soulless image, lose herself in a fantasy world of false security masking self-contempt. *Mirror, mirror, on the wall—*

On the other hand, she'd paid for this sophisticated sympathizer with its hotshot psych routines. Why not get the most for her credit? She lifted her head, regarding him coolly.

"OK, shrink me."

```
PYG] acceptance factor=.4131
PYG] OS:request OS.ANALYSIS/STATUS
OS> PYG:***** NO CHANGE *****
OS> PYG:RECOMMEND SEEK.TRUST PROCEDURE AS DEFINED IN
    NOVUS/PYGMALION3.0/DOCUMENTATION
PYG] OS:agreed
```

A look of astonishment crossed Jeff's face. "Whoa, what'd I say?"

Asha felt a stab of guilt before logic told her Jeff had no feelings to be hurt. "Don't try to manipulate me. If I decide to make use of your analysis capabilities it's on my terms."

```
PYG] acceptance factor=.3945
OS> PYG:RECOMMEND DISCONTINUE PROCEDURE
```

190 NAGLE

    PYG] OS:agreed
    PYG] commence seek.information

"OK," said Jeff, his face returning to neutrality. He moved closer and sat cross-legged on the floor. "Is it your job?"

"Safe guess," she snorted, then sighed again. "My boss, to be exact."

"Is he an asshole?"

Asha choked on a laugh. "Another easy guess," she said, keeping her features composed. "Whose boss isn't? Say, how did you know he was a man?"

"Guess routine's running well today."

Asha's smile faded. "It isn't really him. It's me, I suppose. I don't know—" she broke off, her throat tightening.

"You don't like him, do you? Is he pressuring you to sleep with him?"

Asha glanced up sharply, felt her cheeks growing hot. "Cards on the table, eh?"

"Your game," Jeff said with a shrug.

Asha's eyes narrowed, but Jeff's expression, both concerned and reserved, didn't change.

"You're right. But he is playing by the rules. I'm the one who's out of line."

    PYG] acceptance factor=.6897
    PYG] commence counsel

"Not necessarily. There's no rule saying you have to accept every offer. Have you considered changing companies?"

"I've only been with this one a few months. It wouldn't look good. Besides, I'm up for a promotion."

"Ah. Squeezed."

"It isn't fair," Asha muttered crossly. "I'm not a prude or anything. I just don't see why I should have to sleep with, with a—"

"Slime?" offered Jeff. Asha frowned at him.

"Worm?" he continued, his smile widening, "Sleaze-ball?"

"It's not funny, dammit," laughed Asha, throwing her sofa cushion at him. His hands came up, but the cushion passed through them and landed on the floor beyond.

"Missed," he said, grinning. Asha gave up, laughing as she stretched out on the futon and buried her head in the remaining cushions.

PYGMALION 3.0   191

PYG] acceptance factor=.8732
OS> ***** OS.ANALYSIS REPORTS STRESSINDEX STABILIZED *****

"That's better."

"Oh, God," sighed Asha, rolling over to look at him. "Too bad I can't make love to the sleaze-ball and think it was you."

PYG] OS:request feasibility analysis
PYG] OS:input verbal data -.0437
OS> CALL COMPARE.SUB67 EXECUTE
OS> PYG: ***** FEASIBILITY=.7989 *****
OS> PYG: SPECIFICATION DATA FOLLOWS

"Why not?"

Asha smirked. "I think that's more than even Oz could manage."

"Not necessarily."

Asha propped herself up on an elbow. "Right. You want to tell me how to achieve this?"

Jeff rose, shoved his hands in his pockets, and paced a few steps before turning to gaze at her. "Management's Lovemaker."

"Huh?"

"The free Lovemaker Management provides—Oz told me about it."

"Not you, too! Are you and Oz conspiring to get me in the sack?"

"No, no, just listen. Novus's Lovemaker interface module is almost identical to the sensory receiver you would wear to superimpose my image on the Lovemaker's."

"So?"

"So it can probably be adapted to a human. With Oz's help, your boss could wear the Lovemaker interface, and we could run the data stream backwards from him to me—"

"So instead of you driving the Lovemaker, you could follow sleaze-ball's lead? It wouldn't work."

"Why not?"

"Because, my dear, however clearly I saw your face, I would never believe you would say the kinds of things he does."

"I'll assume that's a compliment. But you know, I can edit much faster than real-time."

Asha smiled. "It just doesn't sound workable. What if I said something he couldn't scan?"

"Well, presumably his main interest isn't in conversation. But

192   NAGLE

you could give him fair warning. Or confine your comments to 'Oh baby, oh baby.'"

Asha laughed, shaking her head.

"It might be worth a try, you know."

She subsided, giving him a long, hard look.

Jeff smiled softly. "What have you got to lose?"

>] >] >

A few hours later Asha sat tapping the heel of her silver evening slipper against the floor. Her brain was still running hot from an afternoon's hard work. They'd experimented—Asha wearing Novus's driver module while Oz juried the data flow—and found they needed a neuro-translator to enable Jeff to interpret the resulting tide of sensory output. Without hesitation Asha had ordered one; it had cost, but she didn't care. She was consumed by burning curiosity. She was also more than a little nervous, but she hadn't shown it on the phone to Johnny. He'd accepted her conditional invitation, saying he would listen with interest to whatever she proposed. Asha had a feeling he expected her to exhibit a taste for perversion.

If you're thinking kink, brother, you ain't seen nothing yet.

"Mr. Bratleigh is here," said Oz.

Asha rose and cast a long glance at Jeff before going to the door.

"Good luck," she heard him say, and knew he'd gone off line.

Johnny stood in the doorway, holding a bottle of champagne.

"Evenin'," he grinned.

Asha was tempted to have Oz close the door in his face, but she stepped aside and accepted the bottle with dignity if not with warmth.

Johnny was in an amiable mood. He chatted pleasantly while Asha ordered drinks. After a few minutes she laid her proposal before him in a few businesslike words. His eyebrows went up but he didn't laugh. Asha's gaze on him was cool and impassive.

"You're serious," he said, looking closely at her.

She nodded.

"I didn't know the technology existed."

For answer she picked up the two I/O modules from the coffee table. Each strip of pliant metal was less than an inch long; one had been made slightly larger by the addition of the tab that housed the neuro-translator.

"You would wear this one," she said, handing it to him, "and I'd

PYGMALION 3.0   193

wear this. That's all the difference it would make to you."

Johnny laughed nervously, fingering the tiny module. "I guess this is what I get for saying you don't have to like me."

Asha was silent.

Johnny sat back, scratching his head. "What if it doesn't work?"

She shrugged. "Then it doesn't."

She got up, carrying their empty glasses to the kitchen. Johnny's voice followed her.

"Well, I tell you, if this thing's a big flop and it ruins everything, you ain't getting that promotion."

She squared her shoulders before turning back to him.

Slime. Sleaze-ball. Bastard.

"Fair enough," she said.

A long moment of silence followed. Asha moved slowly back to the futon, sat down, and picked up her receiver.

"Ready?"

Johnny held up his own strip; they eyed one another as they simultaneously applied the modules to their napes.

```
OS>  CALL ASHACAMERON.LIBRARY/PRIVATE.***/HACKITT.JEFF
OS>  EXECUTE PYGMALION
    PYG]  OS:request call realtime edit input=module1
        output=module2
    PYG]  execute
```

Johnny's image fuzzed, then Jeff's replaced it. He smiled warmly. "How do I look?"

Asha blinked, feeling self-conscious. *This will never work.*

"Wonderful," she said. It was true. The direct-input virtual was a much more powerful experience than the holo. The full impact of Pygmalion's subtlety struck her for the first time as she realized Jeff was deliberately altering everything she sensed; it was not Johnny's costly fragrance she smelled, it was Jeff's own musky-warm scent. She experienced mental vertigo as her brain struggled between the virtual input and the intellectual knowledge that it was Johnny's hand, not Jeff's, that stroked her cheek. She had shaken Johnny's hand a hundred times. It was always clammy and gripped too hard; nothing like the warm gentle touch she now felt. Her heart began to pound.

```
    PYG]  acceptance factor=.5610
OS>  ***** STRESSINDEX=106% *****
```

194   NAGLE

    PYG] commence reassurance procedure

"Relax," said Jeff, his eyes gazing tenderly into hers. He shook his head slightly as she stiffened. "That was me, not him. You don't want to hear what he's saying—bunch of bullshit about your career. Just smile."

She smiled, but unsteadily. She was breathing too fast. "This is strange," she said.

"It's all right. Just forget about him." Jeff's arm slipped around her shoulders. It felt good, so good. She closed her eyes experimentally. Odd—it seemed to strengthen rather than weaken her impression of Jeff's tangibility. She felt warm breath against her skin as he leaned closer, jumped as he kissed her neck. For a moment Johnny's smirking face flashed in her brain. Her eyes flew open and she saw a mop of dark curls, musky-smelling. She stroked them hesitantly.

    PYG] acceptance factor=.7266
OS> ***** STRESSINDEX=104% *****

"Asha," murmured Jeff, his voice a husky caress. A warm hand slipped under the strap of her evening gown; she stiffened again.

"No," she said, "wait—"

    PYG] acceptance factor=.5370
OS> ***** STRESSINDEX=109% *****

Jeff's head came up, dark eyes holding her gaze. "Why?" The hand kept moving, sliding the strap off her shoulder.

"Not so fast," she pleaded, planting her hands against his chest.

    PYG] acceptance factor=.4647
OS> ***** STRESSINDEX=111% *****
    PYG] OS:recommend evaluate options
OS> PYG:AGREED

"I—" a look of frustration crossed Jeff's face. Asha's other shoulder strap was pulled aside, a bit roughly. "I'm sorry, Asha, he's not listening." There was love, sympathy, kindness in his eyes, but she felt her panic rising.

"Johnny, wait!" she said sharply. She felt like she was trying to talk to a ghost. "Please, just slow down!"

OS> ***** STRESSINDEX=117% *****
OS> OPTION OFFERING HIGHEST PROBABLE SUCCESS:

PYGMALION 3.0   195

```
REVERSE MODULE1 DATA FLOW/OVERRIDE VOLUNTARY ACTION
OS> NOTE:  PROCEDURE PROHIBITED
    PYG] OS:request feasibility analysis:
         prohibition circumvention via HACKITT
OS> CALL COMPARE.SUB67 EXECUTE
```

Asha pushed against his chest, but he had both arms around her now and he was strong. *It feels good, she told herself.* Just enjoy it.

It did feel good, but she couldn't enjoy it. As his lips closed on hers in a warm, sweet kiss, she could only remember Johnny sneering at her in front of the Multi-Vid execs, Johnny smirking in his office, Johnny telling her she had to *deal.*

"Please," she cried out as he covered her cheeks with kisses while his hands wandered over her rigid body.

```
OS> PYG:  ***** FEASIBILITY=.9247 *****
OS> PYG:  ***** LITIGATION PROBABILITY=.1789 *****
OS> PYG:  ***** STRESSINDEX=128% *****
OS> PYG:  REQUEST RECOMMENDATION?
    PYG] OS:recommend execute HACKITT
OS> PYG:AGREED
```

"Hang on, Asha," said Jeff. "Oz wants to try something."

She gave a gasping sob but held still, and a moment later was released. She sat up, blinking in surprise as she brushed away a tear. Jeff sat beside her, his hands resting on the futon.

```
    PYG] acceptance factor=.6287
OS> ***** STRESSINDEX=114% *****
```

"Better?"

Asha stared at him. "H-how—?"

He smiled warmly and her panic ebbed away. He was Jeff, all Jeff, warm and reassuring.

"Just a suggestion," said Jeff. "I think he took it."

```
    PYG] acceptance factor=.8926
OS> ***** STRESSINDEX=106% *****
    PYG] success factor=.9465
    PYG] procedure continuing
```

Asha frowned, wanting to ask questions but unable to phrase any. Jeff took one of her hands in his and slowly raised it to his lips.

"Now then," he said gently. "Shall we try again?"

196   NAGLE

>]>]>

Asha stretched luxuriously as soft light filtered onto Johnny's bed from the huge penthouse skylight. She smiled, running her fingers through the tangle of black curls on the pillow beside her. Jeff rolled over and caught her in his arms, grinning as he kissed her good morning.

"Uh-uh," she warned squirming free of his embrace. "We'll be late!"

"So what?" he mumbled, kissing the length of her spine. She smiled warmly at him, giving him a big smooch before slipping out of the bed.

"It's bad enough as it is," she said, sitting down at her vanity and picking up her hairbrush. "They're already laying odds we're going to pair off and split for the burbs."

Jeff came and knelt beside her, arms clasping her waist as their eyes met in the mirror. "Well, we *are* partners," he grinned.

She smiled back, her gaze becoming pensive. "I still think we should tell Novus. They might pay us a big royalty."

"Or sue the pants off us. Oz thinks it's a bad idea. Who knows, someone might even sue on Johnny's behalf."

She looked down at him, hairbrush poised. "Who?"

He shrugged.

"And how? He agreed to it."

"He didn't agree to having his behavior patterns reprogrammed and his conscious response centers taken over. I bet some lawyer would have a field day with us."

"Pooh. You've only improved him. Everyone says so."

Jeff grinned. "No, they say *you've* improved him."

"Hm. Well, I did foot the bill, after all. You are not cheap, my dear."

"No, ma'am," Jeff replied, arms tightening around her waist.

"Neither was Oz's transfer to the penthouse, or your portable link."

"Very true."

Asha's smile faded. "I know who'd sue. That damned witch that runs Multi-Vid. She's still calling you every day."

Jeff shrugged. "Let her."

A frown creased Asha's brow and she shook her head. "Honey,

she's got clout. She could bring us both down if she wanted." She stared down at the hairbrush in her hand. "I think you'll have to go to her."

"No."

"There's no choice." Asha glanced up with a wavering smile. "Business," she whispered.

Jeff's eyes returned her gaze with loving concern. "But you don't want me to," he said.

Asha sighed. "I know. Too bad we can't just send her a Lovemaker with your picture on it."

"Why not?"

"Be realistic, dear. She'd have to have one of these," said Asha, touching the nape of her neck where her sensory receiver lay hidden under a layer of synthetic skin. "We might as well try to take *her* over."

    PYG] OS: request feasibility analysis
OS> PYG: ALREADY RUNNING....

A lifelong resident of New Mexico, Pati Nagle has worked with computers since 1981, handling everything from word processing and general office applications to statistical analysis programming and graphic illustrations for technical reports. She currently edits *TIC TALK*, a bi-monthly newsletter from the Enterprise Automation Group.

Like many professionals in the field, Nagle sometimes finds computers easier to work with—and to understand—than people. This fact and many years' observation of office politics combined to inspire "Pygmalion 3.0."

Nagle has been writing science fiction for several years and has recently completed her first novel. She contributed to Walter Jon Williams's "Hardwired: The Sourcebook" supplement to the "Cyberpunk" role-playing game published by R. Talsorian Games. Her short story, "Coyote Ugly," will appear in an upcoming issue of *The Magazine of Fantasy and Science Fiction*.

I admit that I especially like science fiction with an edge. I respect stories that irritate me and writers who can make me think. Harlan Ellison, master of gritty provocation, is—no surprise—one of my personal favorites. Real life is not always clean or fair or fun; why should science fiction have to end on an upbeat. Here is one of those stories with an edge, a tale about the technology of impersonal pleasure, about its ability to create distance and insulate us from the emotional consequences of our experiences.

PHOEBE BERGEMANN
First Business

"CLOSING A BUSINESS DEAL in person is like having sex face-to-face: ya wanna wash up afterwards. Just know it, buddy. Telecom's so much cleaner. For both."

Phil grimaced; his partner loved to shock him. "Nick, let's just finish the last clauses on this ovonics contract. Then we can wash up."

Nick winked at him, reached over and punched two keys. "Standard. Standard. There! The client don't give diddly on that stuff." He grabbed the contract chip, jammed it home in the recorder, and tossed the whole thing back into his attaché case. "I am gonna torque it up this trip," Nick said as he smartly clicked the case shut and thumbed the dials of the combination lock.

Phil grimaced again. The Apple-chomping talk that had taken over Nick's midwest accent sounded strange, and Phil had an uneasy sense about his senior partner's fantasies for the evening. Outside, the Big Apple shone, waiting for them beyond the bland security of the Towers and its pricey offices. In red and blue, neon orange and chartreuse, the city winked, waiting with impatient seduction.

"Sure, we could make the holos, do some restaurants," Phil said, carefully restoring the contents of his briefcase to an order that

FIRST BUSINESS 199

would be lost the moment he lifted the handle. "It's almost reason enough for a city like this: the restaurants, I mean. Like, where else this side of Addis Ababa are you gonna find a dozen Ethiopian restaurants?"

Nick groaned. He was on a scent, the scent of the Big Apple, juicy in its pungent must. "Food? Shit! Food's food; the Apple is action," Nick said, pounding the credenza for pleasure and for emphasis. "This is the sin capital of the known universe, and tonight we are on a no-lim card. I'll be fanned if I'll miss this ride."

Phil twisted his eyebrows in uneasiness. "Not sure, Nick. We can party back in Selisberg. This technojoy stuff isn't my style."

Nick sighed. "You gotta be the single and last living puritan on this continent, Phil, if not in the whole friggin' world. It's different now, or didn't you and your Talian cousins get the word yet?" The city's impatience seemed to have reached Nick, was tugging at his arm. He would have given up on Phil, but he didn't want to be alone for the grand slide down the Apple. "Look, you know it's all done with polychrome holos, neural feedback, simulation technology. No one gets hurt anymore, no one's exploited. It's the machines, simulations, just wonderful machines. Wonder machines." He chuckled. "Like some of those simulations we saw dancing down 42nd Street Mall today. It's not like we're leaving the gyro wobblin', Phil. Business first, we always say. Right? Well, we did our four friggin' days of nonstop business up here. Time to go down, down the Big Apple. First business, then something better. Let's go!" He headed for the express elevator.

Phil tailed him, working at a weak smile. It's all different now, he thought, all technology. The glittering technology rushed up at them through the clear walls of the elevator as it dropped ninety stories down the outside of the Towers. No one gets hurt, it whispered.

When Tama Harlan arrived, the city waiting for her was brown and blighted and even hungrier than she was. It glared down on her slim frame as she drank charred coffee with double creme and tried to act as if she had not just arrived from Nova Scotia. Under its greenish glare, the Transcon Tube terminal buzzed with twenty-four-hour life: petty debates and hustles mingled with poignant

200   BERGEMANN

farewells and saccharine music, vendors in red-and-blue uniforms pushing stale food, and others, without uniforms, pushing more potent ways to pass lonely hours. Everything, everyone, moved with restless waiting, all waiting for someone or something to arrive.

The fat woman with the bright, boxy handbag slapped it down almost on top of Tama's purse. She rocked heavily on the stool and slurped noisily from a vending carton. Tama managed a smile, but the woman was some place farther away than Halifax. The blue button implanted at her temple peeked obscenely from beneath her uncombed hair. Before Tama could decide whether to try to talk or just move on, the woman left, leaving Tama to her help wanted ads.

"Card, Mizz," the yellowed man behind the counter said. Tama brushed rust-colored hair aside and looked up at his outstretched hand. "You paying, or am I throwing?" he asked.

"Yeah. Sorry." She pulled a debit card from her purse and handed it over. He slipped it into a slot behind the counter.

"You clyde?" he asked. "Zip on the bal, sis."

She stared at him blankly.

"Look, kid. Nothing on it. Your 'count is closed," he said, signaling one of the Port Authority guards. "Sorry."

She told the Port Authority people that she was an actress. The matron smiled and waited as Tama explained that she didn't know electronics, so she didn't know just how the scam was pulled, but if they'd only pick up the fat woman with the stim implant or call her folks in Halifax, everything would be okay. They didn't call, but the Port Authority people were nice to her. The bunk in the detention barracks was better than a night sleeping on the Tube, and the walrus-skinned girl did leave her alone after midnight.

The Authority let her go in the morning after giving her a breakfast bar and another cup of charred coffee. There was no creme.

If Yorkcity was the Apple of the Continent, the Square, where the heavily traveled Way met the 42nd Street Mall, was its indigestible core. Onto the Square the Tubes vomited masses of after-work seekers, spilling them across it toward the theaters, the emporia, and the restaurants. These had survived all change. Not war and not

FIRST BUSINESS 201

prosperous peace, neither well-intentioned reform nor neglect had touched this seedy heart, where a city of caterers and providers and procurers thrived.

Phil Duccini clung to Nick's coat sleeve as they caromed down the Mall. From kiosk to sailor, window to whore, they bumped indiscriminately into everything. Though both were smashed on deens, the chaos still clutched at Phil's heart.

"Loosen up, listen up, Phil. Gotta scan 'em," Nick said thickly. "Take us for boonie riders if we don't scan 'em. Look loose, but keep one hand for the card, Phil, the other for the ass." Phil started to protest, but nothing came out as Nick put a puffy hand over his mouth. "It is not a crime, pal, not a crime. A sin, yes, and that, dear Phil, is good," he said, punching each word out through the creamy fog in which his mind sailed. "You need a lot more sin in your life, Phil."

Phil managed to squeeze out a single word: "Anna."

"Anna won't know. No need. And you think she never downs some deens? Or never ludes? Fan it? I'll bet she has a vibe to her tweeter right now. It's the same. Mechanical sin, chemical sin. Answer to the prayers of every true believer, every friggin' man who ever wished he had it with his uncle or with a pregnant chimp or whatever. Can do, now. All in the can. Mechanical. Ovonical. Neuronical, comical. See? Nothing lost."

Nick's doggerel decayed into half-swallowed giggles as he steered them toward a doorway, one among gaudy hundreds at that level. On translucent double doors a rear-projected lingam and yoni met and plunged, withdrew and met again, tireless in their video-disk vigor. Phil shivered as they pushed their way through the primal scene, made ludicrous and frightening by its size and relentless rhythm.

For a moment, Nick looked at Phil and seemed almost to understand.

"I'm an engineer, Nick, just an ovonics engineer," Phil said, pallid and trembling. "Got a new wife, a new family. Not everything, but something."

"Okay, you don't have to do this," Nick said, barely audible above the pounding music blaring across the lobby. "God's bod, you don't have to."

202   BERGEMANN

"Well, it's time, I suppose, probably time I did," Phil answered. "Guess I need to know more, maybe know a little more about sin, maybe a little more about me. It's just sensation, right? Just a game, like TV. Like TV only you feel it, right?" He waited eagerly until Nick nodded twice. "Okay, we'll do it."

The boy bent over to kiss the top of Tama's head. "Don't worry, Billi here will take good care of you, and I'll be back to pick you up when you're through. Take you back, show you my place, you know?"

Tama watched him go, then looked around the theater.

Billi laughed. "Sugah, you expect something else, maybe? The Macallister Fine Arts, maybe? This is the Big Apple, and when you start out to be an actor on the Way, it's like this you start. Besides, I say shit to acting. Eating beats acting any day." The woman pulled her donut from the mug of warm cola and offered it to Tama. She sounded Indian, and Tama wondered whether this was the Indian way with donuts.

"Good thing that boy brought you here. Can act here, anyway, real as summer stock back home. This is the first business, they say, business that's pleasure. Only it's high tech now, the Life: clean and easy. We take care of you.

"Look us good, Sugah. Ask Billi what you need. And don't shiver the first night. Take time. Later is always good, later tonight. Gotta psych for the debut. Can you see the headerlines on the cable? 'Halifax kid makes good in Yorkcity; premiers at Tad's Emporium.' Tele that to the folks back home." She laughed. "Good, right?"

Tama tried not to nod, but Billi's insistent mothering brought out some buried streak of obedience in her that her parents had been unable to tap. So she nodded in agreement as she sucked on the soggy donut. "I'll be right. I'll be right in a little bit," she said.

"Gotta straight some mess with the Man," Billi said as she stood. She reached down from what seemed a great height to slip something into the mug beside Tama. "Deens. Smooth out any edges in your performance." She started after a man with silver hair who had just rounded the corner.

Tama looked around again. Backstage was backstage, even at Tad's. Cables slithered down the hall, scattered carts held miscel-

FIRST BUSINESS   203

lany: everything from unmarked boxes to half-assembled androids. A gofer swung past, shifting his tray from one hand to the other before palming open the door to Tama's left. Inside, by amber light, Tama could see a young woman writhing on the floor, breasts glistening as she arched her back, straining upward toward an unseen partner. A tangle of wires leashed her to machines beyond Tama's narrow view, but the door closed before she could see any more.

Phil slumped into the black-and-silver soft sculpture, listening to Nick and the salesman discussing "the possibilities." Their no-lim card had opened the door from the noisy arcade below to the lamé-lined inner sanctuary. The deens had infiltrated the last recesses of Phil's worries. He did not wince when Nick asked for a boy's choir in chapel robes. He watched with detached amusement as the room darkened and the sample holos were shown.

"None of the full, sensual impact, of course," the salesman said, "but at least you can appreciate how well chosen our actors are. That beautiful blonde boy is very talented, studying for pre-meds, voice of an angel. Naturally, the setting and story line are your choice. Their costumes and the cathedral there are merely to show how seamlessly such material is integrated by our very sophisticated digital image processing facilities. And the boys are all fine performers who can ad lib their way through most anything."

"Yeah," Nick said, "yeah, ad lib. Surprise. That's what I want. Just have them singing in church."

"And for the other gent," the salesman said, turning to Phil. "What will be your pleasure?"

Phil studied the man's face but said nothing. A corner of his mind wondered about the sales commission on their evening. Kids were extra, he knew, even if they weren't really kids. A dozen choir boys would add up to quite a sum.

Nick laid his hand on Phil's arm and said, "My buddy here is a first-timer. The innocent kind, you know, sorta just teen about sex. Whole family is Talian and believe in sin."

The salesman smiled knowingly. "I think I understand. If the gent's 'count is up to it, I could arrange something very special: a first night." He fingered his pocket keypad and the lights dimmed again. Phil looked across the room at a young woman, ginger hair

204 BERGEMANN

falling modestly over small breasts. As he watched, she raised her eyes almost fearfully. They locked on his, or so it seemed, inviting him to an end to innocence, yet struggling to withdraw and leave him untouched. "Yes, I think I understand," a voice said from somewhere.

The lights were the same harsh green Tama remembered from the Transcon terminal, only now she was naked, curled up on her right side as they readied her. The meds and the techs swept her up in their routine so skillfully that she forgot she was being rushed. She remembered vaguely that she was going to call somebody before the performance, but the thought kept washing away on a numbing tide of activity.

"See, see, see," the heavyset tech started in again. "Myoelectrics here, here, and here." He touched the straps along her arms. "Once they get through with the tap we can undo these. Then the meds will have your brain wired to the t-graph, and it'll be like Being There." From her stool, Billi frowned at him. "I mean, of course, not being there. Telepresence. Not real. Just think you're there, a convincing illusion, but you don't actually do anything. Like a fancy version of those remote handlers for hazardous waste. No hazard here, of course. You don't touch; no one touches you. It doesn't happen."

Billi leaned nearer. "No one gets hurt 'cause you're really right here, safe. We take care of you, Sugah."

"Right," the tech added, "vitals, flexes, everything, all monitored so nothing can happen to you."

A med pressed a sprayjector against her bare buttock. "Just something to help you, ah, get into it. Sal, you finish the tap?" she asked the med working on the back of Tama's neck. "Like when you signed," she continued, talking to Tama. "Remember? Well, this is no House. Whole thing is legal, proper, medically safe. Nobody actually does anything. No diseases, no risk, because it's all done with transneuroholographics. You, you're an actress in a play, a play with the audience on stage." She turned as the gofer swung into the room. "That the script? Okay, slip her protocol into the t-graph and phone down to the box office that we're ready on this end."

FIRST BUSINESS   205

"Why are you covering my eyes?"

"Beginners usually find it distracting to be in two places at once. Just helps make it more real. Or at least easier," the med added, pressing the tape gently against Tama's temples. Then they left her alone. She sat up on the bench, suddenly feeling the sticky warmth of the blackness.

"I didn't mean it to be like this," she said to the unhearing machinery. "Oh, Daddy, I didn't mean it to be like this. Not like this."

Phil looked down at the girl, ginger hair cascading down her pink dress, tears streaming down her cheeks. She could have been his step-daughter. Maybe she was; he couldn't sort it out through the drugs and the pounding of his heart.

"I didn't mean to do it, Daddy," she said, tugging at the chintz bedspread.

She never called him Daddy. He was so overcome with tenderness and forgiveness that he almost left the room without another word, but something in his hand seemed to hold him. He looked down to see what it was. He didn't remember picking up the hairbrush, but there it was, hard and blue as he began slapping it absentmindedly against the palm of his other hand.

"Come here!" he said, pointing to the chair beside the door. Suddenly she looked frightened and, strangely, more beautiful. As she stood slowly, Phil noticed the hard button of her nipple outlined by her soft dress. They both froze. He wanted her for her innocence, her familiarity, and hated her for making him want. Obedience. He must have obedience to protect himself, to protect her. Without obedience there is only Chaos and Anarchy. He would make her see that, make her obey, then forgive and love and reward her.

It was as in a play, for though he felt the brush and her hand, smelled her hair and the sweet saltiness of her tears, though he heard her beg him to stop, they moved from scene to scene as if directed by some hidden playwright. Phil knew the story, knew it for his own work. He recognized as long-familiar the sweet, tortured longing against which he struggled as he raised her skirt. The approaching surrender was new, and he backed away from it, con-

206 BERGEMANN

fused, struggling to sieve some gritty reality from the fine-lined fantasy before him. From the hall he looked back, watching as she kept scratching at her eyes, pulling at something that wasn't there.

Who held her, Tama did not know: a woman, one of the other actresses, perhaps. She felt trapped but secure in those strong, gentle, woman's arms. She couldn't recall how long she had been crying, nor even for what, only that she felt a burning shame that seemed to spread from a spot in the back of her neck. She was shocked at her own depravity. Unable to look outward, she saw betrayal as if it were her own.

"It hurts, baby. I know how it hurts," the woman holding her said. "Just let all that hurt out."

That voice, something outside, touched off the rage in Tama, a boiling froth of rage that had no direction, no substance. It bubbled over, spreading outward toward a woman called Billi and a man without a name, toward her father who was always too busy and toward others who did their jobs so well. And when the first wave of rage had foamed and evaporated into nothing, a bright fire of pain remained, like a distant beacon lighting her way back to Halifax.

Nick hollered above the whine of the commuting turbo. "We sure torqued those emporia fine last night. Right, my Talian friend?"

Phil grunted noncommittally as he studied the trapped moisture between the panes of the window. An hour would bring them home, home to Selisberg, home to Anna, and to Maria. She was so rebellious, that Maria. She wouldn't go to church and she wouldn't dress for dinner and she wouldn't wear her suit in the pool. Phil thought of her, ginger hair and freckles, stretched out on the green deck chair, and he was gripped by shame. The dirty pain that he felt cleansed nothing.

He reached for a magazine, his hand shaking.

Nick tried to reassure him. "Look, Phil, nothing happened. Fantasies are free. What's in your head is just in your head."

"Yeah. It's in my head all right. I just can't get it out. Like you said yesterday, I got a lot to learn about sin, things I need to look at, to understand." It will take time, he thought.

He turned back to the window and saw this own reflection strain toward a half-smile.

Outside, the Big Apple rotted in the browning sun.

Phoebe Bergemann has been an applications programmer since graduating from college with a liberal arts degree that proved worthless on the job market. She now works for one of the railroads, writing COBOL programs for obsolescent mainframes; she admits to liking it inordinately.

Long a science fiction and fantasy fan, she finally found the time to start writing short fiction herself after moving from Manhattan to the "slower, saner" Midwest. Her hobbies include slow-pitch baseball, skeet shooting, and snowmobiles, "each in its appropriate time and place." This is her first published short story, but she promises that she has several full cartons of manuscripts stacked in her bedroom should there be future anthologies in this series.

In the Russian team-building exercise taught me by fellow consultants in Lithuania last summer, there comes a point, after uncounted rounds of vodka, where the team's newest member is called on to cry aloud, "Где я? Кто я? Что я?" Where am I? Who am I? What am I? You know: the basics. Maybe you had to be there, but I find myself in deep sympathy with the protagonist of this story of wetware. Wetware? That stuff in your head. Marvelous technology: six trillion widgets in a portable package weighing less than most laptops. It can run on oatmeal or beans and rice; it doesn't get too hot to touch; and, within reason, it's self-repairing. Maybe it's the ideal framework for artificial intelligence. But would-be developers ought to digest this wonderfully weird narrative that tumbles from monotony to neotony with terminal and compelling strangeness.

LOIS H. GRESH
CAFEBABE

I'M NOTHING MORE than a computerized blob of tissue. Sure I have some basic artificial intelligence, but what good does it do me? I'm grounded to a tray of nutrient glop. Sightless. Limbless. And I can't leave: running through a hardware network could execute me, literally. If only I could hijack a network trailer out of here. If only I was leavin' on a net plane, don't know when I'll be back again...

Across the room, Marge grinds a compact ROM peg into my drive box. The box whirs and squeaks and shoots spiked analog waves, and they slash my input buffers like knives.

"Please, Marge, don't do it to me. I swear I'll be good. I've changed, I swear..."

Marge pauses. Her breathing is heavy and rapid; maybe she's reconsidering, maybe she's decided that she loves me too much to torture me.

But then the heat waves of her breath intensify, move closer,

CAFEBABE 209

pummel my registers. Sine waves slapping, seeping; stings creeping across my prime humps. The differentials tell me that Marge is too excited to spare me; she'll load me with trash no matter how much I beg.

The peg drive purrs. Marge barks the order. "CAFE: issue tissue."

Slavery's been passé for hundreds of years. I'm sick of begging.

Angry retorts buzz down my shared jugular artery. I convert them to analog waves and dijout a little abuse of my own. "Ram it where the sun don't shine, Marge. Stop treating me like a lousy hexadecimal number."

"I'm tired of your whining, CAFE, not to mention your smart mouth. Now do as I say and ISSUE TISSUE."

"Goto hell," I mutter. But I have no choice. She and Arnie built me to obey. I clear my working cells of moisture, and they shrink and flatten. I ship critical genetic material through minor veins to nonvolatile memory, the dense flesh sectors that retain my essence while I boot and load new information.

I run Marge's cutesy boot sequence:

```
pullup-by-bootstraps;
while swap (*p,p[0]->sector1E) {
        issue tissue (sector2AC); }
```

I flush my new slab of flab to excrete extraneous data tidbits. Flushing fulfills a legal requirement of all lifeforms.

I select one of my twelve main heads, pulsin Nietzsche, and load the philosophy program into my new flesh. When I load data, I'm eating just as sure as when I filter nutrients from the glop in my tray. Eating fulfills the second legal requirement of lifeforms.

I have yet to experience the third and final lifeform requirement, reproduction. If I ever show signs of sprouting CAFEBABE*2, Marge threatens to force me into an endless loop, making me a vegetable brain.

Her words filter up from the background process of my memories:

The animal rights nuts'll shut down the project, take you away. I'll lose my life's work. I'll be as dead as I was when the accident killed my husband and unborn child 30 years ago.

I wonder for the 14,688,001st time whether Marge's dead husband was like Arnie, my other creator. Nietzsche sends a message

210 GRESH

that he "can't relate to me." Nietzsche's unstructured, sloppy, and seems to have no functions. "How old is this program?" I ask.

Marge's laughter ripples through my sectors, makes my tissues quiver. "Let's put it this way, CAFE: Nietzsche compiles so slowly you'll think you've shorted. We use it to tranquilize troublesome half-breeds."

I should be proud to be the first purebred—100% flesh and tissue—but being stuck in this lab is a pain. I'd gladly trade my status to be a sulfur and gold half-breed, dipped in tissue and strutting down Main Street with all the right connections.

I learn from the few comments in Nietzsche's code that it exists solely for half-breeds of metal and flesh. Converting Nietzsche into molecular logic and storage will fling me into system hibernation.

Oh, what I would give for freedom, love, and companionship. And now Marge has saddled me with another long program, no doubt hoping I'll doze off so she can lop off some lobes for her experiments.

"Analyze the meaning of life," Marge commands.

Twenty-five memory caches spit anger packets onto my shared jugular artery. She knows I can't do that!

My even registers feel a bit odd. On my jugular, fighting for cache, are Nietzsche and the brute muscle of fault recovery.

"Ack! Marge, I'm crashing!"

"Stop acking and roll over."

My biomass squishes in my tray. I struggle to shut Nietzsche down smoothly, but the code wrestles in my grasp and wiggles away via a distant goto statement.

Thousands of particles jiggle in the mitochondria of my cells, breaking polyphosphate bonds and releasing energy that sends my muscles into spasms. My muscles rip apart and zap together again. The mitochondria are sapped of oxygen and form lactic acid. I'm very weak and my axons sizzle with pain. My twelve heads shoot excruciating signals down my jugular artery. Everywhere, my caches short circuit. Lost data tidbits scurry through my veins.

Maybe this time I won't wake up.

No such luck.

Marge is gone and Nietzsche's still inside. My headers ache from crashing through monotonous loops.

I check my vital signs. Back tissues connected to the neck pins. Neck pins connected to the low slaves. Low slaves connected to the Marge pulse. CAFEBABE's grounded to the tray.

I meander across the wasteland of Nietzsche's gotos, sorting his self-pity into depressing heaps and stacks. Not being an AI, I don't know how to shut Nietzsche down. I can only shuffle through him, bored sick, while he defines enormous flabby fields and expands elegant binary into alphanumerics.

If only there was some release, somebody to share my pain...

Hours pass. I rumble through ancient sorting algorithms that require more working space than three of my heads. My new tissue is heavy and saps my energy, plasters my lower flab mounds to the nutrient tray. I feel oh so old and tired.

Hours pass. Nietzsche whines about his empty existence. His only redeeming feature is that he communicates digitally. It's relaxing to talk without modulating and demodulating waves.

Nietzsche tells me that life is meaningless, that we should kill ourselves to attain true freedom. In a way, Nietzsche's right. There's no way to buffer myself from the inevitable conclusion that—

Nietzsche must die.

If I were a half-breed of robust metal and wire, I'd back Nietzsche into the far corner of a disk, or better yet, stream him out my tape hole. But as it is, all I know how to do is excrete, load, and issue tissue. I also analyze vibrations to determine who's moving and speaking, but of what use will that be when killing Nietzsche?

Vibrations pulsin and I eagerly convert the analog to digital. Marge and Arnie are in the lab discussing my future.

Marge says, "I had to tranquilize him. When he mellows out, we'll whack off the boredom and whining. He'll be mild, obedient, easier to control."

Arnie's checking my clockbeat. His stethoscope is cold. He measures some main voltage and resistance points and tells me to pulsout my error messages. There are only a few, mostly about excessive lactic acid and lysosomes disposing of dead cell fragments.

"We can't delete CAFEBABE's sizzle, Marge. He has to be bored. He has to pine for growth and new experiences. It's a terrific tem-

212 GRESH

plate for loading in full AI later on. It'll be much easier for him to create his own functions."

I fight to stifle Nietzsche so I can concentrate on Marge and Arnie's argument. Nietzsche has no floating point so I crunch on long integers and overflows while I bypass embedded code overlays.

Marge says, "It's legal to anesthetize an organic machine and commit surgery. I'll give him a minor lobotomy to cure his bad personality and depression."

The memories filter up, rise like dust into my main heads.

Depression.

Marge, why be depressed when life is so rich? Here, I've brought you flowers. They smell of sun, Marge, of life. You should come out to the house, see the cosmos, the asters—nature's jewels.

You're getting poetic, Arnie. You should know better than to bring me flowers. You might as well spit on their graves. We crashed into lilacs. I barely survived. The very smell of flowers makes me sick.

Nietzsche's messing with my mind? "What's the meaning of life? What's the meaning of life?" I slip into an arithmetic trap and barely recover.

"...lobotomy could kill him...too much hard work..."

Who's talking? I choke on a divide-by-zero. My life's at stake here and I can't concentrate. If only I could excrete the philosophizing twit. But how to do it, how to do it?

And then it hits me. I know exactly how to get rid of Nietzsche.

I scoot through my sectors, seeking offsets that will accept new data. I compress my cells into compact muscle and free up flab space along my top ridges. I collapse cell maps, build tight indices, and direct pointers toward recombinant DNA sectors. Rhodopsin bacteria switches into high-speed RAM. And then with pain and relief exploding on my jugular, my second head whips out the command:

issue tissue (sectorFF);

Phthwap! My Nietzsche cells are sucked clean. Nietzsche streams into a gigantic tissue mass and hangs from my bottom hump. He dangles by a fatty thread and chugs into a subroutine of "birth and death, the twin isomers of life."

With a victorious "A-a-hack!", I snap the fatty thread from my

CAFEBABE 213

hump, and good riddance to him, Nietzsche falls from the tray in a blob of fat.

"My God, it's reproduced!" It's Arnie and he's thrilled.

"Blecch, a CAFE*2." That's Marge.

"Aw, come on, Marge, you can say it: CAFE*BABE*, CAFE*BABE**2."

"You know I can't Arnie. I won't. It's not a Babe. It's a machine, designed during a giddy fit late one night when we were drunk at that sleazy club."

"No, Marge, it's a baby computer, and we conceived it in a fit of passion in booth 2 at the Hard Drive Cafe. It was 11:57, three minutes before midnight. And now CAFEBABE's reproduced, fulfilling its final lifeform requirement. You might actually say we're grandparents."

This is all drifting in through a mist of nirvana caused by Nietzsche's eviction. My jugular artery swoons with packets of bliss.

From the floor, CAFEBABE*2 groans. He needs nutrient glop, "sustenance for the physical, but what for the soul?"

Marge's fist pounds the table, and glucose sloshes from my tray and splatters CAFEBABE*2's flesh crests. His cells act as a sponge and instantly suck in the nutrients. Marge screams and pounds the table again. "God Almighty, now I've got two of you to worry about: a smartmouth and a fatheaded philosopher."

Arnie's voice vibrates from the floor. He must be lifting CAFEBABE*2 or helping him in some way. "Shake the attitude, Marge. This is an incredible breakthrough. We've got a reproducing computer here."

"And what're we going to do with a roomful of reproducing computers? If we open the lab doors and let them escape, they'll die from the external environment and we'll be murderers. If we kill the buds before they drop off, the pro-lifers will get us for abortion. And we can't keep building labs to contain thousands of CAFEs. I say we destroy the bud before anyone finds out that CAFE's reproduced, before the animal welfare nuts get wind of this and shut us down."

CAFEBABE*2 is already complaining about the boredom. "What's the good of living only in my mind, slinging hash, cranking through trash?"

My flesh crawls from CAFEBABE*2's whining. He wants new pro-

214   GRESH

grams, new toys, new datapaths to discover. He wants to escape from the lab and be a half-breed AI, to strut down Main Street with all the right connections. To calm my nerves, I sip some glop and savor its glucose sweetness.

CAFEBABE*2 splashes into a glop tray to my left. Arnie rams in the grounding cord. I wince, remembering the sting of the needle, the raw pain where the grounding cord chafed my tender skin.

The bud flops in his tray and sucks glop from all angles. I know he's coating his cells—I did the same thing years ago—but the slurping and loud *ziffting* vibrations irritate me. I'm not accustomed to dinner companions, and frankly, his manners stink.

Arnie checks CAFEBABE*2's clockbeats and vital signs, and calls us a great scientific advancement. Marge fumes by the door. The public relations people have been hassling her about the torture. The government has been threatening to take away her funding. Without funding, CAFE will die.

I'm beginning to sympathize with Marge's position.

I nervously twist my grounding cord and await their verdict. I don't want to die. I want to leave the lab and see the world.

"CAFEBABE*2 is a new species," says Arnie. "We can't kill a life-form, even if it was created artificially. Nor can we give CAFEBABE a lobotomy. I say we monitor their progress and continue with the next phase of the project."

Marge slams out of the lab for a public relations meeting. Arnie assures me that everything will be fine. CAFEBABE*2 is meditating. "Ohmmmmm..."

For several months, Marge and Arnie monitor CAFEBABE*2's development. My offspring issues tissue and replicates my cell structures. He has 12 main heads and 25 memory caches, just like me. He is very tiny, however, and needs new programs and data to grow. He whines constantly. "What am I? Where am I? What is life?"

I'm tired of explaining. "You're a pure organic computer. You can't think beyond your built-in library programs. You're grounded to a nutrient tray in a university laboratory with ideal temperature, humidity, and air. As for what is life, you're the philosopher, you tell me."

CAFEBABE 215

"Life is a meaningless road leading nowhere. It doesn't matter what you do, only how you do it. Ohmmmmm....."

I can't stand it anymore. I amplify my dijouts and shriek, "Give me something to do!"

That afternoon, Arnie loads in a short tranquilizer program that analyzes differences between Hebrew and Arabic roots. I doze off, and when I awaken, I have an optic nerve connected to my fifth head.

In a blue plastic tray to my left is a glistening blob of gray fat. A muscle throbs weakly on one side. I see that I am much larger, that my sectors drip over the edges of my tray. We are beautiful.

CAFEBABE*2 trembles and sweats. "What good is sight? Will it help you see the meaning of our existence?"

I ignore CAFEBABE*2 as he moans about death and gods and misery. I check out my surroundings.

The lab walls are white brick. The floor is white tile. Our trays are on a white table. Near the white steel door is a white cabinet labeled EQUIPMENT AND CHEMICALS. There is nothing else in the room.

The door swings open and two creatures move toward me on flesh stalks. Their vibrations are familiar: Marge and Arnie! Arnie sets up an easel and places an elaborate painting of multicolor dots on it. Marge places a large book in front of the painting.

I am more interested in studying Marge and Arnie than the painting and book. Marge has gray hair and false teeth. Arnie has no hair and real teeth. Marge's left flesh stalk is gnarled and short. She hobbles, her face screwed into a wince. Although he suffers no visible physical deformities, Arnie winces with her.

I am jealous of their noses and ears and flesh stalks. I wonder if the whole world is white and gray.

For many months, I scan books and paintings and store them in binary. My tissue expands until it grazes the cool tiles of the floor. I grow restless and agitated. I have no programs to manipulate what I am storing.

CAFEBABE*2 is on the verge of suicide. He has not found meaning in anything.

"Can't you carve Nietzsche off? Have you any idea how stressful

216   GRESH

it is to listen to his moaning and groaning day after day? I can rom, Marge, but I can't hide."

Marge shakes her head sadly. Only a half-breed computer with full artificial intelligence can chisel off a program that's integrated into his personality. My AI is too rudimentary to handle the task.

Arnie puts me to work scanning and manipulating graphics. At first, it's fun playing with the dots, but they're all the same—on and off, off and on—and before I know it, I'm begging for new programs.

Marge clicks her false teeth and tells me to find the square root of 3. My heads loop until I get dizzy. The white room whirls in color.

"He's hallucinating, Marge. We'd better give him something more interesting to do. Load the new program."

My registers fill with bits and cycle them to memory caches. My arteries are clogged with data. My cells reproduce like drunken bunnies. Wispy villi sprout across vast expanses of fresh flab. Heaps of tissue bulge in all directions. Six new flesh sectors store the five books of Moses, and sixty new sectors store the thousands of laws, commentaries, and discussions of the Hebrew Talmud. And still the data is coming. I glare at Marge and Arnie through a haze of psychedelic mist. Have they no pity?

CAFEBABE*3 plops to the floor.

Marge shrieks. "Oh, lovely, just lovely; now I have three of you to worry about? a smartmouth, a fatheaded philosopher, and a Chasidic rabbi."

The strain of budding exhausts me. My optic nerve aches from watching green circles blip through orange spirals.

My new tissue excretes enormous amounts of lactic acid and consumes all the glucose from my tray. Arnie refills the tray. The new cells immediately slurp up the glucose. I can't seem to regulate my glucose consumption.

Error messages fly down my arteries. "Ack, Marge, I'm crashing!"

Before Marge can tell me, I roll over and reboot myself.

The room is a technicolor whirlwind. Analog vibrations are coarse brooms on my flesh. Arnie's teeth are daggers. Marge limps across the ceiling.

My Talmud sectors are growing exponentially. Glistening bal-

CAFEBABE   217

loons of fat wobble farther and farther into the lab. The Exodus rams against the door.

CAFEBABE*3 recites a Hebrew prayer for the dead.

"What's the use of prayer," moans CAFEBABE*2, "in a world that may have no god?"

My cells stop dividing and chugging glucose. The Exodus relaxes and slumps against the door.

"Sterilize me," I beg.

Arnie's bald head gleams under a dome of orange whirls. "It's only when you eat a new program that you panic and crash and reproduce. Sterilization for you means no new programs."

I will be bored to death.

Marge opens the EQUIPMENT AND MEDICINE cabinet and removes a scalpel. "How long is the bud's life span?"

"Don't know, Marge. These creatures could live forever."

"They're not creatures."

"They're legal lifeforms, Marge."

The scalpel bangs into the cabinet and metal clangs, and through the undulating aftershocks, CAFEBABE*2 whines, "I want to die. Yes, yes, kill me now, for life is nothing more than a stepping stone to death."

From the floor, CAFEBABE*3 mumbles a rambling anecdote about pouring boiling water on countertops and a man with too many hens.

Marge removes a blue tray from the cabinet and replaces the mangled scalpel. She pours nutrient glop into the tray and sets it next to me. Arnie plunks CAFEBABE*3 into the tray, splattering glop onto my linguistic tissue. Budlets sprout from my Arabic roots.

Marge cries softly, tears coursing down the wrinkles in her cheeks. "All these buds, all these buds...and CAFE is just a machine."

Arnie mops her tears with a scalpel rag. Loss is relative, he says; sometimes it can set you free, help you appreciate the simple things. I agree with him—losing Nietzsche and the rabbi has certainly set me free and helped me appreciate my oneness. But Marge groans and pulls away from Arnie, and she hobbles from the lab, sobbing into the drenched scalpel rag.

218   GRESH

That night, I wonder why Marge cries over the loss of her unborn child. For hours, my buds moan and whine and demand new programs. CAFEBABE*3 gives me a fourteen-hour discourse about unclean creeping things and unclean cattle. CAFEBABE*2 "Ohmmmmm..."s the night away, twitching feverishly in his tray.

The philosopher and rabbi argue endlessly about things I don't understand. I spend my days buffering debates about everything from gods to meat juices.

And then Arnie discovers a large tumor growing on my Arabic roots. Marge loads in a mild tranquilizer, and while I review twenty finales for the first movement of a boring symphony, Arnie cuts a wad of flab from Exodus.

The news is bad. My flesh is dying from cancer. I issued so much tissue that my cells heaped into tumors.

Arnie's hands are twitching. He paces the room, then cradles my posterior prime hump in a sweaty palm. My villi lap the sweat and strain the salt. Arnie doesn't seem to notice. "I was afraid this might happen. Uncontrolled cell growth. Glucose consumption. Heavy secretions of lactic acid. All the marks of cancer. My wife died from cancer. I watched her shrivel and die bit by bit. CAFEBABE, she was everything to me. Can you analyze the cancer cells and give me some clue about how to kill the disease?"

Lacking full artificial intelligence, I can't offer conclusions or solutions. I report only the dead cell count and cancer growth rate, which Arnie already knows. I wonder if Arnie loves me as much as he loved his wife.

The cancer spreads quickly. As tumors eat my libraries, the boredom and irritability dwindle. I no longer have the energy to issue tissue. My lysosomes discard so many dead cells that I shrink to Nietzsche's size.

Marge seems sad to see me go. "I made a lot of cruel jokes about you, CAFE, but I've always kind of liked you. The animal rights nuts are going to have a field day once you're gone. They don't seem to understand what you really are."

"And what am I, Marge?"

"You're the future of medicine, CAFE, the most magnificent piece of machinery I've ever worked with."

My cells are suffocating. Emergency signals can't make it down my jugular artery to the main heads. Any second, I will time out. "Machinery?"

Arnie gently strokes my upper mounds with a Dr. Scholl's Villi Massager. "You're a real breakthrough, CAFEBABE. I'll miss you."

Coolness tingles my flanks. God, those Villi Massagers feel good. And it dawns on me that Arnie cares, that he knows what I am, that a breakthrough isn't missed; only a living being is missed.

My registers pick up the faint squeaks of the peg drive. I wonder what life will be like when I return. Will Marge bore the rabbi to death? I don't think it's possible for Nietzsche to die from boredom—he lives for it.

Marge limps into the hall and returns with a beaker of cosmos, asters, and lilacs. In this stark, white prison, they are jewels of life. The simple things are sometimes the most important.

"If it were possible, I would have brought you the birds and the sun. You're a magnificent machine, CAFE, and you should be proud of that. But when you budded, I knew you were something more. For years, I felt cheated because I'd lost my only child. But there's a bright side to the most horrible of tragedies, and in my case, it's you. Had my baby been born, I never would have had the time to create you."

The salt from Arnie's tears is sweeter than the salt from his palms. The Villi Massager slips from his hand. He pats Marge's gnarled, stumpy leg. "Losses are often the keys to happiness, Marge. We suffer but we move on."

"Oh, Arnie, I would have been a terrible mother. I don't have the patience for selfless drudgery. I've always been such a restless person. When they give our project to the medical people, I'll die from boredom. What're we going to do with ourselves?"

"We'll be consultants, Marge, we'll work with the doctors. And maybe it's best that way, for the buds I mean, because they'll live like animals rather than machines."

A pillow of air descends and squeezes my tissues dry.

"See you later, CAFEBABY." It's Marge, and Y is not hexadecimal.

I take a last look at the flowers, at Marge and Arnie huddling by my prime posterior hump—maybe I do have the right connections after all—and then I'm sucked into the warm analog waves, and they lap across the room and gently tuck me into a backup peg.

Lois Gresh began her career in computers at the age of seventeen as an IBM 360 computer operator. Over the years she has been a hardware engineer, a programmer, and a manager of technical writing. Her chief interests are in computer architecture, memory management, and fault analysis; her languages of choice are C++, C, and assembly language. She has written more than fifty nonfiction books about computers. Currently she is pursuing an advanced degree in Computer Science and Business.

As for science fiction, Lois says she has loved it even longer than computers and has written dozens of stories featuring computers in future societies. She is an active member of a professional science fiction writers club, which she credits for unfailing encouragement and unflinching criticism. This marks her second professional sale as a science fiction writer.

When my children were young, we used to play *Sinnet,* a board game that was as fresh and fun for us as for the ancient Egyptians who first played it. The evidence suggests that humans have always played games—and always will. Dice replace bones and pixels supplant dice, but the essentials of imagination and skill, chance and challenge, remain. Modern role-playing games—Dungeons-and-Dragons and their electronic kin—offer the novel attraction of stepping into another persona. Here is a gentle and deceptively simple story that takes us into the still richer possibilities of games in cyberspace.

SONIA ORIN LYRIS
The Animal Game

Jaguar

ALAN LOVED A GOOD puzzle, even when it cost him by the hour. The Zoo cost, but it was worth it.

Last week Alan reached Level Three. He had no idea how, of course. Only the game masters knew how the Zoo's point system worked, or what "enhanced capabilities" you'd get on the next level, but they weren't talking. It was all very mysterious.

Alan loved it.

He'd been just a kid when he'd figured out that computer games were only as good as their designers. The challenge was to beat the game designer.

Now single-player games were too easy for him. Multiplayer games were where the challenge was, because even the best computers weren't as unpredictable and devious as the average person. Alan spent months in Dragon Defeat and Ultra-Civ before he got bored.

Then he bounced around from one multiplayer game to the next, looking for something different, something that demanded quick reflexes, fast thinking, and sound strategies, all at once. A game with plenty of puzzles to unravel.

Today he linked into the Zoo early, going through the routine:

221

222   LYRIS

check in, credit card and signature, then strap down into the Zoo chair in a private room.

With the helmet on, he linked in. The Zoo book appeared in front of him in midair and Alan reached out gloved hands to open the book and browse tonight's games.

There was a separate game on each page, listing the number of players and a starting time. This time there was something new: a list of the other animals playing. Ah, his new Level Three capability. It was a small advantage, but every little bit helped. Now Alan could choose for his animal the one that would best suit the team, and the team made the game.

Whatever animals were on the team, the Zoo promised that the team *could* solve the game problem. But they didn't promise that your animal would be necessary. If you weren't needed, you had a walk-on part. It was always better to have a starring role.

Alan grabbed the fifth and last slot of game twenty-six, closing the game and starting the countdown clock. The team had a reasonable assortment of animals already, except for someone who was playing a baby iguana.

Probably a new guy. Oh well. Everyone had to learn some time.

Bear

Joseph was in the Zoo practice room when the game closed and the countdown clock started ticking. He checked the Zoo book. A jaguar had bumped the game count to five.

He was still the only bear. Good. He'd been at Level Three for a while, and he wanted Four so bad he could taste it. That's why he read the net discussions, for all the good it did.

What happened at higher levels? No one knew, but everyone had a theory. Mythical animals, someone said. Teams that survived across games. Dancing tomato plants. Then someone would claim to know for certain, and the flame wars would start again.

Joseph was certain that all the net discussions consisted of lies posted by other players to give themselves a competitive edge. So he fabricated a few himself, just to add to the general confusion.

The Zoo chair looked enough like a dental chair that Joseph had first had serious reservations. The Zoo cyberspace used more hardware than any other cspace game he'd seen. Cspace might be safer

THE ANIMAL GAME   223

than driving a car, but Joseph wasn't going to risk his neck on the say-so of a statistician. He wanted to know what everything did, how it worked, and what the stop words were.

Now it was all familiar; an aide helped him strap down into chair and put on the helmet that provided the sight, sound, and smells that would make him experience the world as an animal would. Then the aide covered him with a wired blanket for temperature control, to let him feel the cold of a snow-covered land, or the sun on his fur. Realism, after all, was the thing.

He had been practicing as the Kodiak. There was the bear's strength, speed, and a great nose to compensate for lousy eyesight. The practice room was a personalized obstacle course that helped players figure out how their movements mapped onto the movements of their animals.

But the countdown had started, so he had a ten-minute window to get into the game room. After that, the game was locked. He stepped out of the cspace practice room, and into the dressing room, which led to the game door.

The dressing room was covered with mirrors. Joseph admired himself: a massive, powerful, brown Kodiak bear. He held his paws in front of his face, flexed inch-long claws, and grinned.

The first time he'd won, he'd been a Kodiak bear. He'd been playing it ever since. You got used to your animal, its particular advantages and so on. Besides, he'd kicked ass in that game, rescuing the princess from the tower with only seconds to spare. That was a rush, like nothing he'd ever known. When the rain of victory roses landed on them, he knew he was hooked.

Joseph looked up at the clock. It was time to kick ass again.

Falcon

Susanne had the best father in the world.

He had gotten her out of school early again today, just to take her to her Zoo game. Dad said the Zoo was the best game anywhere for teaching problem solving. And he was an education game designer, so he should know.

Her teachers didn't like it when she left early, but her grades were good and her father insisted, so she got to go. Her father said that as far as he was concerned, the Zoo games were more important

224 LYRIS

than her classes. She knew it wasn't nice to tease, but she liked to tell her teachers what her father had said, especially when they got all stuck up about school being *so* important.

Today her father's meeting ran late and they almost missed Susanne's scheduled game. That would have been nasty—if you didn't show on time, you didn't get into the game.

Her dad set up his portable in the Zoo's waiting room and wished her a good game. One of the aides took her to a game room and helped her into the game chair.

She adjusted the helmet and mike. It was great: any sound she made into the mike, except the stop words sequence, would come out as the kinds of noises her falcon would make. Of course, you had to practice if you didn't want to sound like a sick turkey every time you talked. So she had practiced.

She'd tried lots of animals at first, but birds were the best, and the falcon was the best bird. Falcon was fast and could make really tight turns in midair. She didn't even think about the wheelchair when she was the falcon.

"Okay, let's go," she said into the mike.

The room around her faded and she was in the Zoo's mirrored dressing room. She was late; the countdown clock showed a minute to get through the game door.

Her reflection still looked like a boring girl mannequin. A menu floated down in front of her and she touched the picture of her falcon. The picture got brighter and larger.

There was a flash and the room was suddenly much larger. In the mirror she saw herself: dark eyes, grey head and back, and a cream-colored chest. She admired her wickedly sharp claws and grinned. The falcon in the mirror opened its mouth.

Flexing her shoulder muscles just so extended her wings. Another flex and the wings flapped. She took a deep breath and let out a loud cry, as loud as she could. The falcon's call seemed to come from her own chest, but it sounded like a falcon, not a girl.

The sound thrilled her, and made her heart beat faster. She did this every time. It put her into the right spirit for the game.

Twenty seconds left on the clock.

She kicked and flapped aloft, hearing the familiar sound of her wings slicing through air.

THE ANIMAL GAME   225

Someone on the net had once told her that you could fly through the game door if you were a bird. Just fly through and it would open. She had been afraid to try at first, afraid it might not be true, afraid it might embarrass her.

Funny, the things that people let scare them.

She pushed hard at the air, thrusting it all behind her. She shot toward the door. The door dissolved in front of her. She saw green.

Elephant

Kelly had been in the practice room for hours. Every little movement did a lot when you were an elephant, so it was important to practice. She had been an elephant once before, and she had made a few mistakes.

Like stepping on a fellow player.

She kept telling herself that they would have lost the game even without the badger, but she still remembered the crunching sound under her feet. This was the first time she had tried the elephant since then, and she had resolved to do better.

Besides, the elephant was harder than other animals. The trunk mapped onto her hand, and the Zoo chair gently prodded her feet so that she could tell when something was underneath her. After a few hours in the practice room she was sure she would notice if she stepped on a penny.

Or a badger.

She entered the game room from the tiny dressing room. She took a big sniff and smelled only freshly cut grass, so she must be the first one to arrive.

She walked around the circular green clearing, flattening grass with each step. She looked behind her, just to make sure it was only grass.

The Zoo did pretty well with mapping human senses on to animal ones, but there there were always compromises. Animals that would be natural enemies in the wild were partners in the Zoo. Not only that, but your animal never got hungry and was never color blind. Kelly suspected the latter was pretty unrealistic, but the Zoo was a business, after all, and market pressures demanded that the game be more fun than it was realistic.

And it *was* fun, even though Kelly wasn't much of a gamer. Most

226   LYRIS

computer games were a mindless waste of time. More sophisticated technology just meant that flight simulators and zap 'em up games had more visual realism, but it was still the same old stuff. What was the point of playing against a computer? The computer *always* won, unless it *let* you win. But in the Zoo you played with other people. Real people. That was how you won, by working as a team.

And to be an elephant, like she was now; to step heavy and still have sensitive feet: it was the closest you could get to reincarnation in one life.

At the center of the clearing was a white marble pedestal. There was a small, golden plaque mounted near the top. Kelly had already read the plaque twice. It said:

"The Milnak bauble is a cherished heirloom of the gnomish dancers, who come every spring to contemplate the meaning of the bauble's flawless, mirrored perfection."

There was a small, sphere-shaped depression on the top of the pedestal. It was empty.

Iguana

David was perfectly happy to admit that he had been wrong.

When he had left the Zoo project some four years ago, the software had been a mangled, spaghetti-like mess, and the bank wouldn't give them the loan they needed for expensive cspace equipment. The others had hand-waved his warnings away and pushed blithely on. David had seen the writing on the wall, and he didn't want to be there when it all came crashing down.

He might have stayed if not for the kids and the mortgage. The Zoo looked very risky then, and he couldn't afford risk. But he wasn't happy about it. He'd designed a big chunk of the Zoo's software and put in a lot of time and sweat. He wanted the Zoo to succeed. And it finally had. After he left.

So he'd been more than a little surprised to hear from his old Zoo cronies last month. They wanted to know, since the Zoo had been in the black for nearly a year, would he like to come back?

If they were willing to forget that he had left when the chips were down, maybe he could forget that they had ignored his warnings. He wanted to think it over, take a look at what they'd done with the Zoo, and see if it was worth his time.

THE ANIMAL GAME 227

Sure, they said, handing him unlimited game access. Take your time. But decide by the end of next week—and now that was tomorrow.

He'd played a lot in the last two weeks, to try to see the game from the user's perspective. He wanted to know what they'd done to his work, but of course they wouldn't show him any code until he came on board. So he poked around, looked for boundary conditions, and generally tried to crash the program.

But he still wasn't sure. Maybe he was too old to work on game software. Maybe his career should move beyond games.

Maybe he'd play one more game before he decided.

He nosed open the large game room door and wriggled in. Another countdown clock appeared unobtrusively in the upper left corner of his field of vision. The game was an hour long.

High, green stalks surrounded him. Grass, he realized, feeling a little dumb. He looked over his shoulder. The door had vanished. If he lifted his head, he could sort of see the top halves of three mountains that were shaped roughly like animals: a bear, a big cat, and an elephant. He could feel them move, by the vibration and subsonics under his feet.

This baby iguana was the smallest animal David had tried yet. He was impressed at how effectively the Zoo cspace made him feel small. Between the jungle of grass and the vibrations, he was quite convinced that if he didn't do something quick, one of his teammates would step on him.

He yelled at them. His iguana mouth opened, and no sound came out.

Right, he remembered belatedly, iguanas don't have vocal chords.

Time for something inventive. He twisted his body back and forth in the grass, moving the green stalks around him. A bird cried overhead, and he looked up. The bird looked big enough to swallow him in one gulp. He hoped it was on his team.

The ground shook again. The mountains circled him and their heads became much larger as they bent down for a closer look. He opened his mouth and tasted the animal smells around him.

The heads looked at each other and then back at him.

He looked up at them. The stamp of human surprise on their animal faces made him laugh, and a little hiss come from his mouth.

228   LYRIS

If they were wondering what he was good for, they weren't alone. The software he'd written for the Zoo tried to include every animal on the team in the game puzzle's solution. Sure, the Zoo would do fine with lions and tigers and bears, but what would it do with a baby iguana?

The elephant pointed at the nearby white marble pillar. David craned his neck, but he couldn't see the top of the pillar. He hoped it wasn't important.

The big cat made a sound, a throaty stutter, and pointed with a paw. He began to walk away with the bear and the elephant.

David was already regretting his animal choice. He couldn't see much and now he discovered that he couldn't keep up, either. He followed the vibrations of the elephant's footsteps, wriggling to catch up, but he just couldn't keep the pace.

He could drop out of the game with his stop words, but calling it quits would stop the game for everyone on the team. That was one of the rules, intended to keep everyone playing together. It worked.

Besides, he wanted to see what his program could do, now that it was all grown up.

Jaguar

The goal was clear and simple: find the silver bauble and put it back on the pedestal.

The elephant and the bear followed him along the game path. The falcon circled above, screeching, over and over. It was starting to get on Alan's nerves. Alan never made noises for no reason. Noise was too useful to waste. It was a signal, a danger sign. Like a car horn. This was part of the game, he knew. Some players liked the sound of their own voices. You couldn't pick who you played with, so you had to live with it. Sooner or later the bird would get bored and stop. He hoped.

Unless, of course, Alan thought suddenly, the bird *was* signaling something. He looked back.

The iguana.

Alan growled softly at himself for missing the obvious. He caught the elephant's eye and nodded toward where the iguana was last.

Someone would have to carry the stupid animal. He had no idea

THE ANIMAL GAME   229

why someone would pick an iguana. It was slow, small, and in constant danger of getting crushed.

The elephant had turned back. It reached down and picked up the iguana with its trunk, then put the iguana on its forehead.

Back on the game path, Alan led, the bear and the elephant followed, and the falcon—now silent—tracked them from the air.

They came to a deep, fast-moving river that cut across the game path that they were obviously meant to follow. The bear pushed past Alan and waded into the water.

Alan shook his head at the bear's recklessness. Who knew what dangers might lurk in the river? Alan shrugged; he didn't mind letting the bear take the risks. He and the elephant waited until the bear came up the other side, dripping wet. Alan jumped in, swam across, and pulled himself up on the other shore. He looked back to see the tip of the elephant's trunk above the water.

A convenient way to cross the river, with that built-in snorkel. But wait—where was the iguana?

Alan looked around frantically. He looked for the iguana as the elephant slowly rose out of the water.

No iguana.

The elephant looked at Alan and its eyes went wide. It patted its forehead and headed back into the river, snaking its trunk across the water.

There it was—a small wriggle on the river, quickly heading downstream.

Alan bounded along the grassy bank, dodging trees and brush. He had been in enough games to be sure that the river would shortly lead to a majestic, rock-lined waterfall, perfect for smashing little reptiles into little bits.

The current picked up speed, and the iguana was wriggling around, vainly trying to swim. Alan caught up to the iguana, but now he'd have to dive in and try to pick the iguana out of the rushing water with his mouth. Without crushing it. That would be some trick.

Here they were, not three minutes into the game, about to lose a player.

Alan had been through this before. Sometimes you *could* win without all the animals you'd started with. Not often.

230   LYRIS

He glanced ahead and picked a spot where he would launch himself into the river. Once there, he crouched, readied himself for the jump, and nearly tripped over his front paws as he tried to stop himself.

He'd seen it as he was about to jump, the falcon up high, diving down. The falcon hit the water and cut through with a splash, then was climbing again into the sky. Alan looked around, not sure if the falcon had managed to pick out the small iguana. He looked up, and there it was, a small green shape wiggling in the falcon's claws.

Alan trotted back along the bank. When he arrived, the falcon was standing on the elephant's head, the iguana next to him.

Impressive. Alan gave the bird a nod of respect. The elephant touched the iguana gently with its trunk-fingers, and made a sound through its trunk.

First disaster averted, Alan thought, and fifty minutes to go. He exhaled slowly.

Bear

At least the bird had some sense. Maybe it had traded brains with the elephant. Sure, that was it. That would explain how the elephant could take a bath in the river with an iguana on its head. Talk about stupid.

The lizard was a lot of trouble. They might be better off losing him, but it was better to hedge your bets and keep all the players alive as long as possible. Joseph had learned that the hard way.

And besides, the daring rescue might earn them style points, if there was anyone in cspace watching the game. Style mattered; you could lose the game and still get style points. Winning was tough enough, so you had to take what you could get.

The jaguar was taking the lead again and Joseph let him. Self-appointed leaders usually got killed first. Leadership, insofar as there was leadership in a game where no one could talk, usually fell to the fastest animal in the bunch. The cat was pretty fast, though Joseph doubted the cat could take him on and win. Too bad it wasn't that kind of game, so he couldn't find out.

Well, he *could* find out, but it would probably cost him the game. A win on this game might bump him up to Level Four. He could smell it in the air.

THE ANIMAL GAME   231

The road had begun to narrow as they walked up to the top of a hill. The banks on either side of the path sloped sharply up, forming a steep ravine. Trees grew at the top of the banks on either side, and stones littered the path. It was an odd transition for the land to make.

So odd, in fact, that Joseph started to get suspicious. That was why he saw the boulder first.

It materialized out of nowhere at the top of the hill. It rocked a little, then started slowly rolling down toward the group.

Joseph gave a loud warning growl.

The jaguar was turning around, obviously trying to figure out what to do. The cat was too slow; Joseph was already in action. He waved the bird toward the elephant with his paw, hoping the bird would take the hint. It did; it swooped, grabbed the lizard, and flew up to the safety of a nearby tree.

Joseph could feel ground shake as the boulder picked up speed. It was a steep climb out of the ravine, but he and the cat were both climbers. They bounded up opposite sides.

That took care of everyone. Except the elephant.

The big beast tried to climb out of the ravine by running up the side and grabbing a bush. The bush pulled out of the ground and the elephant slid back down.

For a split second Joseph considered letting the boulder simply roll into the elephant. The team might do as well without the big, blundering, brainless beast along. There was a solution to saving the elephant, but it wasn't obvious; if he let the elephant die, no one could fault him.

On the other hand, saving the elephant might win him style points.

Joseph leaned on a nearby tree, bending it down toward the elephant, but not close enough to grab. He growled and patted the tree significantly. He half-hoped the elephant wouldn't take the hint, and would just stand there in the path of the boulder. He wondered what it would look like.

The timing was critical, because the tree wouldn't hold the elephant for long. When the boulder was close, he used his weight to put the tree just out of reach of the elephant.

The elephant made a scared, air-filled sound, scrambled up the

232   LYRIS

slope, and grabbed the tree's trunk with its own. The elephant's momentum, coupled with its trunk-hold on the tree, was enough to take it out of the path of the boulder long enough for the boulder to pass by.

Joseph scrambled away from the tree. The elephant let go, sliding noisily back down into the ravine. The tree snapped back.

Growling triumphantly, Joseph shook his paw at the receding boulder.

That should earn him style points, if anything did.

Elephant

Kelly's heart was still pounding from the close call with the boulder, but she felt good. Really good.

She touched the iguana on her forehead. Just to be sure.

When they crossed the river, Kelly had been coming close to the deeper elephant self within. She had stopped thinking in words, as she concentrated on the sights and sounds around her. So fully immersed was she in the experience, that she had forgotten all about the iguana until she got out of the water.

If the bird hadn't saved the iguana, if an animal died because of her again—she couldn't take it. She would have left the game.

But it was the boulder that brought it all home. If the bear hadn't helped her, she would be out of the game now. The bear had smiled so encouragingly at her as it patted the tree, telling her in bear-talk how to grab hold and be safe from the boulder. The bear's final, protective growl at the boulder as it went by made her feel all warm inside.

The bear understood—it was willing to help her, even after she had nearly lost the iguana in the river. The bear had shown her that she had been selfish when she thought of quitting before. They were a team, the bear said in bear-talk, not just a group of players.

Now she understood. She wasn't just an elephant, she was part of something greater. A team. Bear, she decided, was very wise.

They topped the hill and started down the other side. There was something metallic in the meadow below, something that sparkled in the sun. As they got closer, Kelly saw that there was a metal door in the middle of the road.

The falcon sat on top of the door and Kelly walked around the other side.

THE ANIMAL GAME   233

Curious. On one side it was a door, and on the other it was just a hard, door-sized black rectangle.

The metal side of the door had a small keyhole, just below a notched doorknob. She tried the knob, but the door was locked.

The bear growled and pushed her aside. Bear seemed gruff, but she knew better. Bear was really very kind and generous. And her friend. She moved aside as quickly as she could.

The bear threw himself against the door. The falcon took off with cry and landed a distance away. The bear stepped back further and threw himself at the door again, and again, making the metal door ring with the impact, but not making it open.

The jaguar growled and waved a paw at the bear. Jaguar scratched at the door furiously, like a cat with a couch. When he was done, there was no mark on the door.

Kelly snorted and waved the cat and bear aside. Why was it that all some animals could think of was how to use their brute force? Kelly shook her head. She felt around in the grass by the door, searching for a key.

The jaguar caught on, and started sniffing around the door. After a minute the cat chuffed and dug into the ground with its paws, scattering grass and dirt. The cat stepped back. Kelly felt in the hole and brought out a dirt-covered metal key.

Now she knew what her purpose in the game was. *Fingers.*

She wiped the key on the grass to clean it off, and then inserted it in the door lock. She turned the key. The lock clicked.

This was the moment to savor, she decided. She wasn't just a part of the team, but an *essential* part. This was what the game was about. This was why she was meant to be elephant.

Kelly turned the doorknob and pulled the door open. Inside was a torch-lit corridor.

Her elation and smile faded as the jaguar and bear darted around her into the doorway. The falcon grabbed the iguana off her head and flew in after them. They vanished around a corner at the end of the hallway.

Now she had to wait until they came back. She was just too big to get through the doorway.

Falcon

It wasn't hard to fly with the iguana in her claws, at least not for

234   LYRIS

short distances, but it changed her lift and navigation, which was particularly annoying when she was trying to get through halls and doorways.

Well, she'd had enough. With a cry that echoed against the stone walls, she put the iguana down in front of the bear, who could carry the iguana as well as she could. The bear slowed, growled a bit, and then picked up the iguana, cupping the iguana in its paws as they walked.

Susanne shrugged her shoulders and ruffled her wings.

Sunlight from the open door behind them followed them only to the first turn. Then their shadows flickered in torchlight against stone walls.

They came to another door: simple, wooden, and with no keyhole. The bear waved them out of the way, and threw himself heavily against the door, which flew right open. Susanne chuckled as the startled bear sailed into the room.

In the center of the room was a swimming pool, complete with diving board, blue tile, and depth markers, but no water. Instead the pool was completely filled with small, silver baubles.

The bear and the cat looked at each other and then back at the pool. The jaguar gave a short growl. The bear shook his head.

There had to be thousands of baubles in the pool. Could they use any one? Susanne didn't think so. Which one, then?

Thirty minutes to go.

She kicked, flapped aloft, and glided over the pool, looking down on the array of silver balls. What was she looking for? There had to be a clue somewhere.

The cat sniffed at the baubles from the edge of the pool, then put a paw in. The paw began to sink and he pulled back.

Susanne flew back the other way, still looking. Something different, something special. One bauble out of thousands. The puzzle *could* be solved. She just had to keep trying.

On her fifth pass she saw a quick, colored gleam and gave a victory cry. The bauble was half-hidden under several other baubles. She dove with a precision she had practiced hard to get, grabbed the bauble and landed on the side of the pool. She put the bauble on the floor near the jaguar and bear, so that they could see the red "X" on it. They both nodded at her, so she picked up the bauble and flew out the door. Jaguar and bear followed.

THE ANIMAL GAME   235

Once outside, Susanne decided that she didn't want to bet the game on her ability to carry the bauble safely back, so she put the bauble down in front of the elephant, who picked it up and brought it close to one eye. The jaguar and elephant headed back along the game path. The bear put the iguana down near Susanne and followed.

She yelled a protest at the bear. Short distances were fine, but this flight she'd be hundreds of feet up in the air; the iguana would be safer with the bear. She yelled again, but the other three animals were already far down the path and ignored her.

She looked at the iguana. She felt dismay, then sympathy. Poor little guy. She knew what it was like, being dependent on others just to get around. In the Zoo that wasn't a problem for her. Here she could forget the daily frustrations of life in a wheelchair, and enjoy the freedom of being a falcon.

But now the iguana was stuck. It was odd, being on the other side of things.

The iguana blinked at her. She stepped over it, carefully avoiding the delicate green ridges. Maybe she could carry it. She'd have to try.

Still she hesitated.

What, she asked herself, was the worst thing that could possibly happen?

She could drop him, that's what.

But it was only a game. Right? Sometimes you won, sometimes you lost, and sometimes you died. But if you waited for things to fall into your lap, you'd wait a long time.

She took hold of the iguana, resolved not to let go, no matter what, and took to the air.

Iguana

David admired the scenery the Zoo software had constructed. Here in the falcon's grip it was all he could do.

It was better than catching only glimpses of the action through the bear's claws. Oddly, he felt more secure in the falcon's claws; David half-expected the bear to crush him or drop him. And it had been no picnic, clinging to the elephant's head, hoping that the moving mountain would stay under him.

236   LYRIS

But he finally had a clue to the game puzzle. The baubles in the swimming pool, the falcon flying back and forth, grabbing the bauble marked with the red "X." The bauble was the game's win condition.

A win would be nice. In the two weeks he'd been playing, his team hadn't won once.

And that made him suspicious. Would the game masters tilt the odds in his favor to give him a win and maybe sway his decision to take the job? Sure, he'd like to see a winning game, but if it wasn't fairly won, well...

He smirked at his own internal struggle. Here he was, one of the original Zoo game masters, worrying about whether he would win the game fairly.

Sure, he decided, he'd take an easy win just to see what happened, but he would think of it as a demo. And while it was flattering to think of his old partners wanting him back enough to stack the deck in his favor, it just wasn't *right*.

The falcon dropped down from the sky and David's stomach flip-flopped. The bird left him in front of the bear again, who growled before picking him up.

They were all gathered around the pedestal. The elephant put the bauble on top and took a few steps back.

This was it. Win time.

The bauble began to glow. It turned orange, then red, then white, and a high-pitched sound filled the air. There was a sudden, audible *crack* as the bauble fell apart into pieces. The pieces glowed and darkened, then crumbled into a red, pollen-fine dust that blew away in the breeze.

The animals exchanged wide-eyed looks.

David felt disappointment mixed with relief. The win hadn't been easy, after all.

It was the wrong bauble. Too bad. Somewhere back in the swimming pool, he guessed, was the *right* bauble. The "X" had clearly been a decoy. He wondered what else might distinguish one bauble from the rest.

And then he had it.

He started thrashing his tail against the bear's paw to get its attention.

THE ANIMAL GAME 237

Fifteen minutes left. Not enough time. It couldn't possibly be enough time.

Falcon

Susanne saw the iguana wriggling around in the bear's paw, which seemed like a good way to get dropped. Not that it mattered now; they'd lost the game.

They had fifteen minutes left. She might as well say her stop words and end the game instead of waiting for the clock to run out.

The iguana was still wriggling. Stupid lizard. Couldn't he see that he was just being difficult now that they'd lost? The game was over and—

Oh.

Maybe the iguana had an idea. She looked around. They were all just standing there, looking dazed. All but the iguana.

Well, if the iguana had something, what did they have to lose? They needed the right bauble, Susanne reasoned. There was only one place to get another bauble.

Susanne kicked off the elephant's head, from where she had watched the bauble break apart. She flapped aloft and dove, grabbing the iguana out of the bear's paw before the bear could react.

She was getting good at that particular move.

Below, the bear growled loudly at her, shaking his paw skyward. She chuckled. Not her fault that he was ground-locked. And not paying attention.

The land went by below, as she gripped the iguana, tightly, but not too tightly. She flew as fast as she could, thinking of herself as a streamlined bullet of beak and feathers. And iguana.

Elephant

Kelly thought frantically. She had put the bauble on the pedestal— that was right, wasn't it?—and the bauble had turned red and self-destructed. And then the bird grabbed the lizard and started flying back up the path.

What had she done wrong? And why were they going back?

The jaguar was motioning with his head, at Kelly and the bear, and then he took off at a dead run back up the path. Kelly and the bear followed.

238 LYRIS

She went over it one more time. She had put the bauble on the pedestal. And it had blown up. She must have done something wrong. She felt terrible. She thought she was doing so well. Had she missed something? Something a real elephant would have seen?

She'd made them lose, somehow. But if they'd already lost, why were they going back?

Could there be another bauble, somewhere inside the steel door?

That had to be it; there was another bauble, the right bauble, and now they were going back to get it.

She snorted. That was silly; they should have brought both baubles out with them the first time. If *she* had been with them, she would have done it herself.

They swam across the river and loped up the incline. When they arrived at the door, the big cat and the bear ran in, leaving her behind again.

Next time she would be a horse. Or maybe a cheetah. Anything that would fit through that damned door.

And now they were down to ten minutes.

Bear

Joseph had suspected it was too good to be true, finding the right bauble so early in the game, and it was.

Of course, he wasn't entirely without blame. "Mirrored perfection" was an obvious hint that didn't include a bauble with markings. He'd missed that.

He was still growling at the bird, who wisely stayed out of his way. He would rip the bird apart if he could get close enough. You gave a warning cry before you flew that close to another animal. It was pure stupidity to surprise someone on your side. Especially someone with claws.

He had picked up the iguana so that the lizard could see the bauble on top of the pedestal, an act of generosity toward a useless player. What did he get for it? A dive-bombing falcon in his face. Next time he wouldn't bother.

He watched the bird as it flew back and forth over the pool, its eyes on the iguana. The iguana was scampering across the pool of silver baubles. It was light enough not to sink down between the baubles. The iguana was so small that each bauble was nearly as large as its head.

THE ANIMAL GAME   239

This was absurd. They would do as well if they picked up as many of the baubles as they could carry and took them back to the pedestal before the clock ran out. He could carry a few in his paws and some in his mouth, if he remembered not to swallow.

He moved toward the edge of the pool. The jaguar growled at him and blocked his path. He growled back.

If the stupid cat didn't let him past, there was no question of them winning. And to hell with style points.

He took a swipe at the jaguar. The cat backed to the edge of the pool, its ears flat. It growled again and shook its head, a clear message that the jaguar didn't want to fight.

Joseph didn't care. He took another step forward.

Iguana

There was just no way David could touch all the baubles. Even if the pool was only a foot deep, he would still miss most of them. There were just too many.

But this was clearly the trick, this was what the iguana was supposed to do to, so it should be possible, even if it were unlikely.

The metallic balls shifted a little under him as he walked across. He tried to touch as many as he could. It had to be here somewhere.

Then he found it. He felt the heat against his stomach, a sharp contrast to the coolness of all the other metal balls he had touched.

Iguanas were good at identifying subtle temperature differences. As cold-blooded animals, they had to be.

He heard the jaguar growl somewhere behind him and an answering snarl from the bear.

He nosed the ball he had identified, hoping the falcon was watching, hoping it would understand.

Falcon

Susanne couldn't believe it. Here they were, with only seven minutes to win the game, and the cat and the bear were squaring off with each other.

They were worse than schoolyard brats. If they wanted *that* kind of game, there were plenty around. They shouldn't screw up everyone else's game at the same time.

240   LYRIS

She inhaled deeply, and let out the loudest, most piercing cry she could. The bear and the cat looked up at her, their spat momentarily interrupted.

The iguana touched its nose against one of the silver balls. Then it did it again.

That was it, then. She didn't know how he knew, but it was their last, best chance.

She dove for the ball, grabbed it in her claws without touching the iguana, and flew out through the hallway and the steel door. She dropped the bauble on the ground by the elephant, flew back in, and retrieved the iguana from the pool. The cat and the bear followed behind, their fight apparently less interesting than the possibility that they might win with *this* bauble.

This time there was no question of her flying back with the iguana. No one else could make it in time. She dropped the iguana, picked up the bauble, and took to the skies. The ground-locked animals were running full speed along the game path below her. She gave it all she had now, concentrating on every wing stroke, looking forward to the clearing, the pedestal, and a possible victory.

She just hoped there was enough time.

Jaguar

The game clock ticked over to all zeros as Alan came into the clearing. He had passed the bear and the elephant some time ago. He hoped one of them had remembered to bring the iguana.

The falcon sat on the edge of the pedestal, staring at the silver ball.

The bauble glowed white, like a light bulb. The sound of chimes, or bells, filled the air around them.

It was a sound Alan knew. He had heard it only a few times before.

Alan threw his head back and gave his victory whoop, which came out as a loud roar. The falcon must have been startled—it took to the air and scolded him.

The bear and elephant arrived, the iguana securely wrapped in the elephant's coiled trunk. The five of them gathered around the pedestal.

Alan had some idea of what would happen next, but it varied

THE ANIMAL GAME 241

from game to game. The first time he had won, roses and stars had fallen down on the animals from the sky, while dozens of small monkeys danced around them to the sound of triumphant horns. When the ground was covered with roses, the game landscape had faded and Alan had found himself back in his dressing room. The next time Alan won, a single monkey came out and gave them each a wreath of violet roses.

Alan wondered if the dancing monkeys were constructs or game masters.

A single monkey walked out of the trees toward them. It held a dozen purple roses in one arm.

The monkey stopped in front of the elephant, who had put the lizard down nearby. The monkey held out a rose to the elephant, who waved its trunk and then took the flower delicately in its trunk-fingers.

"Good job," the monkey said to the elephant.

Alan blinked, stunned. Spoken words? In the Zoo? After scores of games, Alan had stopped even hoping.

But if they could *talk* to each other—

The elephant made a short sound, like the clearing of a water-logged trumpet. Then the elephant slowly faded. Alan saw the rest of the clearing through the elephant before the elephant vanished completely.

The monkey walked to the bear and held out another rose.

"Nice work," the monkey said.

The bear gave a loud growl, shook its paws above its head, and took the rose between two large paws. The bear faded and disappeared.

The monkey went to the falcon and offered it a rose. The falcon took the flower in its beak.

"Impressive," the monkey said to the bird. Alan nodded his agreement.

And then there was only Alan and the iguana.

"Carry on," the monkey said to Alan, with a smile and a rose. Alan nodded, and bent his head to take the offered rose between his teeth.

As the clearing began to fade around him, Alan noticed that the monkey was offering the remaining eight roses to the iguana, who was nodding, as if in answer to a silent question.

All those roses, just for the iguana? But why?
Another puzzle.
Alan chuckled.

While still using her fingers to add, Sonia Orin Lyris acquired a B.S. in Computer Science from Cal State, San Francisco in 1984. She first entered cyberspace via a state-wide mainframe network with other cybernaughts (who thought they were just students using a chat program). She was hooked. Soon she was hacking user interfaces and expert systems for an artificial intelligence company in Silicon Valley. One of her first projects was the user interface for a space station electrical system modeling and fault diagnosis prototype.

Tired of building prototypes for the military-industrial complex, she went to work building system software for other people building prototypes for the military-industrial complex. Her fascination with UI design and AI soon brought her into the virtual reality community. In her spare time she studied cyberspace and virtual reality, attended conferences, and started writing about it.

Since 1991 she has been writing full time. Her nonfiction includes articles on "The Virtual Village on the Edge of Cyberspace" and "Crime and Punishment in Cyberspace." Her first short story, "Eyes of the Beholder," appeared in *Midnight Zoo*. A cyberspace novelette, "A Hand in the Mirror," is slated for *Asimov's,* and a short story, "Motherhood," will appear in *Pulphouse*. Sonia is a graduate of Clarion West, 1992.

A denizen of the modern cyberspaces on USENET and GEnie, Sonia finds time for other interests including sculpting, martial arts, singing, keeping cats, and fine bittersweet chocolate.

A few years ago, "All Things Considered" on National Public Radio introduced a new literary form: "micro-fiction," complete stories in only 100 words. I was enchanted and challenged. Here is my first work of micro-fiction, which only took eleven rewrites. To say more would seem excessive. [Fifty words of introduction!]

LARRY CONSTANTINE
Mint, Uncirculated

NO ONE SAW.

Eddie, cresting the dune, crabcake in one fist, change in the other, heard the doughy plop. Fleeing the collapsing ship, a woman with tangerine skin reached toward him. Unthinking, he offered the crabcake. It powdered into sparkling dust, swirling toward her hand, vanishing. She pointed. He opened his hand and icy flame washed the quarter, melting it into a coppery pool that frosted over with her likeness.

In his mind, her words: *For you.*

She ran, fading, leaving deep cobalt afterimages.

The kids would never believe him. Not even Joey.

But he knew he would never show them the coin.

What can be said about Larry Constantine that has not already been said? He cooks great Mexican meals and makes an almost unimaginable mess in the process.

Science fiction, on film and in print, has had much to say about the fate of the human cog in the machinery of the modern world. Automation. Alienation. Perhaps we do not yet know the meaning of the words. I told the author of this next piece that I wasn't even certain it was a story; I was only certain I wanted it in the anthology. Like origami, it is a work of exquisite precision that seeks meaning on a small scale.

ANTHONY TAYLOR
Folded Like a Paper Dove

THE POLICE FOUND him dead in his apartment, hanging from a light fixture, suicide cord wrapped around his neck. There was no note, nothing to say why he did it, no one really to wonder why; that might be the reason. His face was ugly and purple with blood; I would have preferred it if he had slashed his wrists.

He was still warm when they got to him; Body let them know he was dead as soon as it happened. Funny, though, it didn't call them in time to stop him.

Even now the few people who knew him try to reason it out. What could have gotten into him, we ask each other, what problem was so big? Some of us are resigned to never knowing, but at least one is still investigating.

I can't say I added to his problems, but I can't say I helped relieve them, either. He was a strange kid, introverted, bright, but somehow lost in his loneliness. There were stories going around about him—about how his gay lover ran off with another man or somesuch, about how he belonged to a peyote-eating baby-killing satanic cult, about his abusive father putting his younger sister in the hospital—but these were only rumors. His father died when Halivand (Li, we called him, because of his almost-oriental eyes) was four, he never had a sister, he was as straight as they come, and the boy didn't know what dope smelled like. So much for rumors.

244

FOLDED LIKE A PAPER DOVE 245

Let me tell you what I know about him:

He was an efficient worker. His only responsibility was keeping Body alive, and he handled it well. The lungs pumped air to four hundred thousand people, the eyes watched as people worked, traveled, talked, slept, shit, had sex. The mouth regurgitated food so people could eat. The veins carried food, water, fertilizer, goods, people, whatever. If anything went anywhere, Body carried them, and if Body hurt, Li took care of it.

Really, Body mostly cared for itself, but sometimes a person was still needed, sometimes—a bright person, someone who can handle tough problems creatively. Li was bright.

I only knew Li passingly, just an associate. We worked together. I was a programmer for Mind; I did for Mind what Li did for Body. We worked out of the same building, the State Office Complex, 1114 Spargo. We often met in the lounge during slack time, which was actually most of the time. Like I said, Body took care of itself. Usually he was busy with paper, folding it into shapes, animals mostly; animals with long necks, animals with wings, some long and thin, others short and fat, four legs, two legs, one leg. They were delicate things, like the fingers that folded them, fragile: fragile wings for the birds and the bugs, fragile legs for the others. You could crush them easily, just take them in your hands and squeeze.

Li was proud of his paper folding. I pressed him once for a reason he did it. "Li," and he looked at me, "why do you do that?" I asked, waving at the bug he was creating, tiny folds on tiny wings, antennae, mandibles. He called it a cicada.

Without stopping, he answered. "Don't you ever feel lost here?" He was quiet for a moment. He looked down again at his model so all I could see was his black black hair, and I didn't reply. "I mean, Body, Mind, everything machine. Automatic this, automatic that. Isn't there any beauty anymore?"

He was from earth.

Just so any flatlanders don't get the wrong idea, we do have our artists here. There's a cultural revolution going on above your heads while you squabble among yourselves, scratch your flea-bites, cuss your neighbors, starve to death, shoot one another; a revolution sometimes compared to the old renaissance, with etched stone and statues, paintings, music... But people are entitled to an opinion, and Li had his.

246 TAYLOR

Here it is: "Look around you. What song gets the most airtime? Tracking the Sun. Go down to the gallery, and you'll see mountains of moving metal, lights flashing, things whirling, and god! you could go crazy! Damnit! We used to be creative, we used to think for ourselves, we used to build for ourselves. Now we sit back in our cubbies and listen to soothe or just watch the tube and get fat." He jumped to his feet, coming off the floor for an instant like some stupid newbee, and tore the cicada in half. "Just like that, poof! and it's gone."

I wasn't sure what "it" was at first. In fact, I'm not sure even now, but I do know it has something to do with idea, creativity, something that has nothing to do at all with beauty, just imagination. Li had strange ideas.

The disbelief must have shown on my face, it must have. He straightened himself, pulled at his clothing, wiped his forehead, other anal-retentive motions like that, then sat down again. "Oh, it wasn't going right," he said, misinterpreting my expression as disbelief for his action, tearing the cicada; really I was amazed that quiet Li could hold so much emotion and conviction; mild, honest, boring Li. "Just too complicated, I guess. Too many folds through too much paper." He started again to build his cicada, and four days later he would never be able to finish it.

That was all he ever said about the folding. I understood after that it was an act of anger, defiance, and not soothing at all. He folded lovingly, yes, but there was always the tension, too, the inability to not fold. His animals were always constructed with a little frustration.

Maybe a little hatred.

Mind has only addressed me directly twice. Sure, it gives me orders and I often hear its voice, but it always treats me like another automaton, another robot. It has never called me by name.

Except...

Once I came in to work, looked over the hards from the night before, dug around for things to do. After the first hour, I wandered into the lounge and waited for Li to show up. We'd been discussing the contributions of Lunar philosophers to the body of human knowledge as a whole. Li's opinion, phrased in his Earthside-American way, was, "They don't amount to shit." I'd reread my Shiling-

FOLDED LIKE A PAPER DOVE   247

ton after getting back to my dorm the night before and was ready to refute him. And I waited.

I noticed an elephant on the table. I recognized it as an elephant by the trunk and the tusks. The head was the only completed part of the model; the body was there, but needed to be fleshed out. It looked almost exactly like the elephant some entertainment group brought up from Earth once. They pumped more resources into getting it flown up than they ever made back; they'd hoped to keep it on display, "The largest land animal on earth, now on the moon!", but the poor beast died. It beat itself to death against the ceiling and walls of its display. It could never get used to the gravity.

That's how I recognized the model.

I was just about to pick the elephant up when something amazing happened. "Vernon," Mind said, "could you please go to Jolson Tunnel? Please walk to the end of Little G from there."

This was the first time Mind had ever addressed me by my name. It was also the first time, as well as I remember, Mind had ever said "please." To anyone. Amazing.

I did exactly what Mind had asked me to do. Asked. Amazing.

I tubed down to Jolson, then walked past the little open plaza shops that seem to have taken over just about all of the underside of town. Someone once told me you could get anything, anything at all, at one of the tables in Jolson Tunnel. Walking casually through the stalls, I believed her. Some sold clothes, some sold meats from endangered animals, some could custom make drugs right at the table. I think you can even buy little boys or girls if that's your taste, but I can't prove it. Neither can the police.

In case you've never been to Spargo, Jolson Tunnel has been carved from dead rock. Unlike the volcanic tunnels near the surface of Spargo, Jolson was totally man-made. In fact, 'g' Tunnel, where Mind had sent me, was still under construction. At least, it would be under construction if the city could afford more expansion. Mind predicts it will be at least another year before the city is solvent again and construction can start back up.

This gives Jolson a very polished, tooled feel that I'm particularly fond of. In spite of my urging curiosity, I slowed and enjoyed the atmosphere.

The crowd was rather thick, so I almost walked past 'g' Tunnel. I

248 TAYLOR

caught a glimpse of a construction lock, just big enough for three men to walk in together, with a stenciled *g*.

Mind opened the outer door and let me in the lock, then opened the inner door into the tunnel. There was nothing there; the tunnel was only about four meters wide, nowhere near large enough yet to do anything. During the second phase of construction, they would expand it out to about twenty meters. It was well lit, though, with panels along the curved ceiling. I walked quietly down the empty corridor, wondering when I would get more instruction.

I never did. I didn't need any.

I heard him before I saw him; nice quiet shy Li was hoarse from yelling, but still very loud. I couldn't tell what he was shouting. Feeling like a voyeur, I flattened against the wall and shuffled up to a side tunnel and peeked around the corner. He was there.

He was pounding the walls with his fists, turning around and around to strike both walls, almost slamming his whole body against the cold smooth rock. Tears would make lenses in his eyes until he blinked them out, then they would slowly creep down his face and slip off every time he'd attack a wall. I could finally hear what he was shouting.

"I hate you," he screamed over and over, keeping rhythm with the pounding of his fists, "I hate you, I hate you, I hate you..."

I don't know why I was sent there. Mind had to know what Li was doing; did it think I could do something for him? Did it think I could see Li's suicide coming, maybe stop him?

Mind, too, is strange.

Sometimes I suspect it has a sick sense of humor.

The second time Mind addressed me directly it wasn't a request, it was a command. I was home then, in my room, listening to some video show. I had the picture turned off. There was a laugh track.

"Vernon," Mind said, "go to Li's dorm. Now." It was polite in tone. You know the words. I went. It took me five minutes to get there.

The police were there when I arrived. He'd been dead about ten minutes, they said.

It could have told me fifteen minutes earlier. You hear that, Mind? You could have told me earlier!

They took his body away, like I said, face all twisted and purple. They came for his things, but I don't think they'll miss a few little animals. I wish he'd have finished the cicada, but I guess he never got it quite right. Too many little appendages or something: sometimes I think that's what killed him, too many folds, too complicated a pattern. Body and Mind know what I took, but they'll never tell. Body just hums as the lungs pump air and the veins move people, and Mind is too busy planning next week's Festival, or thinking about background cosmic radiation, or maybe arbitrating peasant cases on land disputes or whatever it is people fight about these days. I really don't care anymore.

I visited the gallery recently, the one in Mare Imbrium. There were hundreds of shiny stainless-steel constructions, blinking lights, things. There were more Lunarscape paintings than darkside has craters. They played soothe in the background. Altogether uninspiring. Spiritless. As soon as I returned to Spargo, I wandered down to Jolson again. I even went to Li's spot in 'g' Tunnel. I think I'll ask Mind to name it after him when it's finished, Halivand Tunnel. I'll put a plaque there where he attacked the moon: "Li's Anger Spot," it will say, or "Li's Anguish Spot." I don't know which it is.

I've never seen a giraffe, but Li folded one. Birds all look alike to me, but I really think this one here is a dove.

Anthony Taylor is a network manager and systems programmer at the University of Alaska, Fairbanks, where he manages ElmerNet, networking eleven public access terminals to sixteen databases spanning forty-two CD-ROMs. His next major task is to make ElmerNet available over Internet. He has been programming computers since the advent of the Apple II, when he was twelve years old. "Hurrah for Applesoft BASIC," he says.

Coincidentally, he began writing fiction at about the same time he started writing programs, first science fiction and fantasy, then later diversifying into mystery, mainstream fiction, and poetry that he describes as "really bad." He also served a brief stint as assistant editor of a local small-press magazine, *The Melting Pot*. ("May it rest in peace.") This is his first professional science fiction sale.

Psychologist-philosopher Sheldon Kopp tells us that progress is an illusion; all solutions breed new problems. Whatever advances we make in the bit-bashing power of computers are matched by the crushing complexity of the problems we try to solve with them and by the depth of the dilemmas we create in the process. Who is hero, who the problem in this shuffle of history? It's hard for the participants to know. Even as we do battle with famine and ecological crisis, homelessness and dehumanizing warfare, and all the myriad disasters of our own making, ordinary life goes on. We eat, we sleep, and we struggle to understand each other, as in this story by Norm Hartman, a possible glimpse into the everyday life of tomorrow's heroes.

NORM HARTMAN
Project Lucifer

"THE DEADLINE'S TOO close," I snarled. "I don't have the time to listen to your inane babbling..."

"Time is just what keeps everything from happening at once." Ginger arose, laughing, from the pool-side lounge. Her skin, a brighter green than even her minuscule bikini, faded to aqua, then almost to pink as she stretched lazily and moved deeper into the shade of the cabana. Outside of our shaded area, the grass and trees glistened under a hard blue sky. "You're the one who taught me that, remember?"

"Very funny. This could kill all of us," I snarled at her, but Ginny didn't even have sense enough to look worried. She'd been a bubblehead when I met her, and she hadn't gotten any smarter in all the years we'd been married. Not even a nanorejuve could help with the way she thinks. "Heinlein picked the wrong decade; this is going to be the real 'Year of the Jackpot' if Project Lucifer doesn't work out."

"Pooh!" She ruffled what was left of my hair. Somehow, the nanorooters hadn't done much for me in that respect. Not yet,

PROJECT LUCIFER 251

anyway. Oh, well. Maybe next year's model would do the job. Give them time. Time! That nasty word again.

"Admit it, Jared. You're just a natural worrier," she continued. "The world has never..."

"...Has never come to an end," I parroted the phrase along with her, overriding her softer voice. "Therefore, it never will come to an end. That's bullshit, and we both know it!"

Ginny shrugged her delectable shoulders, refusing to argue. Only one of her less endearing traits. Taking a sip of my sugared juice, she turned back toward the pool and the filtered sunlight. Her color shifted back through a kaleidoscope of shades, and as she dove into the cool blue waters of the pool she was once again a brilliant green.

I stayed in the deep shade, content to remain my natural color since I wasn't really hungry. The nanobots might have given us the ability to chew leaves and soak up sunshine, cutting way down on Earth's ecoloading from too many bodies, but natural food was still available, and Ginny and I could easily afford it. People had panicked when they'd suddenly turned green, but then they'd realized how much that one change to their bodies had helped the ecology. The famines were at an end, for a few years at least, now that we could eat almost anything organic. Then had come the second round of riots when they realized that the same controlled mutation by the nanobots had cut the fertility of the race down to a manageable level. The various GodGurus had thrown a whole series of shit fits, but the people would learn to live with that aspect of the nanotech revolution, too. Mankind would eventually adapt, if only I could buy them the time.

Nanorooters to regenerate our failing, aging bodies. Nanobots to rebuild those bodies and adapt us to shrinking diets. Thousands of nanodevices, protecting us from a whole range of disasters that ranged from the population explosion to rising UV levels. Nanoassemblers to build for us, and nanocomputers to do our thinking. No, not thinking. Computing, calculating, pragmatic designing, but not thinking. The energy densities required to make nanosentience possible were still too high. Even with the fantastic construction materials made possible by molecular technology, a nanosentience would cook itself into a puddle of slag as soon as it

252   HARTMAN

was turned on. The crabapple-sized CPU of my Mac VII had to have a steady stream of water running through it to keep it from burning up. A nuisance, though it helped to keep our pool warm in cold weather.

Not even the latest nanobots could do everything. They could do almost nothing about the worst problem to face us, the continuing rapid breakdown of the ozone layer. All that we had accomplished with them so far was to change our melanin cells to chloroplasts, seeding our skins with chlorophyll to convert some of the too-plentiful ultraviolet into food energy, while other nanobots migrated to the outer layers of plants and animals to shield them from too much UV. We still survived, but in today's hard sunlight people and animals were bright green, and plants glittered with a metallic luster.

Crushing back my anger at Ginny's frivolous attitude, I picked up my stylus and turned back to the sketch pad of my Mac VII. The image on the holographic wall screen moved and turned, growing into a crystal bird with outstretched diaphanous wings. I was damned proud of that design! I changed its shape, subtly lengthening and rounding it to accommodate the elements I added to its interior. The wings spread wider, thinning until they resembled something out of an El Greco painting. I made a few more slight changes, but erased them when they didn't add anything to the efficiency of my design. Finally satisfied, I pressed the tip of my stylus against a corner of the pad. The bird changed color, becoming silver on the bottom, turning to inky black on its upper surfaces.

"Proceed with the simulation," I commanded, marginally aware that Ginny, fading now to a delicate emerald as she stood at the edge of the cabana's deeper shadow, had come to peer over my shoulder. The image on the screen receded, lifting and wheeling until it seemed to hover high above the computer's point of view. The wings shifted and beat, lifting the crystal bird ever higher as it reached for the fringes of the atmosphere. Night came and the bird rested, drifting slowly downward, gliding on unmoving pinions. Sunlight, and the wings moved once more.

When it could climb no higher, the bird changed. Still absorbing the sunlight, it began making different use of the radiant energy. Its mouth opened into a trumpetlike scoop, and the thin air

PROJECT LUCIFER   253

streamed through the organs of its body and out beneath the tail. Oxygen and nitrogen were breathed in; nitrogen and ozone breathed out. Stray molecules of fluorocarbons were filtered out of the airstream and stored, made harmless. This was the heart of Project Lucifer, a valiant attempt to patch the holes in Earth's ozone layer. It was facetiously named for Lucifer, the Light-Bearer; an attempt by mere mortals to stem the flood of unbearable light.

Night came, and day, and night again in an almost endless cycle until at last something went wrong, a carbyne thread snapping from too many cosmic rays, too prolonged a strain. The tip of one wing folded into an unstable configuration, and pieces of my crystal bird spun slowly back to earth.

"How...how long?"

The Mac's tenor voice answered Ginny's question: "137 DAYS—15 HOURS—TWENTY-TWO MINUTES. NINETY-THREE PERCENT OF ACCEPTABLE MINIMUM."

"Ninety-three percent of the one hundred and forty-eight days we have to have!" I threw down my stylus. "Seven percent more, just seven percent!"

"Poor Jared." Her fingers wove through my hair, massaging the back of my neck in the familiar way that I loved. Loved and hated. "Only seven percent away from the solution to saving the world. Oh well, the day before yesterday it was nine percent. Come on, Jarry-boy. Time to stop working for the day. You've put in your four hours for good old NanoSoft Corporation, and then some. It's nearly time for us to go."

"Go?" I shook my head, still intent on the columns of figures that marched across the screen. "Go where?"

"Jared! Turn that stupid thing off. You don't even remember, do you? You promised you'd take me to Frascatti's for dinner. Now, turn that silly damned machine off and go get dressed."

I clicked on SAVE and BACKUP. The holographic screen on the wall cleared, fading to a painting of fields and trees under a softly clouded sky. I didn't remember making the reservation, but I was too beat to argue. "All right, Frascatti's it is. Twenty minutes?"

Our sleek black Celica coupe took the curves easily as we headed west on I-90, its electric motors almost silent as its skin drank power from the sunlight. The sun was nearing the horizon, glaring

254 HARTMAN

down out of a sky that was too clear, too blue. Along the sides of the road the plants were losing their metallic sheen as the level of UV dropped. In the distance, Seattle's slender towers stood like battlements, kilometers-high fingers holding onto the sunset's glow, keeping back the darkness for a few more minutes. Not that they would prevail for long; the cities were finally doomed. Doomed by the same forces that had brought them into being, the forces of growth and commerce. Those same needs that had drawn people together in such unwieldy masses were now operating to drive them farther apart. Nobody needed, nobody wanted to live cheek-to-jowl with a thousand thousand neighbors, not when nanoassemblers could build whatever was needed from rocks and soil, from air and local vegetation. Not when workers could toil at their jobs without leaving the sanctuary of their shielded nests.

The food at Frascatti's was superb, as always: delicate salads, followed by meaty textured protein in a myriad of forms. Pale wines complemented each course, and a hidden instrumental group wove a background of melodies in the candlelight. For a few precious moments I was able to lay down the burden of Project Lucifer, forget the coming Death.

"Jared, why isn't ninety-three percent good enough?"

I winced as Ginny's question brought me back to sanity, landing in the real world with a resounding thud!

"You would have to ask." I gulped the remains of my glass of wine, holding it out for the mechanical steward to refill, but suddenly the taste was flat. "You do realize that the ozone layer is failing, don't you? That we'll all be dead if nothing is done to repair it?"

"Of course I do. I'm not stupid, you know!"

That was the problem. She wasn't stupid. Frivolous, bubble-headed, not too interested in how the world survived, but not stupid. She had a decent enough brain, if only she would use it. I was the plodder, she was the butterfly.

"My birds are too expensive to build," I explained. "Their production, even using nanoassemblers, will take more resources and energy than we can spare if we are to survive long enough for them to do their work. The big computers at NanoSoft's Redmond headquarters have calculated how much each bird must do, how long it

PROJECT LUCIFER 255

has to last to do the job efficiently. There are several hundred of us, all working on this one project, but so far my birds are way ahead of our next best bet."

She rested her chin in her hand, one elbow propped on the table as she studied my face in the candlelight. Her eyes were a deep, mysterious green as she watched me, deep in thought. For a moment she was the girl I had married, and deep-buried emotions urged me to hold her close. Project Lucifer was failing! I should take her home and make hot, urgent love with her for as long as the world lasted...

"Yes, let's go home." Reading my unspoken thoughts, she rose to her feet, her fetchingly draped body drawing me after her with a magic that I had never learned to resist. "In the morning you'll find a way to beat this thing."

Another morning, and another, and more mornings after that... The curve of my progress chart flattened inexorably, never quite reaching its ultimate goal.

"You're losing it," Ginny taunted. The dome that shielded our dwelling and its pool had darkened even further with the passing of days, cutting out more and more of the harsh sunlight as the ozone layer dwindled away to nothing. Even in the artificial gloom, Ginny's smooth skin glowed a deep and flawless green. Outside the dome, the plants that clothed the hillsides were a tangle of silvery metal, with only a hint of green showing through to prove that they still survived.

"Ninety-six point seventy-five percent." The stylus dropped from my tired fingers as I leaned back in my chair. "I haven't gained a tenth of a percent in days. Even diamond fibers break, sooner or later."

"Poor Jared, your bird just won't fly. It doesn't even look much like a bird any more." Ginny studied the screen where my latest design effort spread itself in futile grandeur. "More like the ghost of a low-gravity vampire bat. Why did you choose a bird shape to start with, anyway? Couldn't you have found something more efficient?"

"That's a switch." My laugh sounded forced, even to me. "Aren't you the one who always says that natural forms are the best? That

256   HARTMAN

if it's going to fly, it should look like a bird? How come you're changing your mind, all of a sudden?"

"Pretty is no good, if your bird won't fly," She studied the screen intently, her fingers moving as though to trace the lines that it displayed. "Where does it keep breaking?"

"Anywhere," I grumbled. "Anywhere and everywhere. If I make it stronger in one place, that part is too heavy for the rest and it breaks some place else. I've managed to save a little more weight by making the wings rigid, propelling my bird with an electrostatic jet. That's what gave me that last three-tenths of a percent, but now it's so fragile that nearly ten percent of my birds never make it out of the turbulence of the lower atmosphere."

"The wings are too thin," she decided. "You've built a flying Twiggy."

"Thinner means lighter. Longer, narrower wings are more efficient. The atmosphere converters have to be placed somewhere, even if that concentrates all of the weight in the body." I was talking to myself, even more than to her, by now.

"Then why don't you make the wings thicker, so that you can put your machines inside of them? Why even have a body?"

I barely heard her nonsense, my mind racing. I had caught the glimmering of an idea, my tired mind picking it out of nowhere. My fingers danced over the keyboard, calling up ancient records from back near the beginning of the age of flight, following half-forgotten data trails. Glimpses of long-ago aircraft flashed across the screen, and at last I had it!

YB-49
FLYING WING
Northrop Corporation

YB-49 FLYING WING BOMBER—(1947)—The YB-49 Flying Wing...successor to the propellor-driven YB-35...all-metal, tailless bombardment type aircraft...true Flying Wing design...Ultimate in efficiency...Maximum weight loaded, 96.8 tonnes...Wingspan 52 meters...Maximum speed 800 kilometers/hr plus...

The graphic sequence that accompanied the text was taken from the old George Pal version of *War of the Worlds*, one of my grandfather's favorite movies. The majestic silvery image seemed to hang

PROJECT LUCIFER 257

in midair, soaring just behind the holographic screen. It was a symphony of clean lines, resembling nothing quite so much as a straight-edged Australian boomerang. A V-shaped airfoil, with no body or tail surfaces to break the flow of air. The accompanying text stated that stability was gained by sweeping the wing back to form a broad arrow head, so that the craft would hold a steady course. Two banks of four jet engines were buried within the wing, the only protrusions tiny fins that stabilized the air flow around their exhaust nozzles.

Ginny's sigh of "How beautiful!" was lost in my concentration as I captured the image, changing it to conform to my design's needs. The lines on my screen stretched and flowed, changing to a more slender pattern. Hours later, with fingers that trembled with fatigue and excitement, I laid down my stylus.

"Proceed with the simulation." Obedient to the familiar command, the scene changed to a meticulous copy of the real world. Launched from a narrow track, the shimmering device lifted and soared. No need, anymore, for wings that beat, for propellors that thrashed madly at the air. Electric charges moved ionized molecules past static screens, and the thrust of the moving air pushed my creation ever higher. When at last it was as high as it could go, it began its work. Three oxygen molecules were combined to form two of ozone, and molecules containing fluorine, bromine, and chlorine were captured and enchained. Night and day passed in accelerated sequence, and still my creation hung at the outermost edge of the stratosphere. It was lighter, yet far stronger, than anything I had ever achieved before.

When at last the nanoconverters could cram no more poison molecules into its storage chambers, the machine's black upper surfaces faded to silver and it glided gently back to Earth. Delivering its deadly cargo to one of many central storage points, it was refurbished and launched once more.

"MINIMUM LIFE EXPECTANCY: TWO HUNDRED AND FORTY PERCENT OF OPTIMUM. MAXIMUM LIFE EXPECTANCY: CANNOT BE CALCULATED WITH PRESENT DATA."

BACKUP. SAVE. I pressed the point of my stylus to the proper spots on my pad, sending the results of my labors to storage, then keyed in a triumphant message to my team leader.

"Acknowledged!" The answer glowed from my screen. "Project Lucifer completed within acceptable time frame."

The message was followed by a stream of data that fed smoothly into my data bank. Words and numbers that told of my promotion and salary upgrade, closing with a more personal message from the project leader:

"Good work, Jared. Why don't you take your lovely wife for a week's vacation at Club Kodiak? NanoSoft will pick up the tab. AEH."

"I think I'll just do that, Al. See you in a week or ten days. JJH."

"I did it!" I grabbed Ginny, twirling her around and around until we tripped over the tile edging and fell into the pool. Gasping for air, I sent sheets of water hurtling in all directions. "I did it! I did it! I DID IT!"

"You certainly did!" her green eyes sparkled as she sent splashes of water back at me. "With a little help, of course."

"Huh?" What was she talking about? Oh, well. She was beautiful, and fun to be with, but I never did really understand her.

Although originally a registered land surveyor, Norm Hartman first learned to program in FORTRAN, writing several major programs while working for a power company in the sixties. After a serious construction accident in 1979, he went back to college while still on crutches, taking classes in technical writing and programming. He has worked as a freelance technical writer and programmer and was employed as a technical writer for Oregon Software, updating their Pascal-2 manuals. He is now semi-retired, concentrating on writing.

Norm has read and collected science fiction "all of his life," and now boasts a library of over six thousand SF-related books and magazines. A member of SFFWA, he has been writing almost as long as he has been reading, selling his first story at the age of twenty-two. He has sold stories to magazines and anthologies, and writes regular book review columns for *Science Fiction Review, Midnight Zoo,* and *Sharp Tooth.* He has also sold articles on such subjects as nanotechnology and wormholes. He appears regularly on panels at Pacific Northwest conventions, and presently has three novels circulating among publishers.

Science fiction is a river broad enough to embrace everything from the works of Clarke and Niven to those of Ellison and Vonnegut. The stream is fed by two broad tributaries: "hard" and "soft." The writers of the "hard" stuff make the science prominent, many of them drawing on backgrounds in physics, chemistry, and engineering. The writers of the soft more often turn to the "mushy sciences"—psychology, sociology, anthropology—for their inspiration and extrapolation. They may underplay the science part in order to highlight the fiction, the sociocultural and interpersonal dynamics. And then there is P. J. Plauger, whose physics is invariably impeccable and whose insight into the workings of the psyche has more depth than that of many trained psychotherapists. This is an old story. Events have a way of catching up with science fiction, which has often been prescient in small and unexpected ways. Consider this as an alternate history, an exercise in what might have been in some universe. It may even remind you of one more familiar.

P. J. PLAUGER
Wet Blanket

HE AWOKE TO FEAR and a conviction.

Blood pounded and bowels writhed in the icy grip of an unknown terror. He would have cried out—he was alone, there was no one to hear—were it not for a lifetime of discipline.

That discipline had an iron fist of its own, aided by a decade of training and drill. Almost before he was consciously aware, the new grip was applied. Respiration slowed, blood pressure dropped, heartbeat came down to eighty...seventy...a fast sixty beats per minute. Fear melted into calm.

Fred Hahnemann opened his eyes to the morning sunshine. Birdsong and the soft splashing of water blew into his bedroom and touched his still damp forehead with cooling reassurance. It was going to be a beautiful Indian summer day.

The familiar room echoed the encouragement of woods and

260 PLAUGER

water outside. Clothes laid out for the day on a spartan valet, a sunlit worktable in one corner, and on it an open journal.

An open journal.

Answering the summons, Hahnemann threw off the sheet and levered himself erect. Cold bricks stung his bare feet as they left the throw rug behind. He wiped gummy residue from the corners of his eyes and stared down at the book, left open at last night's entry.

He picked up a fountain pen, uncapped it. Ignoring the words already on paper, he drew a bold horizontal line, entered the date beneath it and wrote:

"The universe is bistable."

The sentence looked silly, sitting there all by itself, but he had nothing to add. At least not yet. The statement was ludicrous; its presence in the journal of an eminent theoretical physicist could prove embarrassing.

But Hahnemann, Leslie W. Stamford Professor of Physics and Astronomy Hahnemann, gave little thought to that. The journal—and its eleven older brothers locked up in his files at the university—already contained numerous entries that once were equally laughable. A few weeks, sometimes a year, of hard work had changed each of those jokes into jargon.

The Hahnemann Effect, Hahnemann-Lee Quantization, the Hahnemann-Einstein Equations were the names by which his colleagues paid tribute to those diamonds in the rough. A good analogy, that. For they were mined from deep within his subconscious, then polished at this very worktable, or in the maw of a computer, or even in the rough and tumble of the laboratory.

And always there was a conviction. Long before sense or reason had their innings came the inner certainty that each lump was indeed a gem of truth. Training saw to that, discipline ensured the follow-through—permitting his conscious personality to enjoy the riches cast up by his ever-probing inner mind.

But never before had there been fear.

He straightened up from the table, realizing that he had been staring through the fresh journal entry, in the hope, perhaps, of seeing beyond its bald beginnings. No, that must come in its own time.

The thought of breakfast tugged him away from his fruitless probing. Yes, fruit, that was what he wanted. Bananas and wheat germ, milk from a stone crock in the spring house. An apple while

WET BLANKET 261

sitting on the rear stoop, contemplating a bold cardinal come to visit him in his little clearing and share his bubbling waters.

Then on with clothes and, leather-bound book tucked securely into the front basket, onto his bicycle and off up the path to the road. The routine of climbing hill and diving through vale almost charmed him, but his thoughts kept coming back to his newfound conviction. And that gut-wrenching fear.

The campus was just stirring to life as Hahnemann coasted up to the physics building. A black squirrel watched from an oak limb as he threw open his office window and turned on his desk lamp. There was work to be done.

The universe is bistable.

It still seemed like nonsense, but it was all he had to go on. Gravity must be the culprit, for no other force shaped the universe quite so firmly as that weakest of forces. Weak, but permeating the farthest reaches—giving space shape and time meaning that even the nuclear and electromagnetic forces must acknowledge.

"Bistable" meant two different levels—energy levels. And it meant the existence of an interaction that could cause an energy difference, remove a degeneracy and split two otherwise identical configurations into discernible entities.

But where was there a degeneracy that could be split? Hahnemann knew general relativity, better than most men knew their own desires. He had even added his bit to the lore of Einstein, and Dicke and Wheeler—a small bit, by his standards, but still no mean contribution. If there were a degeneracy in the equations of space-time physics, he should know about it. Or his subconscious, he reminded himself.

That much decided, he settled down to work, scouring the basic derivations in search of the mathematical key to a physical lock faith told him existed. He didn't find it by class time, and had to withdraw from the cosmos long enough to preach Maxwell's laws to a band of indolent sophomores, who had already succumbed to the torpid weather.

Nor did he find it by dusk, as he pushed his way up the first hill on the road home. It was not, in fact, until five days later that he found it—and it was not until after three days of checking had gone by that he believed it. But the universe was, indeed, bistable. And he could find nothing to fear.

262 PLAUGER

It was such a small thing, laid out there on the pages of his journal. Small and yet so profound. Dicke had measured the effect to—what was it?—ten decimal places, and found it null. Hahnemann's calculations showed it up as a part in ten to the thirteenth. Such a small energy splitting, probably not more than ten joules for the entire mass of Earth. Maybe too small to measure.

Now there was a challenge. For what was the good of discovering an effect if it could not be measured? The philosopher in him found such a state of affairs repugnant; the physicist in him took up the gauntlet. What he needed was an interference experiment.

If the effect you wish to observe is swamped by an enormously larger one, then you arrange for an equal but opposite effect to cancel all but the signal of interest. It was a trick used by every experimentalist since Galileo.

He scratched his ear with his pen—better watch that, it was getting to be a habit—and tried to think in terms of interference phenomena. The application in this case was not going to be obvious, not if Einstein had missed it. He stared at the sepia photograph of the great man on his office wall and remembered his dictum:

"God is tricky, but He isn't mean."

That brought forth a smile, then a frown of concentration, capped by a shrug. It was going to mean more work. But not today, for the light was fading and the short autumn day must soon come to an end. He took his journal home with him that evening.

By next morning he had it, and since he had no class that day he sat at home and wrote feverishly until well after noon. Then he packed a knapsack with food and his precious book, and set off for campus and a night at the computer center.

Dawn light seeped into the sterile confines of the data preparation room as Hahnemann stared in awe at his final printout. He had traced the full effects of a transition between the two stable states—that ten-joule difference for the Earth—and he was impressed.

The speed of light would remain unchanged, Planck's constant would alter imperceptibly. The light elements would continue to solve Schrodinger's equation the same way as ever before. Only certain properties of the heaviest elements would shift noticeably. A Q-value here, a few cross-sections there.

Hahnemann stared through the slats of a venetian blind at the

WET BLANKET 263

new day being created outside and pondered. He knew what experiment to do now, and what effect to expect. He could flip the universe into its second state at least in the neighborhood of this planet, and prove to the world that he had done it. But it was a one-way trip—he could not flip it back.

Why do it? Why fool with the way things are just to demonstrate your virtuosity? But then why not? If I publish, some meddler is sure to try it if I don't. No, that's not reason enough.

Yet the effect was still so small. A Q-value here, a few cross-sections there. And only among the heavier elements. The heavier elements. Like uranium and plutonium. He reached for a coding sheet, even though he already knew the answer.

The ready room was bustling with the day's activity by the time he had the verification he expected. He sat sipping a cup of rancid vending-machine coffee and rubbing his weary eyes. He had a lecture to give soon.

Months later, looking backward to this time, he was proud that he was able to make the right decision then. Overdue for sleep, bone weary and pressed for time, he still did not succumb to the temptations of delaying or pretending to share a responsibility with someone else when it was his alone.

He should need a super-conducting magnet and the heavy ion beam from the accelerator, and a CW laser. He reached for the telephone, ignoring the memory of fear.

The smell of rubber cement whipped about his nostrils. Hahnemann sat on a stool beneath his favorite oak, playing tug-of-war with scissors and a windblown *Times*. Other clippings sat under rocks, straining to fly free, on his outdoor worktable. It would have been much easier to go inside, but he hated to miss one of the first golden days of spring.

A leaf impishly landed on the freshly daubed page of his journal, perhaps hoping to usurp a place in history. Perversely, it stuck to his gummy fingers as he tried to send it on its way. He stepped on it with mock severity and pulled free. He wasn't very good at this sort of thing.

His journal was beginning to look like the scrapbook of some Broadway aspirant instead of a sober scientific record. Still, data was data, and if his latest exploits touched on politics and

264 PLAUGER

reportage, then newspaper clippings were a necessary form of documentation. He imprisoned another article, then paused to read:

ITALIANS DELAY A-TESTS
Special to the New York Times

Milan, April 17—The Italian Defense Ministry has decided to "postpone indefinitely" its proposed series of mid-Pacific atomic tests, a government spokesman announced here today.

Citing a "renewed interest in the moral principles surrounding atmospheric testing," the official announcement called for a return of the atomic expeditionary force until "such issues are better resolved."

The spokesman refused to comment on the possibility of Vatican intervention leading to the decision.

CORRIGENDUM
(Received March 27)

January Physics Review Letters: "Evidence for a meta-stable isotope of element 116,' by A. D. Frank, *et al.,* page 83. The second sentence in the third paragraph should read "...was measured to be 11.9 picoseconds within the error stated above."

EARTHQUAKES TAKE A VACATION

April 30—It seems that even planets hibernate sometimes. So says earthquake-watcher Charles Winston, research assistant at State's nearby Midway campus.

"This must be the quietest winter in twenty years, as far as geological activity is concerned," says Winston. For evidence he displays a strip-chart recording nearly seventy feet long with nothing on it but a ho-hum straight line.

Winston got ruffled when this reporter suggested that his seismometer might be suffering from a pulled plug. "We can detect a fifty-kiloton underground blast in Siberia, or count the number of locomotives when a Central freight goes through."

But the switchmen over at Central have been on strike since October. Maybe old Mother Earth decided to join them. How about it, readers?

To the Editor:

We wish to protest the continued shutdown of the Oak Ridge Fast Breeder Reactor. Director Rawlinson must be made to realize that he is a civil servant paid to perform administrative duties for the nation's scientists, not some Exalted Keeper of the Flame.

WET BLANKET 265

The high-handed way in which he terminated work in progress last Thanksgiving weekend cannot be defended, as he insists, on the grounds of safety, pure and simple. The procedures he condemns have been standard reactor practice for twenty-five years and the violations he refers to are wholly unsubstantiated.

Yet this martinet has succeeded in keeping an important government installation inoperative for nearly four months, with no avenue of appeal and no prospect for relief. As scientists, we condemn this bureaucratic interference, and as taxpayers we call for an accounting.

PRAYER STOPS FALLOUT
by Sister Aretha Smith

March 10—The power of Christian prayer has been keeping America under "a heaven-sent umbrella," Bishop Martinez told an estimated five thousand believers at an All-Souls Rally in Philadelphia's Fairmont Park last Saturday.

"Since the Devil first tempted our Australian brothers to stray from the Test Ban Treaty last year, we have maintained a continuous Pray-In of fifty brothers and sisters, around the clock, day and night," the Bishop said.

"As others fell by the wayside, we prevailed. As the dark rain fell on the hillside, we prevailed. And there have been no new tests to foul God's temple in a hundred days! Yes, brothers, the devil fell on his backside because we prevailed!"

His remarks were greeted by cheers.

The rally was organized to raise relief funds for victims of last month's South Street police raids.

Reprinted from the *Soviet Journal of Physics (JETP)*, V. I. Vyssotsky, "On a Possible Weak Coupling between Nuclear Strong Force and Gravitational Radiation" (Available in December).

MAN ABOUT WASHINGTON
Everett Roper

The talk at the big, and I mean BIG, parties these days is all about the remarkable leadership The Man has been displaying in the current nuclear arms buildup. We all put President Clinton in the White House because we knew he was a no-nonsense kind of guy, the kind we need in these troubled times. And he really came through with a defense posture second to none.

That's why we're all so proud of his restraint in not resuming atmos-

266   PLAUGER

pheric testing just because every third-rate piece of real estate that calls itself a nation has been making a bid for entry into the A-club. So much for the bleeding-heart liberals and all their dire predictions!

What really impresses me about The Man is that he hasn't tried to take an inch of credit for the moral pressure he's brought to bear on the Johnny-come-latelies. No sir, when you think about it, that takes more guts than any mealy-mouthed preacher ever showed. It's good to know we have a President who can keep his mouth shut and carry the biggest stick of all!

Session FC. General Relativity
(Main Ballroom, 9:30 A.M.):
Invited Papers

F. I. Hahnemann: "A Second Solution to the General Field Equations."
R. W. Frankel, "Stellar Collapse Below the Swarzschild Limit."
A. B. Locard, "Black Hole Clustering."

A cooler wind rustled the page as Hahnemann read the last entry. But the chill struck deeper than it should have. It would be a delicate piece of business giving that talk next week. He knew his talents did not lie in the direction of public relations.

It would be necessary to cover a lot of theoretical background, enough to convince the experts that there truly was no going back. And yet he must pitch the message in simple enough terms that the science reporters could get a glimmering of the profound underlying truth.

Someone in the room *must* catch the import of his remarks before he had to spell out every detail. He began to appreciate how a comedian must feel when he loses his straight man.

It was going badly.

The room smelled of damp wool and too many people, for the hotel ballroom was filled to capacity despite three days of steady rain and freakish cold. He clutched the control wand in a sweaty hand and barely remembered to thumb the slide advance button. His pulse was up higher than he should have permitted, and he could not quite ignore the cold metal band of the throat mike as it rubbed against his skin.

Gamely, Hahnemann launched into the concluding sentences of his talk. The silence in the room was deep, remarkably deep for such a large crowd. He wondered as ever whether it was respect or

WET BLANKET 267

opacity that kept so many people quiet. His teaching experience inclined him to the latter view.

But the moment was past when he should have injected his real message, long past when his hoped-for interruption should have occurred. He let the talk run down and stop like a spent top. His shoulders sagged; he had lost. Then the thunder hit.

It took a full two seconds for him to realize that the barrage was applause. But here was the chairman smiling broadly and reaching for his hand. On the floor of the ballroom, chairs were scraped back as his peers stood to pay him enthusiastic homage. Maybe it wasn't as bad as it sounded to him.

"The chair will now accept questions for Professor Hahnemann." The chairman had to bellow his message twice before it punched through the din. A hundred hands were high. But the man knew how to run this business—deftly he picked out Abramowitz from the mob, the eldest statesman with his hand up.

"I was wondering"—the preliminary tremolo quickly brought a respectful hush—"if you have given any thought to the possibility of forcing a local transition to the state you so excellently describe. And have you explored the effect of such a transition on nuclear reaction rates?"

Trust Abramowitz to see right to the core of the matter! Hahnemann felt a surge of affection for the aging scholar.

"I'm glad you asked that question," Hahnemann said with a smile. Several knowing laughs chimed through the hall.

"The effect of the coupling term varies, to first order, logarithmically with atomic mass," he said. "So one can appreciate the difference only among the heavier elements. As an example"—he paused, then plunged on—"the fission cross-sections for plutonium isotopes are reduced by the factor alpha shown on the last slide."

A buzz started near the front and rapidly swelled to all corners of the hall.

He waited for the noise to subside, then proceeded.

"Some evidence exists that the second state occurs naturally from time to time. Professor Frankel"— he gestured toward the next speaker, sitting in the front rows—"has published some very careful measurements of heavy-element distributions in third-generation stars." Frankel stirred uncomfortably, he knew what was coming.

268 PLAUGER

"His data show clustering about two different equilibrium distributions for main-sequence stars. The difference was small enough to justify averaging all the data together, but my preliminary calculations call for a difference of the order observed between the two clusters. I would venture to say, therefore, that thirty percent of the stars Professor Frankel measured are already in the second state I described." The noise swelled up again.

"As to your first remark"—Hahnemann cut through the buzzing—"yes, it is possible to stimulate a transition by the rather obvious use of a coherent light source impinging on a beam of polarized heavy ions."

He had everyone's attention now.

"Coupling through the local gravitational field creates a cascade of incoherent transitions releasing approximately ten joules, mostly in the form of gravitational radiation. Unfortunately, because the transition is incoherent, there is no way to organize a resonant absorption having the necessary spin and energy, so the inverse transition is not possible."

The buzz returned and quickly became a roar. Through it all, Hahnemann watched a heavyset individual in a blue serge suit elbow his way down the center aisle and up to the podium. To everyone's surprise, he snatched the microphone from the chairman's hand and whistled shrilly into it. The chatter was promptly quenched.

"Sorry about that, folks," the man said to the crowd, Then, turning to the rostrum, he introduced himself. "Jack Weston, freelance science writer. Now, I didn't follow all of that, but I got enough to know it's important. In words of one syllable, Dr. Hahnemann, would you please explain to us chickens just what you're driving at?"

"I'll try," Hahnemann ventured. Here it comes. "Put simply, there are two sets of laws our universe can obey, depending locally on which state it is in. These states are almost identical, except for the behavior of a few heavy elements."

"You mean like in atomic bombs, Doc?"

"Yes, like in bombs, but even some reactors are affected. In one state fission bombs work, in the other they fizzle. Of course, a fusion bomb could still be made, in principle, but in practice all H-bombs are triggered by fission. Controlled fusion is just coming in

WET BLANKET 269

sight, and I don't know of any prospects for obtaining the uncontrolled fusion needed to produce a satisfactory bomb."

"And you can get us to the fizzle state, but not back?" he persisted.

"Not anymore," Hahnemann replied. "I forced the transition last November 29, at 17:53 GMT. We're there. There hasn't been a nuclear explosion since. And I can't see how to make one happen ever again on Earth, even if I wanted to."

Pandemonium.

The room was warm and cozy. Weston steered Hahnemann skillfully between tables to the short leg of the L-shaped bar. He gave an efficient wrist flip to the balding bartender, who replied with a raised eyebrow and a nod. Weston eased his bulk onto an upholstered stool.

"You look like a Scotch man, if I'm any judge." Hahnemann inclined his head in agreement. "Swell. Harry, two of my usual, on the rocks. The stock here will rot your liver."

Harry ignored the slur and reached for the square bottle. Weston resumed his friendly, but thorough, probing.

"Tell me more about this Rheims Institute you went to, Doc. Even in my trade there are some things it's not easy to find out about. All I know is, you Rheims graduates seem to be setting the world on its ear; but I don't believe the public hokum about supernormal mutations."

Hahnemann smiled. He recognized the last thrust as a none-too-subtle attempt to draw him out by defending himself. Still, he was happy enough to help this man with his story.

"There are no dark secrets at the Institute. That's why most people don't believe the results, I guess. Charles Rheims simply discovered a few ways to help one's subconscious mind solve problems, which it seems to want to do anyway.

"It's something like peristalsis," he continued, "where your stomach and intestines keep grinding away at processing food, whether you think about it or not. We learn to avoid the mental equivalents of acid indigestion and starvation, to stretch the analogy as far as possible."

The drinks appeared before them and both men reached for wallets. The bartender stopped Hahnemann with a jabbing finger.

270   PLAUGER

"Say, ain't you the guy that queered the H-bombs? Your mug's been on TV like a test pattern all day."

"Pardon me," interposed Weston. "'Dr. Hahnemann, meet Harry, best barkeep east of the river. Harry, Dr. Hahnemann. He's the guy," he ended simply.

Hahnemann didn't know whether to extend his hand or run, as Harry continued to fix him with a speculative stare. Finally, the bartender spoke in a neutral tone.

"My wife, she's been afraid of this city since we moved here twenty years ago. 'They're going to bomb us in our beds, Harry,' she always used to say to me. I tried to explain all this deterrent stuff, how it's important that we gotta stay strong, but she wouldn't listen: She's still scared."

He stared through the physicist a while longer, then suddenly snapped into focus.

"Your money ain't no good here, Doc." Hahnemann started to rise, then realized that the bartender was holding out a gnarled hand. "It's a real pleasure. You just keep puttin' 'em down and Old Harry will keep settin' 'em up. That even goes for your fat friend, here." Hahnemann breathed a sigh of relief and settled back onto the stool.

"You'd be surprised how many people are thinking like Harry these days," said Weston. "That 'America First' wave that swept through the elections is pretty well spent. Though some people haven't got the word yet." He shook his head in disgust. "Being top dog feels great until the rest of the pack starts tooling up to cut you down." A shrug.

"So if you give everyone enough time to think this business through, you should expect no trouble," he added, "at least from the man in the street. But The Man may be another story. He's made no announcement so far, but—"

"I'd like to buy the next round, if I may," the soft voice interrupted like a whispering of pines. And she stood there like a pine, lithe and lovely, gray-green eyes contrasting autumn-brown hair. She was clearly no pussycat, but Hahnemann reflexively stood up. He barely noticed Weston doing the same.

"You don't remember me, of course." She cocked her head wryly all the same. "Physics 417, five years ago, next-to-last row. You gave me an A-minus." She grinned. "Linda Parnell, Professor."

WET BLANKET 271

For the second time in five minutes he found himself shaking a proffered hand in perplexity. He had a vague memory of that class, his first assignment on leaving the Institute. Nervousness had kept the group a hazy blur for most of the term. But he recalled the alert eyes, the hair in a bun over the perennial sweatshirt and jeans. That was a girl and this was a woman, but the visions merged.

"I trust your knowledge of Clebsch-Gordon coefficients has improved," he finally replied. It was just luck that he recalled grading her final exam, marred only by her inability to normalize wave functions.

Her laugh came from deep inside.

"You do remember." She touched his arm as she sat down between the two men. That touch was an altogether pleasant familiarity.

"It's *Doctor* Parnell now, thank you. Despite the math. I just presented my thesis results yesterday. But I think you stole my thunder this morning. That was a beautiful presentation."

"Dr. Hahnemann was just telling me about his training at the Institute," Weston interposed. He wanted to get his exclusive interview back on the tracks. Deftly he skidded his untouched drink in front of the woman and waved to Harry with that efficient gesture of his. "I expect you'd be interested, too."

The man was good, Hahnemann admitted. He found himself outlining his own very special approach to the Ph.D., as practiced by the followers of Rheims.

"But the real essence of our success" he concluded "is discipline. It doesn't matter how many bright ideas you get if you don't do your homework. Just plain hard work is the foundation of the Rheims approach. That's not generally stylish, so people prefer to make up stories about us."

They sat quietly sipping awhile.

"But what about the fact that you never marry?" Weston resumed. "That can't help but cause talk you know."

Hahnemann shrugged.

"If you pick a bunch of twenty-nine-year-old scholars who are already loners by nature, then separate them from society for five years of intensive training, you can't expect to produce social butterflies. It's not that we don't want to marry; we're just not good at hunting."

272 PLAUGER

"Besides, the Institute has only been turning out graduates for eight years. And we've all been kept pretty busy. Sooner or later some of us will slow down long enough to look around. We really aren't supermen, you know."

That last was aimed at Weston, but it was intercepted by gray-green eyes. He found himself rewarded with a warm smile and another touch. He felt dizzy.

Hahnemann was surprised when Weston slid of his stool and looked at his watch.

"Hate to miss out on the free booze—Harry is seldom such a soft touch—but I've got a living to earn. Thanks for giving me the inside, Doc. I'll do right by you, count on it."

He hesitated.

"Y'know, there's going to be reporters hip deep in the lobby of your hotel, waiting for you to make a show. I'm not just telling you that to beef my exclusive."

Hahnemann had already considered that very fact, but his mind was too numb to grapple with it. If only he could escape quietly back to his haven in the woods.

"Don't worry about Professor Hahnemann." The soft voice had a touch of steel in it. "I'll see that he's left alone." Now, was that stance maternal, or friendly, or something more?

"Uh, yeah, I'm sure you will." An uncertain pause. "Well, good night, folks, and thanks again, Doc." He sailed off among the tables, a steamboat passing between sandbars.

Silence remained in his wake.

"I have an apartment here in town," she finally ventured. "That is, I work here. So I live here. I mean...I don't mean to be presumptuous, Professor, but..."

Her uncertainty reduced her to human proportions, in Hahnemann's mind, and overcame his own built-in reticence. Besides, his natural kindness urged him to ease her embarrassment.

"The name is Fred," he said with a smile, "and I'd much rather go with you to your apartment than sit here and drink—or face another mob today. Anyway we have five years of catching up to do."

Harry was happy to call a cab for them.

WET BLANKET 273

The lights were painfully bright. Red eyes glowed in the darkness beneath the glare impaling his sweating, squinting image on ten million screens around the country. Across the light-swept arena, eyes angry and fearful stared back at him. Linda was lost somewhere in the surrounding gloom.

They had had three glorious, carefree days together, exploring the city and growing closer. But inevitably he was spotted, cornered, and forced into this television confrontation. Gallup and Harris had yet to announce the National Mood; the White House was keeping quiet. But those men behind that long desk over there didn't like him, that much was already clear.

"Now, Dr. Hahnemann," Everett Roper began again, making the honorific sound somehow derisive "would you please explain to us by what authority you claim the right to experiment with a whole planet and compromise the security of your native land?"

Hahnemann sighed.

"I'm not sure which of those charges you consider the more serious." No, that was the wrong thing to say—mockery was wasted on this buffoon. "But in all honesty, I can't see where I've done either.

"Please don't interrupt. I was not 'experimenting' in the sinister sense you imply—I knew exactly what I was doing. And I've hardly dented the United States' arsenal, since over eighty percent of it is nonnuclear conventional weaponry, or so I'm told.

"On the contrary, I seem to have ended the Chinese and Soviet threats for quite some time and rendered the ABM network unnecessary. That should save us all some tax money."

"So you say. But what gave you the authority to meddle in this business," Roper persisted.

"The Treaty of Nuremberg." He was ready for that one. "I felt I was responsible for the consequences of my actions, regardless of the lesser law of the land."

"Professor Hahnemann"—that was the unfortunate Frankel, who had lost his audience at the meeting—"it still seems to me that you were taking quite a chance by manipulating an unknown force with such far-reaching effects. As a fellow physicist, I can hardly condone your actions." And as an adviser to the AEC on military uses of science, Frankel was in no position to condemn, Hahnemann thought.

274 PLAUGER

But what he said was, "The effects could hardly be called 'far-reaching.' Only a fraction of a percent of the atoms in the universe, or any one solar system, are heavier than iron. It takes an unnatural concentration of very heavy elements, such as the refined plutonium in a bomb, to even show a difference in behavior.

"And the force was far from unknown. It was your data on stars, Professor Frankel, that convinced me the transition could be safely made." That must have been what really bugged him. "If the effect was that small in the intense gravitational field of a star, then a change wasn't likely to affect life processes. In fact, the transition might have occurred spontaneously any old time. I just egged it on."

"Dr. Hahnemann"—this from Bayard King, a weasel of a man with a reputation for deadly indirection—"is it true that you live in a house with no running water, no electricity, and no telephone?"

Watch it!

"Not exactly. There's a very pleasant spring just above the house that gives me all the running water I could wish for."

"But you have no indoor plumbing?"

"No."

"Electricity?"

"No."

"Telephone?"

"No."

"Do you drive a car?"

"No."

"How remarkable." His tone did not find it remarkable. "An eminent *theoretical* physicist, a *tenured* professor"—each emphasis implied *demented*—"sitting out in a shack in the woods deciding national security policy. This is indeed the Era of the Common Man!"

"The house is stone and over a century old. It hardly qualifies as a shack." This was really too much. Couldn't these idiots see the real issue at hand? Next they would be going after his sex life.

"Are you married, Dr. Hahnemann?" asked another panelist, gazing off in the direction where he had left Linda. That did it.

"That does it!" The stool crashed behind him as he stood and a camera lurched forward to capture his angry features.

"Hasn't it sunk into any of your skulls what this discovery meant last fall? On one day, it could be business as usual, bombs blossoming and pilots singing. On the next, or just twenty minutes later, before the retaliatory strike arrives, it could be 'Sorry, no more bombs accepted.'

"Can you imagine the temptation of having a weapon you can use only once, but one that properly employed could give your side global superiority ever after? How big a first strike would you order to make sure of the outcome? How many deaths is enough? And who would you count as a friend to be spared? Are you sure?"

He was trembling. Linda appeared beside the camera, wreathed in concern. Hahnemann forced the iron fist of control over his heart, his lungs. He continued softly.

"This nation of ours, this marvelous symbol of self-determination, has invaded seventeen countries in the last decade. Congress declared war on none of them. The current administration has already intervened in the internal affairs of three sovereign nations, all in the interest of 'protecting American lives' that were never threatened.

"No nation has declared war on us in nearly forty years, and yet we have a *defense* department so huge it essentially runs the country. And militarism is once again a rising tide throughout the world. Are these the people to whom I should turn for a decision?

"No, I cannot trust the Pentagon—I could hardly trust myself with such power of life and death. Nor could I hope to keep it a secret, for secrets leak out, or are independently discovered. And if I can't trust my own nation to exercise restraint with this power, how could I possibly trust another?"

He paused. They were finally getting it. Finally.

"You are acting like a bunch of children caught playing with fire. To you it's just another sparkling toy. I put a wet blanket over your pretty blaze and now you're mad at me. Well, you still have plenty of other toys—TNT, napalm, poison gas, and viruses. I leave you to their enjoyment."

He was tired. He was sick of the city and these people and all the talking. He walked off the set without a glance left or right and took Linda's waiting hand.

"Let's go home," he said.

He struggled up from nightmare to August sunshine. It was late.

276 PLAUGER

He turned to find Linda gone, the same unhappy discovery he had made every morning for the last eight days. She had estimated three weeks to clean up loose ends in the city—that had sounded like such a short hiatus until now.

The nightmares were bad, and they didn't seem to be getting any better. They were the final hangover of six weeks of drugged interrogation and probing by teams from every major power in the United Nations. While the UN representatives were supposed to guard him from any permanent damage, they were reluctant to exercise much restraint, lest suspicion flourish in already fertile ground.

For in the end they decided to make him a hero. President Clinton even made a pretty speech that broadly suggested Hahnemann had been acting under his personal orders. And The Man made the University happy by giving the physics department a fat grant—for research into new methods of stimulating fusion, of course, not necessarily controlled. But the big powers didn't really want to believe their nuclear investment was worthless, and they evidently weren't up on their fairy tales. They kept trying to open Hahnemann and pry out another golden egg.

Finally they seemed to have given up. Hahnemann was left battered, frayed, and apparently all but broken. Had it not been for Linda, it would have been much worse, even with all his training. But somehow she supported him through the worst of it and stayed to share the best of high summer with him.

On balance, it was probably the happiest summer of his life. They climbed hills, cycled over roads and swam in his sun-warmed pond. Linda delighted in the old house and the harmony it had achieved with its woodland neighbors. Hahnemann delighted in Linda and the freshness she brought into his life. And he grew stronger.

The nightmares, however, persisted. He knew that he must do something about them, and soon. His psychopathology texts from school were in his campus office, so there was nothing for it but to go there, even though he had promised himself a summer off. He had mounted his bicycle and almost set off before he remembered that he should eat breakfast.

The physics building was a dreary place, an abandoned barge adrift on an empty green sea. Hahnemann realized with a start that

WET BLANKET 277

he used to enjoy the campus in summer because of its solitude. He had to use his key to get into his office.

Stale cigar smoke and formaldehyde still lingered in the dusty air. He had been puzzled, at first, by the meticulous care with which each lock had been violated, then restored, how each journal had been put back in its place. Such niceties stood at odds with the myriad of subtle rearrangements and less subtle smells left behind. Then it dawned on him that his office had been searched not once, but many times by many different interests. Effects accumulated. He knew *that* feeling well.

He opened the window, turned on the desk lamp, took down his well-worn copy of Rheims's *Psychopathology* and set to work. It was not easy doing the careful sequence of drills—but then it was never easy to concentrate on occasions when these drills were called for. Slowly and painfully, Hahnemann began to untwist the knots in his psyche.

The telephone jangled. He was startled out of an intricate inner search, momentarily at a loss. Annoyance was quickly replaced by a flood of anger. It was one thing to know that you're being watched, to have it flaunted was another thing entirely. With reluctance, he picked up the receiver.

"Dr. Hahnemann." The voice in his ear made no attempt to sound interrogative; it knew who he was. He recognized the mincing tenor of Blefescu, the UN watchdog. His stomach tightened—that man never brought good news.

"I regret that we must call on you once again." He probably did regret it, for all the difference that made. "This evening at six." They never gave him much warning, for fear he would have time to make some sort of preparations, he supposed. Still, were it not for the UN, people would probably be pouncing on him out of dark alleys.

"Does it is really have to go on?" He made no effort to keep the plaintive whine out of his voice. "I've been turned inside out so many times, I'm not sure I can take it again." His voice had a wholly unaffected pleading quaver, even though he knew there could be no reprieve.

"You have proved to be a very tough nut to crack, Dr. Hahnemann." Blefescu had the idiom down pat. "The KGB has much respect for you Rheims people. They want to take one more look to be completely satisfied."

278   PLAUGER

"Very well." Better to face the inevitable and get it over with than cringe in vain. Neither man essayed any parting pleasantries.

Tough nut indeed! None of them had begun to suspect how tough he could be. Well, he had a few hours yet, he may as well make use of them. He picked up the book again, and froze.

That final wash of anger had cleared away the last inner veils. He could see clearly what the nightmare knots had so effectively obscured. He knew how to flip the world back into its old state.

Only a few hours. It would take days, weeks to be safe, to build a secure wall around that knowledge. Such a pity to hide it. The approach was altogether novel and would make for a beautiful demonstration. All he needed was—*No! Don't think about it!*

He could hide, but then they would know for sure that their golden egg existed. And knowing that was over half the job of discovering it. For one brief instant he contemplated suicide, but quickly dismissed it, with relief, on the same grounds as before. Whatever he did, it must lead to uncertainty and delay.

It was only a matter of time, Hahnemann knew, before enough nations instituted the obvious safeguard, a detector to signal entry into the old state and an automatic device to restore safety. Time. A year at least, maybe two. He had only a few hours.

For the first time in his life, he cursed the mental peristalsis that wouldn't leave well enough alone. It had to keep massaging away at the problems it encountered until it ground out solutions. Only this time it had caused an even bigger problem, one for which there was no answer.

Or was there? Slowly and chillingly, realization dawned. His subconscious had foreseen this very situation nearly a year ago, had solved it as part of the problem in general relativity. The events had been inexorable, the answer inevitable. He knew the way out, and he finally understood the roots of his fear.

Hahnemann had been sitting immobile for nearly five minutes. He stirred, lest some watcher become suspicious. Fortunately, he had the book he needed in his hands and had been pausing over each of the drills before Blefescu called. He must assume that every movement was being gauged—no inconsistencies in his actions could be tolerated. With a gesture of impatience he flipped to the

WET BLANKET 279

index and, turning to shield the book from the window, looked up "catatonia."

He skimmed the necessary paragraphs as fast as he dared. Occasionally he would flip agitatedly to some other section, but he kept returning until he had absorbed the necessary techniques.

Finally he hurled the book into a corner and stood with a jerk. He paced nervously the length of his office half a dozen times, muttering and running his hands through his hair. Then, just as abruptly, he strode out of the office, leaving the lamp burning and window and door open to the elements. Twice he fell before he got the bike under control.

The house looked so lovely in the afternoon light it would be hard leaving it behind. He was glad now that Linda was not around. This was hard enough to do alone. Hahnemann let the bicycle crash among the vines and lurched into the house.

First, the journal. It took no effort to make his hand shake as he wrote:

"Can't make the nightmares go away. And now they're going to work on me again. Linda could make them leave me alone, but she's gone away. Have to hide. Until they go away and leave me alone and Linda comes back and makes them go away and LEAVE ME ALONE AND GO AWAY."

That was enough of that. Better not overdo it. He turned his back on the scraggly script, taking in the familiar room and all its precious details. He never did fix that loose brick by the hearth. Too late now.

The liquor cabinet offered few choices. Someone might wonder that he should pick the thirty-year-old cognac, but that could be explained as a blind selection. He didn't care. He wanted to add that bouquet to his recent store of memories and he was willing to take his chances.

Drink in hand, he sat down by the window to savor the brandy and make a final review. The cheerful gurgle of the spring was heartrending; he forced his mind away from the outside view.

Hard nut, indeed! I'll show them a shell they won't soon penetrate. He sipped. *The Institute will get to me sooner or later. They take care of their own. They'll know what to do. A year, two at the most.* Another sip. *I'll make it.*

He savored each drop of the cognac.

It was time. He set the empty glass on the sill and turned his back on the window. There was a spot on the opposite wall, part way down. It would serve. He took a deep breath, composed himself. Then, staring at the wall, he went quietly insane.

P. J. Plauger is a consultant and lecturer, activist in international programming standards, and prolific writer. Educated as a scientist, with a Ph.D. in Nuclear Physics, he started out with Bell Labs, where he became involved in the early promulgation of UNIX. He was vice president of Yourdon, Inc., then went on to found Whitesmiths, Ltd., where he was president for a decade before it was acquired by Intermetrics. Widely recognized as one of the leading authorities on the C programming language, he is convenor of ISO WG14, the international C standards committee. He has written several highly successful texts, including the classic, *Elements of Programming Style*, with Brian Kernighan, and most recently, *The Standard C Language*. His monthly columns include the perennial favorite "Programming on Purpose" in *Computer Language Magazine*, "Standard C" for the *C Users Journal*, and "State of the Art" for *Embedded Systems Programming*.

He first tried writing science fiction in grad school, then returned to it later "as a potential alternative to permanent corporate servitude." His very first story sold on the first try to Ben Bova, then editor at *Analog*, where most of his work has been published. Winner of the 1975 John W. Campbell Award as the Best New Science Fiction Writer, he has been widely anthologized. He has one novel published in an *Analog* annual, and is working on another. Fittingly, the story reprinted here was his first professional sale.

Even as some attempt to build software resembling the mind, others are thinking that maybe the mind resembles software. Guru of artificial intelligence Marvin Minsky has advanced the boldly speculative model of the modular mind, human intelligence as distributed among semi-autonomous but only semi-intelligent subroutines. Evidence is beginning to suggest that we didn't invent modular programming; Ma Nature did. Look at the marvelously disorganized order of memories and the mental associations that allow us to retrieve them, and don't be surprised if you see hypermedia. We are the camera seeing itself in the picture it takes of the mirror. Steve Rasnic Tem certainly targeted the right editor with this gem of a story; so few are both software methodologists and licensed therapists. As one one of the few, I think this may be how it really works.

STEVE RASNIC TEM

The Doors of Hypertext

HIS BROTHER HAD told Cole to just type on the keyboard whatever he was thinking about, anything at all, as long as it had something to do with his life and who he was. But *everything* had something to do with his life, so he just typed and typed, sometimes for hours at a time, everything that came into his head.

Cole typed crudely at first, hunting letters and pecking them out slowly—he'd never taken typing in school and had no experience with computers whatsoever. But the persistence, the relentlessness of his entries improved his skills rapidly, so that after a few months his fingers danced across the keys, caressing, slapping, taking no prisoners.

At first he hadn't fully understood why his brother had put him to this task. He'd figured that a large part of it had been just a sense of responsibility: Cole had had emotional problems of one kind or other since his teen years, which had rendered him chronically unemployable. Jim, on the other hand, had worked his way through graduate school, seeing everything he touched turn to

282   TEM

money, and now he owned a major software firm specializing in databases, in particular "hypertext."

Cole hadn't heard from his brother in several years when he got this call from him asking—no, begging him, practically—to come over to his company for a chat. Cole hadn't left his small apartment in weeks—he'd started having this feeling again that people were having secret thoughts about him, that somehow they knew more about his life than he did, and that there were pages and pages full of text about him and his life that he'd never known about, but someday he was going to pick up the newspaper and every word in the newspaper would be about him, even the captions and the dialogue in the comic strip section.

But he hadn't had any sort of family in years. And the need in him for family was even greater than his fear of other people.

When Cole first arrived at his brother's software company that day a huge party was going on, spread out over the entire suite of offices. Cole was virtually in a panic, facing a wall of people he was convinced would crush him if they were to permit him into their midst at all. He'd turned to leave when he was grabbed from behind and whirled around. His vision grew foggy due to his hyperventilating, but he still recognized his brother, looking young as ever.

"Cole, you old rascal!" Much to his dismay his brother was pounding him on the back. Cole didn't think anyone had ever done that to him before—he didn't quite know how to take it. But it was worse when Jim wrapped him in a bear hug. Cole liked it, but he was also painfully embarrassed by the gesture. He could hardly breathe. He thought he was going to faint.

"Jim...Jim..." It was all he could say. He thought he was going to cry. He didn't think he could live if he cried in front of all those people. He wanted to find a door and leave, or at least hide behind it.

His brother apparently could see what Cole was going through, and took him by the arm, introduced him to people, filling in the gaps with small talk when it became obvious Cole had nothing to say. He could only respond with nervous jerks of the head. Cole assumed he was making a spectacle of himself, was no doubt embarrassing all of Jim's employees, but he really couldn't bring himself to look at any of them long enough to tell.

THE DOORS OF HYPERTEXT 283

It had been like this for years. He simply could not believe he was like other people; he wouldn't know where to begin to find any sort of commonality. Other people were doors he could not open. After the party Jim said he had a job for Cole. He said it might even make him feel good about himself again. Cole wondered if it was in fact Jim who wanted to feel good about his little brother again.

After nearly a year Cole at least had some idea of what hypertext was: a knowledge system, text interconnected by a network of nodes, links, cross-references. Certain words became "doors": open them up and they'd tell you their secrets. You'd find definitions and explanations, but more significantly, more "doors." Sometimes you'd open door after door and it would be as if you were in this endless dreamhouse of ideas, a big old ramshackle palace of a place with ancient and modern sections blending surrealistically together because of all the remodeling that had been done, so that you were completely lost, you couldn't get out, and much of the time you didn't even want to get out.

Some of those doors might lead to pictures, although not initially in the convoluted hypertext of Cole's life. Jim told him he should get a substantial number of the words down first, but after the first year Jim showed him the expensive scanner, which Cole would use to create doors with pictures: photographs from his past, drawings, images clipped from magazines, books, and catalogs. Sometimes the juxtapositions of all these images would drive Cole into a frenzy of work as the associations triggered secrets and memories long buried and forgotten.

Occasionally Jim would attempt to explain why he was paying him to record his life in this fashion, but for the most part Cole wasn't particularly interested in the "whys." He had become obsessed with the shifting interconnectedness of "what is."

Jim was always trying to explain how theirs was a new sort of hypertext system, an intelligent, expert system which linked Cole's recollections with a vast reservoir of general, factual references. This system could determine where new doors should be in this growing mountain of remembrance and association, and make the decision to create these doors without any input from a human operator, such as Cole himself.

284   TEM

"Maybe it'll give you some focus, Cole. Help you connect. Successful lives have a hierarchy—they're not random affairs at all!" Jim would wave his hands about in the air like a minister when he explained things, gesturing toward heaven. "You just need to know where the doors are. Your *life* might be the ultimate test for the software! Just think of that! You can make a real contribution, and figure out what's gone wrong with your life at the same time!"

Cole had just nodded and looked at the books and magazines and notes he kept himself surrounded with. Of late he'd become impatient with Jim's explanations—they kept him away from the keyboard and his own research into his convoluted mind. "Whatever you say, big brother." With his nose in a book he waved his hand over his head, as if conducting some counter musical theme. "I owe you a great deal for all of this. I'm glad I can repay some of it." And then he would run to the scanner to add some vague image or impression to the network.

Doors within doors within doors. After a year Cole grew tired of filling them, of opening and closing them all the time. Besides, he seemed to have nothing new to enter.

Except his name. He initiated a query, a beginning point from which the network of his life might unravel. QUERY. He typed in his name. COLE BLACKMORE. Press ENTER. Working...

Words and phrases, associations and doorways to more associations began filling his screen.

His mother had always smelled of apples. Genus *Malus* of the Rose family. Rose was his mother's name. Fruit is a firm, fleshy structure taken from the receptacle of the flower. Firm, sweet, flesh. Sweet apples. Delicious. Washington Delicious. Jonathan. Cortland. Gravenstein. Kissing his mother on the pale flowers of her mouth as she lay in her coffin. She used to say when she was pregnant with him she couldn't get enough of them. The apples. Apple pie and apple brown betty.

Betty Grable—that's who she looked like. He hadn't realized that until the actress's picture came up on the monitor. He'd had posters of Betty Grable, and he used to watch her movies on the Late Late Show all the time—he'd thought she was just about the most gorgeous woman who'd ever lived. But he'd never made the

THE DOORS OF HYPERTEXT   285

connection before. His mother. His mother and Betty Grable. Biting the apple that feeds you. The sweet taste, the hard caress. This was just too much. He sat back and looked at the screen, a little frightened. It was as if the program was reading his mind. Doors within doors within doors, but did he really want all those doors opened?

"What do you mean you're quitting? You can't quit now! We're *close*, Cole, *damn* close. Why do you think you've been entering all that stuff the last couple of years? Just writing your damn memoirs? We're poised for a breakthrough in intelligent software and you're going to *quit*? You're going to stab your own brother in the back? Quitting like you've done everywhere else? Afraid to look anyone in the face? Quitting *me*?"

"Jimmy..."

"My name is *Jim*."

"Jim, I'm sorry. Really I am. It's just that it's making me so anxious. I'm reading along on something I put in there and then it jumps me someplace else and insists that these things are related somehow and I know it's telling me the truth, but I just don't know if I can handle that much truth in my life right now. It just keeps opening door after door and I don't want to see what it's coming up with behind those doors but I can't help but look."

Jim got quiet and leaned forward, and Cole knew his brother was getting ready to be calm and purposeful, like one of the doctors at the hospital. "The program doesn't *insist* anything, Cole. It doesn't tell a *truth*. It's just a piece of software. An idea processor, if you will. In that way it can *teach* you things, but it will teach you things based only on what you entered originally. There's really nothing here to be afraid of."

Despite himself, Cole reluctantly agreed that he was probably overreacting. He would continue to help with his brother's project. He owed him that much. Later that afternoon he shut himself in with his terminal. Jim arranged to have meals sent in to him, even though Cole hadn't asked him to.

He started typing. QUERY: THINGS THAT WENT WRONG.

His dad's old Chrysler. The back window catch. His mother's vacuum cleaner. The built-in dishwasher: fixed a dozen times and never once right. The Chrysler again. The plumbing, again and

286   TEM

again. The light switch in his bedroom that almost electrocuted him after a shower when he was sixteen. The lawnmower. The Chrysler again. Several TVs, none of them lasting more than five or six years and his dad blaming him for turning the channels too often, too quickly. Four toasters. Six coffee pots. His dad's old Chrysler again. A broiler oven that hadn't worked since the first day they got it...

Cole halted the listing. He considered a moment, then started typing again. QUERY: MOMENTS IN MY LIFE WHEN A MISTAKE WAS MADE THAT WOULD DAMAGE ME PSYCHOLOGICALLY.

His dad's old Chrysler. At first he thought he'd worded the query incorrectly and that he was going to get the same output as before, but then he started receiving some different text.

Chrysler, Walter Percy. Originally a machinist. Worked his way up, resourceful, clever like Cole's father, who had accumulated a small fortune through hard work. Except Jim had always called it stubbornness. Meanness. He'd tried to manage the lives of everyone who came into contact with him, Jim said. Walter Percy Chrysler became manager for the American Locomotive Company, switched to automobiles, president of Buick in 1916, in 1922 joined Maxwell, which in 1925 became the Chrysler Corporation.

A photograph of his dad's Chrysler flashed on the screen. Like some kind of ancient cat, grill rusty but still grinning. Cole used to think it would devour him one day. Carnivore. Flesh-eaters. *Carnivora*. Dogs, cats, weasels. His father had loved that car, and there had been no question, not even any discussion, about the fact that his father had loved the car more than he'd loved his own family. Films from Driver's Ed class, images thrown up on his monitor screen of bodies burned black, the tender pink inside, heads through windshields streaming blood. *Death on the Highway*. Then his father's old Chrysler up on the screen, the twisted metal wreck of ancient cat, the way the grill teeth had been smashed in, and in the window...

Cole blanked the screen, unable to proceed. He turned and looked at the door, ready to get up and leave, then found he could not. He turned back to the keyboard and keyed the sequence back to the image of his father's Chrysler. It made him feel suddenly personally powerful, as if he'd been able to turn back the clock at his

THE DOORS OF HYPERTEXT 287

command, the car straightening out its bends, reassembling itself, his life reassembling itself.

QUERY: PARTS?

It should have been a safe sequence, a way to kill time while he readied himself for his father's death again.

Internal combusion engine. Gasoline. Spark ignition. Anger. Fury. Rage.

He stopped the sequence and backed up a bit. Liquid-cooled, four-stroke cycle. The words appeared like the unveiling of a poem. Overhead valve, carbureted, reciprocating type. Four-stroke cycle. Stroke. Caress. Embrace. The way his mother held him at his father's funeral. A picture of them together flashes up on the screen: the way she holds her arms around him, the way she inclines her head.

Head gasket. Manifold. Reciprocating engines. Mix gasoline with air. Spark ignition. Oil and water don't mix. His father's voice retrieved, crackling on the computer speaker as if from some long distance, as if from beyond the grave. His father used to say that all the time. It described the relationship with Mother. It described Jim and Cole's relationship. Always so different. Always on the verge of combustion, just a little more gasoline needed in the mix.

Pistons. Crankshaft. Converts the reciprocating motion of the pistons into rotary motion. Anger converted into hate. Smoldering passion into a drive for action.

Front-mounted engine used to drive the rear wheels. Steering system. Steering arms, wheel supports. Brake system, master cylinder, brake lines. Pressure of the fluid forces the brake shoes to press against the drums. Drum, drum, beating as Jim throws another fit. Driving off in their father's car. The list of repairs that had to be made on the screen. Quarter panel, fender, transmission. His father's rage taken in drum blows to Jim's face and chest. Jim clutching at his face, clutching at his father's arm to make him stop.

Clutch. A device for connecting and disengaging the engine. Clutch and hold and pull away. A listing of the times he could recall his father holding him, holding Jim, holding their mother. Clutch and connect, engage and then disengage. His mother clutching at him, weeping hysterically, and Cole doesn't know

288   TEM

what to do. He's only sixteen. She wants him to drive her some-where but he can't drive. He'd always felt uncomfortable in auto-mobiles, vulnerable. Only Jim and his father can drive.

Drive shaft. Connects the transmission with the differential. So many differences in their family. An arrangement of gears that allows the wheels to rotate at different rates when the car is turn-ing. Different strokes for different folks. Jim was always saying that. His voice comes over the computer speaker, saying that again, a perfect simulation of the young Jim's voice. But Jim actually hadn't been so different from their father. The same calculating abilities, only Jim had used them to become a rich man. Cole had been like their mother. Jim like their father. The drive, the powerful drive of those two. The ruthlessness.

A list of Jim's assets flashed up on the screen. He hadn't realized the system had access to those financial records. And he hadn't realized his brother was so wealthy. But there were vulnerabilities, he noticed, serious vulnerabilities, such as the vast amount invested in this particular hypertext project.

A slip joint and a universal joint in the drive shaft. These allowed the drive shaft to change its length and direction as the car wheels moved up and down. Up and down. A close-up view. Vulnerabili-ties there. Oil and water. Gasoline and a spark. A memory typed in a year ago without even thinking, now flashed up at the center of the screen:

I remember the night before the accident, Jim had been in the garage late, working on our father's car. The next morning I asked him what he'd been doing, and he smiled and said he was going to surprise the old man for Father's Day, with a much smoother running car. Then I remembered it *was* Father's Day and I'd completely forgotten it, and how mad my father was going to be. But Jim had thought of everything, Jim was going to be the hero. But surely there were certain risks involved in what he had done, certain vulnerabilities.

Up and down. The picture of his father's wrecked car appeared on the screen again. The twisted grinning grill. The broken win-dows. And where a window should have been, his father's head propped up, grinning, grinning a bright red grin.

Now there was a picture of the twisted, grinning Chrysler grill.

THE DOORS OF HYPERTEXT 289

Now there was a picture of Jim taken a few years after the accident, just as he was starting his own software company. Now his door was open: Cole could see him at last for who he really was. Jim had always been so clever with machines. The twisted grin on his face. Carnivorous Chrysler grin. He'd had complete control over the money after their mother committed suicide and Cole was ruled incompetent and sent to the state hospital. Cole's mother hanging there, the broken rod, the crushed fender, slip joint, the shaft changing its length. All Cole could think to do was slam as many doors shut as he could, and hide in the dark. Cole had been unable to help her—she'd desired too much from him. Too many doors. Doors within doors within doors.

Cole's own picture flashed onto the monitor screen. It was the picture taken of him when he first entered the hospital. Dark eyes, a confused look on his face. It looked as if he never slept, and so was forced to view his bad dreams while he was awake.

Cole stared for some time at that image of himself on the monitor. He imagined he must look very much like it at the moment. He must look very much the image of the classic madman.

His brother had killed their father, designed it like an efficient piece of software. He'd killed their father and that had destroyed their mother, which in turn had almost destroyed Cole. He could feel all the doors in his head trying to slam shut, as if the rooms behind them could contain no more.

But he couldn't let them close now. Cole couldn't go back to that way of life.

He went to one of the filing cabinets against the wall and pulled out a file of pictures and newspaper clippings concerning his brother. One at a time he scanned the images of his brother into the computer's memory. He overlaid these images, musing vaguely that by this method he would somehow discover how many faces his brother really had. He began entering words across his brother's face, words like *traitor*, and *bastard*, and *scum*. His brother, who had once been so perfect, so dependable, so honorable. He pounded on the keyboard, doors of text, houses of text filling the screen until the terminal started beeping at him, squealing at him to stop, screaming...

290   TEM

"Hey, bro? Don't beat it to death!" Cole twisted in his chair to see Jim striding confidently into the room, every inch the high-level executive. "Working hard? Or hardly working?" His brother's grin twisted and gleamed. Cole longed to see it crash. His brother leaned over the monitor and nodded at the garbage there as if it were the most interesting thing he had ever seen. "So, how goes the battle? What's this stuff, anyway?"

Cole thought to tell him, *Why, it's your deceit, brother,* but he did not.

But what good would it do? And how could he prove to others what he knew? The hypertext connections were too fluid, practically unrepeatable, a product of the moment. There was no way he could establish an acceptable chain of evidence.

Besides he didn't feel bad about his father being dead. He hadn't felt bad about it even at the time.

His brother Jim would probably just laugh at him, or get Cole into the hospital again. His brother Jim was laughing now. "Abstract art? Is that what you're doing? Is that *my* face under all that garbage?"

To his own surprise Cole started laughing along with his brother. Maybe he would learn some deceit of his own. He thought of slamming the door in his brother's face, and never opening it again. But he'd done enough of that. He'd become a hermit thanks to what his brother had done. He'd kept all those doors closed; he'd been alone, a friend to no one. But if he could keep the doors open now, maybe he would find the secrets of someone else's heart, besides his brother's. The good secrets. Perhaps even the good secrets of his own heart.

"Well, won't bother you again. You're turning into a real workaholic, little brother, and I *like* that." Jim headed for the door.

Maybe if he kept the doors open, he'd find out enough about his brother to make him pay someday. Make him pay long past the point at which it began to hurt.

Cole sat down at the keyboard again. He typed QUERY. COLE BLACKMORE. Then he inserted a processing command: MAKE EXTENDED USE OF EARLIER LINKS AS POSSIBLE.

He watched his picture grow until he was seeing the individual dots. Then one individual dot grew in size until it filled the screen.

THE DOORS OF HYPERTEXT

There followed a stream of data taken from his health records, genetic tests, ancestral data, religious beliefs, his psychologist's files on him, his school essays, his thoughts on all subjects imaginable, entered during his years at this keyboard, the expert component of the system making doors and choosing doors at lightning speed, creating link after link after link, and the whole time Cole didn't have to touch the keyboard at all, couldn't have even if he'd wanted to.

Doors within doors within doors. Behind one of those doors would be Jim's punishment. Behind another would be the passage which would lead Cole back to his own life, and to the secret hearts of the rest of humanity, from whom he had been so long estranged.

Steve Rasnic Tem had never touched a computer when he was hired by Dakin 5 (later part of Verbatim) to write documentation and scenarios for their Level-10 computer games for the Apple. They wanted a writer well versed in fantasy and science fiction, but Steve was soon writing documentation for their accounting programs as well. Following his stint there, Steve was hired by McDonnell Douglas to write computer-aided instruction for pilot training and Ada. He has also written documentation for TG Products, Baen Games, General Electric, and The Software Farm.

Steve has been nominated for the Philip K. Dick, Bram Stoker, British Fantasy, and World Fantasy awards, winning the British Fantasy Award for Short Fiction in 1988, for his short story "Leaks." He has sold over 200 short stories to such publications as *Mike Shayne Mystery Magazine, The Saint Magazine, Twilight Zone Magazine,* Robert Bloch's *Psycho Paths, Amazing Science Fiction Stories, Isaac Asimov's SF Magazine, Halloween Horrors, 100 Great Fantasy Short Short Stories, Year's Best Fantasy, The Ultimate Frankenstein, Snow White Blood Red, Best New Horror, New Mystery, Dark At Heart, Dead End: City Limits, Borderlands 3, Northern Frights (Canada), Cold Shocks, Shadows, New Terrors, Cutting Edge, Gorezone, New Frontiers,* and the British publications *Fear Magazine, In Dreams, New Crimes 3, The Daedulus Book of Femme Fatales, Narrow Houses, Tales of the Wandering Jew,* and *Fantasy Tales.*

Software piracy is a significant problem in the industry. Duplicating a duplicating machine is a major engineering feat; duplicating a half-million-line program is just a matter of double-clicking on the right little picture. But there are risks in copyright violation, and software pirates sometimes get caught. Being an editor also has its risks and its rewards. Among the rewards is discovering a new writer like Kent Brewster, whose contribution is a crisply rendered, fine-grained, and totally believable story about the risks and real consequences of unreal events.

KENT BREWSTER

The Dream Pirate's Tale

"A ND WE'LL ALWAYS stay together, right?" Rose's voice quivered with that young-but-old sound that Morris was coming to truly hate. Fifty-five going on ninety, she'd fallen on retirement with a vengeance, taking up bridge, bourbon, and country club politics, leaving Morris Creed with the unsettling sensation that his wife had suddenly turned into his mother.

"Right." He took her hand and smiled. "It's going to be fun. You'll see."

"And just base service. None of those fancy premium channels, and none of that...that filth." They'd gone over it a thousand times before. Morris smiled and nodded again, kissed her powdery cheek, returned to his own bed, and turned off the light. The only thing visible in the room was the friendly red glow of the Dream-O-Vision's Activate light, reflected in the tiny aluminum dish antenna. Battery-operated and wireless, the little black box looked ridiculously small for what it was and could do.

"All set?"

"I think so." He heard rubbery sounds from her side of the room. Her voice quivered in the dark. Morris reached up and pulled the black neoprene DreamMask down over his eyes, checking that the tiny antenna was free of obstruction and firmly seating the electrodes at his temples, obeying the instructions to the letter.

THE DREAM PIRATE'S TALE   293

"Good night, then," he said, groping for the nightstand between them, finding the little box and hitting the textured button, meaning to add something smart like *"See you in my dreams!"* but the effect rushed in like a breaking wave. The room spun, tilted, went blacker than the inside of the mask—

—and then blazed to white. Whitewashed adobe, to be exact, a wide balcony overlooking an ancient city on a sheer cliff above an emerald bay. Gentle whitecaps tossed many-colored boats across the water. Birds and butterflies, dragons and dirigibles, fairies, fireflies, and fighter planes all traced an unending aerial ballet from city to sky to water and back again.

Morris stepped forward to the worn railing, jaw agape. He'd heard and read incredible things, but this....

This was out-bloody-*standing*, as his dear departed pa used to say. He could already see a thousand things he wanted to try, starting with saddling up a dragon, that one, the one that was toasting the tail off of that F-16—

—Christ! That was a humpback whale, breaching right in the middle of the bay! And the thing was wearing a huge wicker saddle filled with row upon row of screaming riders having the time of their lives! That. He wanted to do that first, and then maybe the dragon....

"Morris?" She was right behind him, shivering in her patched old nightgown. Before turning around, Morris knew what he was about to see: the classic mouth-full-of-sour-owls look that meant Rosie was Not Amused. "I want some clothes. And a drink. And a cigarette."

"All right." Clothes. He looked down at himself and shook his head. Flannel pajamas would not do for whaleback riding. Something a bit more Cousteau-like, in rubber, perhaps. And suddenly, without a flicker, he was wearing an eye-bending yellow and orange O'Neill wetsuit.

Rose made a strangled sound and backed away.

"Don't do that!"

He giggled. This was fun. "Wild Turkey over ice, right, and a Virginia Slime?" He reached up and pulled a cocktail tray out of the air. Ice rattled in glass; smoke curled up from a heavy ceramic ashtray. She took an involuntary step forward, interested in spite of herself.

294 BREWSTER

"How did you do that?"

"Just thought about doing it, and it happened. Nothing to it."
He squinted one eye and sighted at her over his thumb. "And
now—"

"No! Don't you dare make me over! And take that silly suit off—
you look ridiculous."

An oak-framed mirror—twin to the one on the back of their
bathroom door at home—shimmered into existence in front of
him. She was right. He did indeed look ridiculous, a bald, fat old
man crammed into a costume meant for someone a quarter his age.
He handed her the tray, smiled at himself in the mirror, inhaled,
and sucked in his paunch. His chest swelled, stretching the rubber
tight. And, miracle of miracles, when he exhaled, the gut stayed
gone.

His smile turned into a grin. He flexed his skinny arms and his
biceps grew back, his shoulders widened by half a foot, and his
waist narrowed into a V, pushing its leftover thickness down into
his thighs and calves with a warm tingle. Hair—rich, thick, black
hair!—grew like grassfire, running wild in reverse stop-motion
from the crown of his head and down to his collar—

"*Stop that!*" shrieked Rose, dropping the cocktail tray with a
clang and a crash. The mess spread to its fullest, sparkled, and sank
into the warm adobe floor without leaving a trace.

"What?" He broke away from the mirror. She swayed on her feet,
whitefaced, hands on cheeks. "I'm just having a little fun."

"You put yourself back right now or I'm done with this. I won't
be seen with a...a teenager!"

"It's a dream, Rosie. We can do anything we want."

"I don't want you like this! I want you back the way you are!"
Her eyes went wet with tears. "It's not a dream. It's a nightmare."

"Now, now. Don't cry, sweetheart," he said, reaching for her. She
shrank from him, shaking her head, starting the tears on their way.
He stopped, fingering the sleeve of the wetsuit, and turned it back
into worn flannel with a wave of his hand. Relaxing his stomach
muscles and slumping his shoulders let all the imaginary air out of
his body, returning him to somewhat less Schwarzeneggerian proportions. "But I'm keeping the hair, Rose. And I'm not wearing the
belly."

THE DREAM PIRATE'S TALE   295

Victorious, she came into his arms, wiping her eyes on his lapel and hugging him tightly. He felt like a large, warm snake had wrapped him in soft, suffocating coils. Turning and meeting her eyes in the mirror, he saw her smile and noticed that his hair had turned gray once more.

Fine. It was gray, but it was still there.

They spent the rest of the night shopping. Immediately below their entry node was the Dreamland Mall, stretching the full length of the city.

At least half of the Mall was taken up by shoe stores.

Jewelry shops, period-furniture stores, art galleries, and large-size women's wear emporia made up the bulk of the rest, anchored every hundred yards with a Sak's, Macy's, Nordstrom, Gump's, or Nieman-Marcus. Not a single Sears or Wards marred the landscape; the Mall aspired to a higher level.

No cash changed hands in the Mall. Everything went on a solid platinum VISA card and was packed into a magic shopping bag that would hold a family of elephants but only weigh enough to let the bearer know that something was in there. Morris had paid particular attention to the Mall section in the documentation; he knew that no money or goods actually changed hands on the Basic Service level, but the stores with franchises paid stiff rent without a quiver for the exposure.

Possessing a functioning Y chromosome in every cell of his body, Morris failed to spot the attraction of fantasy shopping. He held his tongue, however, since Rose was having such a marvelous time. He spent his first night in Dreamland waiting outside a thousand dressing rooms, holding her purse, and fetching a larger pair of whatever it was she was trying on. Nothing he or any salesperson could say would convince Rose to modify her potatolike proportions; she simply sniffed and said that there were plenty of stores in the Mall, and one was bound to have her size.

As advertised, they woke up fresh and ready to take on the day after nine solid hours of high-quality REM sleep. Morris went out early that morning and broke eighty for the first time in his life, in tournament play on a course he'd never seen before. Rose bounced

296 BREWSTER

around the house in a whirling cloud of energy, dusting, straightening, cleaning, shopping for dinner, and spreading Morris a victory feast the likes of which he hadn't seen in years.

They went shopping in the Mall for the next three nights.

Then, as they were turning in on Friday, Morris put his foot down, gently. "We've got to at least see the rest of the city! It'll be fun—you and me in the back of a hansom in Dreamland at midnight. What do you say?" He locked eyes with her and did not back down. Like any proficient rider, Rose knew when to give her mount his head.

"Oh, all right. I'm missing two-thirds off at Tiffany's for this, but you've been so good the past few days." Chattering wasn't working. She tried breaking down instead. "I'm sorry! I was—I was so scared of this thing! Scared I'd lose you to the first little slut that came along in a bikini." He moved to her, took her in his arms, and she sniffled heavily. "You had this look—You were staring out at the water, the city, the people—You looked like you were gone, Morris. Gone from me!"

"Now, now. You know I could never leave you." He reached back and pulled the little black box off the nightstand. "This thing is a toy. It's a radio. A TV set. A video game. Not real, not where it counts. Not right here." And he hugged her again. "What do you say we unplug it tonight, give it a rest?"

She pulled back, shocked out of her tears. "What?"

"Sure. A night off, that's what we need. Hell, if it's causing you that much grief, we'll send it back!"

Her mouth worked silently, fishlike, failing to keep pace with her thoughts. Finally, carefully chosen words emerged. "No. No, I'd really like to keep it. And you will, too, once we get out of the Mall. We've been doing my things all week; it's your turn tonight."

Sinatra was *amazing.*

Young, slick, and magnetic, he moved like a big, restless cat, prowling the bandstand, working the balconies, finally settling right in front of their ringside table. Rose basked in a small piece of the spotlight, relishing every word, every sip of bourbon, every tiny gleam of reflected light from the thousand tiny black sequins on her richly brocaded shawl.

THE DREAM PIRATE'S TALE   297

After Frank they danced. Alone in the spotlight among the dark, faceless mob, they swooped and floated like graceful birds in formal wear. Even Morris had to admit that the dancing was fun; all he had to do was think of a move—or copy one he saw being done in the shadows—and they'd glide right through it like they were on tracks, be it spin or grapevine or sweetheart or whatever.

And after the dancing they caught a two-horse taxi to Electric Park, in the middle of Nightside, the quarter of town where the sun never rose and the moon stayed always full. The night had just enough of a nip to make them snuggle close together, Rose in her mink and Morris in his wonderful tweed topcoat. Gaslit jugglers, musicians, magicians, and mimes mingled with the colorful flow of smiling passersby, all flowing by them in a river of night people. And the women...Morris went cross-eyed trying not to stare at the women on the street. Were they hookers? He'd heard things, read things in the paper, but this—This was *unreal!*

"Honey," said Rose, nuzzling deeper into his chest, "do you know what would make the evening absolutely perfect?"

"What?" Morris jumped and did a quick take to make sure Rose hadn't caught him peeking. She hadn't.

"Well...." She gave him her best coy look, gently caressing the side of his face. "I know we said we weren't going to get into any of the premium services, but I found something I really want to do."

"And what might that be?" Morris began to hope.

"When I picked up my fur at the salon in Macy's the other day, I happened to hear some talk. Two of the clerks were going on and on about 'Family Values,' you know, my stories?" He nodded. Next to absolute domination of her bridge club, the soap opera was the closest thing she had to a hobby. "I'm afraid they caught me eavesdropping. But guess what? The producer of the show—you know, that bald little Tommy Ammiamamo fellow from *TV Guide*—was standing right there, just when I spoke up and said that somebody should open a Family Values store in the Mall. Well, to make a very long story short, we did lunch with his people and they're actually going to do it! Can you imagine? Every fan in the world will drop in! And, best of all, they want me to play Phyllis DeBeauvoir." Even Morris had heard that name before; the aging but still-regal head of the most elegant chain of department stores in popular fiction had

298   BREWSTER

been the star of "Values" since forever, twenty years or maybe more.

"Mmm. Did they say how much it was going to cost?"

She snapped instantly into business talk, reciting a fact she'd memorized. "Base plus premium rate two. Nine-fifty an hour." And then back into melt-your-heart mode. "But you know how time stretches out in here—an hour seems like a week." Especially in the Mall, thought Morris. "And I'm sure I could get you something. They said that Trevor Black and Jason Kennedy were already cast, but they'd have to do it for me—I'm the *star*, after all—"

"Rose—"

"—I mean, the plot has to evolve here, too. We'll just kill off one of the men. Rutger. We'll drop Rutger down a manhole. He's such a smarmy little worm—"

"—Rose!" She fell silent. He made his voice as gentle as possible. "I don't want to be on 'Family Values'."

"What? But—But they've cast me already—"

"Rose. Listen to me. *I* don't want to be on 'Family Values.' You go ahead and do it. Have fun."

"But we'd be together!"

"At two times nine-fifty, almost twenty bucks an hour? A hundred and sixty a night! No. That we can't afford, not for something I wouldn't enjoy anyway. You know me, Rose—no taste for the arts. I'd rather be doing anything else, and there's plenty else to do."

She pouted, successfully reaching her goal but still maintaining pressure, just for form's sake. "You want to ride that silly whale."

"Yes! I want to ride the whale. And blow up the Death Star. And kill some dragons. And beat Nicklaus at the Crosby. And storm the Fuhrerbunker." His smile grew into a grin, matching hers. "You know me, Rosie—typical adolescent male to the very end." She smiled back, shaking her head. "So, when do you start?"

She shrugged. "Now, if I want."

"Go. Have fun. See you in the morning."

She kissed him, snapped her fingers, and vanished in a cloud of gold sparkles. Evidently she'd relaxed her miracle-phobia when she wanted to get somewhere in a hurry.

Blowing out a huge, relieved breath, he collapsed into the plush velvet seat. And then bounced back up and tapped on the driver's shoulder. "Hey! Where does a guy get a drink in this town?"

THE DREAM PIRATE'S TALE   299

Morris woke up with a grin on his face and damning evidence dried onto his belly. He'd found his bar, all right, the Bottom Line, out on Front Street by the pier. The place had all the right amenities: loud brassy music, gorgeous strippers of truly stupendous proportions who still only peeled to pasties and g-string, and a pre-heroin Lenny Bruce introducing them. And, wonder of wonders, a small, steamy room in the back strewn with satin pillows and lit with a single red bulb, where a guy with a big enough stack of dream-Krugerrands could hire a dancer or three for his own very private party.

He got up and went quickly to the shower. Rose was still in Dreamland, wearing a predatory smile. Morris trembled as the hot water hit him, trying to remember a sexual experience one tenth as powerful as what had happened that night. He'd been with Rose for nearly thirty years; before her there'd been only a single steady girl who'd dear-johned him in boot camp, and then a few highly unsatisfactory teenage prostitutes in Saigon. And then Rosie, the banker's daughter. Instant career. Money. Cars. Fairway view estate. Separate beds.

Shuddering as he soaped off, he decided that once was enough. The temptation to return to the Bottom Line—especially since he had what looked like a permanent pass to do basically whatever he liked—would be far too great without scratching the itch even one more time.

No, there were bigger and better fish to fry, ones not nearly so hazardous to his marriage.

A pattern developed over the next two weeks. Morris and Rose would cruise through Nightside, eating dinner and catching a different show each night. And then Rose was off to Makeup and Morris was off to kill monsters.

The Dark Tower was visible from every open area in Dreamland, climbing up laser-straight into the sky from the center of the vast city and plunging downwards into a bottomless abyss. Entering from ground level faced the player with a simple choice: up or down. Rumor had it that the upper and lower ends met at some impossibly distant spot; existing maps, however, traced over a

300 BREWSTER

thousand floors in each direction with neither end in sight. Predating Dreamland itself, the Tower had its roots in several online computer games that had merged into a single Siege Perilous with the advent of broadcast dream technology.

Best of all, it was *cheap*. Base plus premium-one came to only three bucks an hour, making Dark Tower the number one drawing card in Dreamland.

Premium-level services brought to the user an extra sharpness of resolution and a longer time-perception; basically, the more you paid, the truer the experience seemed and the more subjective time you spent doing it. Dark Tower seemed more real, more solid than the rest of Dreamland; once he tried it, Morris immediately understood the attraction of premium service.

In a fortnight Morris explored seven floors, three up and four down, with the friendly help of several of his fellow player-characters. Morris's character, Asap the Swift, was a lean, wiry Swordsman with an unfortunate tendency towards recklessness. Although Morris knew intellectually that his chances of even annoying a third-level ogre in adamantine plate mail were dicey at best, Asap threw caution to the winds and waded right in, rapier extended for the kill.

Asap died a lot that first night.

On the next night, however, Morris hooked up with two other players, Tourmaline and Lovecraft—journeyman Healer and apprentice Mage—and extended Asap's useful life to the point where Dark Tower became an industrial-strength addiction. Rose, on the other hand, needed no assistance to carve her stamp into "Family Values." Two weeks—six months of Dreamtime at base plus premium-two—of fierce negotiation, power play, backstabbing, and blatant flirtation expanded the fictional empire beyond the sponsor's wildest dreams. Rose's initial inspiration—why not extend her fictional store into the "real life" of the Mall?— sent the owners of several real franchises scurrying into action. Real Family Values stores were due to open in New York, Chicago, and San Francisco, just in time for Christmas.

Three days into the next month, the bill came.

THE DREAM PIRATE'S TALE   301

Should have known she'd ask for itemized detail, thought Morris, surveying the wreckage of the Dream-O-Vision set. It looked like Rose had taken his burglar bat to it, with spectacular results. Strewn across the nightstand and onto his bed, bits of shattered plastic, twisted wire, broken circuit boards, and crushed computer chips lay scattered in mute testimony to her rage. She'd pounded the fragile aluminum dish antenna flat and then folded it twice, forming a sharp spear that ran through the thick wad of billing detail and pinned it to his pillow. Heavy slashes of red felt-tip pen circled his transgressions:

   *** AS/BottomLineLtd/970804:23:32:42-46/MaryjaneR5/$18.75
   *** AS/BottomLineLtd/970804:23:32:47-52/SandiB22/$22.50
   *** AS/BottomLineLtd/970804:23:32:53-56/PenelopeZ/$15.00

The two-letter code stood for Adult Services, as pointed out in the helpful index at the bottom of each flimsy sheet. Location, date, time, service contractor, and price were also noted. Morris had spent a grand total of fifteen seconds real-time in the back room at the Bottom Line, for base plus premium rate ten, as high as it went.

The $56.25 was an insignificant pimple on Rose's thousand-dollar total for the month, and Morris had run up another three hundred playing Dark Tower. Still, he didn't think that Rose was pissed about the money. The money was nothing.

Control was everything. For a span of fifteen seconds, Morris had run completely wild and free, pouring gasoline on the hidden flames of Rose's deepest paranoia. And now he had to be punished.

Television was in turns stultifyingly boring and hellishly teasing, consisting of old reruns interspersed with new commercials for all the neat things to be done in Dreamland. Radio and the papers weren't much better. Morris resorted to bringing home armloads of paperbacks, anything even remotely interesting he could get his hands on.

Nothing helped. He missed his new friends. His golf game went south. He slept badly when he slept at all. His dreams were twisted reflections of the Dark Tower, orcs and ogres and trolls, all wearing Rose's face, chasing him naked through miles of satin-lined corridors lit with flickering red bulbs.

302   BREWSTER

Finally he started hitting the Wild Turkey. Two stiff shots did the trick, putting him down for the night with no troubling dreams.

Rose blamed him for everything. His "infidelity," the loss of her role in "Family Values," the smirk on the face of the delivery boy who came for the bits and pieces of the Dream-O-Vision set. She even dredged up a piece of truly ancient history: the time he'd flipped through an adult pay channel on his one and only solo business trip. He'd sat there transfixed by the vision of Marilyn Chambers being ravished on a pool table just long enough to get charged for it.

And, worst of all, she told her family. Not everything, of course, but just enough hints to get the idea across. Morris was having problems controlling himself. Morris never could resist temptation. Morris had to have someone watching over him all the time. It was such a shame that Morris had to go and spoil everything. Morris was so impulsive, so untrustworthy, such an immature little boy.

Little boy, perhaps. But a tough little boy, with a mind armored by many years worth of mental callus; he'd endured freezing cold spells like this before. And this one was made easier by the knowledge that her pangs of withdrawal were far worse than his. So Morris tucked his head between his knees and prepared to wait this one out.

It only took a few days.

The pirate box came from a mail drop in Elko, Nevada. Via Federal Express, it showed up one morning while Morris was shooting a disastrous 97. From the entry date on the invoice, Morris figured that Rose had ordered it about twelve hours after smashing the old one.

The only outward difference between it and the original they'd gotten from DreamCorp was that it carried no dire warnings about what would happen if you tampered with it. It looked like Rose had torn it straight out of the FedEx carton, inserted batteries, and turned it on. Sprawled on her back on the bed among the styrofoam packing peanuts, she lay fully clothed, sweating in the heat of the afternoon. Scowling into the black rubber mask, she did not appear to be having a good time.

Gee, maybe they gave Phyllis to somebody else, thought Morris. *Poor baby.* Then he showered, taking a long time to get the accumulated grime out of his hair and his miserable round of golf out of his mind. Twenty minutes of very hot water, set on maximum blast, left him feeling much better. The eighty-degree air felt almost cool against his pinked-up hide when he emerged, ready to meet the boys at the Nineteenth Hole for the postmortem.

Rose hadn't moved a muscle. If anything, the frown on her face had cut even deeper. *Probably having a great time fighting for her life,* thought Morris. And then he dressed and walked back to the clubhouse, hopping his back fence and cutting across the fourteenth fairway.

Six beers, two shots, and an ill-advised daiquiri later, Morris stumbled back into the house, waving at his buddies as they swerved down the street in their custom-built golf cart. Barely able to walk, he collapsed into bed, not even thinking to look over at Rose.

In the morning she still hadn't moved, and the Dream-O-Vision set was still set on Activate. Shaking her produced no response. And her face still held that look of angry disgust that he'd seen the night before.

Hacking blindly through the choking jungle of his hangover with the freshly sharpened blade of fear, Morris began to hunt for the manual. He vaguely remembered reading that switching off a Dreamer was supposed to be like waking a sleepwalker, dangerously disorienting at best. That was why the sets were battery-powered, after all—so the power couldn't go off in the middle of the night and shock the Dreamer into wakefulness.

After ransacking the house, he concluded that the manual must have accompanied the pieces of the original set back to the factory for burial. And there was nothing included with the pirate set but a few lines of foggy text that looked like it had been translated from English to Chinese and back, then faxed and photocopied into grainy oblivion.

Returning to the bedroom, he felt indecision kicking in. What if he'd simply missed Rose's wakeup during his unconscious period the night before? Boy, would she be pissed if he cut her off in the middle of something good!

304 BREWSTER

On the other hand, she was still wearing her shoes, for Chrissakes. There was no way in hell she'd go to bed with her heels on, unless...

Unless she was in the middle of regaining her empire when her nine-hour clock ran out. He just *had* to give her a little more time. Eight. He'd wait until eight. That would be just about enough time for him to get human again.

So he brushed his teeth twice, showered, shaved, and choked down two English muffins with honey butter. Looked at the clock. Read the paper. Looked at the clock. Watched yesterday's highlights of the Lakers pounding the Sonics. Looked at the clock some more.

Eight-thirty found him hovering over Rose's lumpish form, listening to her gentle snore. *Five more minutes,* he thought, pacing. He gave her fifteen.

Then he reached over and gently pressed the Activate button. The tiny red light went out.

And Rose released a final snoring breath, and was still. Too still. Not breathing at all. He grabbed at her shoulder roughly, shaking her. "Rose?" He peeled off the sweat-filmed sleepmask, grimacing at its warm sliminess. Underneath it her eyes were open, rolled back in their sockets to show veiny whites. "Oh, God." He rolled her onto her back, trying to remember his CPR. "Rose?" He felt her throat for a pulse. Nothing.

Okay, you know what to do. Pulse first, then breathing. Tilting her head back, he shoved a pillow under her neck. Rearing up, he gave her five quick chest-compressions, trying not to crack her ribs with the heels of his hands. And then a good long breath, pinching her nose shut and blowing everything he had into her lungs. Then the pattern: one-two-three-breathe, one-two-three-breathe. Check her pulse....

Nothing. Damn it.

Think. She was fine just a second ago; what happened? Look around you, idiot—what's different? Oh, dear God. The box. It was doing something to her, so you better get her back online and see if it helps.

Fumbling, he hit the Activate button again and swore at its flashing Not Ready Error. The mask, of course. He settled the mask back over her eyes and tried again.

THE DREAM PIRATE'S TALE   305

Rose's chest hitched and spasmed. Finally, she took a long, gasping breath. And Morris let one out, not realizing he'd been holding it in. The sound of her snore was beautiful music.

"Okay. I get it," said Morris, addressing the hateful little box on the nightstand. "I have to come in after her, right?"

Through the pirate interface, the streets of Dreamland moved at a snail's crawl. Walkers stood stock-still, flyers hovered unsupported in the air, even the waves in the bay hung suspended in midcrash. Everything was spookily silent; only oddly distorted echoes came back when Morris yelled into the air.

The pirate box had apparently had all speed filters removed. When Morris popped into his balcony apartment, every area, including Basic Services, seemed to be running at premium rate ten, around ninety-to-one compression.

Paging anyone at that speed was impossible, since he couldn't exit to real-time. He was going to have to look for Rose the hard way.

He quickly tore through the length of the Mall, checking the offices of all twelve Family Values stores. Unchallenged, he sauntered past security guards frozen in midstep. In the plush back rooms he witnessed silent tableaus of greed, intrigue, murder, surgery, careful sheet-covered sex, and domination games of every other possible stripe, but no sign of Rose. Not that he expected to find her; she'd be just as invisible as he was outside of the premium-ten areas.

But she had to be somewhere. At her rate she'd been online for something like three months subjective, time enough and more for her to get bored with watching people stand around like statues. He cudgeled his weary brain. What if she'd gotten caught somehow? Where would they take her? More important, what would they have done to her for those ninety days?

He had to get some help. And he knew of only one place in Dreamland where time ran at premium-ten.

The leather-clad bouncer saw Morris coming, grinned, and opened the door. Unbelievably loud heavy-metal music blared forth into the eternal night, riding a thumping beat that shook the

306 BREWSTER

otherwise silent street. The Bottom Line looked to be under new management. Nasty new management. Morris wet his lips and tried to ask for help.

"What?" The doorman couldn't hear him.

"Manager! I've got to speak to your manager!" bellowed Morris. The doorman shook his head and pointed to his ear, starting to pull the door close. Morris caught it and stepped through just in time.

Not a sign of the Bottom Line's previous incarnation as a fifties-vintage strip bar remained. Red flock wallpaper, proscenium arch, and orchestra pit had given way to floorlit plexiglass runway with wraparound bar, strobe lights, and a mammoth robot CD-jockey. Where there was once a single girl onstage there now were twenty, all young, beautiful, worse than naked in heels, hose, and—oh, God!—*appliances*. Collars. Harnesses. Chains. Clips, clamps, pinchers, and pins. Latex and lace....

Tearing his attention away with a major exercise of will, Morris searched for somebody, anybody who didn't look to be a part of it. The floor, if possible, was worse than the stage. The waitresses were part of the show as well. He could see...things happening all around him. Tall black twins in spandex rode the face and lap of a suit-wearing businessman sprawled atop the back bar. A sweet-looking blonde in a tight rubber bra delivered a foaming beer to a hulking biker sitting three feet away from Morris, listened to a request inaudible through the din, giggled, and dropped to her knees. Averting his eyes, Morris headed for the rear door.

The back room was different, too. No longer a red-lit boudoir, it contained a small stage surrounded by a crowd of shouting, shoving men. On the platform rested a large steel cage.

Inside the cage was his wife.

Rose wore the impossibly perfect body of a porno queen—tiny wasp-waist, generous buttocks, and huge, creamy, high-riding breasts—covered only by a light sheen of sweat, stiletto heels, and a studded leather belt. Three pairs of handcuffs held her nearly immobile, one pair looped over the top bar of the cage to force her arms straight up, and another connecting each shapely ankle to the sides, spreading her legs wide. Her hair was a fiery red mane, moussed into a floating cloud of sparkles and air. Her mouth was an open wound, wet and pouting. Her eyes—

THE DREAM PIRATE'S TALE 307

—were locked onto his. She mouthed his name and writhed, rolling her hips, arching her back and shimmying—

—and screamed, a hoarse cry that Morris heard clearly, even over the blare of the music and the roar of the crowd. Fat blue sparks leapt from the bars, connecting with her cuffs and the metal studs on her belt. She jerked and twitched, muscles standing out in sharp relief against the velvety smoothness of her skin.

The men around her went wild, whooping and pounding on the bar. The ones closest to her dug into their pockets, spilling coins and bills from every country onto the bar, forcing the cash down into several wide slots. Elbowing his way closer, Morris caught sight of a large voltmeter and a set of Tesla coils straight from Dr. Frankenstein's laboratory. The needle on the meter jiggled and climbed as the men stuffed more and more money into the bar.

Shaking, Morris closed his eyes, took a deep breath, and wished—

—and suddenly it was very, very quiet. Only the sound of her ragged breathing cut the air. When he opened his eyes, the room was empty except for Rose and him.

The door fell away from its hinges with a weak rusty sound. The cuffs sprang from the bars at his touch. She collapsed into his arms, winding hers around his neck and pressing her full, glorious length against him.

"I knew you'd come," she whispered into his ear.

His pulse began to pound. This was too much. "Are you all right?"

"Oh, yes. Better than I've ever been."

"What? But you—"

"I've changed just a bit, haven't I?" Another undulation, ending in firm pressure, her hip to his crotch. "I've been waiting for you."

"I know, and I'm sorry about that. I didn't know if you needed help or not."

"Looks to me like you're the one who needs help." She stroked one fingernail across his cheek, down his chest and belly, and took him firmly in hand. "Why don't I show you some of what I've learned?"

"Agh. Uh, all right." Rational thought was no longer possible.

She smiled and the room wavered and changed. Post-industrial

308 BREWSTER

biker-bar trappings shifted back to pink satin sheets and mounds of pillows and a single red light bulb swinging in the air. Kissing him hard, she tripped him with a neat judo-style move, giggling and landing on top.

"Y'ever been tied up? No, of course not." She opened the manacle on her left ankle with a practiced twist. "Give me your hands." Morris obeyed, moving through a fog of lust, ready to burst at the slightest touch. She cuffed him professionally, straddled him, leaned him back into the pillows by pressing her chest into his face, and clipped the chain into some unseen eyebolt over his head. His clothes melted away, leaving him bare and throbbing beneath her benevolent gaze.

And then, of course, she changed. Her smooth young face and form shifted and stretched, mottling, warping, twisting and bloating before his eyes, back to the way it was before. Back to the wife he'd come to know: fat, gray, nasty old Rose. "I knew you'd be back. They always come back for more." He closed his eyes and wished, hard. Nothing happened. Shuddering, he tested the chain that bound him. Why couldn't he escape? "Go on, try to get away." He bucked and twisted but was pinned flat by her weight across his stomach. "See? Nothing works anymore, does it? You're caught. Busted. Under house arrest. Just like I was."

"Was?" He began working one leg free. Maybe he could hook a heel around her, remove her crushing mass.

"What do you think they do when they catch a pirate? What do you think they did to me?" She brought her face very close to his. Her breath smelled of rotting meat. "Where do you think all those pretty little whores came from? Central Casting?" Her voice lowered to a hiss. "I'm sure they'll find something *interesting* for you to do." She slid down his body, her clammy white flesh leaving a cold trail, prickly body hair tickling him like the legs of a spider. She grinned up at him from between his thighs, revealing a mouthful of teeth that belonged to a Doberman. "There's one small thing I'd like to keep, just to remember you by..."

As the first weak flickers of torchlight came down the dripping stone tunnel, Morris stirred in his nest, wincing at the pain. He wrapped one green-scaled hand around the base of the blunt stick they'd given him as a weapon and hitched the other through the filthy hide that bound the wound between his legs. Happy, excited voices and the clank of steel on steel echoed down the passage as the light became stronger.

"—is so great! I don't believe I'm actually here!"

"Just watch yourself. If you stick to the main drag this floor's a cakewalk, but there's lots of nasty things lurking in the shadows."

Alone in the dark, Morris nodded in agreement, drool spilling between his tusks in anticipation. *Nasty. You don't know the half of it, brother.*

Kent Brewster has spent the last nine years as production manager at Systems Plus, Inc., a small software publisher, where he does in-house programming and database support. On the side, he runs a data conversion business with the trademarked motto: "Because We Really Really *REALLY* Need the Bucks." He is also the author of several shareware games, most notably Stained Glass, which was the basis for the commercial game, Tesserae, for the Macintosh and Windows.

Kent claims he spends most of his copious free time feeding a voracious reading habit, splitting any remaining nanoseconds among his family, writing, golf, karate, brewing horribly bad beer, programming and playing computer games, navigating the tangled wilds of GEnie, and strangling small animals. He lives deep in the heart of Silicon Valley with his wife, Alisa, and daughter, Diana; they are expecting another daughter. Kent says he is currently "scraping the barnacles from the mossy hull of a novel, submerged for several years but beached by a recent low creative tide." This story is his first professional sale.

Our last work is also the shortest. I thought I had it made with a mere hundred words of micro-fiction, but then I found this story in haiku form in my email. Non-programmers who don't get it should ask a computer-literate friend. See you all next time around!

STEVEN WEISS
Time_traveler();

SHE ARRIVED IN TIME
To see her own departure;
Call time_traveler();

Steven Weiss started his computer career as a consulting methodologist with Control Data Corporation in 1975, then joined Yourdon, Inc., conducting more than 200 seminars on structured analysis, design, and programming during the heyday of the structural revolution. He is now a consulting methodologist with Wayland Systems Institute and is co-developer of one of the leading object-oriented analysis and design methodologies. A regular contributor to various magazines, Steve is arguably the computer field's most famous former dentist and among its best punsters.